"*Necessary Measures* left me with chills. Hannah Alexander possesses an incredible storytelling gift that makes it unable to read just a little. *Necessary Measures* becomes your constant companion until you're finished, and even then, it leaves its mark."

Kristin Billerbeck, author of *Blind Dates*

"Fast-paced and full of realistic characters dealing with the challenges and ethics of modern medicine and modern life, *Necessary Measures* is the perfect sequel to *Second Opinion*."

DeAnna Julie Dodson, author of *In Honor Bound, By Love Redeemed* and *To Grace Surrendered*

"*Necessary Measures* is true-to-life ER action that envelops and engages. Hannah Alexander paints a broad and detailed picture of a small town emergency room and the relationships of those who serve there. Great family dynamics and realistic professional tension."

Kristen Heitzmann, author of *Twilight*

"In *Necessary Measures*, Hannah Alexander presents a well-crafted, fast-paced drama centered around life in a hospital emergency room. Alexander skillfully drew me into the personal lives of doctors, nurses, and patients, taking me on a journey through their sorrows and joys. Woven throughout the tension-filled stories is a tapestry of friendship, growing love, and abiding faith."

Yvonne Lehman, the WHITE DOVE ROMANCES series

"The Hannah Alexander writing team had done it again with *Necessary Measures*—a town so real you'll be looking for it on the map, characters so endearing you'll think of them as friends, and struggles so compelling and genuine that you'll identify with each one. Most importantly, the truth of God's intimate involvement in lives shines through on every page."

Deborah Raney, author of *After the Rains* and *A Vow to Cherish*

HANNAH
ALEXANDER

THE HEALING TOUCH ✛ BOOK TWO

Necessary
Measures

BETHANYHOUSE

MINNEAPOLIS, MINNESOTA

Necessary Measures
Copyright © 2002
Hannah Alexander

Cover design by Lookout Design Group, Inc.

Published by Bethany House Publishers
A Ministry of Bethany Fellowship International
11400 Hampshire Avenue South
Bloomington, Minnesota 55438
www.bethanyhouse.com

Printed in the United States of America by
Bethany Press International, Bloomington, Minnesota 55438

Library of Congress Cataloging-in-Publication Data

Alexander, Hannah.
    Necessary measures / by Hannah Alexander.
       p. cm. — (The healing touch ; bk. 2)
Sequel to: Second opinion.
    ISBN 0-7642-2529-4
    1. Single fathers—Fiction. 2. Physicians—Fiction. 3. Hospitals—Fiction. I. Title.
    PS3551.L35558 N43   2002
    813'.54—dc21   2002010726

"You have heard that it was said,
'Love your neighbor and hate your enemy.'
But I tell you: Love your enemies
and pray for those who persecute you. . . ."
MATTHEW 5:43–44

In loving memory of

Leo Vernon Latshaw,

June 6, 1923 — June 1, 2002,
who was willing to be
"father of the bride"
one more time.

Books by

Hannah Alexander

FROM BETHANY HOUSE PUBLISHERS

Sacred Trust

Solemn Oath

Silent Pledge

THE HEALING TOUCH

Second Opinion

Necessary Measures

Web site for Hannah Alexander:
www.hannahalexander.com

HANNAH ALEXANDER is the pen name for the writing collaboration of Cheryl and Melvin Hodde. They have seven previous books to their credit and currently make their home in Missouri, where Melvin practices emergency medicine.

CHAPTER 1

Mr. William Butler, administrator of the Dogwood Springs Hospital, flexed his left arm and wiggled his fingers. An uncomfortable tingle, like a weak electric current, pulsed beneath his skin. He shifted in his seat, trying to ignore the sensation. Now was not the time to give in to petty irritations.

The husky voice of Jade Myers, Dogwood Springs' mayor, emanated from the speakerphone on William's broad desk. "I refuse to be manipulated, Will. You know we can't allow the insurance company to go unchallenged."

William grimaced at the sound of her anger, but he identified with it. "I won't let them push us around, Jade." He worked to keep his voice calm and reassuring.

"Then would you please talk to them again?" Jade asked. "If they knew you and I were in agreement they might not be trying so hard to—"

"I've already spoken with them twice this morning. I think we'll see another check in the next couple of days."

"They told you that? Specifically?"

"Yes. Until then, could we please relax a little?" He drummed his fingers on the desk, then stopped. Jade's sharp ears would detect his newly acquired nervous habit.

"Those people have lied to us before, and we need those funds, Willie. I can't count how many times . . ." Her voice droned on as William focused his attention, instead, on the tinny jingle of the Christmas music that had accompanied her calls today. The holiday season was slowly drifting upon them, in spite of the warm sunshine and balmy weather in this protected area of Missouri, so close to the Arkansas border. Thanksgiving was less than a week away, and Dogwood Springs would soon be enduring the same tired music that was always broadcast over the outdoor speakers downtown. No wonder city revenue was dropping.

A knock at the closed door of William's office suite punctuated the mayor's flow of words, and William's secretary entered with a yellow sticky note on her finger. She stepped across the silent carpet and pressed the note to the surface of the desk in front of him.

While Jade continued to fume, he read the words, *Dr. Caine on line two. Better take it, he's mad.*

William sighed. That was nothing new. He nodded to his secretary and leaned forward as she retreated. "Jade, would you hold for a minute?" he asked gently, poising his finger over the blinking button of his telephone.

"But Will—"

"Just a moment. I have a fire to put out on the other line. I'll be right back with you." He punched the other line and forced a smile to his face so his voice would sound friendlier than he felt. "Yes, Dr. Caine, what can I do for you today?"

"First I want to know why my lab reports can't be faxed to my office in a timely fashion." The voice clipped through the speaker in typical Mitchell Caine complaint rhythm, low and growling, no niceties. "Your people don't seem to realize I have patients to answer to."

"I'm sorry you're having—"

"Is there any reason why the chief of staff is the last doctor connected with this hospital to receive his daily reports?"

Another streak of energy shot down William's arm. He was sick of Caine reminding everyone within hearing distance that he held the title of chief of staff for Dogwood Springs Hospital this year. Thank heaven that debacle would only last another month or so.

"I'm sorry, Mitchell, have you spoken with the lab about your problem?" He kept his voice pleasant with difficulty. "I'm on another call at the moment—"

"Excuse me, but troubleshooting for your outpatient services isn't my job, it's yours," Mitchell snapped. "And I would think my concerns should take priority over—"

"Mitchell, you can talk to the lab director about these problems yourself. You *are* the chief of staff. I, on the other hand, am keeping the *mayor* on hold." Against his better judgment, William depressed the button and cut Mitchell off. Let him blow steam on his own time—it would come out one way or another anyway.

He pressed the mayor's line. "I'm sorry, Jade, you were saying?"

"Did you put the fire out, Willie?" Jade asked. She sounded a little peevish.

He bristled at her nickname for him. No one else ever called him that. "It'll be okay."

Jade Myers, the attractive thirty-four-year-old mayor of Dogwood Springs, Missouri, was tenacious. She had political clout, and she was a formidable ally in this battle with insurance companies. For some reason, she had a tendency to look to William for advice and balance.

If William had his druthers, he'd be holding a hunting rifle snugly beneath his arm right now. Instead of arguing with an obnoxious box on his desk, he'd much rather be tramping through a cedar forest of green dusted with sunlight this nice November day.

"Willie, they're holding *our* money! Do you know it's been six months since the disaster? That's half a year! Legally, we could take them to court right now."

Half a year. Had it really been that long since the mercury leak?

The tingle in William's left arm led to numbness. He flexed his fingers and shrugged his shoulder, frowning at the strange sensation. "Jade, you're doing a good job. The citizens of Dogwood Springs are glad you were the mayor when the poison hit this summer."

In a town of seven thousand, this hospital had treated thousands of their citizens in the weeks following the discovery of and subsequent panic over the mercury-tainted water. It was a financial and legal nightmare, and the brunt of it was falling on Jade's shoulders—and his. So far, not a single person had sued the city, thanks to Jade's obvious concern and compassion for the victims.

There was a static sigh, and then Jade said, "I've done all I can do." William wished she meant that. "Then why don't you leave it—" The tingle spread up to his shoulder and across his chest. It didn't hurt, exactly, but it certainly caught his attention. He shrugged. He'd been sitting in the same position too long.

"Willie?"

He grimaced, hating that nickname with sudden ferocity, and then wondering at his irritability. But how would she like it if he were to call her Jadie? Or worse yet, honey?

"Is everything okay?" she asked.

"Yes, everything is fine." Or would be as soon as she hung up. "I wish you wouldn't worry about thish—" He clamped his mouth shut in shock. His tongue felt as if it had suddenly thickened. Tingling down his arm . . . pressure in his—

"Willie?" Jade's voice sharpened. "What's going on over there? Are you okay?"

He exhaled in a rush. "Nothing, Jade. Gimme a—" He squeezed his eyes shut, banking down the fear as he concentrated fully on perfect enunciation. "Wait a moment."

He felt as if a cat had just curled up on his chest for a nap. An overweight cat. With that sensation came increasing fear. He exercised, watched his eating habits, kept an eye on his cholesterol and blood pressure. There was no history of heart disease or stroke in his family. It was probably nothing more than stress, but what if it was something else? Heart trouble *and* stroke symptoms, at the same time?

"Jade, lemme—" Blast the timing! *Focus on the words.* "Call back. I'm tired." He pressed the disconnect button. Dr. Sheldon was on duty in the ER. Time to pay a courtesy call.

"Slow down a minute, Brooke. I want to get my laptop." The dismissal bell had not yet rung when Evan Webster dialed the combination of his locker and opened it.

Brooke Sheldon pivoted from her typical race-pace down the hallway and clearly expressed her impatience with little more than a whispered sigh. "Okay, but hurry. Beau and I volunteered to help out at the health fair at the hospital this afternoon, and he's secretly hoping they'll let him do blood pressure readings."

"Just walk slow. I need a ride home, and Beau won't drive off and leave *you*."

"He won't leave you, either, silly."

"Just give me a chance to catch up, okay?"

She shrugged and retraced her steps—this time more sedately— toward the sunny end of the building, her silhouette etched against the light in shadowed detail. Evan risked a few extra seconds to watch her as she walked away. She was beautiful, and at five foot eight, she was taller than he by an inch. She also had better developed muscles and much better developed social skills.

The two of them had just completed some vital research for his best- ever series of editorials for the *Dogwood High News* about all the stages of illegal methamphetamine addiction. Rumor had it that the town paper, *The Dogwood,* might even pick them up. Miss Bolton, their cre- ative writing and publications teacher, had announced to the class that someday Evan would be a Pulitzer Prize winner. Her words still echoed in his mind.

He couldn't have done the articles without Brooke. She knew the right questions to ask during their interviews, and she wasn't afraid to get pushy. If Evan got pushy, people got mad. When Brooke got pushy, teachers listened, female students obeyed, and male students drooled and competed with each other for her attention. She and her twin brother, Beau, were Evan's best friends in the whole world. What amazed him was that they liked him—and that Brooke didn't even expect him to share his by-line with her.

Sergeant Tony Dalton, who was in charge of the county's special task force on meth production, had actually called Evan two days after the article came out last week. What a rush! The sergeant had wanted to know how much more Evan and Brooke knew about drug activity in the school. So now, not only were they in the public eye, they were also private eyes!

A door closed nearby, and Evan stashed his crumpled jacket on top of the books, pulled the small voice-activated recorder out of the locker, and slid it into the pocket of his jeans.

He sensed a nearby presence without turning. "Brooke, I said I'd catch up. You can—"

"Webster." The deep male voice came from so close behind him that he jerked and banged his elbow on the locker door. This was not Brooke.

He turned and nearly rammed his nose into the muscles of Kent Eckard's steroid-stuffed chest. The high school junior's bulk blocked light from the hallway, but that didn't disguise the glower in his expression.

"Uh, hi, Kent." *Be nice. Save a life—your own.* Evan couldn't force a smile. Hard to believe they'd once been friends. "What are you doing out of class so early?"

"I saw you and your *girlfriend* out snooping for more dirt. Give it a rest, Webster, while you still have a future, or you'll be history." Eckard smirked at his little pun, his shoulders squaring.

Kent and his gang of borderline-psycho friends were a tad displeased by the articles that had so enraptured Miss Bolton and Sergeant Dalton. Evan's initial idea for the articles had begun immediately after school let out last summer—when he had trustingly taken two pills Eckard gave him. Those pills had turned out to be illegal. Speed. The emergency room experience had given Evan a close encounter with the police, and his life hadn't been the same since.

Evan cleared his throat, emboldened by a rush of resentment at the memory. "If there's no dirt to dig up, there won't be a problem, will there, Kent?"

Eckard's brows formed a thick V across his forehead. "For a scrawny runt, you've got a big mouth."

Evan closed the offending orifice. Because of his articles, the superintendent and school board had initiated locker searches and issued a ban on book bags. The searches had resulted in the expulsion of two students so far—buddies of Eckard's.

Evan swallowed. He had discovered in the past few months that Kent was not the kind of person one wanted to irritate, and Evan had done so in a big way when he gave the police Kent's name last summer.

Kent's hands bunched into fists. He leaned into his frown. "You were in the boys' locker room yesterday."

"I was in classes yesterday."

"Not after the last bell. What did you hear, runt?"

"Hear? Was I supposed to hear something?" It wasn't what he'd heard, but what he'd seen—and documented with the help of his wonderful little camera—that counted. Evan stood on tiptoe to see if Brooke was anywhere around.

Eckard moved to block his view with an overdeveloped shoulder. "I asked what you heard."

Evan didn't reply.

Eckard grabbed the neck of Evan's shirt and jerked him forward. "What!"

"A good reporter never reveals his source—"

A blurred fist slammed into his right cheekbone. The impact smacked the back of his head into the open door of his locker, and he felt a bite of metal in his scalp. He didn't have time to cry out before a freight train rammed his stomach and shoved him backward.

His voice betrayed him, and he heard the high pitch of a squeal, then a whine before the force ejected all remaining air from his lungs in a pitiful hiss of weakness. His posterior got stuck in the locker, and he couldn't scramble out before Kent's fist hit him again, this time in the jaw. He saw darkness. He saw sparkles of light. He heard a scream. Humiliated by his own cowardice, he wondered if he would lose every scrap of dignity and wet himself.

But the scream wasn't coming from him. And it wasn't one of fear— it was one of outrage. Before the fist could strike again, the scream grew in volume, and a blur of fury lunged into Evan's attacker from the side with a blast of speed and flying hair that could only be Brooke Sheldon.

The surprise attack knocked Eckard sideways, and he stumbled. Before he could recover she dealt him a blow to his left temple with her elbow. Hard.

"Help! Somebody help us!" She slammed him again with her elbow as she screamed, "Help!" But at the same time the first dismissal bell rang.

Eckard shook his head and turned on her, raising his right fist. But before he could plow forward, she gave him a vicious, well-placed kick that she must have learned from her brother.

He grunted and dropped forward on his knees.

In a haze of pain, Evan saw the doors fly open along the hallway and students come out.

Brooke pivoted toward Evan. "Are you okay?"

He was dying. "I'm fine. Let's get out of here before his buddies—"

The wounded bull growled. "Webster!" He braced himself to stand.

Brooke grabbed Evan by the sleeve and jerked him out of the confines of his locker. "Let's go. Hurry!"

All Evan could do was slam the locker door behind him and follow in Brooke's wake, praying that his skull was intact and that he wouldn't pass out before they made it to the car.

William made his way slowly along the hospital corridor, into the elevator. When the doors swished shut and the floor moved beneath him, though there was still very little pain, he felt as if his fluttering heart might take wing and burst from his rib cage.

Panic attack?

What nonsense. He had never been a jittery person. If he had, he wouldn't have made it far in this business.

When the elevator came to a stop, he felt a wave of black dizziness and leaned against the wall with a catch in his breath. This was no panic attack. Something else . . .

The doors whispered open and he stood gawking out at the lobby, where nurses, techs, volunteers, and visitors walked in different directions. No one noticed him.

Before the doors could close again, he took a deep breath and stepped out. It probably wasn't good politics for an administrator to collapse in the lobby of his own hospital, but the alternative—dying alone in the elevator—would be unconscionable. He thought of asking a passerby to fetch him a wheelchair, but at the last minute he pressed his lips together and continued walking on his own steam. The ER wasn't far. He could make it.

CHAPTER 2

The final dismissal bell of the day rang at Dogwood Springs High, echoing across the large publication department, signaling the end to creativity—or rather, what *should* be creativity, but was, for most students, an opportunity to gossip, goof off, and let the editorial geeks and creative-writing nerds do all the work.

Beau Sheldon, who didn't mind being an editorial geek when he wasn't studying or working at the hospital, relished the arrangement. He anticipated at least a few more seconds of peace to complete his printing job before Brooke and Evan came rushing in, late, as usual, from their research wanderings across campus. Brooke would be chattering, even faster than she walked, about their research or the unfairness of homework or the latest, hottest guy on campus.

Beau pushed his wire-framed glasses to a more secure position on his nose, then sighed. He loved his twin sister, but she was not a peaceful person.

He leaned back in Miss Bolton's comfortable chair and watched the students scatter across the broad front lawn in a race to see who could hit the streets of Dogwood Springs first in the after-school cruising parade.

The dwindling chaos of laughter, talk, and the shuffle of feet gave way to the *clink-shush-clink-shush* of the old Heidelberg "Windmill" letterpress as it printed and numbered, in ascending order, three hundred tickets for the junior-senior play. It was almost done. Maybe he would get the printing finished tonight. Only about fifty tickets to go and he could shut down, clean the ink from the—

A slamming door and a raised female voice blasted through the comforting rhythm of the press, and Beau heard the *slap-clatter* of feet out in the hallway. Two pairs. Coming closer. The wandering reporters were back.

Brooke's words spilled over one another in their race to escape her mouth. "Your mom can't blame your dad for this, Evan. He wasn't the one who attacked—oh, will you look at that! You're bleeding! That does it—we're going to the hospital right now. Dad's on duty, he can check you out. That monster's getting expelled."

Beau tensed. What was she talking—?

"Your dad?" squeaked Evan.

"No, silly, Eckard. I mean it. We can go straight to the superintendent with this. He'll trust our word over Kent Eckard's any day. Really, why is the guy even still in school? It isn't as if he's passing any of his classes." She burst through the double doors of the department ahead of Evan and immediately noticed Beau at Miss Bolton's desk.

"Beau!" She grabbed Evan's arm. "That jerk jumped Evan in the hall and tried to stuff him into his own locker."

"What jerk?"

"Kent Eckard. Haven't you been listening? Look at the blood!" Her dark gray eyes were nearly black with outrage, her face flushed. A smudge of . . . of something . . . was that—

"Brooke, did he get you, too?" Beau rushed forward to check her face.

She waved him away. "Not me, silly. Look at Evan's head. Turn around, Evan."

Wincing with obvious pain, their friend did as he was told, and Beau saw blood matting the short brown hair. A wound about an inch long continued to ooze.

"It looks like a pretty clean cut."

"Don't you think he should go to the hospital?" Brooke demanded.

Beau took a closer look. Evan definitely needed a doctor, but he didn't need to be frightened about the severity of the wound. "I don't guess it would hurt—"

"I don't think it's that bad," Evan protested. "If I end up in the emergency room again, Mom's going to freak, and she'll make me live in Springfield with her and Dork-face. I can't go to school up there, guys. If they can do this to me here in Dogwood Springs, what would they do to me in a bigger school?"

"You need sutures or staples or something, and I doubt your family practice doc will be able to fit you in this late on a Friday afternoon." Beau raised his hand before Evan could protest again. "When was your last tetanus booster?"

"Tetanus? When I was eight or so, I guess."

Beau noticed that the flesh along the left side of Evan's jawline had begun to color with a developing bruise. No telling what other injuries he had. Dad needed to see him. "I told you to stay away from that guy. What else did he do?"

Brooke held up Evan's left elbow. "Rammed him into a locker. And look at his cheek. He'll probably have a black eye."

Evan's face flushed, and he pulled away from Brooke. "I'll be okay."

"Maybe," Beau said, "but we'll let Dad decide."

"Shouldn't we at least talk to a teacher first?" Evan asked. "You know, report it?"

"While you bleed to death?" Brooke exclaimed. "Forget it. We can tell them later, after Dad sees you. Maybe we should call an ambulance, or—"

"No!" Evan's bruised face tinged an even brighter pink. "This is already embarrassing enough. Come on, let's just go and get it over with."

Brooke went to her workstation and pulled out the suitcase she called a purse from beneath a stack of books. "I've got the keys. I'll drive."

"No, you won't," Beau said. Brooke's driving would scare Evan to death long before they reached the hospital. "I'll drive—you sit in back with Evan and keep pressure on that wound."

"Not me, Beau! You're the one with the medical training."

"And *you're* the one who dented Dad's fender last month."

Evan cleared his throat. "Uh, guys?"

"We're on our way." Beau grasped Evan's upper right arm with one hand while holding the other out for the keys Brooke dug out of her humongous purse.

With a final glare she gave them up and walked beside Evan to the car.

"Lauren! I need you in two." Dr. Grant Sheldon grasped William Butler by the shoulders as the sweating, gray-faced administrator swayed forward. "Will, what happened?"

"Shick . . . chesh . . . urts . . ."

"Your chest hurts?" Hiding his alarm, Grant guided William into exam room two, helped him onto the bed, removed his tie, and unbuttoned his shirt.

Lauren McCaffrey joined them seconds after she was called. If she felt shock at Will's gray appearance, she didn't betray it. "Hi, Mr. Butler. Have you been eating onion rings again? I told you they'd give you indigestion."

"Lauren, put him on oxygen, nasal cannula," Grant said. "I'll hook him to the monitor."

She nodded and eased their patient's upper torso onto the pillow while she reached for the oxygen. As she worked over him, Grant noticed that the right side of Will's face seemed to droop a little. Not a good sign.

"You sound a little slurred, my friend," Grant said. "Do you feel pressure or weakness anywhere else? Any numbness?"

Will nodded, and for the first time since Grant came to work here in May, the unruffled hospital administrator looked frightened. "Left shide numb."

"We'll see what we can do." Grant grabbed monitor patches and placed them on his friend's chest and left side. "You lie back and take it easy. Let us do all the work." He attached the leads to the patches, switched on the monitor, and studied its screen. Will had a regular heart rate and rhythm, with nonspecific ST changes. That meant heart trouble until proven otherwise.

"Lauren, get an IV established and draw some blood. I want an immediate sugar level." He didn't want to wait for the lab to get that.

Even stat lab could take fifteen to twenty minutes. The bedside glucose test would give them the information they needed in ninety seconds.

He raised his voice and called out through the door to the secretary, "Vivian, I need stat CBC, electrolytes, and coags. I also need an EKG." They couldn't risk taking Will out of the department for a CT scan just yet, but if this was a stroke, he needed to be transferred as quickly as possible. "And get me Mr. Butler's chart from Med Records."

Almost before he finished his orders, Lauren had an IV established. As Todd, the LPN, joined them in the room to help, Lauren drew blood from the IV site into a 12 cc syringe. She filled it and set it carefully on the stainless steel tray.

After hooking the plastic tubing to the IV and attaching the bag of saline, she left Todd to do the vitals while she placed a needle on the syringe of blood she had just drawn. She ran the first blood test, then reported the results.

"Dr. Sheldon, the sugar is 82."

Nothing there. "Thanks. Give him normal saline."

Once again, Lauren had read Grant's mind, and he relaxed. Instead of waiting for the lab tech to come in and take the blood, she took the sterile tubes and stabbed the first of three rubber stoppers, then filled it with blood. The tube with the purple top was for a complete blood count, the tube with the green top was for electrolytes, and the tube with the blue top was for coagulation studies. She had just finished when the lab tech came rushing in, breathless.

"Sorry, Dr. Sheldon, I was detained by a grumpy doctor. You can always tell when Dr. Caine is in the build—oh . . . hi, Mr. Butler." She grimaced, then turned her attention to work. "Thanks, Lauren. I'll get these taken care of right away." As she took the tubes and rushed back out the door, she nearly collided with Gina Drake, from Respiratory, pushing an EKG machine in front of her.

The attractive respiratory therapist, with wavy red hair and a scattering of freckles across the fair features of her face, smiled at Todd, then frowned at the hospital administrator as she pushed the machine to his bedside.

"Well, hello there, Will. Checking out our bedside manner, huh?" With smooth expertise, she connected the EKG. "You picked a good shift. You couldn't have gotten a better doc." She winked at Grant, then nudged Lauren. "Had to poke his arm, huh? Hope you were gentle, or it'll show up on your permanent employment record."

"Just be glad you didn't have to get a blood gas on him," Lauren teased back. "I think I hear Vivian calling. Take good care of our favorite administrator."

Grant saw Will relax a little as Gina set up shop beside his bed. Ever since Gina's scare with low blood sugar this past summer, Mr. Butler had taken the young single mother and her two little boys under his protective, grandfatherly wing. They had an excellent relationship. Like Lauren, if Gina was worried, she would never show it in front of Will.

While Gina connected her equipment, she and handsome, sandy-haired Todd kept Will entertained with lighthearted stories about shows they'd seen on television, books they'd read—anything but hospital news. Todd was in the middle of a story about his children when the EKG machine gave the results Grant needed.

There were nonspecific ST changes, same as the monitor.

Todd glanced at the printout and nodded. "Looks good, doesn't it, Dr. Sheldon?"

Grant watched the printout a moment longer. "Let's just say I'm cautiously optimistic. This doesn't entirely rule out the possibility of an irritable heart, but it helps. We'll wait until someone from Med Records brings his old chart for comparison."

While Gina and Todd stayed to watch Will, Grant stepped out into the hallway and walked toward the central desk. "Vivian, how soon before we get that chart on Mr. Butler?"

"It's on the way up." The middle-aged secretary gestured toward the ambulance radio. "Meanwhile, you have another patient who should be arriving in about six minutes, and two just came in for triage." She glanced around and lowered her voice. "One guy stinks like the dump, and he's panicking because he's having trouble breathing. Everybody around him is having trouble breathing, too, if you know what I mean." She waved her hand in front of her face and wrinkled her nose.

"Who's with him now?"

"Lauren's getting him to a bed."

"Good. Thanks, Vivian. Gina's in with Mr. Butler, so I'll tell her to get a stat breathing treatment started on the newcomer."

———————

"Beau, you drive slower than Grandma!" Brooke's aggravated voice seemed to reverberate through the car from the backseat. "Evan could bleed to death before—"

"Evan isn't going to bleed to death. His bleeding had almost stopped before we got in the car." The streets were congested with after-school cruisers, and he knew better than to let his sister distract him.

Something else did get his attention, however. The past three times he'd checked the rearview mirror, he'd been disturbed by a big tan 4x4 pickup with wide wheels and dented, rusty fenders following too close to his back bumper. If he slammed on the brakes too quickly they would be rear-ended. He hated being tailgated, and that hovering presence almost seemed ominous, considering what had already happened.

"Do you guys have your seat belts on back there?" He knew they didn't.

"Who needs a seat belt?" Brooke snapped. "We could walk to the hospital faster than—"

"Put them on." He used his deepest, most commanding voice. "Now."

"Beau, we'll be at the hospital in five—"

"Do it, or I'll pull over." The guy behind them was inching closer again—Five feet . . . four feet . . . *What is he going to do, ram us from behind?*

"Oh, fine," Brooke said. "Come on, Evan, we'd better do it or you'll—"

"Now!" Beau gunned the motor as the guy's front bumper seemed ready to chomp a bite out of the trunk of their Volvo wagon. On impulse, Beau swerved and turned onto a side street.

"Ow!" It was Evan.

"Beau, what are you doing?" Brooke exclaimed. "Now he's hit his head again. Are you crazy? We're buckling up, okay?"

"Sorry." While Brooke and Evan scuffled with their restraints and clicked them into place, Beau checked the rearview mirror. To his relief, a school bus now followed directly behind him at a discreet distance.

He'd never been so happy to see that bright yellow monstrosity in his life. He couldn't see behind it, though, didn't know if the truck had followed.

"Evan, what did you do to make Kent so mad *this* time?" he asked. That wasn't Eckard's truck that had been behind them—it didn't look familiar—but the muscle-bound bully had friends who didn't go to school, and they were the kind who looked for trouble just for the fun of it.

"It doesn't take much with Kent these days," Evan said. "He's getting really grumpy. You know that editorial I wrote last week?"

"How could anyone forget?" Brooke said. "Miss Bolton won't let us."

"Well, it wasn't fiction, you know. I really do think the mercury poisoning in Honey Creek was only the warning smoke from a smoldering volcano. That was a dump site for meth cooks."

"Nobody's going to attack you for some wordy article in the school paper," Brooke said.

"Wordy?" Evan sounded offended.

"If Kent really is friends with meth manufacturers, that article's going to ring *somebody's* bell, Evan," Beau said.

"Just before he smashed your face, he asked what you heard in the boys' locker room yesterday," Brooke said. "What was that all about?"

Evan's only response was a long, heartfelt sigh, then silence.

"What happened, Evan?" Beau prompted, watching the bus behind him as it flashed its lights and stopped to drop off children. Whoever was stuck behind it would have to wait.

"A transaction," Evan murmured.

"What?" Brooke snapped. "You saw a drug deal and didn't tell me?"

Again a slow sigh. "I got a picture. I'll show you later."

"No, Evan," Beau said, "show Sergeant Dalton. Don't drag my sister into it." Another movement in the mirror caught his attention. In spite of the bus's flashing warning lights, the truck that had been following them passed it. What disturbed Beau most about the pickup was its tinted windows. He couldn't see who was driving, but the truck was closing in again.

In another desperate attempt to lose the pickup, Beau quickly turned left and headed downtown, right into the middle of Dogwood Springs traffic.

Brooke gasped. "Evan, your head's bleeding again. Beau, now look what you've done."

"It doesn't hurt," Evan protested. "I'll be fine."

"I'm still seeing blood," Brooke said. "Beau, you need to be back here."

"I told you what to do," Beau said. "Just put pressure on it, and stop trying to analyze the rate of flow. We can't do anything about that right now anyway."

"Uh, Beau," Evan said, "didn't you just pass the turnoff to the hospital?"

"See?" Brooke said. "I told you I should have driven."

Ignoring them, Beau glanced in the rearview mirror again, and relief rushed through him. Someone had pulled in front of the truck. He turned around to look for the blood Brooke insisted had appeared on Evan's head, and he found Brooke holding Evan in a headlock.

"Don't squeeze his *throat*, Brooke, just put pressure—"

"I know what I'm—"

"Look out!" Evan cried.

Beau turned back in time to see the blurred image of a stop sign. He slammed the brakes and winced at the squeal of tires on blacktop.

"That's the way, kill us all before we even reach the hospital," Brooke snapped. "If you and Dad hadn't insisted on buying this monster car that won't go faster than a paddle boat—"

"This paddle boat is safe. We need safe."

"Obviously, with your driving."

Beau's hands tightened on the steering wheel, and he waited for a car to cross in front of him before he pressed the accelerator once again. He glanced in the side-view mirror and saw a little red Mazda Miata buzzing impatiently behind them.

Things would settle down. Everything would be okay—as soon as they got Evan to the ER.

CHAPTER | 3

_____

Throat's on fire." The patient held his left hand to his neck, his unshaven face contorting as Lauren McCaffrey angled him onto the exam bed.

Lauren's eyes smarted from the aroma that permeated the air around him. "Mr. Proctor, I'm going to set you up with something to help you breathe, but I need to check your oxygen saturation level."

"Just hurry!"

Lauren did so gladly. This was ridiculous. A nurse worked with bad smells all the time. This man, however, didn't just smell dirty or sick. There was another odor she couldn't define and didn't have the time to analyze. She raised the head of the bed so he could lean back and still be seated upright, then she laid a hand on his shoulder to help ease him back.

She reached for the package of plastic tubing and ripped it open. "Did you say this is a flare-up of your asthma, Mr. Proctor?"

Gil Proctor nodded. Sweat lay thick across his forehead, and tears dripped down his face from obviously irritated eyes. He didn't behave like an asthmatic. Someone who was experiencing an asthma attack sat up straight and still to concentrate on getting the highest airflow they could manage.

She attached the probe to his finger to check his oxygen.

"What're you doing that for?" he demanded. His voice grated, probably from some kind of physical irritation.

Lauren explained what she was doing while she connected him to the automatic blood pressure cuff, all the while trying not to gag. She chided herself for her squeamishness. This guy was in trouble. She needed to forget about her own dropping oxygen level and be as compassionate as possible—he needed help.

"Where's the doctor?" he snapped. "I want a doctor. My lungs—"

"Dr. Sheldon will be here in a moment, Mr. Proctor. This oxygen should help a lot, and our respiratory therapist is on her way to give you a breathing treatment." She adjusted the tubing, careful to avoid dislodging it when he coughed again. "Don't worry," she soothed. "We're going to help you. Just try to breathe through your nose, and relax if you can. Do you want me to call your wife from the waiting—"

"Ain't my wife!"

"Your friend, then."

"Yeah, get her back here. Tell her to get me a drink."

"I'll bring you some water as soon as the doctor has checked you."

He grunted and tugged at the tubing.

She stepped to the entryway and peered out to find Grant and Gina talking with the secretary at the central workstation. She waved at them and caught their attention, then gestured for them to come. They nodded. Gina carried a nebulizer unit.

From the time Grant Sheldon had come to work here in May, he seemed to move with an aura of calm. His presence soothed overstressed staff and patients alike. As he stepped into the exam room, a barely discernible frown around his eyes revealed that he noticed the smell.

On the other hand, Gina Drake's pretty, copper-colored eyes widened, and she looked hard at Lauren. Lauren gave her friend a short nod of acknowledgment, then turned to give Grant the chart.

He studied the information for a moment, then introduced himself to the patient. "I understand you're having trouble with your asthma today?" He looked again at the chart, eyes narrowed, as if seeking something that wasn't there.

Gil nodded and coughed again.

Grant looked at the blood pressure reading on the monitor, then looked at Lauren. He'd picked up on the readings right away. "When did your breathing start getting bad?"

The patient frowned. "I don't know. Couple hours ago."

"Have you ever been admitted to a hospital for your asthma, or have you ever been placed on a ventilator to help you breathe?"

Gil gave an irritated shake of his head.

Grant pulled out his stethoscope. "And who is your family physician?"

Gil slanted him a glance, then slid it away again. "Don't have one."

"I see. What medications are you presently taking for—"

"Look, I'm not on no medications, all right?" Gil snapped. "What's with the twenty-question stuff? I just need you to help me. My lungs are killing me."

Grant nodded and placed the chart on the counter. "Let's get you started on a breathing treatment." He turned to Gina, who was already assembling the nebulizer unit. "Gina, let's do 4 milligrams of Decadron and 2.5 milligrams of Ventolin."

"Ready to load, Doctor." She stepped to the oxygen line, connected her medicines, and adjusted the flow. As she placed the mouthpiece of the unit in Gil's mouth she indicated for him to hold it, then leaned toward him and tapped at his front shirt pocket. "Got some cigarettes there, I see. You smoke?"

Lauren suppressed a smile. Gina was an outspoken opponent of smoking, and she seemed to lack fear when it came to confronting patients about their bad habits.

This patient glared at her, then laid his head back against the pillow. "No law against it."

"Gil, let's listen to your breathing." Grant eased the patient forward and raised his shirt to press the stethoscope against the man's back. He listened a moment, then straightened. "You say your lungs hurt? What's the sensation? Are they—"

"They burn, okay?" Gil snapped. "It's my throat, mostly."

"That doesn't sound like an asthmatic reaction. You might need—"

"Hey, I think that stuff might be working. It doesn't feel so bad now."

"Good. It's fast-acting medication," Grant said.

"So you're feeling better, Gil?" Gina asked.

He closed his eyes and nodded. "Yeah. So give the lady a medal."

Gina stepped to the far side of the exam room and rubbed her nose.

"Now, Gil," Grant said, "I need more information about the onset of your breathing problem. I noticed you were holding your throat. Did you accidentally inhale something that set off the—"

"Yeah, that's what happened," Gil said. "My girlfriend gave me some . . . you know, some caustic stuff to clean the tub, and I breathed too much of it."

Lauren saw Gina's sudden expression of disbelief, then the shake of her head. No way had this guy been cleaning a tub when he didn't even bother to clean his own body.

Grant reached for a tongue depressor. "I don't think this is an asthma attack. We need to see if there's some other cause of distress. Let's get a look at your throat." He took the nebulizer mouthpiece out of Gil's mouth and handed it to Gina to hold for a moment. "Open wide, Gil."

The patient's eyes narrowed. He darted a glance at Grant, then at Lauren, then slowly opened his mouth. Lauren caught a quick glimpse of rotten teeth and a fiery red mouth and throat.

Grant nodded. "Mm-hmm." He took the unit from Gina and placed it back in Gil's mouth, then turned to Lauren. "Let's go ahead and establish an IV for some Solu-Medrol. Draw for blood."

Lauren was already prepared. She reached for Gil's left arm and unbuttoned the sleeve of his shirt. There were no appreciable veins. She moved the sleeve further up above his elbow.

"No!" He jerked away. "I hate needles!" He grabbed at the sleeve, but not before she saw the scars.

Gina gasped softly. Lauren stared. The man had some nasty . . . track marks?

"What're you looking at?" he demanded. "Just leave me alone and let me breathe awhile. Can't you people just help a guy feel better? Do you have to go sticking your nose where it don't belong?"

Vivian knocked at the open doorway. "Dr. Sheldon, we have another ambulance arriving outside, and Med Records brought me you-know-who's file."

Grant placed his stethoscope around his neck. "Thanks, Viv. I'll be right out." He turned to the patient. "Gil, I'm going to—"

"Yeah, yeah. Take a hike, pal. I'll be fine." Gil waved his hand at Grant as he replaced the nebulizer and continued to inhale the soothing medication.

Grant gestured to Lauren. "Why don't we go check on our other patient?"

She followed him out of the room, relieved by the sweet smell of the air in the hallway. He leaned close. "Call Sergeant Tony Dalton and tell him about our patient. It's possible this could be a police matter. At any rate, Tony will want to have it checked out."

"A police—"

"From the smell of things, that man's been cooking methamphetamine. I'm guessing he got the recipe wrong and had a little accident. Notice his eyes?"

"You're saying something exploded on him?"

"More likely he mixed the wrong things together and caught some caustic fumes."

They reached the central desk, and he gestured toward the phone. "I want to look at Will's chart. You go ahead and call Tony."

"Do you want me to go back to the room and keep an eye on Gil after I call?"

"No. If this guy's an addict between fixes, he's likely to be paranoid. Notice how defensive he got with three of us in the room?"

"I'm not crazy about leaving Gina in the room alone with him," Lauren said.

"Gina's safe as long as she's helping him feel better. We don't want him to think he's being threatened in any way. That's when he could become dangerous."

"Oh. Well. Then why don't I just call the police?"

Grant smiled at her and winked. "Good idea."

———

"Will our children all be dead by the time we wake up? Hold it, no, make that . . . awaken and see the battle around us? Will it be too late for this generation to survive? There's a war going on, my friends. The stakes are high. The enemy is blinding our souls, it's—"

"*What* are you doing?" Brooke snapped. "Evan, give me that thing."

Beau heard a scuffle and then a click in the backseat as she turned off Evan's handheld recorder. "I thought you were hurt."

"A writer doesn't let a little thing like blood stop the flow of the story." His voice cracked with the intensity of his passion.

Brooke groaned.

"We're almost there." Beau checked the mirror once again. No truck. Maybe they'd lost it for good this time. "Just hang on a little longer."

"We would already be there if you had turned when you were supposed to," Brooke complained. "But no, my brother has suddenly transformed into a social animal who wants to go cruising with the rest of the kids after school."

"I'm not cruising." He just hadn't wanted to get caught on a deserted street with that truck munching on their bumper. He wanted witnesses, just in case . . . of course, he was imagining . . .

Another mechanical click. "Dogwood Springs is a town of survivors. When the encroaching evil of drug lords and demonic forces attempted to poison this fair city with—"

"Evan, stop!" Brooke snapped. "Why are we even bothering to take you to the hospital?"

"I told you I didn't think I needed to go—"

"You were scared enough a few minutes ago."

"I thought Beau was going to kill us."

"Well, at least find a new angle. And watch your purple prose."

Beau covered his mouth to stifle a soft chuckle. They would soon be at the hospital. Dad would be there. Everything would be okay. Evan was obviously not wounded as seriously as they had thought. He wasn't bleeding to death, he hadn't lost consciousness, and no one was—

"Beau!" Brooke screamed. "Brake it!"

He caught movement to his right and looked up in time to see the truck racing toward them from a side street. He stomped the brake and pumped to keep from sliding. Too late, he realized the truck had aimed for them. He jerked the steering wheel hard to the left to the sound of squealing tires and screaming passengers. He saw the pickup's big front bumper lurch forward, across a curb, and into their right front fender. Metal hit metal in a raucous collision, and the world tilted sideways.

Beau's seat belt caught him hard, and a burst of airbag pillowed his face, ramming his glasses hard against his flesh. The roar of the monster grew louder, and the truck reversed with another squeal of tires on asphalt. They were driving away! Their stalker was getting away!

"Beau, are you okay?" There was a metal click and a whisper of material, and then his sister's hands touched his face. "Beau!"

Lauren sat at the central desk listening to the ambulance attendants, Christy and Bill, grumble to each other as they completed their report on their latest run.

"We've been on calls, nonstop, all day, and these clowns decide their little girl needs an ambulance because she lost a tooth," Christy muttered. "We've got better things to do with our time."

Vivian turned and shushed them. "The exam room door is open. They might hear you."

The five-year-old in exam room six had been brought in with blood on her face and shirt, but the only evidence of injury was in her mouth. She had been riding in the backseat with her head and upper torso leaning out the window, when a piece of rock had flown at her from a passing car. She had lost a tooth.

While Grant reminded the parents about the illegality of allowing a child to ride in a car unrestrained, Lauren had called a dentist.

"I don't get paid enough for this kind of grunt work," Bill said.

"Oh, quit complaining," Christy said. "You didn't have anything better to do. It isn't as if we have a right to eat dinner or anything."

" . . . can't replace the tooth in the socket?" one of the parents was asking Grant.

To everyone's amazement, the parents had found the tooth and saved it.

"No." Grant's reply was firm.

Christy nodded in emphatic agreement. "You tell 'em, Dr. Sheldon," she muttered, this time softly enough that the parents couldn't hear even if they were trying. "I mean, I can't believe they let her ride unrestrained—but to let her ride with her head out the window? I don't even let my dog do that. At the speed we drive these days, a flying bug could put an eye out just like that." She snapped her fingers. "Look at the splats on your windshield if you don't believe me."

Lauren sighed. What a cheery crowd they had here today.

Christy slumped back in her chair. "Sorry, guys. I'm a little wound up. It's that cold medicine I'm taking."

Bill's radio went off. He pulled it off his belt and listened for a moment. "Yeah, sure, we're on our way." He hung up and turned to Christy. "Wrap it up and get ready to roll. We've got another hot one."

Christy scowled at him. "What now? Somebody with a gooseberry up his nose?"

"Hit-and-run on Third. Three teenagers."

She grabbed her charts and jumped to her feet. "Let's get to it."

CHAPTER 4

Grant strolled into William Butler's exam room with the chart from Med Records in his hands. "Only a minor change from your routine physical a year ago, Will." It was a relief, but he was mystified.

"So I'm not having an MI or a stroke?"

"I don't want to rule anything out yet. Sometimes the body is a more accurate barometer than a clinical test about what's going on in your system."

Will scowled at him. "You're a nice ray of sunshine today."

"How are you feeling now? Is the pressure still there?"

The administrator shook his head. The droop in his facial features had not changed, but his pronunciation had improved markedly. "Gone. Could it have been a TIA?"

Grant checked the numbers again. "I don't know yet. The CT scan came back clean. You do have a first-degree heart block that wasn't there before."

"You know that isn't uncommon, Grant. It probably came with my sixty-first birthday last Saturday, much as I hate to admit it. I could even be reacting to stress."

"Could be. You've been through a lot these past few months. As you said, it could also be a TIA." Those little stroke-like episodes could be terrifying, and they could be precursors for something worse to come, but they didn't ordinarily leave lasting damage. Still, Grant didn't want to dismiss anything without careful consideration.

He lowered the sidebars of the exam bed and pressed a button to raise his patient to a seated position. "I want to send you to Cox South for a complete work-up. I'd like both a neurologist and a cardiologist—"

"No." Will raised a hand, as if to ward off a blow. "You're not shipping me out of here."

"But you need further—"

"You know the mess we have on our hands right now."

"I also know it won't improve if something happens to you. We need you healthy."

Will closed his eyes. The paper-pale color of his skin made the dark circles beneath his eyes stand out, and his bushy salt-and-pepper eyebrows accentuated the pallor of his face. "Jade Myers has made a depressing habit of calling an average of three times a day since the first of November to discuss our city's finances."

"You have my deepest sympathy."

A shadow of a smile passed across Will's face. "Don't get me wrong, Grant, I love the young lady like a daughter. Her father and I were in Vietnam together, and he was a good man. She has a lot of his positive qualities." He opened his eyes and caught Grant's gaze. His smile deepened. "A guy could do worse."

Grant caught the implication. "Huh-uh." *No way.*

"She has a tender heart underneath that tough exterior."

"I know. She cares a great deal for Dogwood Springs."

"She has a high opinion of you, too," William said. "She'd love it if you gave her a call."

Grant tried not to dwell on the thought of Jade Myers spending any time under the same roof with his strong-willed daughter. Brooke already had her heart set on someone else. She could make life uncomfortable for anyone who stepped between her and her long-term goal of making Lauren McCaffrey a member of the family.

A few months ago, Grant would not have thought that possible, but Brooke could be unpredictable. Lauren's attitude of friendly detachment had piqued Brooke's interest. Now they were close friends.

Grant had to admit to himself that Lauren's kindness, her vitality, her natural love for others affected him much more deeply than he let on, and he had no interest in looking further, even though their friendship was just that—friendship.

"I happen to know Jade would love for you to give her a call and ask her out to dinner," Will said.

"Tell you what, I'll call her and explain the effect her telephone calls are having on you."

"No!" Will's voice held a touch of its old vibrancy. "If you tell her I was here, she'll have the whole hospital in an uproar—not something we need right now. Not something *she* needs right now, with the battle she's waging to keep Dogwood Springs in the black."

Grant was greatly relieved by William's improved enunciation. "Then we'll swear our nurses on the floor to secrecy, because I'm admitting you here if you won't go to Springfield."

Will's thick brows lowered, and he studied Grant's face. "You know I trust your judgment, but is it absolutely necessary? I can't afford to be out of the office."

"And I can't afford to let you go home like this, Will. I want a carotid Doppler ultrasound and an echo at the very least. We need to keep you in fighting condition, especially now. Stress isn't going to do you any favors."

As Grant released the lever and lowered Will to a more comfortable position, he heard a light rap at the door. "Yes?"

The door cracked open and Gina Drake leaned through. "Dr. Sheldon, can I speak to you for a moment?" She turned and looked back over her shoulder, her freckled face pale, mouth tense with concern. "Sorry, William, I hate to interrupt, but I—"

"Go ahead, take him out of here. He's determined to keep me tied to this hospital bed." Will waved them both away.

Grant followed Gina out into the hallway, leaving the door open behind him so the nurses could keep watch. "What's wrong, Gina? Is Mr. Proctor okay?"

She glanced both ways along the hall. "I'm sorry, Dr. Sheldon, I blew it," she whispered. "I think he took off."

No. "Proctor?"

"Yes. The smell got so bad in there I stepped out for fresh air. I couldn't have been gone more than . . . I don't know . . . a couple of minutes, long enough to clear that stink from my lungs while he continued his treatment. I wasn't out of view of the door for more than thirty seconds, tops. When I went back to his room he was gone." She covered her face with her hands. "Dr. Sheldon, I feel awful about this!"

He took a moment to catch his breath and recover some calm. "Why should you feel bad, Gina? You're a respiratory therapist, and you did your job." It wouldn't do any good to make her feel worse than she already felt. Maybe he should have called Todd in for help with the man, but Proctor probably would have picked up on their surveillance.

"We both know he was probably a longtime drug abuser," Gina said. "I mean, I'm surprised he didn't ask for a script for narcs."

Grant had always appreciated Gina's knowledge about these kinds of things. "The police will want your input on his description, Gina, so don't leave the hospital until someone has spoken with you."

She left, obviously still upset.

Lauren stepped out into the main corridor that led to Respiratory from Emergency and saw her copper-haired friend pushing a cart of respiratory supplies, walking slowly, head down, as if she was in deep concentration.

"Hey there, stranger," Lauren called.

Gina glanced up and then her shoulders slumped. "Hey." She stopped and waited for Lauren to catch up with her. "I know, I know, the police are on their way. I'm hanging around. I can't believe I let the guy get away."

"You didn't *let* him get away, he took off on his own. You could have been standing right there in the room and he would have done the same thing."

"No, I wouldn't have let him."

"And that would have been dangerous."

"Don't be dumb," Gina said. "I don't mean I would have physically stood in his way, but I think I might have been able to convince him that if he removed the oxygen tubes from his nose, his sinuses would swell up and implode into his brain."

Lauren grinned at the dark humor. "You have a disgusting way with words."

Gina slowed her steps. "Maybe I should start writing horror stories. It seems like I've been living in the middle of one lately."

"Here at the hospital?"

"Sometimes. Too many adults with drug addictions, asthma, cancer. I prefer working with kids. My dream is to work in a children's hospital, where I don't have so much contact with adult monsters. If it had been up to me, I might have been tempted to let Gil fry in his own poison. I recognized that smell as soon as I stepped in the door."

"So why don't you tell me how you *really* feel." Lauren laid a hand on her friend's shoulder. "Come on, I'll walk you to your department."

"Evan Webster gave me a copy of his article in the school paper last week," Gina said as she walked beside Lauren. "I guess I never realized that it was probably the discarded leftovers from several batches of meth that poisoned so much of our water supply with that mercury."

"I try not to think about it."

Gina frowned up at her. "But you realize, don't you, that people like Gil caused the contamination in the first place? All the financial problems this town and this hospital are suffering were caused by people like him. You nearly *died* because of people like him."

"Your face is getting red," Lauren warned her friend. "Calm down. It does no good to preach to me about it, and you don't need the additional stress."

Gina took a deep breath and let it out slowly. "Sorry. But still—"

"I know." Lauren had learned from the experience. Gripped suddenly by the sickness while she was out in the wilderness by herself, she had discovered what loneliness truly was for the first time in her life, and the experience had changed her whole perception about being single. What she'd learned had brought her closer to God, and to His will in her life, than she had ever realized she could be. That did not excuse the ones responsible, but she couldn't do anything about them; all she could change was her own attitude.

"Are you going to Dr. Sheldon's for Thanksgiving next Thursday?" Gina asked. "He invited me, and I think he invited the Websters."

"Yes. I'll be there." Lauren automatically matched her steps to

Gina's shorter ones. "My parents are having the family gathering this Sunday, since so many of my family members have to work next Thursday, you know, being in the medical field. You and your boys are welcome to join us Sunday, too."

Gina cleared her throat. "Nah, that's okay. I've got . . . um . . . other plans."

Lauren glanced at her. "So tell me where you've been keeping yourself lately. We haven't had lunch together in a month. Every time I call you're too busy to eat."

They turned a corner in the broad hallway in silence, and when Lauren looked at her friend's face again, she saw the glow of a blush across the freckled cheeks.

"You know things are busy lately." Gina swallowed. "We're working short in the department, and I . . . um . . . take my lunch later now."

"Okay," Lauren said, giving her friend a thoughtful look. "How late? Maybe I can adjust my break time."

"Uh, three in the afternoon."

"Well, no, I can't take mine then. That's when Todd Lennard always insists on taking   Todd takes his break at three every day." Todd Lennard, the LPN who had helped with Mr. Butler, worked in the department most often from eleven in the morning to eleven at night—the high volume hours.

Gina's blush deepened, and Lauren felt her first wash of alarm. "Gina?" She waited for—hoped for—a quick denial. The last Lauren had heard, Todd Lennard had a wife and two young children. In fact, he'd been telling Mr. Butler and Gina about his kids in the exam room earlier.

Gina looked away. "Tell the police I'll be in Respiratory when they need to talk to me." She increased her pace down the hallway.

"Gina Drake, we need to talk." Lauren followed her. "You never said anything to me about this."

"Because I knew what you would say." Gina didn't slow down.

"So you really are seeing Todd? You're *dating Todd Lennard*?" Lauren knew outrage sharpened her words.

"No." Gina pulled the heavy cart to a stop, raising a finger to her lips. "Would you lower your voice? I'm not actually dating him. We eat lunch together, that's all."

"If you eat lunch together here in the hospital—"

"Shh!" Gina glanced both ways down the corridor. "We don't eat in the cafeteria. There's a conference room up on the second floor. We eat there. That way there won't be any silly rumors. You know how this place can be."

"Gina, you're ignoring a very obvious problem." And Lauren couldn't believe she would do that. Not Gina. Not after what she'd been through. "Why don't you try explaining a little more so I can at least sleep tonight."

"Look, Lauren, I know what you're going to say, but I've learned that things aren't always what they seem to be."

"So you aren't really spending time behind closed doors with a married man?"

"He's separated now. He left his wife two weeks ago. And we're just friends."

Lauren gently grasped Gina by the shoulder. "Honey, how long have you been seeing him? What about that promise that you would never have anything to do with another man as long as you lived, particularly an undependable one?"

Gina shot a quick glance along the empty hallway. "Would you keep your voice down? I didn't promise . . . exactly."

"No, that's right. What you said to me was, 'Lauren, if I ever look at another man as long as I live, just knock me in the head.' So you wait right here and let me find a nice, hard—"

"Would you relax?" Gina chuckled, though the sound was forced and the smile on her lips barely touched her eyes. "It isn't as if we're serious or anything."

"Then why do you hide it?"

"Because people would think the wrong thing, just like you did. Todd Lennard is one of the best LPNs in the ER."

"What does that have to do with anything?" Lauren asked. "He also has two little girls. Do you truly want to get involved with a man who would leave his family for another woman?"

Gina's copper-colored eyes flashed a warning. "That isn't—"

"Don't even say it, Gina. I know that look. Are you forgetting how you felt when *your* husband left you to raise *your* two children alone?"

"Stop it! I told you Todd and his wife are separated."

"And how long have the two of you been having lunch together?"

Gina looked away, but her grimace betrayed the truth.

"Let me guess," Lauren continued. "Longer than two weeks."

"I told you, we aren't dating. We talk. He needs a friend, and so do I."

"I'm your friend. You have other friends. And what about Todd's wife? Don't you think she needs a friend? Gina, please, think about what you're doing. It's wrong to—"

"Stop it!" Gina jerked away from her.

At that moment they both stiffened at the rattle of metal on plastic and the labored slap of heavy footsteps. Black-haired, sharp-eyed Fiona Perkins waddled around the corner ahead of them, carrying her tray of lab supplies.

She slowed her steps when she saw them and glanced from Gina to Lauren, then back again, which made her triple chins jiggle. "Hi, you two. Break time?"

"The break just ended." Gina reclaimed her grip on her cart and pushed it away without another glance behind her.

Lauren watched her go. Gina was a new Christian, and she had a lot to learn about walking in the Light. Todd was a young man in his late twenties who loved his patients, loved people, and apparently loved women a little more than he should.

Fiona continued to stand in the middle of the corridor, the beauty of her wide blue eyes marred by the sly cunning in her expression. "Did I just miss a catfight?"

"No, Fiona," Lauren said wearily. With deepening regret over her words with Gina, Lauren left Fiona standing there and went back toward the ER, praying Fiona hadn't overheard any of their conversation.

Fiona had the well-deserved reputation of a gossip—not just a casual gossip, but one who lived to spread dirt and humiliate her co-workers. She'd managed to come up with a doozy in the summer when she drew the erroneous conclusion that, since Lauren obviously had a crush on

Pastor Archer Pierce, and because she was sick a lot at that time from undiagnosed mercury poisoning, she must, of course, be carrying Archer's child. That vicious rumor had nearly cost Archer his job and his relationship with Jessica Lane. The fallout had only cost Lauren a broken heart, which God had mended.

What was Gina really doing with Todd? *And what business is it of mine?*

But it was her business if she was really Gina's friend.

This had not been a good day, and although Lauren couldn't imagine how it could get worse, she also didn't see how things could improve.

———

Grant sat at his desk with the telephone receiver propped between his chin and his shoulder while he jotted notes on a yellow pad. "I'm sorry, Tony. We had several other patients at the time, and I couldn't stay with the suspect."

"Could you tell if this guy was tweaking?" Tony asked.

"It's possible." Grant was far too familiar with the term Tony used. A "tweaker" was a high-intensity methamphetamine abuser who was between drug-induced highs. Depressed and deprived of sleep—sometimes for as long as two weeks—he would be frantic for another hit and would be more dangerous than a hungry grizzly. If the tweaker was using alcohol to dull the sharp edges of depression, he could be doubly dangerous.

"Okay, tell me this," said the police sergeant, "did he go by the name Peregrine or Simon Royce?"

"No, he said his name was Gil Proctor. I would have recognized Peregrine, I think. I got a good look at him this summer when they brought him in on a backboard after an accident. Is Simon Royce another suspect?"

"It's Peregrine's real name."

"I thought that guy left town last summer."

"He did, but he might have returned. He had a lot of customers, and his greed might well have overridden his sense of caution."

"Any new leads?"

There was a pause, then Tony said quietly, "A couple of promising ones." He sounded reluctant to say even that much, and then he changed the subject. "Lauren told me this patient of yours smelled like a dirty cat-litter box."

"The air was pretty rank," Grant said. "That's why our therapist stepped out of the exam room for a moment, to get some fresh air."

"By your description of him, it sounds like a batch of meth could have gone awry," Tony said. "I'm glad you called."

"I'm just sorry we lost him."

"It happens. Don't let any eyewitnesses leave until my men get there."

"I won't."

This wasn't the first time a suspected drug trafficker had escaped the hospital before the police could arrive. Peregrine—a known pusher and possible kingpin of meth production in and around Dogwood Springs—had been brought to the ER last summer, strapped to a backboard. The fact that he had managed to escape from that situation attested to his physical strength and possibly to the additional power afforded to him by whatever drug he'd taken. It was a scary thought.

Grant leaned back in his chair and stared across the manicured lawn and sculpted cedars and holly shrubs at some of the early Christmas decorations that trimmed the houses across the street. "Tony, I feel as if we're under siege."

"Then you're sharper than most people in this area."

"It disturbs me that I see some of the same evidence of drug abuse I saw in St. Louis on a daily basis."

"Good. I want it to disturb you. I just wish more people were disturbed by it. Maybe you can help us rout it for good from this part of the Ozarks."

"I'm a doctor, Tony, not a police—"

"You're an expert, and I need as many experts as I can get, in all categories. You can recognize signs of drug abuse—and obviously drug-manufacturing accidents—before we have any other clues. I can count on you to sound an alarm as soon as you see something."

Grant had met Tony Dalton several times. The sergeant had been brought into this emergency room on a gurney last summer, blinded by a booby trap of ammonia that his partner had accidentally tripped during a drug raid. Grant could picture the tall, dark-haired police sergeant encouraging his men, issuing commands, and catching criminals. The word on the street was that Tony Dalton had been rough on Dogwood Springs' criminal population the past few years.

Because of one of those criminals, Tony was blind, but that didn't stop him. It barely slowed him down. Tony managed an elite force of men devoted totally to shutting down meth manufacturers that took refuge in the wilderness of forest that checkerboarded the Ozarks.

"When my guys get there they'll be out of uniform, as you know, but they'll show you their badges," Tony said. "Grant, the evil is spreading. Every time we catch one or two drug producers, three or four new ones pop up somewhere else."

"Your men can expect our full cooperation."

"Thanks, Grant. Keep me posted if you get any more suspicious cases or any patients with respiratory problems, particularly someone who might work in places at risk for fumes from the production. I've spoken with several members of the housekeeping staff from our area motels, and they are keeping a close watch."

"Will do, Tony. I'll be in touch."

Grant had just replaced the receiver when someone knocked at the door.

"Come in."

Vivian entered. The expression on her round, tense face arrested Grant's attention immediately. "Dr. Sheldon, you'd better brace yourself. That ambulance that was called out a few minutes ago? There was a little accident downtown. The patients don't look too bad, but the car was an older model Volvo."

He felt ice along his backbone. "Brooke and Beau?"

"And Evan Webster. They're being transported here."

CHAPTER 5

Archer Pierce stood in the shadows of the church auditorium, enthralled by the graceful movements of his fiancée, Jessica Lane, as she counted the steps from piano to pulpit to organ in deep contemplation.

"Think we'll fit?" he teased.

She nodded. If she caught the humor in his voice, she chose to ignore it as she returned to the piano for another check. "Think there's a way to downsize the stage so we can make more room for the congregation?"

He forced himself to be serious, not an easy task for a man so close to marriage. "If we use the stage for the whole wedding party, we can easily put two extra rows of seating in the front. If we do much more than that you'll have to cut the train on your dress."

The humor in his voice apparently reached her at last, and she turned a frown on him. "Careful, Pierce, or I'll call the tailor and tighten the waistline in your tuxedo. Better yet, I'll order you a pink shirt with ruffles and lace."

"I'd wear it if you really wanted me to."

A smile broke through, and it felt to Archer as if the tiles of the ceiling had slid aside to reveal bright afternoon sunlight.

Jessica Lane was the most beautiful person in the world. Not because she was a physically attractive woman—which she was—but because she had a more vital spirit than anyone Archer had ever met.

He stood staring into her lively hazel eyes and tried hard not to get lost in them while she described, with her typical theatrical gestures, the ambience she wanted to create at the church for their wedding. She was thrilled by the fact that the auditorium would already be decorated for Christmas.

In three weeks and one day Archer would be a married man—not only that, but he would finally be a *legitimate* pastor in the eyes of his church. Several of the more conservative members had questioned the wisdom of having a single, thirty-four-year-old pastor lead them, even if he was engaged to be married. When Jessica broke their engagement last spring, he had almost lost his job.

He couldn't believe that the day of his dreams was finally in the last stages of planning. Dad would officiate, and most of the congregation would be in attendance. Actually, it seemed to him that half of Dogwood Springs would be here. The balcony would probably crash with the extra weight.

He added a mental note—requesting that the ushers seat only skinny people upstairs—to the thousand others he'd made over the past few days.

Archer had found himself wishing, more often as time passed, that they'd planned a short—very short—engagement. Maybe they could still elope. All he wanted to do now was take the most beautiful woman in the world into his arms and hold her and tell her how much he loved her and—

"Heather will stand here when she sings." Jessica gestured to a mike stand in front of the piano. "She'll be wearing green silk, and the other bridesmaids will wear pale pink and green with an overlay of eggshell lace. I know it sounds old-fashioned, but I don't care. I would like to cover the piano with matching material and candles and—" Jessica paused and wiggled her fingers in front of his face. "Archer, are you listening?"

He took her expressive hand and drew it to his lips for a kiss. "I'm listening. Heather is wearing a lacy piano with candles and—"

"Archer!" A gleam of ill-suppressed humor lurked in her eyes, and she didn't attempt to pull away.

"It all sounds beautiful," he murmured. "I'm just so glad it's finally going to happen, I don't care if the best man wears ribbons and lace, or if we kneel at an altar covered with satin bows and baby's toes, or whatever that stuff is they—"

Jessica chuckled gently—whether to reassure him that she appreciated his juvenile sense of humor or simply because she was giddy with nerves, he couldn't tell. She kissed him on the cheek, then drew back and looked into his eyes. As usual, riotous waves of hair, the shade of autumn oak leaves, fell across her high forehead. She appeared every inch the beautiful singing star of Branson, but right now, at this moment, she gazed into his eyes as if he were the center of her universe. He knew better. God held that position.

Lately, they had begun to spend more and more time together, but in accordance with the advice Dad had given to prenuptial couples for the past thirty-odd years, they spent less time *alone* together. Archer loved and respected Jessica. He knew they would remain physically pure in every way. They both longed for more opportunities to know each other better on a mental and emotional level—and so they talked on the telephone a lot. And they exchanged e-mail constantly.

Remaining physically pure was not the problem. Archer wanted to remain mentally pure, as well. He wanted to honor Jessica with his thoughts as well as his actions. And since his church had a weakness for spreading gossip, he and Jessica both arranged their schedules to avoid that gossip, while he took special pains to protect the image of her in his mind.

Jessica turned and surveyed the far corners of the large auditorium. "We'll never fit everyone in here."

"Maybe we should hold our wedding the way we hold Sunday services—do it twice."

"I am not getting married twice in one day. Once is enough to last me a lifetime." She stepped down from the stage and wandered out into the center of the church. "I just hope Heather doesn't get silly and start flirting with the ushers or the groomsmen. Do you know, when she was asked to sing at her best friend's wedding, she made a few slight adjustments to her dress, and—"

"Please, don't tell me. Knowing Heather, she did a dance down the center aisle after the ceremony."

Jessica chastised him with a look.

"Oh, no. She did it *before* the ceremony?"

"Archer."

"Sorry, but I'm nervous enough without wondering about what kinds of practical jokes your baby sister's going to play on us."

"Relax, it won't be that bad." Jessica frowned. "Probably. Heather isn't a baby anymore, and she has her professional reputation to think about."

Archer continued to shrink from thoughts about what the undisciplined Lane sister might do, but he would let Jessica take responsibility for her. Even worse, he shuddered to think about what his own church youth might pull . . . or Hardy and Roger, Lauren McCaffrey's two younger brothers, who had agreed to serve as ushers.

A fine thread of tension deepened the exquisite lines of Jessica's face. She had endured more than one episode of doubt about becoming a pastor's wife. She was coming to terms with it now, but the pressures of responsibility could be overwhelming at times. Even Archer felt the pressure, and he was a preacher's kid, accustomed from birth to living in a fishbowl—actually, in this particular fishbowl, since his father had been the pastor here when Archer was born.

Jessica, on the other hand, had little church experience. She had gone to vacation Bible school every summer as a child, and that was it, until she moved to Branson for her music four years ago. Her baby sister, Heather, had dropped out of college and moved in with her. When Heather attempted suicide a year later, Jessica turned to a church in Branson for help. Archer had been serving at that church as a youth minister and had found help for Heather while developing a great friendship with her older sister.

"We have more RSVPs than we have seats now," Jessica said. "I'm just glad we have a large reception hall."

"We could still rent a theater for the service," Archer said. "That way everyone—"

"Too late to book a theater. Besides, if we did that, more people could attend, and we would become more of a spectacle than we are now." She turned to him, her generous lips pressed together in a resolute line. "If we hadn't already made the plans and sent out the invitations,

I would be very tempted to take you up on your offer to elope."

Archer had felt that pressure too often in the past not to understand her struggle. It made their relationship that much more precious to him, knowing the sacrifices she would make to share his life. "They already love you, Jessica."

"They don't know me." The final threads of laughter had died from her eyes, and her gentle grip eased from his. "Not the real me. Not the me who needs privacy, who doesn't react well to telephone calls at two in the morning, who refuses to be the chairperson of every committee they think I should join. I know they're already angry with me for forcing you to marry me so close to Christmas."

"You didn't force me to do anything, I—"

"They'll see it that way. I already heard Mrs. Netz muttering about it to her Sunday school class."

He felt a sudden rush of anger. "I'll talk with Helen."

"No! No, please, Archer. You know it'll just make things worse."

Ouch.

Old questions darkened her gaze as she walked toward the altar. "I'm trusting God with it," she said softly.

"You've made the right choice." He fell into step behind her, whispering a familiar prayer for Christ's spiritual healing and continued strength as they entered a new relationship together.

Jessica didn't have the solid foundation of a successful marriage as an example of the wonderful things God could place between two people who loved each other. Her parents had fought for years, then her mother died when Jessica was eighteen.

"Pastor Archer?" The church secretary stepped from the shadows at the back of the auditorium, her silver-gray hair reflecting the overhead lights like a halo. "Got a call for you. Can you stop by the hospital in a few minutes?"

He heard Jessica catch her breath, then let it out with a near-silent sigh.

"What happened, Mrs. Boucher?"

"Some of our church kids had a fender bender. Nothing serious, apparently. Those Sheldon twins and that Webster boy who hangs around with them."

Oh, no. And Grant was on duty today. "Tell them I'll be there."

"Tell them *we'll* be there," Jessica amended. She took his hand, squeezed it, and looked into his eyes. "You might as well start training me now. This is one job we're going to share."

Grant saw the boxy orange-and-white ambulance negotiate the final curve on Oak Street with sedate caution. No lights flashed, no siren sounded, and he slumped against the building in relief. They weren't coming in hot.

He hadn't been able to accept anyone's assurance that his children were safe, and he wouldn't rest until he had checked them out for himself. As the vehicle approached the bay where he stood waiting, he caught sight of Brooke sitting in the passenger's seat. She didn't appear frightened.

She looked mad.

As soon as the ambulance pulled to a stop, she unbuckled her seat belt and shoved the door open. "Dad, don't freak, we're all okay." She came bouncing from the ambulance in full-speed monologue. "It wasn't Beau's fault, we were just driving through town minding our own business when some *blind maniac* plowed into our front bumper, and Mr. Gaylord—you know, the pharmacist?—made us get out of the middle of the street while he called for help, and nobody got the *blind maniac's* license number because it happened so fast, but—"

Grant reached for his daughter and pulled her into his arms, then held her back so he could see her. "Is that blood on your face?"

"It isn't my blood, it's Evan's, and his bleeding stopped before the truck hit us, but Christy made him let her strap—"

"What happened *before* the truck hit you?"

Brooke lay a hand on his arm. "Don't blow a fuse, he got beat up at school, and we were on our way here anyway, so we thought it might be a good idea—"

"He was beaten up at *school*?" Grant's voice had suddenly developed a will of its own, and he could not control the horror that quaked through his words. "Brooke, that's assault. Did you call the police?"

"We didn't take the time."

"Dr. Sheldon, they all looked pretty good," Bill called from the back of the van as he slung the doors open and reached in to help Christy.

"He's fine, Dad," Brooke said. "He was composing his next editorial just before that *maniac*—"

"Your girl refused treatment—no surprise there." Bill raised his voice to be heard over Brooke's continued nervous chatter. "But we got both the boys to cooperate and put them on long spine boards with C-spine immobilization according to protocol. Vitals are what you'd expect, normal as you can get for sixteen-year-old kids." His casual Ozark drawl curlicued around the words and numbers of vital signs as he pulled Evan out.

Christy reentered the van. Grant wanted to go with her, to check Beau for himself, but instead he leaned over Evan's stretcher.

"Dad." Brooke tugged on the sleeve of his white coat. "Now, Dad, I told you not to freak."

"I'm not freaking. Evan, where's the blood coming from?"

"Head mostly, I think." He squinted up at Grant. "I lost a contact lens. This backboard is hard. Do I have to stay on it?"

"Give me a chance to check you out first, Evan."

"Brooke and I ran all the way across campus after Eckard hit me. If he'd damaged my spinal cord, I couldn't have done that, could I?"

"It depends, Evan. Sometimes you won't realize the extent of your injuries or your pain when your adrenaline is pumping. Hang on for a few more minutes." Grant wanted to go to Beau. He *had* to see for himself that Beau was okay.

The hospital entry door slid open, and Lauren came racing out of the ER, her face pale. She stopped when she saw Brooke, and relief registered in her eyes.

"Lauren," Grant said, "take Brooke to an exam room and check her out. On your way in tell Vivian to call the police. There's been an assault."

Brooke huffed at him like a nine-year-old. "But, Dad, I told you—"

"Sit on her if you have to." He ignored his daughter's protests. "Just do an assessment."

Lauren reached for Brooke's arm. "Gotcha. Come on, Brooke, you heard the man."

Brooke evaded her grasp. "Why won't anybody listen to me? I said I'm fine!"

Lauren outstepped her and put an arm around her waist. "Humor him, Brooke. He's your father. He's upset. This will make him feel better." She wiggled her brows and winked at Brooke.

At last, Grant's unmanageable daughter allowed herself to be managed. No one but Lauren could do that these days.

Grant shifted into automatic, leaning over Evan's stretcher, doing a neurologic check on him while surveying the surface damage to the boy's face and head. Reflexes were normal. The blood caked on his face and hair had come from a cut on his scalp.

After what seemed far too long, Christy pulled the last stretcher from the back of the ambulance. In spite of Bill's warning, Grant felt a sharp tug of alarm at the sight of his son strapped to a backboard, encased in a stiff-neck collar. "Beau?"

"Yeah, Dad," came Beau's studiously uninflected voice.

"Are you okay?"

"I'm alert and oriented times three, I've got a Glasgow Coma Scale score of 15." He rattled the terms off as easily as he could verbalize his trigonometry exercises from school. "I don't think I have any focal neurologic deficits."

Bill chuckled. "We can tell that's your kid, Dr. Sheldon. He can almost treat himself."

"Brooke and Evan are fine, too, as far as I could tell after the wreck," Beau said. "But since I was the driver and got them hurt in the first—"

"Beau, don't think like that," Grant said.

"He's upset," Evan whispered. "Just remember, the wreck wasn't his fault."

Grant laid a hand on Evan's bony arm and called again, "Beau?"

Christy and Bill rolled him forward.

"Yeah, Dad." There was a catch in Beau's voice this time. "Don't worry, it'll be okay."

Grant swallowed. He should be the one reassuring his kids, not the other way around. "I know, son."

There was a stretch of silence, then Beau said, "I'm just . . . sorry."

As Grant pushed Evan through the automatic doors into the ER proper ahead of Beau's gurney, he fought a vicious flashback, reliving mental pictures of the nightmare his family had endured two and a half years ago. The car coming toward them across the median . . . Beau's shout of horror from the backseat . . . Annette's gasp and her, "Oh, dear Lord, help—" . . . the sudden explosion of sound and pain . . . and then the darkness of heart that seemed to last forever.

"Dr. Sheldon, are you okay?" came Evan's gentle voice.

Grant gave himself a mental shake. "I'm fine. Let's get that head checked out." He wheeled Evan into the laceration room and looked up in time to see Christy and Bill transport his son down the hall.

What nightmares must Beau be reliving? What went through his mind upon impact?

Evan reached for one of the straps that secured him to the backboard, his thin, bony arm flexing with underdeveloped muscles. "I can't believe I left my tape recorder in the car. Do you think the police will hold it for me?"

"I'm sure they will."

"I hope so. I got a lot of good, up-to-the-minute stuff on that. Do you think if I call them they'll find it for me?"

"I'm hoping they're already on their way here."

Vivian stepped to the open doorway. "Evan, you're living with your father now, aren't you?"

"Yeah, Mom's remarried. She lives in Springfield."

"So does your father have legal custody of you now?"

Evan scrunched his lips into an awkward bow, emphasizing the dark bruise across his cheek and jaw. "Mom still does."

"Then I need to call her."

"No, you don't. Mr. Gaylord already did that while we were waiting outside the pharmacy." He gave a dramatic sigh. "That's the drawback about living in a town this size. No privacy. You don't have to call Dad, either. He's probably on his way here now. With my luck, they'll both get here at the same time. Get ready for the Great Christmas Clash. It happens every year around the holidays. If they can't find something to fight about, it ruins their Christmas."

Grant nodded at the LPN who came in to assist him. "Todd, set up for staples. If the cut is straightforward enough, we'll use them, and that way we won't have to shave so much hair."

"Thanks, Dr. Sheldon," Evan said. "I already have enough trouble getting people to take me seriously." His prominent Adam's apple took a bumpy ride up his throat and back down. "Uh, it's not going to hurt, is it?"

"It'll be over before you know it. Todd, I need to go take a look at Beau. I'll be back."

Lauren pressed the bell of her stethoscope against Brooke's chest. Except for an abrasion on her arm, the sixteen-year-old showed no signs of injury from the accident. Of course, Grant would want to see that for himself as soon as he finished with Evan and Beau.

"Your heart's still beating a little fast, Brooke." Lauren raised the stethoscope and stood back, studying the consciously stoic expression Brooke had adopted as soon as they entered the exam room. "You still upset about the car?"

"Wouldn't you be?" The firm yet delicate line of Brooke's chin took on extra definition. Her dark gray eyes focused into Lauren's with that characteristic Brooke Sheldon stare. "Beau and I worked hard for that down payment."

"Yes, but that car can be fixed."

"It won't be the same."

"I don't think that's what's bothering you." Lauren dabbed the abrasion on Brooke's left forearm with a gauze pad soaked with surgical cleanser. She had come to know Brooke too well these past few months to be fooled by the tough-girl stare. Deep within those eyes were tears that she was too stubborn to shed. "You never wanted that particular car in the first place."

The stare shifted to the closed door. "Beau wanted it. He loved that car. He's the one who drives so carefully. He's the one who makes us buckle our seat belts." She gave Lauren another quick glance. "He'd just finished making us buckle up before impact. Why did this have to happen to him? Now he'll start having the nightmares again."

"Again?"

"He had them after the wreck that . . . killed Mom."

Oh. Of course that would be horrible for him. For a strong, masculine young man who looked and behaved like a mature twenty-one-year-old, Beau Sheldon had the soulful sensitivity of a poet. "Then we'll have to be there for him, Brooke."

"Did you see the way he's acting, though? Can't you see that he's blaming himself?"

"I didn't get a chance to check him out before I brought you back."

"Before the ambulance got there, he was just sitting there, staring at the punched-in fender." Her words were soft and low. Sincere.

"I think there's more bothering you," Lauren said.

Brooke reapplied her steady stare. "I'm fine."

"I'm sorry about the car, Dad." Beau felt worse than sorry. He felt like a failure. Years ago he had quietly taken on the responsibility of keeping Brooke out of trouble. This time he'd driven her straight into it—not only her, but Evan, too.

Dad squeezed his arm, and something told Beau he would have gotten a big bear hug if not for the backboard restraints. "Son, you're all alive. You didn't cause the collision, and it's impossible to predict someone else's actions."

Beau wanted to cry, but he refused. He felt like a weakling. Grant Sheldon was a strong man, with broad shoulders that his family had always trusted to carry the load of life, especially since Mom's death—and in spite of his own struggles. Dad shouldn't be expected to carry the full responsibility all the time.

Still, he could handle just about anything.

Beau hesitated as his father released his arm and stood back. *Tell him.* That guy had probably followed them all the way from the high school. He had *stalked* them. Someone needed to know about it, the police needed to know. The man was more than crazy. He was scary.

"Son, if you hadn't been at the wheel, things could have been a lot worse."

"You mean Brooke didn't tell you about the car I almost hit when I ran a stop sign?"

Grant's shoulders lost some of their taut definition. "What caused you to run a stop sign?"

Beau hesitated. "I was trying to show Brooke the right way to hold pressure on Evan's head." *Tell Dad about the guy.*

But did he really need to know? Didn't he already have enough to worry about? If Sergeant Dalton knew about it, wouldn't that be enough?

Maybe not, because that stalker was probably tweaking. A meth abuser who was desperate to find his next high would stop at no crime to get what he wanted, and he had no conscience. He had probably followed them from the school because Evan had witnessed a drug deal. Maybe they knew he'd taken the pictures. If that was the case, then Eckard was probably involved.

Beau would talk to Brooke about it if he thought she wouldn't freak. She probably wouldn't; Brooke handled herself well when she needed to.

"Beau, are you okay?" Dad asked. "Your glasses—"

"I think Bill has them."

Dad reached forward and touched the bridge of Beau's nose. "They didn't break the skin, but it'll probably be sore for a few days."

"I know." *Don't tell him now. There'll be time for that later.* "I'll be fine, Dad. I hope they can repair the car."

"That car is a tank. I'd be surprised if they couldn't fix it up as good as new. It probably made quite a dent in the other vehicle. You say it was a truck?"

"A big, tannish one with rusty fenders."

"You noticed *that* much while he was getting away?"

No, he had noticed that much in the rearview mirror while the stalker followed them. "How's Evan doing?"

"I think he's a little more traumatized than he wants anybody to believe."

"Probably." *Poor Evan.* "I don't know why people pick on him so much."

"Of course you don't." A film of sudden moisture deepened the glow in Dad's eyes, and he blinked it away. "It isn't something that would ever occur to you." He gently touched one of the places on Beau's face where the cosmetic surgeons had made—and ultimately failed at—highly skilled attempts to restore the broad Sheldon smile after the accident that killed Mom.

"Son, I just got off the phone with your teacher, Miss Bolton. She spoke with the principal and superintendent, and if everything checks out with your story, which it will, Kent will be suspended from school for the remainder of the semester for attacking Evan in the hallway."

Somehow that didn't make Beau feel any better. It made him nervous. At least with Kent in school they could keep track of him and his friends.

"Beau? I thought you'd be relieved."

"I guess I should be, but knowing Eckard, this will just make him mad." Beau made the decision then. He would tell the police about the stalker, but Dad already had enough to worry about, and today's wreck would only make things worse.

Maybe Archer . . . No, he was too close to Dad. So was Lauren. Sergeant Dalton knew how to keep his mouth shut. Beau would talk to him and no one else.

Beau felt responsible, no matter what anyone said. If he'd driven straight to the police station instead of trying to play hero and duck the guy, maybe none of this would have happened. And he should have told Dad about it as soon as they got here.

"Are you feeling okay, son?"

"I'm fine. Evan's probably still shook up, though. You know how his parents get when they're around each other. It would be worse if they didn't call his mom, but he doesn't want to face her right now."

Todd knocked at the threshold, then stepped through the door to Dad's side. He nodded to Beau, then leaned toward Dad conspiratorially. "Dr. Sheldon, just wanted to give you the heads-up. There's a threat of an uprising in three. The people can't figure out why their baby's broken tooth doesn't take priority over a teenager's broken head. I wanted to ask them why their child's life didn't take priority with them in the first place, but I didn't want to get us sued."

Beau saw the infinitesimal movement of Dad's jaw—a sign of controlled frustration.

"I'll be okay, Dad," Beau said. "Don't worry about me."

Dad nodded and caught Beau's arm with another squeeze, then leaned down and kissed him on the forehead. "I love you, son. I'm just glad you're safe."

He turned and followed Todd out of the room.

CHAPTER 6

Archer led Jessica through the staff entrance to the emergency department and directly into the milieu of organized chaos that had become increasingly familiar to him these past six months. He was never totally at ease here, because he couldn't predict what situations he would witness. But he had come to realize that more people acknowledged eternity in this place of physical trauma than behind doors of stained glass, so he would go where he was needed.

He prayed that Jessica would realize that the volunteer position he held as a part-time chaplain for this department was as important in his service to God as his Sunday morning sermons.

As he led the way along the bustling hallway, he saw Grant in the laceration room with Evan Webster. Evan's face was the color of pre-baked sugar cookies, complete with red sprinkles. His acne-scarred cheeks seemed to shrink away from his prominent nose and cheekbones.

Evan Webster was not one of the beautiful people, but he was one of those people with promise, who might be very charismatic when he matured and filled out in all the right places and learned to control his tongue with a little more decorum. Now he was just an awkward teen-ager who had a way with words. And there was something about those puppy-soft eyes . . . squinting eyes. He must have lost a contact lens again.

"So the rumor was true." Archer strolled into the exam room ahead of Jessica. "Evan, I heard you and the Sheldon twins played bumper cars with the wrong person this afternoon."

Some of the tension relaxed from the teenager's face. "Hi, Preacher."

"Archer?" Grant didn't look up, and he obviously couldn't take his hands from the medical staple gun he wielded on his patient, but his voice engulfed Archer with welcome. "I didn't think you were on call until tonight."

"I'm always on duty for my own." Archer didn't react to the sound of the staple being shot into position in Evan's scalp, but he reached down and took Evan's hand with a firm grip.

Evan squeezed back . . . and squeezed . . . and squeezed.

Archer endured the pain without expression. It was an occasional hazard of this ministry. "Evan, your dad called us at the church while we were planning the wedding service, and I thought I'd bring Jessica along."

The pressure on his hand eased a little, and Evan smiled. "He told me he'd called. Dr. Sheldon sent him to the waiting room for a few minutes. Dad thinks staples belong in paper, not scalps, and he started getting dizzy, so Todd told him he couldn't watch." Evan grunted as the final staple struck its mark. "Mom's on her way here with Dork-face."

"Should I have brought my flak jacket?"

"Maybe you should just hide."

"Nope, I'll face her like a man."

Jessica cleared her throat softly, and Archer could feel the questions in her eyes without looking at her.

As Grant put the finishing touches on his handiwork, Evan's tension eased and color returned to his face. Archer gave the teenager another pat on the back and led a most curious fiancée from the exam room.

"Okay, I'm sure you'll enlighten me," Jessica said as she stepped around a gurney in the corridor.

Archer put his arm around her shoulders. "It's nothing new. I met Evan the night he had a bad reaction to some speed he was tricked into taking."

"Evan Webster on speed? I don't believe it."

"As I said, he was tricked by a so-called friend, Kent Eckard. His parents were as bitterly divorced then as they are now, but Evan was living with his mother instead of his father. I was in the room with Evan and his father, Norville, when Lucy entered that night. For some reason, that woman does not like preachers, and the introduction went downhill from there."

"Why doesn't she like preachers?"

"Evan doesn't know, and I never got a chance to ask her. Evan and his mother don't exactly have the closest of relationships. The night we met I made the mistake of trying to call a cease-fire to a battle between Norville and Lucy, and Lucy caught me between the eyes."

"That bad?"

"It seemed bad at the time," Archer said. "It was my first experience as a volunteer chaplain—and as an emotional punching bag. It seemed as if I could say nothing right to Lucy. My presence only made things worse for Evan. Let's go out to the waiting room so we can reassure Norville about Evan's condition. We may have to lay low when Lucy arrives."

Jessica preceded him through the entry door. "*You* may have to lay low, Brother Pierce, but remember, I'm not a pastor. And I'm not even a pastor's wife, yet." She smiled up at him. "In fact, this time maybe I can intercede for you. Don't forget, I know how to deal with feuding parents. I navigated that minefield for the first eighteen years of my life."

"Yes, but—"

She raised a hand to silence his protest and smiled lovingly into his eyes. "Archer, you're a fantastic counselor, you're a wonderful preacher, and I admire the way you stay on your toes with those kids in church, but you have been woefully deprived of something I've had in abundance."

"I don't know what musical talent has to do with—"

She pressed a finger against his lips and chuckled. "You have been forced to endure childhood memories of a loving family and parents who were still madly in love with each another after thirty-five years of marriage. That means you've been deprived of the necessary firsthand knowledge of a dysfunctional childhood."

She turned as Norville Webster came toward them from the far corner of the waiting room. "Hi, Norville, Evan's doing fine and the doctor has him all fixed up." She took his hand. "You've got a talented young man there. I've been reading his articles and editorials in the school paper."

As she continued to charm the look of sick helplessness from Norville Webster's white face and perspiring high forehead, Archer could only watch her with growing trepidation. She didn't know what she was getting into. Norville was a gentleman. His ex-wife, on the other hand, was no lady.

With a heavy sigh, Archer braced himself for the coming storm. He was about to tangle with Lucy again. *Lord, protect us all.*

Lauren spread antibiotic cream on Brooke's arm, taking care to be as gentle as possible. "You've had a rough day. You want to tell me about the attack on Evan?"

"Kent Eckard, that jerk." Brooke sucked in air.

"Sorry, does that sting?"

"Nope. Kent has hated Evan since last summer, when he gave Evan that speed. I mean, he*llo?* What did he expect? That Evan wouldn't tell the police about it when he almost died? It isn't fair! School isn't safe." She blinked hard and ducked her head. "Dad thought it would be different here, but it isn't. At least in St. Louis security's tighter. This stuff shouldn't be happening here."

"There are bullies everywhere." Lauren bandaged the wound and gave Brooke's arm a reassuring squeeze. "I understand how you feel. I had two little brothers I had to fend for when we were growing up. The other kids finally learned that when they messed with the McCaffrey boys, they also messed with me."

Brooke's expression revealed that she was not impressed. "So?"

"Bullies learned to scatter when they saw me coming."

"Hmm-mmm. You'd never hurt anybody."

Lauren flexed her right biceps muscle. "See that? I'm a farm girl, born and raised. I could bottle-feed a family of motherless piglets and milk the cows and haul hay out of the barn, and I could swing a mean fist, all between the time school let out and the sun went down."

The first inkling of humor spilled from Brooke's deep gray eyes. "Ever hit a guy?"

"Sure did, when he tried to bully Hardy, my brother."

"Did the guy hit you back?"

"He didn't dare."

Brooke glanced toward the door, then beckoned Lauren to lean closer. "I put a couple of moves on Eckard he's not going to forget." She pointed to her knee and elbow. "Didn't even get a bruise. He didn't expect me to know how to handle a bully."

Lauren giggled and reached for Brooke in an impulsive hug. "I probably shouldn't say this, but I'm proud of you."

Brooke's feminine yet muscular arms returned the hug with some force, and she laid her head, momentarily, on Lauren's shoulder. Lauren relished the bond that had grown between them these past few months—in spite of their initial meeting when Brooke had made her feelings clear about her widowed father's interest in dating again.

Now a week seldom went by when Brooke didn't hint that Grant and Lauren could use some time alone so they could get to know each other better. She was never shy about speaking her mind, or venting her frustration when the camaraderie between Lauren and her father remained unchanged over the months.

Never having been married and never having had children, Lauren found it easy to relate to Brooke as a friend—perhaps easier than it might be if she'd been a mother, with a mother's instinct to guide and teach and discipline. As it was, she didn't have to worry about that. She worked with the church youth because she enjoyed teenagers, not because she wanted to build endurance for motherhood.

"Lauren?" Brooke pulled away and looked at her. "Do you think Mom would be upset with me if she were alive?"

"Upset! For what? Your courage? Or maybe your loyalty to a friend?"

"Dad doesn't even know I attacked Kent, and he's all freaked."

"So am I," Lauren said. "But not because you did anything wrong, Brooke. I'm proud of you, and I know your mother would be, too."

Brooke closed her eyes. "I hope so." She slumped back down. "This whole day stunk."

Lauren frowned. Brooke seldom remained in one mood for more than a few minutes at a time, and Lauren was acquainted enough with all of Brooke's moods by now to know this was not a normal reaction to stress. Usually she talked, sometimes she shouted, and once in a while she got hyper and giggled uncontrollably, and then before anyone realized what was happening the stress was gone and Brooke was happy again. Lauren had become too close to this particular teenager not to be able to read the signs of something deeper than stress.

"The incident with Kent Eckard must have upset you a lot." Lauren leaned closer to Brooke's bedside.

For a moment, Brooke wouldn't open her eyes, and that squeezed at Lauren's heart. The expression in her face had that distant look that Lauren hadn't seen since the first few weeks after the Sheldons moved to Dogwood Springs from St. Louis—it was the look of someone on alert, closed in on herself because she had lost the ability to trust.

"If it's that bad, Brooke, we need to talk about it some more."

Brooke opened her eyes then, revealing tears. "There's nothing to say. I can't explain why I feel so . . . weird about all this. Something just struck me wrong."

"Uh-huh. You mean something besides the truck, right?"

Brooke scowled at Lauren's lame attempt at humor. "I feel responsible. I mean, not for the accident exactly, but for Evan getting beat up. You know how sometimes you feel like you could have prevented something from happening?"

"I'm pretty sure Evan wouldn't agree with you, especially after you dealt Eckard such a powerful blow to his ego."

Brooke shrugged the comment away. "It didn't exactly help Evan's ego, either, you know." She leaned toward Lauren and lowered her voice. "Evan isn't very popular. He irritates people because he has this bad habit of saying the wrong thing at the wrong time to the wrong person. But deep down he's a sweet guy, and I don't want him to get hurt, so I kind of . . . tag along after him sometimes. Kind of like a bodyguard. I'm bigger than him, and stronger. Did Dad tell you I took some self-defense classes in St. Louis?"

"Yes." Lauren reached up and wiped a smear of mascara from Brooke's cheek. "Want to talk to your father about this?"

"He's got enough to worry about. You saw how upset he was when we came in."

"Do you blame him?"

There was a knock at the entrance to the exam room, and the door slid open. Grant stepped in, drying his hands on a paper towel. "Blame me for what?"

"For being upset," Brooke said.

"I thought I was handling it pretty well, all things considered." There was an undercurrent of tension in his voice. He reached up for his stethoscope around his neck. "Doing okay?" He pressed the bell against his daughter's back.

Brooke grimaced. "Oh, Dad, I'm fine." She crossed her arms over her chest. "Just mad."

He nodded, and a grim smile passed over his face. It didn't settle in his eyes, but drifted away as quickly as it came. "No change there."

She curled her lip at him, then gave him a reluctant smile.

"Brace yourself," he said. "Evan's father is here, and his mother and stepfather will be here soon."

Brooke groaned, then put a hand on her father's arm and leaned toward him. "I know how you can stop them," she said in a stage whisper. "Call the police to set a speed trap on Highway 65. Evan said she drives at least eighty on that stretch. As if it isn't bad enough that he gets attacked by the school bully and gets caught in a wreck, now he has to deal with his neurotic mother."

"She has a right to be here, and I think she'll feel better when she sees Evan. His head wound is already stapled." Grant watched his daughter for a moment, then tossed his paper towel in the wastebasket and pulled her against him in a fierce hug. "Don't worry so much. The car can be repaired."

Brooke hugged him back and patted him on the shoulder, but her eyes remained open, and she looked at Lauren. "It's going to be okay, Dad." She stared hard at Lauren, and the doubt that clouded her eyes belied her words.

———

Evan's mother, Lucy Tygart, made a full-blast entrance through the ER doors forty-five minutes from the time the kids were brought in by ambulance. Her lanky, somber husband trailed a respectful three feet behind her.

Archer saw her through the reception window from the doorway of Beau's exam room. "She's here."

"Better duck," Beau said.

Archer grinned at him and stepped into the corridor to look for Jessica. He saw her standing in Evan's room at the end of his bed. She should at least have the opportunity to be formally introduced to Lucy.

He'd expected another thirty minutes before Lucy and her husband arrived. This meant they had probably broken the speed limit. He hoped they had left no victims along their path. He hoped they left no victims here in the hospital, either—particularly her son, who had suffered from her misdirected anger in the past.

The secretary pressed the automatic unlock for the door to allow the visitors access to the emergency department proper. Lucy's stress-bright gaze scanned the workstation with cool intensity as she entered, still ahead of her husband. The gaze dragged and stopped when she saw Archer. Her eyes narrowed.

Lucy Tygart was reputed to be an attractive woman when she was trying to be pleasant. Archer had never experienced that particular quirk in her personality. She could be downright ugly when the mood hit. He knew ugly.

Time for the introduction. Archer stepped forward at an angle to intercept, reminding himself, as he had done before, that Evan's mother was a confused woman with a lot of pain in her life, and a lot of anger. She had made Norville a target of that anger for too many years, and Norville and Evan were still coming to grips with the damage—not that they were total innocents in battle.

"Hello, Mr. and Mrs. Tygart," he said. "We've been waiting for you." Like a fly waiting for a swatter.

Her husband stepped up to her side and smiled. "Are you the doctor?"

Lucy gave her husband a look of tired amusement. "He's a *reverend*." She pronounced the word the way Jessica would pronounce *stinkbug*.

Her husband reacted like a well-raised churchgoer and held his hand out. "Hi, I'm Stan Tygart, Evan Webster's stepfather. Do you know if he's still here?"

Before Archer could reply, he caught sight of Jessica walking toward them, gearing up with her most charming smile as she approached the couple. Archer tried to catch her attention without catching anyone else's.

"Mr. and Mrs. Tygart?" She held out her hand. "I'm Jessica Lane. I've been visiting with Evan for the past few minutes. Would you like to—"

"Jessica . . ." Lucy gave a start. Her mouth formed a sudden, surprised *Oooh,* and her eyes sparkled. "*You're* Jessica *Lane.*"

"Yes, please call me Jess or Jessica, anything will do. May I call you Lucy?"

An expression of pure joy transformed Lucy's face. "Of course," she whispered. She looked down at Jessica's outstretched hand and reached for it as if she were caught in a dream. "I love . . . your music. Stan's taken me to two of your shows this year, and I have your CD. 'Daddy's Story Time' is my favorite. . . ." She caught her breath and released Jessica's hand, as if she had suddenly realized where she was.

Jessica chuckled softly. "Thank you. That's my favorite song, too. Why don't we go see Evan?"

Archer watched in dumbfounded amazement as the two women preceded Stan down the hallway, talking like old friends. The door to Evan's room swung shut behind them, and Archer continued standing there. His nerve endings twinged with some unnamed surge of emotion that he struggled to identify.

It should be joy, even pride and admiration that the woman he loved had revealed yet another God-given talent to the list that made her so special. Jessica had always been good at fitting into every social situation the church threw at her, in spite of her misgivings.

Another emotion should be relief that she had been able to tame Lucy's tongue before it turned to acid. But to his utter mortification, Archer realized, as he analyzed his own heart, that the emotion that caught him in its grip wasn't a positive one at all. It wasn't exactly jealousy. It wasn't exactly wounded pride. It was a mixture of those two nasty emotions with a third, less frightening one—disappointment.

He'd had no chance to leap to the rescue of his helpless bride-to-be. He'd had no chance to prove yet again the power of his love for her. Instead, he had been left behind, feeling—as he had the first time he came to counsel others in this emergency department—as if his presence here was superfluous.

Now he understood how Evan must have felt when Brooke fought off his attacker. Jessica's status as a well-known Branson singer had calmed the waters and soothed any negative reactions she might have received from Lucy. She hadn't needed his support or his presence.

She hadn't needed him at all.

———

Beau kept his voice low as he finished telling Sergeant Dalton about the harrowing experiences of the day. Evan had already been interviewed, and it looked as if Kent Eckard would cease to be a problem at school, at least for a while.

Tony switched off his handheld tape recorder. "Let me get this straight, Beau. You think the attack on Evan and the accident downtown were connected."

"I'm not sure, but I don't think what happened downtown was an accident."

The dark, muscular sergeant shook his head. "It doesn't sound like it."

"Please don't tell Dad. He'll just worry, and there's nothing he can do about it."

Tony leaned forward in the straight-backed chair, his heavy-browed, unseeing eyes seeming to focus on Beau's with uncanny accuracy. "I won't make any promises."

"I understand."

"I think you underestimate your father."

"No, I just don't want to worry him. You think this is drug related, don't you?" Beau asked. "Otherwise you wouldn't be here."

"I don't know yet." Tony shoved the recorder into his front shirt pocket and stood up, reaching for his cane. "I'm also following up on a case your dad had earlier. It seems as if half the cases this ER gets these days are drug related." He pushed his chair beneath the table and turned to feel for the doorknob. His fingers found it with ease. "Keep in touch, Beau. And keep an eye out for Evan Webster, would you? He's a bright kid, but he might be making some enemies."

"Sure sounds that way." It occurred to Beau that Evan Webster probably wasn't the safest friend to have—but sometimes people didn't pick their friends, they just kind of got put together, as if some bigger hand guided them.

Tony said good-bye and stepped into the hall, where his wife waited to drive him back to his home office.

Through the open doorway, Beau saw Stan and Lucy Tygart leaving Evan's exam room with Jessica Lane. Mrs. Tygart was all smiles. She seemed pretty happy to be in the presence of one of Branson's biggest celebrities. Jessica handled the star-worship with kindness. She was used to it. Beau would have chafed at that much attention. Jessica just took it in stride.

Beau also saw Brooke skitter down the hallway and slip into Evan's room, and he followed. Mrs. Tygart had been in Evan's room a little too long for him to escape unscathed.

"Well? How'd it go?" Brooke was asking as Beau walked in. "Was she mad?"

"I don't know." Evan reached up and fingered the short spikes of hair around his wound. "Does this look stupid?"

Brooke gently slapped his hand away. "No, I think you should cut all your hair that short. Leave it alone or you'll get it infected. What did your mom say?"

Evan gave a pleased grin at Brooke's attention. "She was worried. She wants to call an attorney and see if Eckard can be sued. She didn't get too bad, though, because Jessica wouldn't leave the room. Anyway, she seemed okay."

"Maybe marriage agrees with her."

"Could be." Evan frowned, then sighed. "You know, Dork-face may be okay, after all."

"That's what I've been telling you," Brooke said.

"Couldn't you call him Stan?" Beau asked.

"Hmm. Stan. You know he was on that business trip last week on my birthday?" Evan held up his arm, from which jutted a clunky wristwatch that gleamed like gunmetal. "He gave me *this* today. Can you believe it? He ordered it from the airline magazine. Isn't it great? Mom griped about it a little. Said he was spending too much money, but he said a guy only turns sixteen once. I bet it set him back more than a hundred."

"Don't forget he gave you the cell phone the day of their wedding," Brooke said.

"Yeah, but that was to buy me off, keep me from moving in with them." He held the watch up for them to get a better look at it.

"It's a watch," Brooke said in her "big deal" voice.

"No, it's a camera. See?" He gave her a quick tour of the tiny tool. "Cool, huh?"

"Yeah," Beau assured him. "Digital?"

Evan nodded eagerly, the trauma of his injuries forgotten. "Brooke, think of the pictures we could take—and nobody would even know it."

"No, Evan," Beau said. "That tends to make people mad, and you know what happens when some people get mad."

Evan was too enthralled with his new present to pay much attention to Beau. "You know, a guy could get used to this stuff." He straightened the watchband on his arm, then leaned back in the bed with his hands clasped behind his neck.

"Get used to what?" Brooke asked. "Letting someone spend so much money on you? Please tell me that isn't the only reason you've decided to like him."

Evan wilted. "It isn't. I'd think you'd know me better than that by now."

Beau felt sorry for him. "Lighten up, Brooke. At least the guy cares enough to want Evan's friendship, even if he doesn't go about it the best way."

"So what makes him think he's got to buy it?"

Beau gave his sister a warning look, then turned his attention to their friend. "Show me more about the watch, Evan. Can you download it onto your computer at home?"

"I probably can't, but I bet you could show me how. You're the computer genius."

"Let me see it. Do you have the directions?"

"They're over on the counter with my other stuff." He held the watch up and stared at it as if it were made of precious jewels.

Evan's encounter with his mother hadn't taken much damage control today, but Beau still wished they could forget this day ever happened.

CHAPTER 7

Dogwood Springs had settled comfortably into the forested hillside of southern Missouri a hundred and thirty-one years ago, and due to its protected location its citizens enjoyed warmer winters than in other areas of the state. The mature maple, hawthorn, oak, and, of course, dogwood trees, which had been planted when the town was first settled, had been dropping their brilliant leaves during the past few weeks. The autumn nature show had stolen Grant's breath away with its extravagant beauty.

One of the best works of art had recently displayed itself right smack in the middle of town, where thirty acres of cliffs and hollows and three pristine springs of sweet water served as a city park. A few brave leaves continued to cling with stubborn pride to their hosts.

This Thanksgiving Day had dawned so bright and warm that Grant invited his dinner guests to join him and his kids at the park for a picnic, complete with his own special Vidalia onion barbecue recipe to go with the turkey he had prepared in his outdoor smoker. Everyone else seemed thrilled by the change in plans. Everyone else had not been spoiled by Annette Sheldon's Thanksgiving dinners for half a lifetime.

Still, he enjoyed his seat across from Lauren, who sat between the twins, teasing Brooke and giggling with seemingly lighthearted abandon. She had a musical laugh that could melt the coldest of expressions. Of course, he was biased. So were his kids.

Grant assumed that Lauren might not realize the level of attachment the Sheldon family felt to her. He knew she hadn't intended it to be that way, but when Lauren McCaffrey gave her friendship, she shared her very soul. She gave without thought of repayment—like the gardening she had helped them with this summer, and the fishing trips when she had not only showed them the best spots to catch fish but also helped them clean and freeze their catches later.

He silently thanked God for her friendship. It wasn't something he would mention aloud—it would embarrass her—but this was a day to be thankful, and before Annette's death his family had always made a habit of naming aloud all the blessings they could count on Thanksgiving.

Lauren was filled with spirited fun today. Brooke had caught the contagion of Lauren's silliness, and Beau's eyes brimmed with laughter in spite of the damaged nerves that forced an uncharacteristic solemnity to his face. Occasionally he lost himself in the humor of the moment, and his cheeks and mouth contorted with the lopsided grimace that was the closest he could come to a smile. He felt safe—they were among friends. Grant wished there were more moments like this, when his son felt comfortable enough to be himself in public situations. At least he had forgotten, for a while, about last Friday's accident.

There were a few expressions that remained heavy in spite of all the teasing and laughter. Gina Drake sat at the next picnic table staring at her food and jabbing at it with her fork. From time to time she looked up at something Lauren said. Her unique, copper-colored eyes held shadows that Grant hadn't seen for several months.

Gina was a talker, and ordinarily when she and Lauren were together they could hold a chatterbox sideshow that was spectacular to witness, but today she sat in uncharacteristic silence except when one of her little boys, seven-year-old Levi or four-and-a-half-year-old Cody, asked her a question.

Grant finished his last bite of burger and gestured to her. "I hope you're not still beating yourself up about last Friday, Gina. You did the right thing."

The shadows did not go away. "Thanks, Grant. I still can't help thinking that if I'd stayed at my post and endured the stink, maybe he wouldn't have left."

"Or maybe he would have," Lauren said softly. "And if you'd been there, he might have—" She stopped, glanced at the little boys, and fell silent.

Gina's frown deepened. She returned to her study of wood grain on the picnic table without acknowledging Lauren's remark.

With a single look, Lauren expressed her frustration. There was something going on there, but Grant didn't have the nerve to mention it. If there was a problem between the two of them, Lauren would find a way to work it out as soon as possible.

Evan Webster and his serious-faced, balding father, Norville, sat across the table from Gina and her kids. They, too, had been mostly silent as they ate.

Norville tugged at the short bill of his hat. He cleared his throat and caught Grant's attention with a nod of his head. "I've been attempting to convince Evan that it might behoove him to take a prolonged visit with his . . . his mother." The words came out with obvious difficulty. As hard as Norville had struggled—and failed—to win legal custody of his son, it would be painful to let him go live with Lucy and her new husband. "For his own safety."

Evan sighed and rolled his eyes. "Dad, I told you that wouldn't work. I can get myself beat up just as easily in Springfield as I can here in Dogwood Springs. Besides, I've got work to do here. Right, Brooke?"

Grant's impetuous, occasionally clueless daughter blinked at Evan and shrugged. "You can take your computer with you and e-mail your articles to Miss Bolton. Now that you have that cute little camera you can e-mail the photos, too." She nudged Lauren and pushed two potato wedges onto her plate.

Poor Evan slumped. Grant felt sorry for the young guy and feared for the heart he wore on his sleeve. Brooke might break it unintentionally. Since she probably didn't even recognize Evan's crush for what it was, his feelings were in dangerous peril indeed.

Grant looked at Lauren and Brooke, who sat with their foreheads nearly touching as they talked about the upcoming wedding of their pastor and Jessica Lane. Grant could not suppress a quick pang of envy. He would like to have that kind of easy relationship with his daughter, but the parent of a strong-willed child could not let down his guard. At her impressionable age, Brooke needed the guidance of both a father *and* a mother, and so he was scrambling to fill both positions. He knew she wasn't taking it well. She'd become more secretive with him lately.

He was just glad Beau had a logical mind and a mature outlook on life. Trying to keep up with two Brookes would have killed most fathers.

Lauren said something that made Brooke chuckle, and Grant's attention returned to the soft, evenly rounded lines of Lauren's attractive face. As usual, she wore no makeup. Her blond hair tumbled around her shoulders with a golden sheen in the patchy sunlight that worked its way past the few remaining sassafras leaves that fluttered with spicy richness from the slender branches.

Grant felt an uncomfortable kinship with Evan.

With fingers and face covered in barbecue sauce, four-and-a-half-year-old Cody looked up at his mother. "Mommy, is Todd coming to the park?"

Lauren and Brooke stopped talking.

Gina blinked in surprise. "No," she whispered, then grabbed a napkin from the middle of the table and dipped it in her water. "Here, let's get you cleaned up."

"But I'm not done eat—" The rest of his sentence was cut off by his mother's brisk ministrations. Her complexion gradually deepened to an interesting shade of pink beneath the generous sprinkling of freckles.

"Did he have to work today?" Levi asked.

"I don't know." Gina started on Levi, who quite possibly had some sauce in his hair, although with the strawberry blond color dampened to amber by root beer from his brother's cup moments earlier, it was hard to tell for sure.

"Mommy, doesn't Todd like Thanksgiving dinners?" Cody asked.

"Todd?" Brooke asked. "Is he a friend of Levi's from school?"

"No," Levi said, "He's a friend of—" His mother's wet napkin suddenly covered his mouth.

"He's a friend." Gina's color deepened further. "Levi, are you finished with your potato? What a beautiful day. I love this time of year. Maybe it'll stay warm through Christmas. I don't want to drag out my winter sweaters yet. I don't like driving in snow."

"Snow!" Cody shouted. "I want snow!"

"Yes!" his towheaded brother chimed in. "I want to build a snow-man and have snowball fights and make a fort like we did in the moun-tains. Will it snow here?"

"Does Todd make snow—"

"You know, I think you boys need to run off some of your energy," Gina said. "Why don't we go play on the swings at the playground?"

"Yay!" Cody dropped his potato wedge and scrambled from the bench.

Levi frowned at the pumpkin pie in the middle of the table. "But, Mom, we haven't finished—"

"Later. You can have dessert later—that'll make Thanksgiving last longer." Gina picked up the paper plates and napkins and rushed her older son from the table.

"I can take them," Brooke said. "I'm finished. I'll push them on the swings."

"Uh, maybe in a few minutes. I need to get them settled down first." Gina glanced quickly at Lauren, then her gaze slid away. "I'll be back to help with cleanup."

Both tables fell into mystified silence as she walked downhill toward the swings and merry-go-round, holding her children's hands—practi-cally pulling them along.

"What's Gina all freaked about?" Brooke asked. "And who's Todd?"

Lauren drummed her fingers on the table. "You know, Gina's right. Maybe we could go on a walk when we get the tables cleared away. I haven't had enough sunshine lately. This is my favorite time of year. You should see the Christmas lights in the park. Thousands of lights spar-kling from the trees, all different colors. People drive from as far away as Branson and Springfield to cruise through the park after sunset dur-ing the Christmas season. I came from Knolls last year to see it."

Grant watched Lauren. What was she suddenly so nervous about? He leaned back and stretched and stepped from the bench. "I like Christmas lights, and I love autumn colors, but I think this is God's favorite holiday."

"Thanksgiving?" Lauren asked. "Not Christmas?"

"Think about it," he said. "When do we pay the most attention to Him? Not when we're busy shopping for presents to put under the tree.

I think God's signature holiday is Thanksgiving, when we take time to thank Him for all our blessings." And he had so many of those. He needed to remember them more often.

He picked up his plate and cup and carried them to the recycle bin.

"So that would mean that His signature season is autumn," Brooke said. She took a deep breath and looked around at the brilliant leaves covering the ground. "And His signature color is what? Burnt orange?"

"Blue," Lauren said after a moment of thought. "It's the color of the sky, and it represents eternity to me. Besides, it makes a great backdrop for the clouds and the treetops."

"Green," Grant said without hesitation. "It's the color of life." Particularly the color of Lauren's lively eyes, which always held so much kindness and vitality, reflecting the lush beauty of a cedar forest even after all the other trees had dropped their leaves. Ever green.

"If we're talking about God, though," Lauren said, "maybe it's white. You know, purity."

"Green is the promise of continual life," Grant insisted. It was the week after the hit-and-run attack on his kids. That was what he called it—an attack. He wanted them near him. And he wanted to be reminded of that promise of continual—eternal—life. He had so much to be thankful for.

"If you're looking for promises," Brooke said, "rainbows are God's reminder of His promise never to destroy the earth with another flood."

What Grant wanted was a promise from God that his family would be safe.

"Red," Beau said softly. "Blood red. The color of God's final price."

"There you go," Lauren said. "Beau, why don't you preach the sermon for Archer when he and Jessica are on their honeymoon?"

As Lauren, Brooke, and Beau continued the gentle argument, Grant returned to his place at the table and allowed the peace of the moment to flow over him. How long had it been since he'd felt this much enjoyment of a simple picnic? *Thank you, Lord. You are so good to me. I need to pause more often during my day to talk with you.*

In spite of the fear Grant felt after the accident last week, the Volvo had already been repaired, and his kids were healing. Evan bore the marks and bruises of an attack from a schoolmate, but that schoolmate was now expelled from school for his trouble.

Grant's mother was spending the Thanksgiving weekend with his sister in Kansas City, and his father was out traveling somewhere instead of stirring up trouble in the family, as was his habit at least once a year.

"Yoo-hoo, Dad." Brooke waved a hand in front of his face. "Your mind is somewhere on the far side of the galaxy. What are you thinking?"

"I think I need more days like this."

Brooke gave a theatrical sigh and grimaced at Lauren. "See? I told you he wasn't listening. Dad, that's what I just said."

"Sorry." He poured more iced tea and lemonade for his kids. "Tell me something, guys. Do you think I'm suffering from burnout?"

"Maybe," Beau said. "You're under a lot of pressure right now."

"He's not burned out," Brooke complained. "He can handle it, Beau. You know, you could learn to be a little more encouraging."

"I'm not trying to discourage him. It doesn't hurt to be prepared."

As brother and sister tangled in one of their famous debates, Lauren stood from her place on the bench and joined Grant at the cleanup table. "You haven't burned out, you know. Anyone who works with you can see that. Your patients can see it. You still care. You still do your best and go above and beyond your job description."

"But I don't think I'm handling the complaints as well as I did ten years ago."

"Ten years ago I doubt you had the patient load you have now."

"Actually, the emergency department in St. Louis handled about three times the number of patients we get here, and higher acuities for the most part, but we had more staff to take care of them." He pulled out the pecan pie Lauren had baked for dessert and placed it on a serving plate beside the pumpkin pie, which had been Norville's offering for the occasion. "Ten years ago I saw myself as a missionary."

Lauren took the plates from him and set them on the table, then returned to stand beside him. "Really?"

"Don't act so surprised."

"I'm not. The medical field *is* a mission, of sorts. Doctors are called to the mission field of medicine."

"Exactly." He loved the way she understood him so quickly. "When I first realized I was meant to be a doctor, I considered going someplace wild and exotic, like Africa or South America. I believed in what I was doing."

"Obviously you still do."

"When I made the decision to make emergency medicine my specialty, I realized my mission field was right there in St. Louis, where so many uninsured patients turned for treatment out of desperation. I even volunteered at a free clinic a couple of times a month, before the wreck." In other words, in his past life, before so much of it had been destroyed. "Lately I've found myself wondering if I sold out when I moved the kids out of St. Louis."

"No." Though spoken softly, Lauren's reply was immediate and firm.

Grant looked into those green eyes, which held so much assurance for him right now. And as he held her gaze, he felt another stirring of some of the joy he had experienced so many years ago, when he was young and idealistic and convinced he could take on the world.

"You came here because you were meant to come," she said. "I know God is constant, never-changing, even though it might sometimes appear to us as if His plans for us change. But I don't think God sticks us in a rut with the intention of leaving us there forever. He has the ability to use us wherever He places us. It's obvious He's using you here, and that you continue to touch lives, right here in Dogwood Springs. I'll never forget you saved my life."

Against his will, Grant recalled with vivid detail the early morning hours in June when he and Archer conducted a panicked search for her the same night that they discovered the mercury poisoning that had attacked Dogwood Springs. They'd found her lying unconscious on the ground beside her truck, out by Honey Creek, her favorite fishing spot. Had they been any later . . . *Thank you, Lord.*

"She's right, Dad," Brooke came over to stand beside them. "Archer said in last Sunday's sermon that we shouldn't be afraid of changes in our lives, because those changes can be used to help us develop a more deeply satisfying life."

Lauren nodded in agreement, and once again, Grant allowed himself to enjoy the beauty of those eyes. He knew, without doubt, that he was feeling an emotion he hadn't experienced since he was a teenager falling in love with Annette, his best friend.

"To me," he said softly, "green is still God's signature color."

———

Levi and Cody screamed with delight as Brooke and Beau pushed them on the merry-go-round at the playground downhill from the picnic area.

Lauren could feel Gina's gaze on her and wondered at the uneasy truce they had silently called today. It hurt to have this wedge between them. It was painful to be at odds like this, and she could tell Gina still carried some pain from it herself. Still, what other option was there?

Seldom had Lauren confronted someone like she had done last Friday with Gina, but seldom had it been so vital that she do so. She would do it again if necessary.

Gina took a container of Grant's barbecue sauce from the table and walked over to the cooler beside Lauren. She leaned against the bench. "My boys were asking about their father last night." She opened the lid of the cooler and found a place to put the sauce.

"I didn't think they knew him," Lauren said.

"They don't. Levi was a toddler and Cody was a newborn. But the kids in Levi's class at school talk about their fathers. He's started asking questions, and Cody has picked up on it."

Lauren felt a rush of sympathy. "I know that's got to be hard on you. What have you told them?"

"As little as possible. How do you tell your children that their daddy left because he didn't want them?"

Lauren was quiet long enough that Gina looked at her with a silent question.

"I don't know."

"Levi asked me last night if Todd could be his dad," Gina continued.

Lauren ripped two squares of paper towel from the roll. *Lord, what do I say? She's hurting. She's lonely and desperate. How can I tell her how wrong this is without destroying our friendship?* "What did you say?" She cringed at the sound of criticism in her own voice.

Gina obviously caught the sound. She stiffened and turned a resentful gaze on Lauren. "I told them no. What did you expect?"

"I don't know, Gina. I guess I expected the truth from you last Friday."

There was a swift, angry intake of air. "What?"

Lauren met the glare with an apologetic shrug. "You told me you were only meeting Todd for lunch, that's all it was," she said softly. "I believed you. But if you're just having lunch with him at the hospital, why do the kids seem to know him so well?" It hurt to ask the question, and Lauren braced herself for Gina's fury.

It didn't happen. Gina looked away, closed the lid of the cooler, and fumbled with the handles. She folded the foil over some of Grant's homemade whole-grain rolls and placed them into a plastic bag. She glanced over her shoulders, then leaned closer. "Okay, we had lunch at my house a few times when the kids were home. I didn't think it was a big deal. I mean, we've visited with William Butler like that."

"But William—"

"No, Lauren." Gina raised a hand to cut her off. "This is something I have to deal with myself. Why can't you just be a sounding board for me?"

"Because I'm your friend," Lauren said. "Friends care enough to tell you the truth, and this thing with Todd is—"

"It isn't a *thing*, okay?" Gina jerked a knot in the plastic bag that would probably never come loose. "I don't want to tell the whole world about this, you know."

Lauren took the bread from her and set it on the table. "Why not, if it's so innocent?" She took Gina by the arm. "Come on, let's take a walk."

Gina made her reluctance obvious, but she went. They strolled a few yards away from the picnic area, and Lauren released her grip. "Your life has just begun, Gina. God's taking it and making something beautiful out of it, but you need to be patient."

"I've *been* patient. I don't know why you're getting all hot about a simple friendship."

Lauren took a few steps in silence. In all her years of being single— and all the resultant bouts of imagined loneliness—she had dreamed of having a family. Children of her own. A husband. She wouldn't remind Gina of the love she shared with Levi and Cody, because she knew they were never far from their mother's thoughts. Lauren, more than anyone, knew what Gina had endured when she thought she would lose them this past summer.

"I know you're lonely."

"I don't think you know the meaning of the word," Gina snapped.

Lauren winced. That stung.

Apparently Gina realized the sharpness of her words as soon as she said them. "You have parents who love you, brothers and sisters and nieces and nephews and all kinds of friends in another town, and yet you chose to move away from all that. If you were lonely—if you truly understood what it meant not to have those loving ties—you wouldn't give it up so easily."

"I didn't give it up." She hadn't, had she? "I just had to give it some space. You know how much pressure they've been putting on me to get married. Mom gets a little whacked out about it sometimes. Gina, please don't let your loneliness push you into something that's wrong for you. Remember when we had lunch together for the first time? And we talked about the kind of men who attracted us?"

Gina nodded. Her scowl lifted, and she looked up at Lauren with more tenderness. "That was when you told me about your crush on Archer, and Fiona Perkins overheard you and spread the rumor that you were carrying his child."

Lauren didn't need the reminder. "And you told me—"

"Yes, I know what I told you, but—"

"You said you were attracted to the undependable ones."

"I *know*."

Oops. Don't push it. Time to find some common ground. "There are some things worse than being alone. I want to see you happy, Gina. I mean truly happy. Sometimes you have to—"

"Wait." Gina stopped at the edge of a spring that trickled from a cliffside covered in kudzu vine. She placed her hands on her hips. "Stop trying to convince me you know what I'm going through. You don't have any idea what it feels like to be dumped by the one person who knows you better—more intimately—than anyone else."

"You're right. All I know about is being rejected by someone who doesn't even care enough about me to spend time getting to know me." Oh, hold it. She hadn't meant to say that. She sounded bitter, but she wasn't. She was happy for Archer and Jessica. She was happy for Lukas and Mercy.

"But there's someone right back there at that picnic table who would do anything to get to know you better, and all you can do is run away," Gina said.

"You're changing the subject."

"It's true."

"If you're talking about Grant, I'm not running anywhere. We have a good friendship, and I'm there for him and his kids, and he knows that."

"Oh, so you can have a perfectly innocent friendship with a man, but I can't."

"Grant's wife died two and a half years ago. He didn't leave his family so he could be 'friends' with me."

Gina glared at her, and the flush that tinged her cheeks matched the fire in her eyes. She crossed her arms over her chest. Lauren thought she might storm away, but she didn't. Instead, she sighed, closed her eyes, and sank down onto one of the flat rocks that had, thus far, avoided the thick growth of kudzu vine.

Ordinarily Lauren would have apologized again, begged Gina's forgiveness, and tried hard to make amends. She knew she sounded harsh and judgmental, and she didn't want to. But this was too important to back down. She had to remain firm.

"Like I told you," Gina said softly, "you don't know what the rejection is like, Lauren. I thought you understood about my family. Everyone I've ever loved has left me or rejected me. When my husband left me for another woman, I felt so ugly and unlovable. I felt such a deep need to feel approval, reassurance that somebody, somewhere, would still want me."

"Someone does."

"No, you don't understand. I mean *that* way. Attractive. Desirable."

Lauren took a deep breath and sat down on the rock beside her. *Gina's right, Lord. I don't know what it's like. How can I even pretend to identify with her?* "I've never been married, I know, but don't you think it's slightly possible that single people crave that intimacy, too? That need to be attractive to someone else? At my age, when I tell people I'm single, they take for granted I've been divorced, and when I explain that I've never been married, I can see in their eyes that they wonder what's wrong with me, as if I had some kind of strange problem. These days, it's much more acceptable to be divorced than it is to be permanently single."

"You're just a little too choosy."

Lauren felt a prickle of irritation and realized this conversation wasn't going well. She looked up at the kudzu that covered the cliff behind them and trailed into the pool of water that sparkled from the spring.

She broke off a leaf and held it out. "See this? Pretty, huh?"

"I guess."

"I've heard that, years ago, people thought it might be a cheap way to prevent erosion, and so they introduced it here in our country. They soon found out that it was the worse of two evils. Now it covers a huge portion of land in the South and starves out the native plant life. It spreads voraciously, and it's become so prevalent it can't be wiped out. Someone told me that ragweed was introduced the same way. Now look how many people are miserable every summer and fall because of those weeds."

"You're comparing Todd to ragweed?" For a second, Gina's natural sense of humor glimmered in her eyes, and then she pressed her lips together and looked away.

"You're trying to battle loneliness by seeking a relationship that looks inviting at first, but it can kill you on the inside and cause destruction to everything it touches, including your children and his children."

Gina stood up and held her hand out as if to keep Lauren away. "With you it's all cut and dried, isn't it? But it isn't that easy for me. I'm sorry, I've got to go." She turned away and trotted back to her children.

Lauren buried her face in her hands. "Well, God, I blew that."

CHAPTER 8

E arly Friday afternoon, the day after Thanksgiving and a week after his first frightening episode of chest pressure, William Butler battled a wave of depression as he made his way to the ER once again. The mystery remained. The symptoms were back.

He'd spent the first three days this week driving back and forth from Dogwood Springs to Springfield, enduring test after test, consulting with specialists, waiting for results. Nothing. They had found nothing. He had tried to follow the doctors' orders—surrendering much of his work to assistants and attempting to avoid Jade Myers, with her complaints about finances and slovenly insurance companies.

Still, his schedule had been a tight one, and he'd had to take precious time to instruct the staff about proper procedure if, heaven forbid, he should be away from his office for more than a day. He would much rather just do the job himself. But what if that wasn't possible?

Now he concentrated on placing one foot in front of the other with great caution, watching his feet as he avoided curious glances from hospital personnel. Fear threatened to paralyze him. Or was this numbness a precursor to a stroke? What was happening?

He staggered for the first time just as he reached the staff entrance to the ER. His hair felt matted to his forehead with perspiration, and his hands looked pale gray as he reached up to open the door. He stepped into the flurry of activity and apparent confusion that was always evident at this time of day in this section of the hospital—

particularly on a day when family practice docs weren't in their offices because of a long holiday weekend.

How he loved this hospital—his hospital. What would happen to all that had been accomplished by the work and sweat and tears he had invested in this place if he suddenly couldn't do the job? Especially with Dr. Mitchell Caine serving as chief of staff this year.

Caine was every hospital administrator's worst nightmare, with his constant demands for public funding that wasn't available, his complaints about imagined slights from other staff physicians, and his attitude of superiority and exaggerated dignity.

As a hometown boy, Mitchell could get away with a certain amount of ugly attitude, because the townsfolk still remembered him as the smiling young man of his youth. But William had recently been the recipient of more than one report about Mitchell's sudden flares of temper. Patients were looking elsewhere for the kind family physician they had expected when they called his office number. Everyone agreed that Mitchell was not the same idealistic young man who left Dogwood Springs for medical school over a generation ago.

As soon as William stumbled through the staff door into the bustling ER proper, Lauren McCaffrey turned from the drug dispenser and caught sight of him. "Mr. Butler!"

"Lauren, it's happening again." He reached for a counter to catch himself. Thank goodness the slurred speech had not returned. Yet.

"Okay, it's okay." She rushed to his side and took his arm. "I've got you. Here, let's get you to a bed."

He allowed her to support part of his weight.

She turned and called over her shoulder, "Dr. Sheldon! We need you over here."

Grant looked up from a chart on the counter of the central workstation, then shoved his chair backward and rushed toward them.

Will took an easier breath. Grant was on duty again, not Mitchell. With all the pressure Mitchell put on Grant to add hours to his ER shifts, this was a minor miracle. Mitchell must have decided to keep his own office open today.

"It'll be all right, William." Lauren led him gently forward.

"Will, how do you feel?" Grant's strong, reassuring voice came seconds later as he caught William from behind and helped Lauren guide him into an empty exam room.

"Weak. Shaky. Tingling in my left arm." He looked at Grant and was reassured by the expression of calm strength that always seemed to emanate from the younger man.

"Chest pressure or pain?"

"The same as before." Will sighed. "I thought I was going to be okay." He heard the tremble in his voice and felt a slight thickening of his tongue. He concentrated on controlling his speech. "I delegated nearly half my busywork to the secretaries." He sank back onto the bed with a grunt of relief. "I tried to slow down. I even threatened Jade that if she didn't stop calling me three times a day about problems with the insurance company, I would run for mayor myself and lock her out of the office."

Grant gave a soft chuckle. "I'll deal with Jade. You remember the drill from last week, don't you? Lie back and relax. Let us do all the work and all the worrying." He turned to issue orders to Lauren, who had already called Grant's son, Beau, to assist and had begun collecting vitals.

"Maybe this will pass like the last one," William said.

"I don't want to wait for it to pass; I want to find out what it is. Did you keep those appointments I made for you in Springfield?"

"Yes, yes, I did it all. Holter monitor, treadmill, and everything else you said they'd throw at me." He held up his hand to present the bruise from the IV. "First-degree atrial-ventricular block." He closed his eyes. "Nothing life threatening. Said it's probably my age."

"And last week when we admitted you they did the carotid Doppler ultrasound and echo?"

"That's right. Nothing significant."

"How's your vision?"

William opened his eyes to find Grant watching him closely. "Fine, but my tongue is feeling funny." He could tell his speech was slurring again. He felt so frustrated and helpless. "Grant, what can you do?"

"I'm going to connect you to the monitor. Then we're going to keep a close watch on you. I think we need to get a little more history. I must be missing something."

William nodded. "You and the rest of the world."

"Dr. Sheldon," Vivian called from the hallway, "we've got an injured man in a private vehicle in the ambulance bay, and an ambulance is on its way in with an ETA of three minutes."

"Go," William said. "You don't have much time."

Vivian nodded. "And you'll want to see the people in the private vehicle, Dr. Sheldon. Looks like a child at the wheel. They're both covered in mud, and I can't tell if the child is a boy or a girl. Christy's in one of her moods today, and she's likely to run right over that car with the ambulance if we don't clear out that bay before she gets there."

"I'll help with Mr. Butler, Dad," Beau said. "Just tell me what to do."

William raised his hand and waved Grant away. "Get to work, Doc, and let Beau work on me. I trust him." Beau Sheldon had already passed his CPR test, and his knowledge base surpassed that of many of the other hospital personnel. He volunteered whenever he wasn't scheduled to work for pay. William admired the kid. "Go on, Grant. Can't have you loitering back here with the hired help."

Grant gave William's arm a reassuring squeeze. "I'll be back soon. Meanwhile, Lauren and Beau aren't leaving your side."

As Grant walked out the door, William forced himself to relax. He wasn't going anywhere. He needed to calm down. He had to stop wondering what was going to happen to the hospital if any of the fears racing around and around in his mind actually happened. If Mitchell Caine wasn't chief of staff . . .

He felt a hand cover his own, and he looked up into Lauren's gentle green eyes.

"You look like a man with a lot on his mind, William."

"What's new? The old treadmill of business just keeps getting faster and faster."

Her grip tightened on his, and she lowered herself onto a stool beside him. "You want me to call your pastor?"

"I don't intend to be here that long."

"Then I guess it's up to us, huh?"

He knew, before she even bowed her head, that she was going to pray.

The cry of an ambulance whined in the distance as Grant and Todd stepped out into the bay. A muddy pickup truck idled where the ambulance driver would expect to be pulling in any minute. Sure enough, a child, who looked to be about eleven or twelve, sat in the driver's seat, clutching the steering wheel in obvious fear. Tears made dark streaks in the dried mud on her face.

"Todd, get us a wheelchair out here, would you?" Grant opened the passenger door and did a quick visual assessment of the man who occupied the seat.

He was sprawled across the seat with his left leg stretched out, and a white T-shirt was tied around his calf. His jeans were wet, torn in several places, and spotted with blood. The pain was evident in the mud-cragged lines of his face.

He groaned. "You the doc here?"

"Yes, I'm Dr. Grant Sheldon." Grant looked at the child in the driver's seat, then back at the man. "I take it you're the patient, Mr.—?"

"Cameron." The man grimaced in pain. "Call me Cam. I think I need some stitches, maybe a rabies vaccine."

Grant reached into the truck to help him out. "Rabies?"

"Dog bites."

Grant hesitated before moving him. "Any broken bones? Back or neck injury?"

"Nope, they just ripped me up a little."

The ambulance siren blared again, just blocks away, as Todd arrived with the wheelchair.

Grant set the brakes on the chair. "Todd, I'll help our patient out of the truck, but I need you to park it for—"

Cam reached up and grabbed the side of the doorframe. "Don't need help parking this thing. Haley dragged me out of the creek, wrapped my leg with what she had at hand, and hauled me on the ATV eight miles through creeks and trees and hillsides. She's been driving this truck since she could peer over the dashboard." He winced and gasped and grabbed at his leg.

"Dad!" Haley cried. "Please, mister, do something fast!"

Grant reached toward the tear-streaked child. "It'll be okay, sweetheart. We'll take good care of him. Why don't you go ahead and park your truck over there." He pointed toward the patient parking area. "Then you can come into the hospital, and someone can get you a drink and help you clean up a little."

She nodded and gripped the steering wheel with both hands.

Grant nodded to Todd, and together they eased the man out of the truck. As the ambulance rounded a corner and pulled into view, Haley put the truck into gear and steered it out of the bay. Grant and Todd pushed Cam through the automatic doors.

As soon as Cam was out of earshot of his young driver, he moaned aloud in obvious pain. His hands gripped the arms of the wheelchair so tightly his knuckles turned white, and he sucked in his breath with deep, panting gasps. "Do something, Doc. I didn't want Haley to know . . . how bad . . ."

"Let's get him to five," Grant told Todd. "And get those boots off. Cam, I want to give you something for the pain as soon as possible. Are you allergic to any pain medications?"

"Wouldn't know. Never take 'em."

Grant grabbed the clipboard for room five and a T-sheet from the rack. "Any allergic reactions at all?"

"Penicillin. Nothing else."

Grant continued his questions as they pushed the patient into the exam room and set the brakes on the wheelchair. He unwrapped the leg and saw multiple puncture-tear wounds of a vicious bite in the fleshy portion of Cam's left calf.

The patient winced. "I think you found the spot, Doctor."

"I see." Grant palpated the foot and checked the toes. They were warm. No interrupted blood flow. He examined the wound on Cam's right thigh and another on his ankle above his boots. Neither was as deep as the calf wound. "Todd, help me get Cam onto the bed, and let's remove the wet jeans and shirt. Cam, we'll have to cut your jeans off and irrigate all these wounds. I see three, do you know of others?"

Cam shook his head. "I was wearing a leather jacket. Can somebody call my wife? She's going to kill me for taking Haley with me, but I don't want Haley to wait—"

"I'll take care of that," Vivian assured him from the doorway. "We've got an aide taking her to the private conference room. Dr. Sheldon, the ambulance is in the bay."

"Thank you. Would you please call a nurse down from the floor?"

Archer tugged at the bow tie of his black tuxedo, buttoned the coat, and stood in front of the small mirror in his office beside his bookcase. He smiled at himself, then chuckled. His youth group would laugh at him. Let 'em laugh. Jessica would like this look.

He had never been a particularly modest guy, but as far as he knew, he wasn't conceited. Mom and Dad would never have allowed that to happen. Still, even though it embarrassed him when people compared him to Paul Newman in his early thirties, it made him feel good, too.

When he made the decision to follow in Dad's footsteps at the age of seventeen, Dad had warned him that it would be harder for him than most men in ministry, because some people automatically expected a handsome man to be weak willed when it came to women.

Archer had never considered himself handsome, and women weren't his problem, in spite of what some members of his congregation wanted to think.

His problem was getting people in this church to take him as seriously as he would like. Mrs. Warren, who had been his Sunday school teacher for two years and youth director for seven, still called him "honey." If he got too close, he was always afraid she might pinch his cheek or, worse, grab his ear to get his attention if he was doing something she didn't like. He tried to be on his best behavior when in her presence.

Still, the familiarity had been a good protection for him when Jessica forestalled their engagement for a few weeks this past spring. The members of the church who had watched him grow up knew they could trust him, and they had been loyal. For the most part.

One small, powerful faction had tried to stir up some trouble, but it never went anywhere, simply because there had been no truth to the rumors they had heard about him and Lauren McCaffrey.

There was a knock at the door that connected his office to the church secretary's, and he stepped over to unlock it and open it.

"Pastor, there's a—" Mrs. Boucher blinked and stepped back with parted lips. "Why, Archer, aren't you a handsome one!" She, too, had taught him in Sunday school twenty-five years ago, and though she tried hard to give him the respect she felt a "man of the cloth" deserved, she sometimes slipped up. That was fine with Archer. He preferred a casual church office. He felt his neck flush. "Thanks, Mrs. Boucher. It's my wedding tux. Jessica wanted me to try it on to make sure it fits. I wanted to be wearing it when she arrived."

Mrs. Boucher turned and glanced over her shoulder, then back at Archer. "Speaking of Jessica, there's a lady out in the foyer who says she's here for a counseling session."

"A counseling session? Are you sure?" He didn't have it written in his appointment book.

"Her name is Lucy Ty—"

"Tygart." Archer felt his stomach tighten in dread anticipation. What could Evan's mother be doing in town? "You said she's here for counseling? You're *sure?*"

Mrs. Boucher spread her hands in a gesture of confusion. "She didn't want to come to the office—said she'd wait in the lobby for Jessica."

"Jessica?"

"Yes, that's who she said she wanted to see."

"I'll go speak with her." Instinctively, Archer straightened the collar of his coat, wishing he'd waited until Jessica arrived before he tried on the tux. Now he felt silly.

He stepped into the expansive church foyer and indeed saw slender, sharp-chinned Lucy Tygart seated in one of the padded chairs beside the stairwell that led down to the children's classrooms on the second floor. The church was built into the side of a hill, like much of the town, and consisted of three levels. The main entrance was on the top level and had a broad walkway out to the parking lot that crested the hill. The church enjoyed a panoramic view of Dogwood Springs. The auditorium took up the front half of the two top stories, and the basement contained a well-supplied kitchen, as well as a multipurpose room that opened to another parking lot and basketball court.

Lucy stood up when Archer stepped toward her. "Hello, Reverend

Pierce." There was the barest hint of latent antagonism in her voice.

He held out his hand. "Hello, Mrs. Tygart. Please, just call me Archer. Would you like something to drink? Some water or lemonade? Some tea, perhaps? We keep a pitcher of—"

"No, that's okay." Lucy stared at his hand, as if she were afraid he might be playing some kind of practical joke on her, but she took it in a very brief clasp. "I thought your . . . um . . . fiancée would be here."

"Unless she's changed her plans, she isn't due for another thirty to forty-five minutes." He postponed the obvious question—what was *she* doing here?—but held his arms out and indicated his choice of attire. "As you can see, we're making sure everything will be perfect for the wedding. You're welcome to come up to my office and—"

"No, that's okay." She took a step backward and glanced nervously around the foyer, like a tiger trapped in a cage. "When we talked she said she would try to meet with me before the church office closed for the evening. I wouldn't want to put you out."

There was that edge of animosity he remembered so well. The edge was not nearly so sharp as it had once been, but it was still there. This time, however, he thought he detected a quality he hadn't picked up previously—uncertainty.

"You're welcome here, Lucy. Nobody's going to bite you, nobody's going to throw you out." He saw the narrowing of her eyes at his gentle chiding. "I have to admit to some curiosity, however, since I'm aware of your attitude about all things relating to church."

"Particularly preachers," she said dryly.

"That's right."

She glanced once again toward the door, as if hoping Jessica would suddenly enter through it and rescue her from this unwanted conversation. Jessica didn't do so, however, and Archer continued to wait.

"Tell me, Reverend, you live off the tithes of your church members, don't you?" It was an accusation, as if she'd caught him stealing food from a convenience store.

He swallowed his irritation and offered up a silent prayer for wisdom. "The church pays me a salary, Lucy. Pastoring this church is my full-time occupation; it's what I was trained to do, and what I love to do. It's fully supported by biblical principles." He would not debate further with her about the rightness of his calling.

"My parents belonged to a church once, when I was a kid." She folded her arms over her chest. "My father was a stockbroker in Fayetteville. He made pretty good money and gave a lot of it to the church. Problem was, the pastor of that church controlled those people like he was God. So when this guy decides they need a new church building, with all the very best workmanship and most expensive fixtures, he uses his charisma to convince these church members he's right. They build the church, and then you know what he does? He manipulates the right people so that the property is put into his name."

Archer suppressed a shudder. "I can imagine what happened next."

She nodded. "So he gets all caught up in his own hype—I mean, this guy's on radio and they're talking a television broadcast, the works, and he starts dictating what they should and should not do with the extra money coming into their church because of his so-called *ministry*. When the people finally get wise and start asking questions, he gets all huffy and uses the church property as a point of extortion. There's a church split, we lose the building, and my parents never enter a church again."

"I'm sorry that happened, Lucy."

"So now you know why I dislike preachers."

"Actually, no, I don't."

"My parents became very bitter after that."

"And you're continuing a family tradition?" He couldn't help himself.

Lucy stiffened and glared at him.

"Think about it, Lucy. I've seen far too many divorces in my life, but I still believe in the institution of marriage, or Jessica and I wouldn't be getting married in two weeks. Obviously, you still believe in that same institution, in spite of your own divorce from Norville."

"But I've seen too many televangelists use God's name to build their bank account."

"You've only focused on those who lost sight of their first love, much in the same way married couples lose sight of their love when they grow apart."

"Grow apart? That man ripped our church apart, piece by piece."

"You're concentrating on the failures, Mrs. Tygart. You will not see someone fail who puts Christ first and self last. The man who hurt your family and your church obviously gave no thought to God's will. When God truly guides a church, their love for one another and for the One who died for them becomes more and more obvious to those around them who are hungry for the genuine hope they have in Christ."

She was shaking her head before he could complete his final sentence. "I'm not hungry for any false hope, Reverend."

"The hope God gives us is not false. Don't let that one wayward man lead you down the same path of unbelief that he's traveling."

"Hey, is it sermon time?" Jessica came breezing in, wearing jeans and a blue knit sweater with a matching corduroy jacket. She had obviously not taken the time to scrub her face after the show, because her eyes held the dark definition of liberal stage makeup.

She rushed over and grasped the woman's hands. "Hello, Lucy. I'm so glad you could come. Would you like to stay here and talk, or would you rather take a stroll? It's a beautiful day, and the wind is dying down."

"A walk would be nice," Lucy said.

"Good." Jessica released Lucy's hands and turned her attention to Archer. The natural warmth in her eyes deepened, and her smile widened. "Perfect. You look wonderful. The tux is an exact fit." Without a hint of self-consciousness, she stepped over and kissed him firmly on the mouth. "I'm going to take a walk with Lucy, okay? I'll be back before it's time for us to leave."

Before he could reply, she touched Lucy's arm and turned to lead her out the door into the brilliant, late November sunshine. Their footsteps echoed across the concrete walkway for a few seconds before the door closed. Archer stood looking out the narrow windows that framed the doorway. He battled disappointment. He realized he was a little more conceited than he'd thought, because he'd hoped that Jessica would make a little more of a fuss over the tux.

His biggest disappointment, however, was the fact that he'd seen no change in Lucy's expression as he talked, not a hint that she'd "gotten" the point he was trying so hard to make.

Typical Baptist preacher—disappointed because no one walked the aisle after my sermon. I should be ashamed of myself. But he wasn't. It was the way he was wired.

He looked down at his black tux and sighed. "Guess it fits," he murmured as he went back into his office to change.

William studied the mesmerizing blip that marched in a structured rhythm across the monitor screen. He was feeling better again, and the steady beep screamed healthy. He knew enough about medicine to realize they would probably find no answers today.

So why. . . ?

He lay in silent contemplation and listened to the activity in the other rooms. An ambulance had just brought in a patient from a local convalescent home. A nurse was irrigating the wounds on the bite victim's arm and legs, and Grant had everything under control. He had ordered Demerol with Phenergan to control the man's pain, called the sheriff and the local ranger station about the animal attack, and ordered treatment on the ambulance patient.

Sound carried very well in this ER. It made for good communication, even if it did cut down on patient confidentiality.

Vivian had asked Beau to take the man's daughter away from the traumatizing activities of the busy department, and the girl had gone eagerly.

Yes, Grant had everything under control. William didn't doubt that the doctor had the seasoned ability to meet any challenge.

"Tell me something, Lauren."

She stepped to his bedside and laid a hand on his arm. "What's that?"

"What do you think of Grant as a director?"

"Excellent."

"People skills?"

"The best."

He raised his head and gave her a pointed look. "Could he take my place if I'm out for a few days?"

She hesitated. "What makes you think you'll be out, William?"

"Call it my skills of cynical insight. I'm preparing myself for the worst."

"Then you can relax," she assured him. "I've never seen Grant fail at anything—just don't tell him I said that."

"You know, I might just talk to Grant about drafting him for some of my duties."

"Good idea. He'll be back in a few minutes."

He rested his head once again on the pillow. "Maybe things will be okay after all."

Grant examined Cam's wounds as soon as they were cleared of blood. None of the bites had penetrated the fascial sheath. Still, with two surgeons in the hospital, it wouldn't hurt to request a second opinion. Bite wounds were notoriously susceptible to infection. And if the dogs were rabid . . .

"Cam, tell me what happened." He sat down on the chair next to the head of the bed.

The man's head rolled to the side and he gazed around the room. "Haley and I were riding my four-wheeler down a logging trail some of my buddies told me about last week." His speech no longer held the broken edge of pain. "We crossed Pigeon Creek, and Haley was screaming and laughing because she got splashed by the cold water." Cam closed his eyes. "It's feeling better, Doctor."

"Good. Let me know if the pain returns. When did the dogs attack?"

"I guess they heard Haley's voice when she screamed, because they were running full tilt toward us when we rounded the curve just past the creek."

"You're sure they were dogs? Not coyotes or—"

"A Rottweiler and some kind of large shepherd mix. Two of them. I know dogs, and these two meant business. They weren't some hunter's bird dogs." He looked around the room again. "Haley? Where'd she go? Is she—?"

"My son is taking good care of her, Cam. Try telling me more about the dogs and what section of the forest you were in."

Cam gave precise directions and the forest trail number, then laid his head back against the pillow. "I'd seen dog tracks earlier, but I didn't think much about it. I mean, I've been all over the state and never had problems with mean dogs before. I couldn't let these guys get to Haley."

"What did you do?"

"I plowed a new trail through the brush for about a hundred feet, then rerouted to the trail and raced back through the creek. We'd have been okay except for that creek. I hit the water so hard we fishtailed sideways and got stuck in sand. I had to get off to push. The dogs caught up with us just as I got the tires clear. I yelled at Haley to drive back to the truck as fast as she could and not to look back."

"And the dogs attacked you then?"

"They did until Haley charged at 'em with the four-wheeler." There was a hint of parental pride in his voice, "She wouldn't leave me with them dogs. Stinkin' monsters."

"I'm surprised you got away with no more injury than this, even with the leather jacket."

Cam blinked up at him. "Hear what I said, Doc? Stinkin'. They stunk. It gagged me. Wasn't skunk, either. They smelled almost like they'd been rolling in a rotten carcass, but it was different . . . sharper. That scent lingered with me halfway to town after Haley ran them off. Do rabid animals stink like that, Dr. Sheldon?"

Grant hadn't heard about any rabid animals in the county lately. However, he had heard warnings about other activities. . . . He turned and gestured to the secretary again. "Vivian, get Sergeant Tony Dalton on the phone for me. This may be drug related." He leaned toward Cam. "It may not be rabies at all."

Tragically, it could be something much more dangerous and difficult to destroy.

CHAPTER 9

William came awake with a jolt at the edge of a snore and blinked at the white walls, the antiseptic smell, and the mechanical beep that filled the space around him. The door opened and Grant Sheldon stepped into the exam room. He nodded to Lauren, who had kept vigil at the foot of the bed.

"How's he doing?"

"Very well," Lauren said. "He's been asleep."

Grant laid a chart on the counter. "Sorry to disturb you, Will. I know you needed the rest."

"Let me guess," William grumbled, "the results were all normal."

"No change from last time." Grant pulled the stool over next to the bed. "We need to talk."

"Don't you have other patients to treat?"

Grant gave a chiding shake of his head. "When's the last time you took a vacation?"

"This spring."

"I don't mean a working vacation."

"Neither do I."

"How long were you out of the hospital on this break?"

"Three days."

"That isn't a vacation—it's a weekend. Some people get those several times a month." Grant took the stethoscope from around his neck and positioned the cold bell on William's chest.

William waited, watching Grant's friendly gray eyes as they narrowed a bare fraction of a millimeter.

"Sounds healthy, doesn't it?" William asked when Grant completed his examination.

"It sounds normal."

"Then you aren't going to convince me to take time off. Not now."

"Not even if I threaten to call Jade?"

William felt a trickle of fear as he thought about Jade's overprotective reaction. "You wouldn't."

Grant returned the stethoscope to its customary position around his neck. "You're right, but it would be tempting."

"She would hire bodyguards to sit on me."

Grant smiled. "If I think it's necessary, I'll call them myself. What kind of a vacation could you possibly have taken in three days?"

"I went turkey hunting with my nephew in Ohio."

"Did you enjoy it?"

"Most of it. We didn't get a turkey, and the creeping critters were bad, especially for early May, but it was a good—"

"Take some time off. Doctor's orders."

Once again, William allowed himself to consider the possibility. "I might . . . if I knew I had qualified help to keep things running while I was gone. I would need someone with good administrative abilities."

"I'm not asking you to take a month, Will, just a week or so."

William gave Grant a more direct look. "As I said, if I knew someone was here, making the decisions, arguing with the insurance reps, fending off the mayor—or charming her—someone with a good head for business and a medical background . . ."

"I'll take care of things while you're gone, Will, you know that."

"You're serious?"

"Of course."

"Enough to allow me to appoint you as acting administrator in my absence?"

"I don't think you'd need to do that for a short absence."

"It's absolutely necessary." William glanced toward the doorway, then gestured for Grant to come closer. "If any other physician were chief of staff this year I wouldn't worry, but I am sorry to say that I have no faith in Mitchell," he said quietly. "If you're acting administrator, you'll have authority over him. You can keep him in line."

"Then of course you can—"

"Hold it." Lauren looked up suddenly from her chart. "William, what did you say about creeping critters a few moments ago? Are you talking about ticks?"

"That's right. No hunter can avoid them."

"And you were in the state of Ohio?"

A frown marred the handsome, evenly lined features of Grant's face. "You didn't get a bite, did you, Will?"

"How am I supposed to remember that? It's nothing unusual. I do recall that they were all over the place, and it was an irritation. I find it ironic that we were hunting for a tick predator. Turkeys dine on—"

"You don't remember if you received a bite?"

"In our family, you aren't considered to be a hunter unless you've been—"

"Did any ticks become embedded in the skin?" Grant's words came a little more sharply this time.

"Grant, I grew up on a farm. We always had ticks and chiggers and—"

"Will."

"Yes, I know what you're getting at, but I don't remember any bull's-eye rash. I didn't develop flu symptoms or any irritation around a site."

"That only happens about two-thirds of the time. You didn't take anything to prevent Lyme disease after you came out of the woods?"

"If I did that I would be gulping doxycycline every few weeks. I like to get out into the woods when I can." William thought for a moment. "Wait a minute. I do remember one particularly irritating place. But it didn't get infected. You know how hunters like to get out to their site and stay. Well, up in Ohio we drove out to our site as soon as my nephew picked me up at the airport, and we left just in time for me to take a quick shower and change my clothes before I boarded to come home. There wasn't time to do a check—"

"So you did get a bite?"

"I don't know. It was in . . . an unreachable area, which I couldn't actually look at, if you know what I mean. Now that my wife is gone, there's nobody to . . . well . . ."

"Ever heard of a hand mirror?" Lauren asked. "I use one every time I go fishing."

"Excuse me a moment—I need to call the lab." Grant went to the door and disappeared down the hallway. By the time he returned, a mantle of concern had settled itself over his face. "My friend, you could very well be experiencing an advanced stage of Lyme disease. You of all people should know that if it's allowed to invade the body without a fight it can mimic stroke and cardiac symptoms. And those symptoms, even though they aren't the real thing, can be dangerous if allowed to continue."

William slumped back against his pillow, feeling a strange mixture of relief and consternation. And embarrassment. Grant was right. He, of all people, should know better. He just never worried about it that much because it had never happened to him, and now that he lived alone, he didn't keep up with everything the way he would like to.

"Okay." He let the idea soak in. "Test me for it." He held his arm out. "Draw another vial if you have to. If that's what this is, do whatever it takes to get me back on my feet and behind my desk."

"I've already ordered the test. You'll still need medical leave," Grant said. "And if that's really what this is, I would advise more than a week. This could take some significant time to clear up."

William closed his eyes and moaned. After years of healthy service, his body was letting him down.

"Don't worry," Grant assured him, "I'll be here to help with the load."

There was a knock at the door, and at Grant's word of permission, Vivian stepped in. "Dr. Sheldon, there's a private call for you in your office."

"Would you take a message for me, Vivian? I'll return the call in a few minutes."

"I think this might be one you'll want to take."

Something about her voice attracted Will's attention. He looked at her, then at Grant. "Go on, Grant. I think we already know what my problem is. I'm not going to try to slip out on you. Take Lauren with you. I'm obviously not in much danger for a while."

———

Jessica stepped into Archer's office just as he was pulling on his jacket to go out looking for her. Her wavy golden brown hair fell in tangles over her shoulders, her cheeks were flushed from wind and exertion, and her hazel eyes danced with some unnamed excitement. She peeled off her jacket and draped it across two branches of the brass hall tree in the corner of the large room.

"Did you have a good walk?" Archer asked.

"It was very enlightening. I think I'm going to enjoy this business more than I expected." Her long-legged stride carried her across the room with casual grace. She wrapped her arms around him and kissed him soundly on the mouth.

For a moment he forgot everything else and enjoyed the impact of her loving presence, the softness of her arms, the unique fragrance of her lilac perfume combined with the fresh scent of physical exertion from her energetic movements during her afternoon show.

He frowned, however, with one uncomfortable term still ringing in his mind. "Business?"

She released him with obvious reluctance. "Hmm?"

"What business are you referring to?"

"Oh, that. Oops, I should have said ministry. Slip of the tongue. You know, music business, counseling business. At any rate, I think I'm actually going to enjoy this aspect of being a pastor's wife."

"Oh. That's good. I'm . . . glad." He turned away and reached up to adjust a book in the shelf beside his desk. *What counseling business is she talking about?*

Jessica stood in the middle of the office in silence for a few seconds, then she stepped up behind him. "Why do I get the feeling that you aren't as thrilled about this as I am?"

He knew that if he hesitated to reassure her, this was going to become an issue. Still, he would not lie to her. "I guess it's something I'm going to have to think through, because I honestly don't know, Jess." He turned to face her. "This is all a little bit of a surprise. I didn't realize you were going to be meeting with people as a counselor. I thought we'd agreed that the demands of the church weren't going to swallow you alive the way it does some spouses. And what kind of counseling are you doing?"

The light in her eyes lost some of its sheen. "Oh, Archer. I'm sorry. Maybe we should have talked about it before I did this. Of course you'd be upset. Why didn't I think? I mean, you attended school, you studied long hours, disciplined yourself to earn the privilege to listen to the troubles of your church members, and here I am talking about it as if it's just an easy career adjustment for me."

He frowned. "And so what, exactly, is it? I don't get the connection. You were actually counseling Lucy about a problem she has?"

"Not as a professional counselor, no, but she asked me last week when we met if I would be willing to talk to her about . . . something."

He waited. She didn't explain further.

"I hope I didn't hurt your feelings when I went walking away with her like that," she said. "I know this was supposed to be a day for us, but I came early just to meet with her."

"Yes, I understand that." The curiosity was becoming uncomfortable. Did he have a right to ask for more information? Didn't married couples share everything together? Yet, they wouldn't be married for two more weeks.

"So Lucy has a . . . personal problem and asked to talk with you about it?"

Jessica nibbled on her lower lip and studied his face in silence for a moment. "Yes. I'm sorry, I don't think she would want me to betray a confidence."

Ouch. "No, of course not." There was his answer. And she was right, but it still rankled, and for a moment he couldn't figure out why. *Jealousy?*

Could be. Easily.

Or maybe it was something else. "Jess, I . . . I wouldn't want to see anyone take advantage of your relationship with me."

"Take advantage? In what way?"

"I couldn't miss the sudden change in Lucy's behavior when she realized who you were the other day. I think, because of that, she was much less antagonistic to me today. Don't get me wrong, that's a relief after the way she's behaved toward me in the past."

"Then, what's the problem?" Jessica asked.

He sighed. He wasn't wording this very well. "Other than the fact that I'm bungling this badly, I just worry that, as one of your more enthusiastic fans, she might have used the opportunity of meeting you in the hospital to take advantage of—"

"Oh, that." She grinned and waved her hand in dismissal. "I just think she's star struck. If she is, she'll get over it, and meanwhile maybe she'll listen to what I have to say."

That didn't cure his curiosity.

She reached up and gently laid her hand across his jawline. "When I'm your wife, I intend to shoulder some of the responsibilities that come with the territory. I know you feel it would be a burden to me, but I can't help feeling just as strongly that it will be more of a blessing. Don't sell me short, Archer. I can do more than sing, you know."

Archer was about to serve his rebuttal when he was stopped by a knock at the door, and at his invitation Mrs. Boucher stuck her head inside. "Do you mind if I go home, or would you prefer I stay and play chaperone so Netz doesn't drive by and see your cars alone in the parking lot and jump to another stupid conclusion?"

"That's okay, Mrs. Boucher," Archer said. Bless her, she was protective of him since that last uncomfortable misunderstanding with the deacons. "Thanks for the offer, but we're leaving, too. I can hear Jessica's stomach growling."

"Correction," Jessica said, "that growling is coming from your stomach, Archer Pierce. Thanks for the reminder, Shirley. We're on our way out right now."

The secretary said good-night and left the door open.

"Archer." Jessica turned back to him. "Honey, I know you're not accustomed to sharing the pastorate with someone else. You've struggled for years to be taken seriously in this church, because you grew up here and people keep comparing you to your father."

He gave her a reluctant smile. "I'm sure that's one of my deepest, darkest reasons, but there's more to it than that, Jess. I just don't want the more dependent members of our congregation to manipulate your life so you will resemble their own personal idol of grace. They can't force you to mold yourself to their expectations. I hate to see you get dragged in."

"Lucy isn't a member of this church."

"No, she's a fan from Springfield."

"I can handle fans—I've had plenty of practice." She took his arm and walked with him out of the office, then turned and waited for him to lock the door behind them. "And I promise I won't go meddling in your job, but I think I can help with this one."

"I don't think you're meddling." He dropped the keys into his pocket and strolled with her through the foyer and out into the brisk November air. He didn't lock the building, as their dedicated janitor was still on duty. "But how do you plan to help Lucy?" He knew he was being shameless in his quest for information.

"First I need to get to know her better. Then I'll let her get to know *me* better. She needs to understand what Evan's going through, how he feels. I've heard him remark a couple of times that his mom and step-father are glad he isn't living with them. I don't know where he gets that idea."

"They are newlyweds. It's natural for them to want to have some time alone."

"She loves her son very much, Archer, but I don't think she has any idea about how to show that love."

"Maybe she could start by telling him how she feels."

"First, I think she needs to identify those feelings for herself."

"I take it you told her that already."

Jessica slanted him one of her "Do you have to ask?" looks.

"Of course you did. Silly of me."

She grinned at him. "I'm starved. When do we eat?"

He kissed her again. For now those tidbits of information would have to satisfy his curiosity.

Lauren was just completing the last of her outstanding charts when Grant stepped out of his office with such an expression of shock on his face that she immediately thought something might have happened to Brooke. If something had happened to Beau she would have heard about it, since he was here in the hospital.

His gaze roved the department until it focused on her. He didn't need to say a word.

She dropped her chart on the desk and hurried over to him. "What is it?"

He motioned for her to follow him into his office, then closed the door behind her. "That phone call for me was an attorney with General."

"The hospital where you used to work?"

He nodded. "Two years ago a patient died in my emergency room. Six months ago I was served interrogatories for a malpractice lawsuit from her sister. The document named three physicians and the hospital."

"They're suing *you*?"

"Among others. Don't look so shocked," he said. "It happens to doctors all the time. When the sheriff served the papers last spring I filled them out and sent them back, and I didn't think any more about it because I knew from intensive follow-up research that I had met standard of care."

She watched the play of frustration across his face. "I take it someone disagrees."

He pulled a chair out for her, then sat down beside her. "Apparently. I never expected it to go this far. The patient had myasthenia gravis." Lauren noticed the hint of sorrow that was always present when he mentioned the suffering of a patient.

She leaned forward in her seat. "So her muscles wore out, and she became too tired to breathe?"

"That's right."

"Should you be telling me this? I mean, don't the attorneys warn you not to talk to anyone about the case?"

"Yes, but why would they call you to testify? You weren't there when it happened. When the patient—"

Lauren raised her hand for silence. "Hold it a minute. I need to check one thing." She stood and walked out of the office and stepped into the supply room next door. Good, no one was there. She pulled the door shut behind her so they would hear if anyone opened it, then rejoined Grant in his office.

"Sorry," she said, "but you know how voices carry through the vent. We don't want to take any chances with this. So tell me about this patient."

"When she presented to our department she was sick," he said. "But her vitals weren't serious enough to intubate at that time, and she told me she did not want that tube down her throat. I could understand that. I had treated her several months previously with the same condition, and we had a good outcome with high dose IV steroids and breathing treatments. It seemed to be working this time, as well, and I gave orders for her to be admitted to ICU immediately."

"What went wrong?"

"There was a bed shortage in ICU, and we had to keep her in the department until one became available."

"But that could be several hours."

"Exactly. Since this happened thirty minutes before shift change, I gave report to my replacement, Dr. Teschlow. I explained the patient's status and documented what I told him. When I left work that night, I had no reason to believe anything would go wrong."

"What happened?"

"When I returned for my shift the next morning, I received word that she had died. Dr. Teschlow had decided after I left that she needed to be intubated. In order to do that he gave her a paralyzing agent beforehand. It was a depolarizing agent, which is contraindicated for her condition."

"Then that's what killed her."

Grant nodded, and a stain of sorrow darkened his eyes again for a moment. He looked down at his hands. "That's what killed her. Teschlow told me later that I had not properly reported her condition. My documentation showed that I told him about it twice. He also stated that I should have intubated her as soon as she arrived. I disagreed and still do."

"But doesn't your paper work back you up?"

"The copies I have do. I'd made copies of my T-sheet and dictated an addendum to her chart when I heard about her death so I could study my records and see if I'd made a bad call. I hadn't. Later, when I was given the hospital chart to review and sign for the attorneys, my addendum was missing."

"Someone tampered with it?"

"I would hate to make that accusation. There was a copy of Dr. Teschlow's documentation, which, of course, disagreed with mine. Now I need to find a private attorney to represent me, which means I'll probably have to foot the bill for this, guilty or not."

"But I thought the hospital had provided your malpractice insurance."

"They did, but only if I agree to be represented by that hospital's own attorneys. If I'd realized I was risking this mess when I signed that contract, I'd have funded my own malpractice protection, even if it did set me back twenty thousand a year."

"So you're saying you don't have coverage after all."

He leaned backward and rubbed his face. He looked tired. "With the hospital using their own attorneys to represent all of us, I'm afraid there will be conflict of interest. When I met with the attorneys last spring, I was told at the time that there would probably be a summary judgment and my name would be dropped from the suit."

"And it wasn't?"

He shook his head. "I think the attorneys for the defendants have since decided it would be in the best interest of the hospital not to do so."

"But you're innocent! How can they place the blame on you? That's ridiculous!"

His attention was momentarily diverted by her outburst, and his tender gaze focused on her. "You see," he said gently, "Dr. Teschlow is now the ER director there."

Lauren hated the politics played in the medical field. She had always hated them. "Oh, yes, I do see," she said dryly. "You're not on staff any longer, so they're making you the scapegoat, even if it was his action that killed her."

"It's happened before," he said. "I've seen colleagues wiped out because some hospital, or another physician with more political clout, needed a fall guy."

"So who called you today, Grant?"

"The same attorney I spoke with last spring. His tune has changed. The plaintiff's attorney has someone's attention, and he has political clout. I get the feeling he sees dollar signs on this case. They apparently set a trial date several months ago, and it's scheduled for two months from now. The depositions begin next week, and the defense attorneys suddenly want more information from me."

"Next week! They're springing this on you so quickly? How unprofessional."

"As I said, the case in question happened two years ago, so they'll want this wrapped up."

"So what happens? What are you going to do?"

He propped his elbow on the arm of his chair and rested his chin on his hand. "I have to go to St. Louis on Monday. I don't have a choice. I've called a friend of mine who's a malpractice defense attorney in the city. We've got an emergency appointment for Monday evening. I've already called Dr. Caine, and he's taking my shift."

Lauren groaned. "Why won't he be in his own clinic?" She did *not* want to work with that man.

"Since most of the other family docs in the area took today off as a holiday, he agreed to keep his clinic open today in exchange for Monday. He's always looking for more shifts, so I thought he'd jump at the chance. I was right."

"How long will you be up there?"

"I'm not sure. Lauren, I need some help. I can't take the kids out of school for this trip because I'm not sure how long I'll be."

She felt a trickle of discomfort and was instantly ashamed of it.

"I thought of Norville and Evan," he said, obviously noting the hesitation she was trying to hide. "Norville's been working a lot of overtime lately. Archer and Jessica are overwhelmed with wedding plans, and Archer's also helping Sergeant Dalton set up a drug awareness training program." He was talking faster now. "I thought about that teacher at school they like so much, Miss Bolton, but there's only one person I feel comfortable about right now, only one person with whom they will be comfortable."

"The kids are always welcome at my house, Grant, you know that." She couldn't let him down. He needed help. "Just keep in mind I've never had children of my own, so I'm not a great authority figure."

"They are at their best with you. They'll be upset about this lawsuit, and they'll—"

"Of course, they're sixteen, and Beau's a responsible—"

"Thank you, Lauren." He reached down and took her hand. "They care a great deal about you. I know this is asking a lot, and I'm sorry."

"It isn't a problem. Really." Could he hear the doubt in her voice?

"You're a dear friend, Lauren." He gazed into her eyes with such a surge of gratitude that it took her breath for a moment.

She couldn't look away, and she felt a misstep in her heart rhythm.

What was happening here? All her senses were on high alert, as if danger were near. But except for the added responsibility of the twins for a few days, what kind of danger could there be?

Silence ticked past them until the sounds from the corridor intruded—voices and monitors and the telephone buzz. As she listened to the soft murmur of Beau's voice out at the central desk, she realized with a jolt how much she was coming to care for this family. And then she realized why she was suddenly reluctant for the kids to stay with her. Her connection to this family was growing stronger every day, intertwining with a cord of empathy . . . of friendship . . . maybe more if she allowed it.

Grant looked down at her hands, and his grasp tightened on them with a gentle warmth that seemed to spread up her arms.

Her breath caught and she pulled away.

She pushed her chair back and stood. "I should get busy. Discharges to do. You know, now that I think about it, why don't I just pack a suitcase and spend a few nights at your house? That would be better than trying to fit Brooke and Beau into my house on such short notice. Brooke would probably have to pack a steamer trunk, and Beau would miss his computer. They would both be more comfortable at home, I'm—"

"Lauren, I—"

"Sure. It will make the stress a little more bearable if they have familiar things—"

"Please, Lauren." He stood with her. "I'm sorry. I know this is an inconvenience."

Inconvenience? Was that what they called the feelings she was experiencing? "It's okay. Really. What are you going to do about Will? He's expecting you to fill in for him."

"Hopefully I'll only be gone a few days. It's a five-hour drive from here. I can come back between meetings. How much damage can be done in such a short amount of time?"

She suppressed a shudder. "Don't even joke about that, especially with the shaky condition of our hospital right now."

He grinned, and she took sudden delight in that grin, as if she'd never noticed the degree of mischief his gray eyes could hold. So *that* was where Brooke got the playful quirk of her personality.

Oh boy. What was going on here all of a sudden? Why this extra *thud-thud* in her chest?

"Really, Lauren, thanks."

She returned the grin. "By the time you return home, you may wish you hadn't rescued me from the perils of the wilderness. Your kids may never be the same."

The triage bell chimed out in the ER proper. "There's my cue to get to work." She stepped to the door.

"Lauren."

"Yes?" This time she didn't meet his gaze. She wanted her heart rate to stabilize before she had to face a patient.

"I'll miss you," he said softly.

"Of course you will."

He chuckled. "And you'll be glad for a few shifts away from me, right?"

"You're kidding, of course. Do you realize who will probably take most of your shifts?"

"I've called Dr. Jonas to cover for me, and he's down for the rest of my shifts next week."

"He isn't the one nagging you for more hours."

Grant shrugged. "Too bad, the schedule's set. I may get back for some of them myself."

"Let's just pray that the judicial process goes smoothly for once, for both our sakes."

CHAPTER 10

At eight-thirty Monday morning Lauren settled sixteen-year-old Jamey Younts into exam room eight and took her vitals. Jamey was their fifth patient of the day. If the ER traffic picked up as usual, they wouldn't have an empty department for the rest of the shift. Lauren could remember a time, only a few years ago, when she actually looked forward to busy shifts. Lately she dreaded them. Today could be worse than usual, with Grant gone and Dr. Mitchell Caine taking his shift.

"Is the doctor going to be long?" Jamey asked through a raspy throat. "I want to get to school today if I can."

"I'll let the doctor know you're here as soon as I finish with you." Not that he was likely to come running for this one.

Dr. Caine's impatience with the Medicaid system was legend in this hospital. Jamey came from a second-generation family of recipients, and now she was an emancipated minor. She had been abandoned by her father when she was a toddler, and earlier in the school year her mother and stepfather had evicted her from their home when she told them she was pregnant. Now she was six months along, living on welfare and the income she made from a job at one of the fast-food restaurants in Dogwood Springs.

Lauren took Jamey's temperature and blood pressure. Both were on the high side, as expected. The patient's respirations weren't bad, but her heart rate was a little fast. Lauren noted the highlighted warning on the chart of a penicillin allergy. That could make treatment difficult.

"You think it's strep throat?" Jamey asked.

"I hope not. If it is, you'll have to stay quarantined for forty-eight hours."

"Quarantined?"

Some of the other staff members occasionally joked that Jamey was not the brightest candle on the stand. Lauren knew better. "That means you wouldn't be able to go to school for a couple of days, honey. You won't want anybody else to catch what you have."

"Oh." The unhealthy flush of the teenager's face deepened a shade. "No, I guess not."

"Have you been eating right?" Lauren asked. "Swallowing all those vitamins I gave you?"

"Yeah, I try. I can't always keep them down."

Lauren had taken it upon herself to keep in contact with this needy child for the past three months, and at her request, the kids at church had raised money for any emergencies Jamey might have.

"Have you considered the possibility of moving back in with your family?" Lauren asked.

"Nope, can't do it. Mama's too mad. She got pregnant with me when she was sixteen herself, but does she think about that? No."

"Are you still renting a room at the motel downtown?"

"Yeah." Jamey touched Lauren's arm and blinked up at her with big brown eyes. Lauren had trouble believing she would give birth to a baby in three months. She looked like a child herself. "Thanks for the groceries last week."

"You're welcome. We need to keep you and the baby healthy." Lauren patted Jamey on the shoulder. "I'll tell Dr. Caine you're here."

Jamey's expression froze. "*He's* here? *Caine?* I didn't see his car in the parking lot."

"That's because there are no longer any reserved spots for the doctors."

"But why? That's how I can tell when Dr. Sheldon's on duty. He's the one I like."

Lauren shook her head and smiled. Jamey wasn't the only one who did that. Many people in Dogwood Springs used the ER instead of going to the family practice doctors in town. Until William Butler removed the reserved parking signs a few months ago, Grant and two of the other more popular ER docs had been overwhelmed by patients who'd learned to recognize their cars. That made it difficult to triage in order to treat the genuine emergencies.

"We'll get your throat checked out." Lauren suppressed a sigh as she left the exam room. She knew it was the same all over the country. When the ER patients were Medicaid recipients, the hospital's reimbursement was so low it didn't cover the hospital's costs most of the time.

Hospitals were shutting their doors more and more often lately. Dogwood Springs Hospital would probably already be out of business if not for William Butler. He had worked as an RN for twenty years before turning his attention to the administrative side of the hospital world. His business savvy and medical knowledge had kept this hospital's numbers in the black for the past seven years. Would they make it through this crisis?

Lauren found the secretary at the central work island, coding charts. "Hi, Vivian. Did Dr. Caine go to breakfast?"

The plump, blond-haired older woman shook her head without looking up from her work. "He's on the telephone, as usual. Probably talking to his financial advisor. Here, you might as well put this with Jamey's chart." She handed Lauren a sheet with a copy of the patient's mother's Medicaid card. "You know they probably won't pay on this, not with Jamey living on her own. What's the kid got this time, the sniffles?"

"I think it's a little more serious than that."

Vivian clucked her tongue and shook her head. "She's in here every other week, but I don't know where else she's going to go. If you find him, tell Dr. Caine I need to talk to him, would you? He still fills these T-sheets out wrong half the time." She returned to her work, muttering, "You'd think an intelligent man could learn to fill out a simple set of forms. Because of his oversights, we're losing money."

The intentionally melodious bass voice of Dr. Mitchell Caine announced his presence in Grant's office. Lauren felt a tug of resentment as she stepped into the room, which Dr. Caine tended to take over when he was on duty.

"Yes, I'm aware of the tax benefits, Phil, but I have no intention of adding her name to these funds. She has her own money to play with." He glanced up sharply, as if just noticing Lauren's presence. "Just a moment, Phil." He covered the receiver with his hand. "Yes, what?" The prick of his gaze was a little too sharp, the arch of his eyebrows a little too pronounced.

"I have a patient for you in eight," Lauren said.

He nodded, then uncovered the receiver to resume his conversation.

Lauren laid the chart on the desk and cleared her throat, prepared to wait. She would never have been this assertive with the other doctors, but Dr. Caine had been known to leave a patient sitting in an exam room for up to an hour, with no other patients in the department, if he wasn't in the mood to see them.

Dr. Caine, with prematurely silver-kissed hair and steel blue eyes, held a strange appeal for some female hospital employees. Lauren couldn't see any reason for the attraction.

After another moment of conversation he looked up at Lauren and his frown deepened. "Phil, one more moment." Hand over receiver. "What *is* it, Nurse?"

Lauren tapped her finger on the chart. "She's hoping to make it to school if she isn't too sick."

He glanced at the chart, then shook his head. "Did you explain to her that this is an *emergency* department? If she's well enough to want to go to school—"

"It looks as if she might have strep, Dr. Caine. I'll get a culture if you wish."

"No. Don't waste the money." He scowled at Lauren's persistence. "I'll be there in a few minutes." He resumed his conversation with his advisor, and Lauren sighed and stepped from the office.

A familiar feminine giggle heralded the presence of Fiona Perkins, lab tech and resident gossip, who leaned against the central counter with her tray of supplies beside her as she talked to Vivian.

Fiona looked up when Lauren approached. "Hey, Lauren, wasn't that Jamey Younts in exam room eight? Know what I heard? I heard that drug guy was the one who got her pregnant. You know who I'm talking about? The loser that calls himself Falcon?" Her chubby cheeks pudged out in a frown. "No, wait . . . Eagle? Hmm, anyway, some kind of—"

"Would you be, perhaps, attempting to say . . ." Vivian hesitated, looking at Fiona with distaste. "Are you trying to say Peregrine?" She spoke the word as if spitting out something rotten.

Fiona lightly smacked her temple with her right hand and pointed at the secretary. "You get the gold star, Viv."

"Hold it right there." Vivian raised her hand. "Don't go spreading stuff like that around the hospital. It could hurt the girl worse than she's already—"

Fiona's chin dimpled in distress. "But I heard *her* say it! You know? Back when she first got tested."

At that moment, Dr. Caine stepped from Grant's office with the chart in his hand, and Fiona straightened from the counter and started toward him.

"Dr. Caine, you should know. Didn't Jamey Younts get pregnant by Peregrine?"

Vivian caught her breath audibly. "Fiona!"

Dr. Caine stiffened and his steel gaze narrowed on Fiona's face with icy intensity. "Why would you expect me to know something like that?"

"Well, because I thought—"

"What are you doing in this department? I didn't ask for your services."

"Uh, well, I just stopped by to—"

"Your department is already having trouble getting reports out on time, and now I think I can see why. If I don't see an improvement in your department's performance by next week, I will write you up, along with your supervisor, who can't seem to keep his employees on the job where they belong."

Fiona's mouth dropped open. "I'm sorry, Dr. Caine, I—"

"And if I see you standing around gossiping anywhere in this hospital, I will write you up again. Try explaining to your next prospective employer why the chief of staff of this hospital found you so very lacking in discipline that you could not even keep the lowly position of a phlebotomist."

Quick tears flooded Fiona's blue eyes as she grabbed her tray of lab supplies and rushed from the room. For the first time since coming to work at the Dogwood Springs ER, Lauren felt sorry for her. She just hoped the doctor had worked his mood out of his system, or his next patient could fare just as poorly.

Lauren found herself wishing she'd received enough forewarning to change shifts with another nurse. She would gladly work every single day this week to avoid this situation. Unfortunately, Eugene, one of the night nurses, was on vacation, and she was on schedule for tomorrow night. So was Dr. Caine.

How she missed Grant!

Beau looked at his watch, checked it against the clock hanging in the hallway at school, and paced toward the double doors of the library. Again.

It was almost nine o'clock. Where were Brooke and Evan? How could they do this to him? They were the ones who had insisted on coming to school thirty minutes early this morning, ostensibly to work on an article in Publications, but had they stayed in the department? Of course not. Less than ten minutes after their arrival, while Beau was deeply involved in an edit, Evan had orchestrated some trumped-up reason to take Brooke and disappear and do an on-site interview at the elementary school.

First hour would be over soon, and they hadn't even shown up yet. This whole thing stunk of mystery and intrigue, something Brooke and Evan seemed to pursue with relentless devotion.

Beau turned and paced back toward the sunny end of the hallway. He'd looked all over for them. Nothing. What if something had happened? What if Kent had caused trouble again?

Lord, please keep them safe. Someone needed to. They obviously didn't have the sense to take care of themselves, and of course they hadn't bothered to let Beau in on their little secrets. Oh, no. Chicken

Beau would spoil all their fun. Beau was boring. Beau was too cautious. Beau was—

A door opened and closed somewhere behind him, and he swung around to find a girl walking down the hall from the school office. She was in current events and geometry with him.

Everyone called her Dru. She had a friendly smile, shy. She blushed easily. He thought she was gorgeous, and he'd caught her looking at him a few times in class.

Beau glanced at the badge clipped to the neckline of her sweater, and he realized she must work in the office during her free hour. The badge said her name was Deseret.

She aimed a bashful smile at him as she walked past. "Hi, Beau."

"Hello." He braced himself and waited for her to voice the question that was obvious in her eyes—*What are you doing out here in the hallway?* She walked past without comment.

He sighed with relief and pivoted to pace again. What if Brooke didn't come back? What was he going to do?

No, wait, don't get all nervous about this yet. Brooke was sharp enough to avoid getting into too much trouble. Dad always used to say Brooke lived a charmed life, and he was right. She always seemed to get away with a lot. She took chances nobody else would take. She drove like a maniac and didn't get caught or hurt.

Of course, there was the fender bender she had with Dad's car in the hospital parking lot last summer, but that was mild compared to the wreck last week—

"Beau?"

He looked up to see the principal stepping out of the library entrance as the doors swung shut behind him.

Oh, great, he'd just been caught skipping class.

———

Lauren hovered protectively—while attempting to appear as if she wasn't hovering—while Dr. Caine examined Jamey.

He shone a light into her mouth, checked her nose and ears, listened to her breathing and heart. "Young lady, it's obviously a little late for this talk, but has anyone ever told you the facts of life?"

Jamey didn't react to the censure in his voice. "Yeah. My mother told me not to get pregnant because it would ruin my life, just like hers was ruined when I was born."

Dr. Caine's expression did not change, but Lauren thought she saw a reflection of some unspoken thought come and go in his eyes. Annoyance? "I take it you're not married." This question was not gentle, but neither was it harsh.

"Huh-uh."

He straightened and studied her face. "The father is nowhere around?"

"Hope not."

He frowned. "Obviously your mother's words did not achieve the intended impact, but you're old enough to take responsibility for your own actions. . . ." He gestured to Jamey's swollen stomach.

"Well, I can't do much about it now, Dr. Caine," Jamey croaked.

Lauren braced herself.

"You don't seem to know where babies come from," Caine continued, "or what you need to do with one when there's no place for it to go." He pulled a card from the counter and jotted something on it. "Put this in a pocket if you can find one without a hole in it. When you get home, call this number."

Jamey stared at the card for a moment, then reached out to take it, hesitantly, as if it might suddenly strike at her. "What is it?"

"The name and number of someone in Jefferson City who can help you with your . . . problem."

Lauren stiffened.

"What I would suggest," he continued, "although I'm sure you won't listen, is that you wipe this town from the bottom of your shoes and never come back."

Jamey shook her head. "I'm not getting no abortion."

Again he raised a sharply pointed eyebrow. "I am not suggesting that you do, but you're in no position to raise a child properly." He straightened and gave Jamey a hard glare. "I do hope you have the brains to stay away from drugs of any kind. Particularly those of the illegal—"

"I don't do drugs," Jamey muttered.

"You expect me to believe—"

"I *don't*." Jamey winced at the sound of her own raised voice, then looked down at her hands. "I did a . . . a few times last year, but only 'cause I let him talk me into it." She put her hand on her belly. "Same as this."

He studied her face in silence for several seconds, as if weighing the possible truth of her words. "And you've stopped both habits in the interim?"

Jamey blinked up at him. "Huh?"

"You've quit the sex and the drugs?" His voice was growing sharper.

In spite of the edge of impatience in his attitude, Jamey's shoulders relaxed a little. She gave the doctor a look of curiosity and shoved the card he had given her into the front pocket of her shirt. "Yeah. Had to. These people pass out free food or something?"

"No, they provide homes and adoption services for girls who didn't know enough to keep their pants on."

"You mean they'd, like, let me stay with them or something?"

He turned away from the exam bed. "That's what I just said, wasn't it?"

"Could I finish school?"

Dr. Caine's chiseled-granite face softened momentarily, and Lauren caught another barely-there flicker of something in his eyes—was it compassion? Sorrow? "I believe they might arrange that."

"I don't have no phone," Jamey said. "Maybe they'd let me call from school."

"Ask our secretary if you can use the hospital telephone. I'll speak with her," he said over his shoulder.

"Okay."

"Good, I see that we understand each other," he said dryly, then turned to Lauren. "Strep, most likely, and I see she's allergic to peni—"

"Lauren, there's a call for you," Vivian said from the open doorway. "School."

Any softness Lauren might have imagined disappeared from the doctor's expression. Those formidable brows drew together as his eyes narrowed on her, but he said nothing.

It was the high school principal. Beau had been caught skipping class, and they needed to speak with her.

For a moment, she didn't believe what she was hearing. "Are you sure you have the right student?" she asked. "We're talking about Beau Sheldon?"

"Positive." The man sounded tired. "Can you come to the school?"

"No, I'm sorry. I can't leave the hospital."

"Then I'm sorry, too. The rules state that a student caught missing class without a viable reason for it is automatically suspended for three days."

She caught her breath. "No! Please don't do this to Beau. If he was not in the class where he belonged, trust me when I say that he had a good reason for it."

"He doesn't seem to have one at the moment."

"Lauren," Dr. Caine called from behind the curtain in exam room three, "I need you in here."

"Coming, Dr. Caine." She couldn't allow Beau to be suspended. "Look," she said over the phone, "would you call Pastor Archer Pierce? He'll be at the church. If you need someone to go down—"

"Archer Pierce?" The tone of the principal's voice changed. "I had him as a student when I taught social studies."

Lauren gave the man the number at the church, then hung up and rushed to help Dr. Caine. Maybe, if she decided to stay here, she would be an accepted member of Dogwood Springs in about twenty years. Fifteen if she was lucky.

———

Brooke's voice carried well, and it seemed to float above the chatter of the crowd that filled the hallway during the short break between first and second hour. Beau stepped into Publications and saw the sunglow from the bank of windows highlighting the short length of Brooke's dark hair as she and Evan hovered over a computer screen.

"Where have you two been?"

They froze like thieves and looked up simultaneously.

Brooke's mask of cautious penitence dissipated. "Beau! What are you doing here?"

"Risking suspension, thanks to you. I've already been warned."

Evan laughed, as if Beau had made a joke. It was forced laughter. Guilty laughter.

In Beau's present mood that was not a smart move. He stared hard at Evan, who looked at Brooke, who looked at the wall. They both appeared flushed. Excited. Wary.

"Something's up," Beau said. "I want to know—"

"Oh, would you stop with the detective stuff?" Brooke said. "Nothing's up."

"Then why did you skip class?"

Evan gave a long-suffering sigh, as if he were explaining a math problem to a dumb kid. "I already told you, Beau. We were on a fact-finding mission down at the elementary school and working on an article for the—"

"Where's your camera?"

Evan cast his gaze to the ceiling and reached for a very small digital camera partially covered by a stack of papers. "There. Are you satisfied?"

"Beau, you shouldn't be so suspicious," Brooke warned. "Evan's going to be a local celebrity before long. *The Dogwood* is going to pick up at least two of his school editorials, and they're considering more."

He knew when his sister was trying to mislead him. "What's the article about?"

Evan and Brooke made eye contact again.

"That's what I thought," Beau said. "Does Miss Bolton know you're using her good name to ditch class?"

Brooke's eyes narrowed. "We don't have it completed yet, okay?"

"Who's in the pictures?"

"Peregrine," Evan said.

Brooke glared. "Evan!"

"He asked. We are not liars."

"What are you talking about?" Beau demanded.

"Peregrine's back in town," Evan said. "Guess he's been here awhile and nobody knew it. We plan to watch him."

"Naturally. And he's at the elementary school?" Beau asked dryly.

Evan leaned forward, his overly pronounced dark brows drawing together. "He's lost a bunch of weight, cut and bleached his hair, and grew a beard, but we're pretty sure it's him. I got a shot of him with my thirty-five millimeter and with my digital."

Fear trickled up Beau's spine and back down again, like a teasing wraith. "You really took pictures of the guy?"

"Didn't get one with my camera watch." Evan held up his watch. "I've been practicing how to point and shoot, but not—"

"You're skipping school to follow Peregrine around town and take pictures?" Beau exclaimed. "Are you crazy?"

Brooke slapped Beau's shoulder with a little more force than usual. "Would you keep your voice down!"

"Why? If you're going to publish this guy's picture in the paper, everybody'll know—"

"Of course we're not publishing it! How stupid do you think we—"

"You said you were working on an article for the—"

"Well," Evan said, "I didn't exactly say we were doing the pictures for the article. I said we were working on a fact-finding mission *and* working on an article."

Beau took a menacing step toward Evan.

"Someone told Brooke they saw somebody that matched Peregrine's description hanging around near the playground a few days ago," Evan said quickly. "Since I'm working on a feature article about the Christmas program they're doing this year—"

"Meaning," Brooke interrupted, "that we have a good cover for being down there—"

"—and since I already know what Peregrine looks like—"

"Call the police," Beau said. "Let Sergeant Dalton take care of it. What are you going to do with the pictures?"

Evan shrugged, glancing quickly at Brooke. "I guess we'll do just what you told us to. We'll show them to the police."

"Want to know what we think?" Brooke asked. "Peregrine couldn't stand to leave his best contacts behind, so he's come back to town and looked Kent up. I think he's the one who told Kent to attack Evan in the hall. He's behind a lot of the drug traffic, and Kent's one of his front guys."

"Which means Kent and Peregrine are dangerous," Beau said. "Which means you don't have any business taking pictures, Evan. And you don't have any right to endanger my sister while you're doing it."

"Oh, would you stop it!" Brooke snapped. "Evan doesn't drag me behind him on a leash, you know. I make my own decisions, and it was my idea to skip, so stop blaming him."

The tardy bell rang, and Beau groaned. "We're missing another class. Now we'll have to go to the office and get a late pass. I'll be suspended for sure."

Brooke gathered up her papers. "Then let's hurry and get to class. Mr. Barton doesn't usually get started right away, and he isn't as crabby as some of the—"

"Wait," Beau said. He had to tell them. They didn't know how much danger they might be in. "First, we've got to talk."

"What?" Brooke snapped. "We've *been* talking, remember? You've been nagging—"

"I don't think the hit-and-run was an accident. Someone was tailing us, and I don't think they were after me, Evan Webster."

The color drained from Brooke's face. Evan's eyes widened, and he swallowed audibly.

Brooke recovered first. "Why didn't you tell us?"

"Because I'd hoped it wouldn't be necessary. I was naïve enough to think that you'd learned your lesson when Kent beat Evan up in the hallway. I didn't want to upset you more when you were already so—"

"Beau Sheldon, I can't believe you!" Brooke snapped. "You kept it a secret?"

"I told Sergeant Dalton."

"What's going on in here?" came an ominously suspicious teacher voice from the doorway. Miss Bolton stood at the threshold, looking at them over the tops of her reading glasses, hands stuffed into the pockets of her coat. "Your class isn't in here this hour."

Evan leaped to his feet. "I know this is your free hour, Miss Bolton, but we need a little more time to work on this article, and I can't figure out how to download the pictures for it, and I need Beau to help me, and we've already gotten him in trouble because we missed first hour and he came out looking for us. Please give us a little more time. Please?"

"Let me get this straight. You are skipping classes to work on a project on your own for my class, and you want to use me to shield you from any disciplinary measures."

Evan's bravado deflated only slightly. "Well, when you put it that way . . ."

She gave them a final glare and walked to her desk. "Get the pictures downloaded for him, Beau, then I want all three of you in your second-hour class." She jotted a note on a pad of paper. "If I find out you didn't make it to that class, I'll personally turn you in to the office." She ripped the sheet from the pad and handed it to Brooke. "You got that straight?"

"Got it. Thanks, Miss Bolton."

CHAPTER 11

G rant sat in the twelfth floor legal office of Jay Hartmann, M.D., J.D., and stared through the plate-glass window overlooking the Mississippi River. He had arrived in St. Louis in time to catch the tail end of the Monday evening rush, and a jeweled line of headlights and taillights continued to enhance the Christmas decorations beneath the gleaming presence of the Gateway Arch. Grant listened to the muted clatter of a computer keyboard and the soft conversation and laughter of Jay's personnel as they completed final tasks of the day in the outer office. Jay had graciously extended his hours. That meant a lot coming from such a busy man.

Grant had never imagined that his anatomy lab partner in medical school would attend law school after he received his medical license. Back then they had all been so sick of school and eager for residency. . . . But then, who would have thought residency would be so grueling? Nobody quite believed it until they experienced it.

Jay's specialty of choice had been family practice, but three months into residency he'd quit. Now his specialty was malpractice defense law.

The lights of a jet streaked their way west across the center of Grant's view, and he checked the time on the grandfather clock in the corner of the spacious office. Brooke and Beau would be busy at the hospital now. Lauren would go to the house and stay with them after work. She would take good care of them until he could get back. He just hoped things didn't go too badly between her and Mitchell Caine today.

He felt a little guilty for pressuring her to stay with the kids, but he'd been desperate. There was no one that he would trust to care for his children the way he trusted Lauren. He had no doubt that she would do a better job of it than he usually did.

This morning, the kids had been in such a rush to get to school early he had neglected to say good-bye to them properly. That oversight had stung. Ever since Annette's death, he had taken such care to make sure his family knew he loved them, so that if they, God forbid, should die before he saw them again, he would have no regrets. Fortunately, Brooke and Beau knew from long experience how he felt about them.

Didn't they?

He sighed and stared back out the window at the city lights. Already he longed for the peace of Dogwood Springs. He missed the silence of his own home at night, when Brooke and Beau were safely asleep and he could be alone with his thoughts.

But why stop there? He would also like to see physicians be allowed to treat patients by the dictates of a good conscience without having frivolous lawsuits slapped on them. And he would be thrilled to see a health-care plan that really worked. . . .

Grant blinked and shook his head. Time to derail this black mood before it took control.

"Lord, forgive me," he murmured. "I still miss Annette. This trip has just brought it all back so suddenly. I'm no good to Brooke and Beau like this."

"And how might that be?" came a long-familiar Ozark drawl from the doorway.

Grant turned to find his old friend sauntering toward him across the thickly carpeted floor. "Jay." He stood and reached out to shake hands.

Instead, Jay caught him in a hearty guy-hug, complete with back-slapping. Typical Jay. "Hey, Grant. Been a while." He did a final shoulder clap, then stood back and smiled.

Grant knew Jay had never considered himself a handsome man, with the scars of adolescent acne that riddled his face, and a shiny scalp crowned by a bare skirting of pale brown hair, but his eyes had always held a special glow of warmth and maturity, even in his twenties. Now, at forty-one—the same age as Grant—what hair he still had was sheened with silver, and the kindness in his expression was comforting.

"Something's going on with you besides a malpractice suit, Grant. I can see it."

Grant returned to his seat while Jay took the one beside it. "Sorry. You just caught me in mid-whine. It's nothing unusual lately."

Jay leaned back. "The night's open for you, and don't forget I owe you, big time. I wouldn't have made it through Anatomy 101 without you."

"You don't owe me a—"

"You're not paying, Grant." Jay held his hand up. "This one's on me. I read the information you faxed me. First of all, it shouldn't take long for the plaintiff's attorney to discover he doesn't have anything to use against you. Second, even if it does go to court, I expect a short trial." He grinned. "And if it isn't, they'll have me to contend with." He looked at the clock. "You're hungry, aren't you?"

"Starving."

"Do you still like gyros?"

"I haven't had one since we left St. Louis."

"Good, that's what I ordered. It should be here any time. Now, let's talk."

"I don't care what your cardiologist told you. *I'm* telling you to cut the dosage in half!"

Lauren heard the sharp blade of Dr. Caine's voice slice through the door in exam room five. He'd lost his temper at least four times since the noon rush. Now, at evening rush, they had every room full and another patient waiting to be checked in, and at least three of them were high-acuity cases.

Vivian turned from her workstation and frowned at Lauren. "The guy's a grump, and it's only going to get worse."

"It can't get that much worse. He's off in an hour."

"Not tonight. I took a message from Dr. Jonas. His flight was canceled, and he's stuck in Kansas City for three more hours. Dr. Caine will be working until midnight at this rate. He nearly strangled me when I relayed the information."

"Oh-oh."

"I'm just glad my shift's almost over. How long is Dr. Sheldon going to be gone?"

"The rest of the week, maybe longer."

The secretary shuddered. "I don't know if we can take it that long."

The curtain snapped back and Dr. Caine strode out with a steel glare, scouring the landscape for a likely victim. Lauren stiffened, and Vivian retreated to her stack of coding work.

"Lauren, where's Lester? I need a tech to wheel this patient to—"

"He's with Mrs. Barrows in Radiology. Do you need me to—"

"I need *you* to discharge some patients. Where's Emma?"

"She's taking a break."

Beau came rushing out of an exam room that had just been vacated. He had a fresh set of sheets in his hands and a spray bottle of disinfectant under his arm. "You need me for something, Dr. Caine? I can take—"

"I don't want a high-school student touching my patients! Vivian, page Emma. Why is she taking a break at this time of night?"

"Because she didn't have a chance until now, and she was nearly fainting from hunger." Vivian's face reddened. "I'm not paging a tired nurse to come back and do something a tech can do just as well. Let Beau take him."

A sudden, tense silence drifted like invisible ice pellets over the department. Caine focused his steely glare on Vivian.

Beau stepped into the breach. "Room's done, Dr. Caine. What patient do you want to—"

"Take the shoulder in five to Radiology. Send Lester back. I need him *here*." The doctor pivoted and plunged through the next doorway.

Lauren shrugged and glanced at the clock. She would be out of here soon. Unfortunately, she was scheduled to work tomorrow night. So was Dr. Caine.

"So let me get this straight." Jay leaned back in his chair and rolled his sleeves up. "You had no knowledge about the missing information until you read the records this past spring."

"That's correct."

"Vital information was lost."

"I dictated an addendum to the T-sheet, but I never saw a typed copy. I should have been more observant and asked questions when it didn't show up in the chart for my signature."

Jay placed the last page of a report on an inch-thick stack, leaned back, sighed. "My friend, you're being railroaded."

Grant pulled out a folder of papers he hadn't faxed to Jay. "These are my handwritten notes about the patient's symptoms and my treatment, the tests I ordered, and my differential diagnosis. I dated it and filed it away in my home office, as I do any questionable case. Amazingly, the hospital doesn't even have the copy I submitted, so this probably won't fly in court."

Jay read the pages while the grandfather clock serenaded them and the pleasant aroma of Greek food wafted through the office. It hadn't taken long to eat. They'd been starved. It also didn't take Jay long to read Grant's papers.

He stacked the pages neatly with the rest. "You say they can't find the copies you gave them."

"That's right."

"Convenient for them."

Grant rubbed his face wearily. "There's something else you need to know that could complicate this case."

"That sounds ominous."

"It has nothing to do with the particulars of the case, but I'm afraid it might become an ethical concern."

"*Ethical* concern? You? Grant, you're the most ethical person I know. If I remember correctly, you and Annette practically lived in that church of yours when you weren't studying."

"Church doesn't necessarily make one ethical."

Jay leaned forward, elbows on knees, piercing Grant with his gaze. "You live what you believe."

Grant hesitated. Another concern nagged at him—Jay was not a believer. He had a high standard of moral conduct and a compassionate heart, but he had always demurred when Grant tried to speak with him about Christ. What would he think about this deep, dark secret?

"Things changed after Annette was killed, Jay."

"You lost your faith?"

"No, but it hid from me a few times. Or maybe I should say I hid from it." This was more difficult than he'd expected. Why had it been so much easier to share this with Lauren? "Remember when I told you about my drug addiction in high school?"

"Yes."

"And how Christ had healed me from that?"

Jay nodded. "So you said. I personally believe it was your own strong will."

"Not at all." Grant allowed the clock to complete a chime on the half hour. "After the accident, I developed a new addiction."

"To what?"

Grant hesitated again. Was that alarm in Jay's face? "To the prescription pain medication I was taking for my injuries."

Jay's expression relaxed and he shook his head. "Big deal. They can't deny a man legitimate treatment."

Grant gestured to the case information stacked neatly beside their empty food containers. "Jay, that wreck happened six months before I handled this case. Do you honestly think it was legitimate? If they had tested me for drugs the day this patient presented to the ER, there would have been a positive result."

"But that didn't happen, and the drug was legal." He caught Grant's gaze. "Wasn't it?"

"I had a prescription from two different physicians, and I was filling them at different pharmacies, paying for one prescription myself so it wouldn't alert my insurance company. Maybe it was legal, but I question the ethics."

Jay frowned. "Did you question them at the time?"

"No. I had myself convinced that I needed that much medication, and that I owed it to my patients to keep the pain under control. Physical pain wasn't the problem, though. That went away in less than two months. It was the emotional pain that nearly destroyed me."

Fine lines of sympathy cast a shadow across Jay's face. "Grant, I'm so sorry. I should have known. We saw each other so seldom after the accident, and I took for granted you were okay. You were always so strong when we were in school."

"Annette was the strong one. I didn't realize how much I depended on her until she was gone."

"I told myself your church would take care of you," Jay murmured, rubbing his face wearily. "You had family nearby . . . and I got caught up in my own business. I should have kept in touch."

Grant shook his head. "My church tried to take care of me; I wouldn't let them. I probably wouldn't have allowed you to help, either. If it hadn't been for the fact that Beau needed me during his reconstructive surgeries, I still don't know if I'd have come out of it. As it is, I kicked the habit soon after this incident took place." He gestured to the stack. "But that won't help us if they ask me about it."

Jay spread his hands and looked at them instead of Grant. "Obviously it didn't impair your judgment about this case. I know you aren't lying about these notes. You did everything right."

"Do I detect a tone of concern that wasn't there a few minutes ago?"

Jay stared at his hands a few seconds more. "I know it's too late, but I'm going to ask for a summary judgment before the deposition. Your interrogatories are all in order, and since I'm new on the case, and they know I can raise a stink about the way they've treated you, they might accept my request. If the judge reads what we have, there's a slight chance your name may be dropped from the suit."

Grant didn't allow himself to hope that a summary judgment would be granted this close to the deposition date. "Perhaps we should prepare for the worst."

Jay picked up the stack of reports, fanned them in the air thoughtfully, and frowned. "Perhaps we should."

For the third time in ten minutes, Lauren looked at her watch. Her right foot did an impromptu dance on the tile floor. She had already worked an hour overtime. Beau had gotten off thirty minutes ago, and he'd caught a ride with his impatient sister, who wanted the car to go cruising. On a weeknight. When they'd walked out the door of the ER waiting room they were in argument mode, and Lauren didn't have time to referee.

But she couldn't, in good conscience, leave Muriel alone to work with an inexperienced nurse in an ER full of patients. Todd wasn't on duty tonight.

Lauren entered exam room four and saw Dr. Caine completing a lumbar puncture on Mrs. Lindeman, who had come in earlier with a severe headache that had started the night before. The new nurse, Lela, held the patient in a seated position, leaning forward over the tray table with a pillow beneath her chin for comfort.

"Okay, Mrs. Lindeman, we're going to pull the needle out now." Dr. Caine nodded at Lela, who stared back at him blankly. "Bandage, please."

"But that's on the sterile tray, Dr. Caine."

"We've completed the procedure, nurse," he snapped roughly. "We don't need the sterile tray anymore. I need the bandage before I can pull out the needle."

Lela's face flushed, and she reached for the tray. Her hand accidentally nudged the bed railing and sent the tray sliding.

Lauren rushed forward and steadied the tray, pulled a bandage from it, then opened it and held it over the site. Dr. Caine pulled out the needle, and she sealed the puncture site with the bandage.

"Thank you, Lauren," he said. "Aren't you off duty?"

"Not yet."

"If this nurse can't do the job, she shouldn't be here. You don't need to baby-sit, and I don't need you lurking around, telling me to hurry and see patients."

She felt the bite of his words. So he *had* taken offense this morning with Jamey's case. Taking a last glance at Lela's scared-kitten eyes, she stepped from the room.

Becky, the night secretary, was working at the computer as Lauren reached beneath the counter for her purse.

"Home to the kids?" Becky grinned and winked.

"I guess so. I thought I might stick around to help Lela, but . . ." Lauren shrugged.

"Poor Lela," Becky said. "I thought Dr. Caine had scared her off for sure the last shift she worked with him. You should have heard him yell when she got the patients mixed up. He had her in tears before her first break."

Lauren could identify.

"Look at that." Becky nudged her and gestured down the hallway to where Dr. Caine stood studying a chart. "Know what he's doing?"

"What?"

"He's checking to see how the patient is paying before he goes in to see them. Watch him. He's checking the form. If it's a Medicaid he rearranges the triage. He always puts the Medicaids and uninsured last on the list unless it's a life-or-limb threat. The other night we diagnosed a lady with pneumonia who had waited four hours to be seen, and we weren't even that busy."

"That's a COBRA violation."

"Cobra?" came a voice from behind them. "You've got snakes in this hospital?"

They turned to find Archer Pierce leaning with casual grace against the workstation counter. He flashed them his characteristic grin of mischief.

"Just one," Becky replied softly, jerking her head in Dr. Caine's direction.

The doctor chose that moment to look up from his chart, and he caught Archer in his sights. His frown deepened. He tucked the chart beneath his left arm and strode toward them.

"Oh, great," Becky muttered under her breath. "You'd better duck, Brother Pierce. He's looking for victims. I know that look in his eye."

Dr. Caine stepped to the counter. "Reverend Pierce, I didn't know you had obligations with us this evening."

"No obligations, Doctor." Archer held his hand out to shake.

Dr. Caine looked down at it, took it in a brief clasp, then released it and stepped away. "What brings you to our department?"

"I try to make a habit of stopping in on my way home from work, just in case I'm needed by a church member."

"How . . . eager of you. Aren't you taking yourself a little too seriously?"

Lauren stiffened at the barely civil tone of the man's voice.

Archer's smile didn't waver. "Could be. It's a weakness of mine."

"No one has requested your . . . services, Reverend. If a patient should do so in the next few hours, I'll be sure to send word."

"Thanks, Dr. Caine, I would appreciate it. Lauren, if you're getting ready to leave, why don't I walk you to your car?"

She was happy to comply.

"Sorry about that," she said as they stepped outside. "Dr. Caine has a depressing way with words."

Archer walked beside her in thoughtful silence for a moment. "He isn't the same Mitchell Caine I remember from high school."

"You *knew* the guy? He practically treats you like a stranger."

"Let's just say I knew him the way a junior-high kid knows his graduating basketball hero. Mitchell was a happy person then."

"Wow. Life does change people," she said.

"Tragedy changes people."

"Tragedy?"

"He's seen his share of it. Which reminds me, I received a telephone call from the high school this morning about Beau's misdemeanor."

"Sorry I sicced them on you."

"It's okay. Since Beau has never even hinted at truancy, I think the principal felt this constituted an emergency. I assured him that if Beau wasn't where he was supposed to be, he had a good reason for it."

"I never had a chance to ask Beau about it when he came to work," she said. "We were too busy."

"Apparently Brooke and Evan decided to skip their first-hour class to work on an assignment from Miss Bolton—which, by the way, Miss Bolton did not condone—and Beau was so worried he went looking for them. That was when the principal caught him loitering in the hallway."

"The principal told you this?" Lauren asked.

"Brooke called me this afternoon and took the blame herself, told me it wouldn't happen again, and I agreed. I don't think we need to make a special call to Grant about it."

"He has enough to worry about." Lauren pressed the unlock mechanism on her key chain, and her truck welcomed her arrival with a friendly wink of headlights.

"There's definitely something that bothers me a lot more, Lauren."

"What's that?"

Archer peered into the front and back seats, glanced into the pickup bed, then opened Lauren's door for her. "I got a call from Tony Dalton today. He warned me to keep a closer watch on the kids in our church. A couple of teenagers from Dogwood Springs were busted for possession two nights ago in Springfield."

"Possession of what?" She got into the truck, put the key in the ignition, and turned it until the battery was activated, then pressed the button to lower the window and closed the door.

"Speed. Meth crystals, specifically. It's nothing new."

"But why would we need to worry about our own church bunch? We've got good kids, Archer. Aren't you still conducting that drug awareness class every Tuesday night?"

"Yes, and Tony's taking the D.A.R.E. program a step further. His officers are each assigned a school in the area, and they conduct small-group seminars for teachers and students every week. Still, Tony wouldn't call if he weren't particularly worried about something. Were you on duty last week when the dog-attack victim was brought in by his little girl?"

"Yes. Did Tony's men find something?"

"Yes. They didn't find anything on the first run through the woods, but they called the drug dogs in, and they discovered a makeshift lab, suddenly abandoned, within a mile of the place where Cam was attacked. Things are heating up, Lauren. Want me to follow you home?"

She grinned at him. "For what reason? You're not suddenly paranoid about burglars, are you?"

"No, just paranoid, period. I keep thinking I would want someone to make sure Jessica made it home safely from the theater."

"Well, don't take it out on me. You two will be married in less than two weeks, and you won't have to worry about it again." She switched on the engine, said good-night, and drove to the Sheldon home.

CHAPTER 12

In the early hours of the Tuesday evening night shift, Mrs. Lindeman sat forward on the ER exam bed, kneading her forehead with the fingers of her right hand. "I don't think I can take it much longer." Tears gathered at the corners of her eyes and seeped down the faint worry lines that traced her rosy skin. She rubbed her head with her left hand, fingers splayed wide, as if to cover as much territory as she could reach.

Lauren remembered this patient from last night. Mrs. Lindeman had received a lumbar puncture from Dr. Caine just before he snapped at the new nurse about being unfamiliar with the procedure.

"Mrs. Lindeman, your chart says Dr. Caine gave you pain medication for a headache last night. Did that help?" Lauren asked.

"Yes, but this pain feels different."

"When did it begin?"

"I woke up with it this morning, and it just kept getting worse as the day wore on. By midafternoon I'd taken all the aspirin I could safely swallow, and it didn't help. I'd hoped I wouldn't have to come back here after he stuck that awful needle in my back last night. I just put it off and put it off until I couldn't stand it anymore."

Lauren didn't blame her for staying away as long as possible, but if this was what she thought it was, she had endured a lot of unnecessary pain.

She took the woman's blood pressure and listened to her breathing.

The pressure was a little high, but that wasn't unusual for someone in a lot of pain. The rest of the vitals were fine.

"Mrs. Lindeman, I remember seeing you briefly last night when Dr. Caine was doing the puncture. Can you tell me what you did after you were released?"

"My husband drove me home and I went to bed. Why?"

"You went straight to bed?"

"That's what the doctor told me to do."

"You didn't do any household chores or lift anything?"

"Nothing but my purse. I didn't feel like doing any chores last night."

"Did you do any other moving about your house before you went to bed?"

"No. I told you, no. I went upstairs and straight to—"

"You climbed stairs?"

Mrs. Lindeman gave her a level look. "That's where the bed is."

Lauren sat down in the chair beside her. "I'm afraid you might be suffering from something called a spinal-leak headache. When you make any excessive movements within six hours of a lumbar puncture, spinal fluid could leak from the injection site, and that causes a painful headache. That's why we give our patients a discharge sheet with instructions."

Mrs. Lindeman's face darkened. "The nurse gave everything to my husband, and he just shoved it in the glove compartment when he helped me into the car. I should've known he'd get rattled and forget everything. Why didn't somebody warn me about this before I went home?"

"I'm sorry, Mrs. Lindeman. The nurse you had last night was new, and they were busy. I wish I'd taken time to give you some verbal instructions."

"Why didn't the doctor tell me that last night? He could have told me something helpful instead of griping at that poor nurse."

Lauren silently agreed. "If that's the problem, it can be corrected. The anesthesiologist can do a blood patch—he will withdraw some of your own blood and inject that blood into the affected area to seal up the leak."

"You mean I've got to have a needle stuck in my back again?" Her voice rose in conjunction with the flush of anger on her face. "Because the doctor couldn't do the job right the first time?"

Lauren refrained from reminding the woman that the doctor in question had done the job right and had given the proper instructions, though he hadn't explained the reason behind them. "Mrs. Lindeman, the doctor will have to determine exactly what your problem is. I'll speak with Dr. Caine and let him know you're here."

After two and a half years of cooking for his family, Grant Sheldon found his elbows relegated to Mom's kitchen table while she wielded a spoon over the cast-iron skillet.

He watched her work with conflicting emotions of nostalgia and guilt. "Mom, I thought we decided this morning that I would take you out to dinner tonight."

She turned from the stove with pursed lips, with short strands of her gray hair feathering untidily over her forehead. "We did?"

"Yes, don't you remember? You told me you loved that country-fried steak down at Rosie's Place."

Her confusion did not clear before she turned back to her work. "Well . . . I don't like to get out in traffic at this time of night."

"You don't have to worry about the traffic," he reminded gently. "I'll drive." He pulled two napkins from the plastic holder and tried to wipe some crumbs from the faux wood surface of the table. They dragged across a sticky puddle of strawberry jam and became part of the mess. "Why don't we plan to go out tomorrow? I didn't come here to stay so you could wait on me."

"I still don't understand why you didn't bring the family with you. There's room for everybody."

"The kids have school," he explained for the second time in the past fifteen minutes. He pulled another napkin from the holder, then risked Mom's displeasure by getting out of his assigned seat and walking to the sink to wet the napkin. If he didn't get that jam off the table, he'd have a sticky elbow for the rest of the night.

"It's been such a long time since I've seen those twins. . . ." Her voice faded to silence. She gave a tiny sigh, and the permanent frown lines deepened around her eyes and mouth.

The greasy odor of cooking beef assailed Grant along with a wave of guilt. He had never told Mom that hamburger gravy and fried okra had ceased to be his favorite foods when he was twelve. When Dad moved out the first time.

"Does Rita know you're here?" Mom asked. "She'll want to come and see you if she knows you're here."

Grant swallowed his frustration. Mom didn't seem to realize that Dogwood Springs was almost as close to his sister's house as she was to St. Louis—Rita and her family had moved to Kansas City years ago.

He watched Gwen Sheldon struggle with the rusty can opener she'd had for at least fifteen years. "Mom, why don't you use the electric opener we got you for Christmas last year?"

"I never could remember to use it, so I donated it to the senior center." She flipped the lid into the trash and dumped the can of cream of chicken soup into the skillet without draining the grease from the hamburger—just the way he liked it when he was eleven and skinny and had never heard the swear word *cholesterol*. Smoke billowed through the kitchen. Mom stirred, unconcerned.

Grant got up and opened the kitchen window, then turned on the overhead vent above the stove before the smoke alarm could go off. "Does Mrs. Scott still clean your house every week?" Judging by the windows and floors, the answer was—

"No." Tight-lipped. Disapproving.

"But I've been sending her a check every month for—"

"I can clean my own house." Her voice sharpened. "I send her to Mr. Lewis. He's getting old and can't take care of things like he did. I'm not *that* old yet."

Grant sank back into his chair with a sigh. He loved his mother, and that was why she frustrated him so much. She had been set in her ways for as long as he had been aware that there were ways in which one could be set. She didn't believe in many personal luxuries. People who had grown up during the Great Depression never forgot the deprivation. Their practicality could become a phobia.

To the despair of Grant and his sister, however, Mom had also failed to recover from yet another big catastrophe in her life—when her husband left her for another woman. The fact that his relationship with that woman had fizzled barely six months after it began had been no comfort. Mom's bitterness had formed an immovable core of deep anger that occasionally manifested itself in the form of depression, which cast a pall over the whole family.

When Dad apologized and asked permission to return, she allowed him back into the house, but she made it obvious that she did so only for the sake of Grant and Rita. Her lingering resentment soon formed a wall between her and Dad that blew them apart years later. She never allowed him to forget what he had done.

While Mom had developed a habit of complaint, Dad had developed a drinking habit. As teenagers, Grant and Rita avoided both parents, and because of that—or perhaps in spite of it—they developed a close relationship.

Mom set a glass of milk in front of Grant—whole milk, not skim—with a plate of hamburger gravy on toast. She went back to the stove and returned with a pan of fried okra, crisp with tempura batter. She set it on the table with a little flourish.

"Mom, you can still work that stove like a magician." He hoped he'd put enough enthusiasm in his voice.

She allowed a small, pleased smile to touch her lips as she took off her apron. "It's probably been a long time since Annette fixed this for you."

Grant gave his mother a sharp look, then dismissed the remark. He said silent grace over his food, aware that his mother had never understood or condoned the commitment he'd made to Christ when he was a teenager. He'd never been able to convince her that Christianity was not just some secret weapon Annette had used to steal his heart from his mother when she needed him most.

"How is Annette doing?" Mom persisted. "She hasn't called me in a long time, and I'm always afraid to call you down there. With all those night shifts you work, I don't want to take a chance of waking you up in the daytime when you need your sleep."

Grant ignored a little jab of surprise and reached for another napkin. "You mean Brooke, don't you, Mom?"

She frowned, and for a few seconds her gray eyes studied him in silence. The thick lenses of her glasses gave her an appearance of confusion. "I might be a little forgetful lately, but I don't think I've gotten so absentminded that I would forget my own daughter-in-law's name."

A chill of disbelief froze Grant. He steadied himself against the edge of the table as he looked up into his mother's innocent gaze. While she waited in apparent mystification for his reply, he floundered in confusion.

"Mom, are you feeling well? Have you been sick recently? The flu seems to be—"

"Nothing wrong with me but a few aching joints, Grant. You haven't answered my questions—"

"Has your doctor changed your medications?" he asked on a surge of panic.

"Why are you so worried about me all of a sudden? I'm fine." She reached for the small plate she had prepared for herself and carried it around the table to take her customary seat. "Eat your dinner before it gets cold."

He was stunned.

She fixed him with a steady gaze of concern. "You're not having marriage problems, too, are you? It seems like everybody is these days."

It was a misunderstanding. It had to be.

"Mom, I've never had marriage problems, but . . . Annette's dead."

The shock transformed the look of concern on her face to one of horror. Grant felt a reflection of that same horror in his heart.

———

Lauren pressed her knee against the faucet control at the sink and soaped her hands. She was just getting ready to reach for paper towels when she heard Dr. Caine's voice echo through the department—spiked with characteristic annoyance.

"Nurse."

She looked around to find him bearing down on her in the hallway. He wore the frown that struck fear into the hearts of the staff, and it hit her at point-blank range. She switched off the faucet with her knee and dried her hands.

"I need you to explain something to me." He stopped well within Lauren's personal space—a favorite tool he used for intimidation.

"Yes, Dr. Caine, may I help you?"

"I want to know why you placed all the blame on me for the neglected instructions to Mrs. Lindeman last night."

"I didn't." It would do no good to try to justify herself to him.

"Then why did I just receive a pointed reprimand, blaming me for her headache? She said *you* told her it was from a spinal leak."

"I also told her she had received a discharge instruction sheet with the information she needed. I suggested that it might be a spinal-leak headache and that a simple proce—"

"I'll thank you to leave the diagnoses to me in the future."

"I'm sorry. So it wasn't a spinal leak—"

"It was a spinal leak. I've given her pain meds, and she's scheduled for a blood patch in the morning. She's already warned me that she will refuse to pay the bill and that she will call administration and complain about the substandard treatment she received here."

So what's new? "You're blaming me for this?" She resisted the urge to point out that if he had shown a little patience with the new nurse and the proper attitude of compassion with Mrs. Lindeman in the first place, she probably wouldn't have complained—at least not so bitterly.

"Some nurses get reported for this kind of thing," he said coldly. "I choose not to do that, but I wouldn't advise you to push it."

"What would they get reported for?" she asked. "And to whom would the report go?"

A muscle twitched in his jawline. "The report would go to the state board for practicing medicine without a license."

She felt the shock of his words, but she didn't react. *Don't give him the pleasure.*

He stared at her, grim-faced, for another few seconds, then made an about-face and stalked away.

"You know how to push his buttons, don't you?" Becky said from behind her.

"I don't mean to."

"He has no right to talk to you like that, but who are you going to tell about it? I've been told he doesn't mean most of the things he says."

"It's okay, Becky. I'll try to keep my mouth shut." Dr. Caine had a sharp tongue, but his tendency was to take out his frustrations on the staff when a patient got cranky. Part of Lauren's job, she knew, was to boost staff morale when the doctor got testy. This kind of situation wasn't unusual. It came with the territory, but unfortunately, patients tended to heap even more verbal abuse on the nurses than the doctors did.

Lauren just wondered who was going to boost her own morale when Caine and the patients stepped over the line too many times on the same night.

———

Grant listened to the contrast of the silence in the house against the discordance of traffic outside on the busy street. He watched the flicker of headlights reflect through the leaded panes of Mom's living room window and door and travel across the wood grain of the paneling. He sat in the dark room and tried to tell himself his imagination was working overtime . . . tried to convince himself that anyone could make that kind of mistake.

But not about her own daughter-in-law.

Pots clattered in the kitchen. The aroma of grease smoke lingered. As had been the case for forty-one years, Mom would not dream of allowing Grant to help with the dishes. At least that part of her memory remained steady.

Other things had changed, apparently.

Still, it could be a fluke. Something that would never happen again. A little glitch.

He switched on the lamp beside his chair, and found himself staring at a picture of Beau, with a smile that spread across his features and lit his dark gray, black-lashed eyes with joy.

But that couldn't be. There were no recent pictures of Beau's smile. Grant checked the photograph more closely and realized it was a picture of himself. For a moment, he allowed himself to forget the problem with Mom and concentrate on the awe that surged through him.

He had never realized how much Beau resembled him at the same age. It filled him with pride. And then it plunged him into despair. Beau would never have his smile.

Another light came on in the room, and Mom stepped in from the kitchen, drying her hands on a dish towel. "I found that in our old picture box, and it looked so much like your grandpa, and like Beau." She sat down in the wingback chair opposite Grant. "I just wish Beau . . ." She closed her eyes and shook her head. "Someday I hope they can fix his face."

"I don't think he'll want to try again, Mom."

She didn't seem to hear him as she took the picture from him and wiped at a smudge in the top left corner, then hugged it to her chest and leaned back. "There are times I just want to wipe the whole scene from my memory, but then, somehow, it always comes back." She sighed and held the picture out again. "Those gray eyes run in the family."

Grant exhaled a breath and leaned back on the sofa. Maybe everything would be okay.

CHAPTER 13

S ometime after midnight Wednesday morning, Lauren leaned back in her chair at her section of the central desk and looked at her stack of patient charts. The evening rush didn't look as if it would let up for the rest of the night. She and Muriel had not taken a break since they'd arrived at work, and her stomach reminded her of that at every opportunity. A nursing home patient moaned in room three, and a baby with an earache cried in room six.

"I'm well aware you were sleeping, Dr. Morris," came Dr. Caine's soft growl through the open doorway of Grant's office. "May I also remind you, however, that you are responsible to be on call tonight."

Muriel turned and rolled her eyes at Lauren, and the top edge of her lower teeth peeped out from between her lips. "Serves him right," she muttered. "Do you know how many times he's chewed other docs out for calling him in the middle of the night?"

Lauren raised a hand to shush her before the doctor could hear.

Muriel stood up and flexed her shoulders. "Time to check on my baby in six. Lay low while His Majesty is on his rampage." She walked away, muttering under her breath, "If all doctors had his attitude, there wouldn't just be a nursing *shortage,* there'd be a nursing *stoppage,* and I'd be one of the—"

"Lauren." Becky, the night secretary, stepped up behind her and gave her arm a gentle squeeze. "There's a call for you on line three. I think maybe you should take it back in the break room, where it's more private."

"What?" Lauren frowned and looked around at her. "Why? Who is it?"

Becky leaned closer. "It's your mother."

Lauren automatically looked at her watch. It was one o'clock in the morning. She caught her breath and rushed to the break room. This couldn't be good.

When she answered, she heard a watery sniff and the sound of a quavering sigh. "Hi, dear. It's Mom. I'm sorry to bother you at work. I wouldn't have called this late if I thought you were at home asleep, but I remembered you said something about having to work too many nights this week. As it was, I thought I would take the chance that—"

"Mom, what's wrong?" Lauren gently halted her mother's flow of words—a family trait that had been handed down to the McCaffrey offspring and multiplied, it sometimes seemed, ten times per generation. "Mom, are you okay? Is Dad—?"

"It isn't us. We're okay. We're . . . oh, I can't believe this. . . ." There was a shudder of breath and a moment of silence.

"Mom, what is it? What's happened?"

"It's . . . Hardy, honey. He's . . . there was an accident." Her voice dissolved to soft, broken cries.

Lauren stiffened. "Mom, what? Where is he? Was he hurt?"

There was a shuffle of the receiver at the other end and the deep bass sound of a man clearing his throat. Daddy.

"Lauren." He had taken the telephone, and his voice sounded shaky.

"Daddy! What about Hardy? Is he okay?" She knew already that he was not. It had to be bad for her parents to be so upset.

"Lauren, your brother's . . . gone." Daddy's voice went hoarse.

Lauren caught her breath, then pulled a chair out from the table and eased herself into it. For a moment she couldn't respond. She heard the baby cry out as Muriel gave him the injection, and she heard Dr. Caine issue an order to the secretary out in the ER proper, and she felt as if the room had suddenly been depleted of oxygen. Gone . . . that was the euphemism her parents always used for . . . No. It couldn't be.

She squeezed her eyes shut. *No!*

Her father's voice continued after a moment. ". . . accident at work. You know he was working night shifts at the foundry so Sandi could work at the bank and one of them would always be available for the girls." His voice continued to wobble. "Some fool made a mistake with the metallurgy mix, and there was an explosion. Hardy rushed to help, and he got caught in a second blast. They took him to the hospital, but . . . Dr. Bower pronounced him at midnight. They're calling—"

"He's dead?" Lauren felt her hands tremble. She had to speak the word. She couldn't grasp it otherwise. She had to know for sure. "He died an hour ago?"

"Yes, Lauren." There was a sob, and Daddy's voice wobbled and failed. Lauren had never witnessed her father crying, and the sound of it undermined her strength. She pressed her forehead to the table and waited to awaken from the nightmare.

"This is the first time since you moved that I was glad you weren't here," he said at last. "I can't imagine how you would have felt if you'd been on duty when they took him in."

Lauren inhaled and nearly choked. She could feel the tears sting the backs of her eyelids. *Oh, Hardy.*

"We probably should have waited until morning to call you, but your mother didn't want to take a chance that you would hear about it over that ambulance radio."

"I'm glad you . . ." Lauren's throat closed. It couldn't be possible.

"Do you have Archer Pierce's telephone number? He and Hardy were . . . good friends."

"I'll call him in the morning, Daddy." *Oh, Hardy. Hardy! This can't be!* "Don't wake him tonight. He's overworked as it is." And she didn't want him to come to the hospital tonight—which he would do—and make it more real.

"I don't like the idea of you going home to an empty house in the morning."

"I won't." She swallowed and forced herself to remain as calm as possible. She couldn't fall apart now. "Remember? I'm staying with Brooke and Beau Sheldon while Grant's in St. Louis." She had work to do. People needed her.

"Honey, are you going to be okay?"

"I will be, Daddy. Did Dr. Bower say . . . what did it?" She suddenly sensed that she wasn't alone, and she turned enough to see from the corner of her eye that Dr. Caine was stepping toward her from the doorway. She didn't look up or acknowledge his arrival.

"Head injury," Daddy said. "I don't think you want the details. I know I didn't."

"H-how are Sandi and the girls doing?" The thought of her young nieces, Faith and Sierra, facing childhood without their father . . .

"Pretty broken up. They're staying with us tonight, and I—"

"Lauren." Dr. Caine's irritated voice intruded into the room like buckshot. "I need—"

Lauren held her hand up for silence. "What, Daddy? I didn't hear what you—"

"Nurse!"

She jerked around and glared at him, and she saw a flicker of surprise in his eyes.

"Did you hear me, Lauren?" Her father's voice came clearly into the room. "I said don't you even think about trying to drive here without any sleep."

She turned her back on Dr. Caine and pressed the receiver close to her ear to deflect the conversation from the doctor's listening ears. "I won't. I promise. Can I call you in the morning?"

"You call any time. I don't think we'll be getting much sleep tonight anyway. You . . . you be careful now, you hear?"

She swallowed fresh tears. "I will," she whispered. "Thank you for calling. I love you." She said good-bye and disconnected.

A chart slid onto the table and whispered to a stop in front of her. "We have patients waiting." Dr. Caine bent forward with the fingers of his right hand splayed across the chart. "If you can't keep up the pace, you can find your way to the time clock and we'll get a replacement."

The roll of emotions quickened within her with white heat, and she clenched her fists in sudden, overwhelming resentment. "Sounds good to me." She said the words without conscious forethought, and it surprised her how good it felt to say them. She slid from beneath his leaning shadow and stood to her feet, keeping her back to him. She *wanted* to quit. In that instant she resented Dogwood Springs Hospital. She resented this department for putting so many demands on her heart and on her hours, when she could have spent more time with her family, with her *brother*.

In particular she resented Mitchell Caine, and everything within her resisted a horrible weight of Christian guilt for those emotions.

She opened the door to her locker and reached for her coat and purse, knowing with every movement that she would not leave, but receiving dark enjoyment from the sense of freedom it gave her, if just for a few seconds, to pretend that she was. A sense of retaliation stirred her.

Yes, the anger felt good. It soothed the pain for a few seconds to behave totally out of character for Lauren McCaffrey, even if it was just make-believe.

She gripped her purse with shaking hands and turned toward the door.

"Nurse!"

She pivoted back and glared at him. "What!"

Again the shock of surprise as he straightened from the table. Anger warred with amazement in his expression as he watched her. "What are you *doing?*"

Time to back down. Time to stop pretending. "If you want to fire me and bring in a replacement, feel free." *Lauren, stop reacting! Calm down! Behave!*

The low hum of fluorescent lights filled the room, and the chatter of the ER spilled through the open doorway. Reality seeped past Lauren's barrier of anger and stiffened her shaking arms and legs. The telephone rang and Becky answered, and Lester raced past the doorway in response to a patient's call.

"I did not fire you," Dr. Caine said. "I merely reminded you of your—"

"I heard what you said," she snapped. "I've been hearing you all night. Who could avoid you?"

He blinked, and his lips parted. "Lauren, what's wrong with you?"

It was the famous McCaffrey temper, which she had long held in check. It took over when her defenses were down.

She could not leave her patients. "If you didn't fire me, then I'll get back to work." She returned to the locker, shoved her coat and purse inside, and resisted the urge to slam the metal door. She didn't want to startle anyone but Dr. Caine. And she had done that.

She knew she should be ashamed of the unholy satisfaction that filled her at the sight of the confusion in his face. She wasn't. There would be time for that later.

She grabbed the chart from the table and walked from the room. The surge of temper drained, leaving the imprint of grief to plow more deeply into her heart. Those furrows would be filled with tears.

Later.

still miss you so much. Nothing is the same without you here." Grant knelt in the grass beside the pink marble headstone Wednesday afternoon.

He hadn't expected the blast of emotions that had attacked him when he drove into this cemetery for the first time in three months. He hadn't expected the confusion with Mom, the struggle over the deposition. He hadn't expected to miss his children so sharply. And he hadn't expected this sudden inner conflict over his growing attachment to Lauren.

Life was taking him by surprise, and he didn't know how to stop it from flooding over him like the banks of the nearby Mississippi after a week of heavy rain.

He traced the engraved date of Annette's death with his finger. "I don't know how I've made it two and a half years without you."

He understood now that one of his unconscious reasons for moving was to remove himself from so many reminders of his personal failure after Annette's death. Though he had certainly moved from St. Louis to Dogwood Springs to remove his children from some of the threatening influences of the big city and from the conflict that still occasionally raged between Mom and Dad, there were deeper issues. In a way, he was avoiding God. But he hadn't expected to find God waiting for him in Dogwood Springs, and he hadn't expected two special messengers, Lauren McCaffrey and Archer Pierce, to surround him with reminders of the love and forgiveness of Christ.

He continued his one-sided conversation with Annette, barely able to hear his own voice over the roar of a backhoe that was digging a fresh grave nearby. The operator ignored him. The people who kept these grounds obviously saw their fill of mourners who got in the way when they were trying to work, and this was one of the older cemeteries in the city, with some tombstones that rose above the level of the lawn—difficult to maintain, and most likely a source of irritation for those who had to work around them. Annette's marker was set into the ground with a permanent vase attached, and Grant had always kept silk flowers in it when he lived in St. Louis.

He felt himself reverting to the mode of city dweller—closing himself into his own world, avoiding the gaze of other humans so he could fool himself that he was alone with memories of the wife he had loved so passionately for so many years.

"You would have loved living in Dogwood Springs. I remember when we visited there on our last vacation before the kids were born, and you told me you would like to retire there someday." He felt foolish talking to a piece of chiseled marble, but not foolish enough to stop. "It has its problems, but the kids have discovered there's life outside this city. They're learning a sense of community. It might even be a safe place someday if we can eliminate the drug influence."

He stared into the distance at the traffic that served as a constant reminder that he had stepped out of the homey comfort of his new place of residence. "Of course, if you were alive, we would probably still be living here in the city, and you would still be carrying the load of family responsibilities on your shoulders. I wish I had understood . . . wish I'd known what a burden you carried. I wish I'd helped you more with the kids."

The shadows deepened. It was almost quitting time for many St. Louis workers. Rush hour would be starting soon, but he didn't want to leave yet. "You would know what to do about Mom."

He closed his eyes and remembered when he had first met Annette. At sixteen she was so pretty, with laughter just below the surface of her beautiful blue eyes and constant movement of life in her expressive hands—a lot like Brooke's vital presence. Because of Annette's influence he had found Christ at the rebellious age of seventeen. And it was only through the grace of God, with Annette's indomitable support, that he had been able to focus on graduating from high school through the turmoil of his parents' messy separation and divorce.

Because of Annette, Mom and Dad's continued sniper fire over the years—"If he goes to the wedding, I won't be there." "If she's at your house for Christmas, I'll just spend the day alone at home." "How could you let him hold my grandchildren before I even got to see them?"—had been less disruptive than it might have been.

"I wish you could meet Lauren. You would approve of her," he murmured.

As the backhoe operator completed his job and loaded his rig to leave, Grant settled into the grass more comfortably to catch Annette up on the past three months.

"Brooke and Beau already love her." A surprising truth, because though Beau's affection came easily, Brooke's first reaction when he'd suggested he might want to start dating again was a public display of extreme outrage that had the Dogwood Springs locals teasing him ever since.

Small towns had long memories. They also had big hearts, and even though he knew he would probably be referred to as "that new doctor down at the hospital" for the next five years, he had no doubt that he and his children had found their home.

"She's the best nurse I've worked with, and she anticipates my orders before I ask." He paused with a smile. "She's even brave enough to stay with Brooke and Beau while I'm here."

He knew Lauren had some misgivings about allowing their friendship to progress further, but since they had never actually discussed their friendship, he didn't have a good grasp about what those misgivings might be. She was good for the kids, and she was certainly good for him. What would her reaction be if he were to ask her to consider a closer relationship with them? What would she say if she knew how much he'd come to care for her?

"You know, Annette, you told me one time that, if anything were to happen to you, I should find the right woman and remarry. I remember my reaction." He felt grief rush through him at that distant memory. He had told her that, if she died, he wanted to die with her. And she, in her wisdom, had reminded him that someone needed to stick around to keep Brooke out of trouble.

"Now I know what you meant. As always, you were right."

"You're a good driver, Beau." For Lauren, who normally preferred to be the one in control when she was in a car, that was a generous observation. From the edge of her vision she caught his nod of satisfaction in the glow of the dashboard lights.

He turned from the county road onto the quarter-mile gravel road that led to the hundred-and-eighty-acre McCaffrey farm.

"Beau usually drives the same way he does everything else," Brooke said from the backseat.

"Don't start on me," Beau said. "I do not drive like Grandma."

Brooke cleared her throat. "Well, most of the time you do, except for last week when you—"

"Almost got us killed."

"No, I was actually going to say when you probably saved our lives."

"Oh."

"I feel safe riding with you," Brooke said. "Even if I could have gotten us here fifteen minutes sooner."

"If we'd lived through it."

"Beau, I just paid you a great compliment. It wouldn't hurt you to be nice to me sometimes."

Lauren allowed the current conversation to flow over her. She had long ago learned that the argument mode in which the twins usually conducted most of their conversation seldom held anger or aggression. In this particular word battle, she would have sided with Beau, but considered it wise to remain silent.

She felt safe riding with him. He never tailgated, he never lost his temper, he always signaled. He drove with consideration not only for his passengers, but also for the other drivers—as Brooke said, pretty much the way he did everything else. Lauren had appreciated his skill for the past hour as he traversed the twisting curves and steep hills of the highway from Dogwood Springs to Knolls, with Brooke's constant chatter from the backseat of their repaired Volvo. Brooke hadn't called it a boat since the accident.

The better Lauren had gotten to know this wounded family, the more she discovered how similar Beau and his father were in taste and temperament. Even Brooke showed signs of a serious side when she let her guard down. Most of the time, however, she allowed few people past her bold facade.

She could be intimidating, as Lauren had discovered last spring at their first, uncomfortable meeting. She had proven since then that there was a brain behind the beauty, and a very soft heart hidden beneath the humor.

Beau pressed the brake and gave a low whistle. Cars gleamed in the glow from their headlights, lining both sides of the driveway, lurking halfway into the shadows of roadside trees and shrubs. There was barely room to drive between them.

"Where should I park?" he asked.

"Anywhere you can find an open spot is fine," Lauren said.

He pulled in behind the last pickup truck on the right-hand side and parked beneath the overhang of sassafras trees that still retained a few of their brilliant orange leaves.

"Whoa, this place is packed," Brooke said. Yard lights illuminated more cars parked in a strategic circle around the huge front yard where Lauren and her two little brothers had played tag and statue and hide-and-seek after her older sisters had outgrown her.

She recognized most of the cars, but some were unfamiliar. She saw Lukas and Mercy Bower's car and Buck and Kendra Oppenheimer's pickup truck. Most, however, belonged to family—cousins, aunts, uncles.

"Why do relatives always wait until a funeral to get together?" she asked herself aloud.

Brooke unbuckled her seat belt. "Probably because they don't like each other."

"Lauren's family is different from ours," Beau said. "They're nice."

"Ours can be nice for short periods of time," Brooke said.

"Grandma and Grandpa are nice as long as they don't have to think about each other."

Lauren opened her door into the low branches of the sassafras tree, but Beau had left plenty of room for her to maneuver. "I have some relatives like that, too. Everybody does, I guess. The more relatives you have, the more likely it is that there'll be some kind of spontaneous combustion amongst some of them."

As she walked around the car to join the kids on the road, she became aware of a tension tightening inside her. She didn't want to go into the house. She didn't want to see the faces of family and confront the real reason she was here. What she wanted to do was stand out here in the darkness, talking to these two fascinating individuals, continuing to push present reality into some hidden corner of her mind.

She wanted to remain in denial.

Ever since she had left work at seven this morning she had struggled hard to push the pain to a more comfortable distance. She had arrived home in time to help Brooke and Beau with breakfast and give them the bad news. Brooke had announced at once that they would come to Knolls with her, and Beau had agreed—although later Lauren had overheard him accusing Brooke of using this as an excuse to see Lauren's seventeen-year-old cousin Jason McCaffrey.

After they'd walked out the front door in typical argument mode, Lauren had taken two over-the-counter sleeping pills and waited for drowsiness to come. When it did her dreams had been nightmares, and she'd awakened in a sweat long before noon. The day had gone downhill from there.

Thank God for Brooke and Beau.

The fragrant crispness of the air assaulted her with the impact of a country holiday season. The spicy sweet smell of finely aged leaves forced her to remember years long past, when she and Hardy had been in charge of hanging colored Christmas lights around the eaves of the house the week after Thanksgiving.

The crunch of footsteps on gravel echoed against the cars, and Lauren took a deep breath. "When Hardy and I were growing up, it was our job every year to rake the leaves in the yard and throw them out in the feedlot."

"But this is a huge yard," Brooke said. "Didn't you have a riding lawn mower?"

"We had a push mower. With five kids, my parents didn't believe in riding lawn mowers." As they drew closer to the house, Lauren heard the sound of dozens of voices through the screen of an open front window—late November in southern Missouri could be mild, and today the thermometer had reached 65 degrees.

The buzz of several simultaneous conversations drifted out across the front porch. Typical McCaffrey get-together. Lauren's tension mounted, and her steps slowed. From the corner of her eye she saw Brooke glance at her.

The voices grew louder, and a burst of laughter surged through the window screens. Lauren recognized the voice of her oldest sister, Sarah.

Through that same window, cousins Ruthie and Brenda were visible on the sofa in front of the fireplace, and their chuckles joined Sarah's.

Lauren knew they meant no disrespect with their laughter. In fact, in her extended family the pre- and post-funeral gatherings were often accompanied by copious amounts of boisterous talk and laughter, particularly when they shared stories and loving memories of the deceased. Hardy had been such an entertaining character, there would be a lot of stories to tell. Such a gathering had played itself out at several different times during Lauren's life.

But those other times had been for Grandma and Grandpa and Great-uncle Edmund and Aunt Dixie. They had lived full lives. They'd raised families. For them, their deaths had been peaceful passings, rich with celebration and family.

Hardy was different. He'd left a dependent family—a wife and two little girls—who loved him with total devotion. What would they do now?

The shock of loss felt raw inside Lauren. As she walked closer to the yard, she felt more and more as if a part of her had been ripped away and devoured by greedy jaws. She'd left a million things unsaid.

Had Hardy known how much she'd always loved him? Being only eighteen months younger than her, he was a part of her deepest blood ties, her earliest memories. Even though they sometimes hadn't seen each other for months at a time after they became adults, the minute they got together again they could read each other's thoughts and complete each other's old, tired jokes. They were family.

Brooke stepped closer to Lauren and put a hand on her shoulder. "Ready to go in?"

"No." She didn't realize her answer until she'd spoken it aloud. "Not yet." Her throat closed with fresh, cutting grief. Tears spilled over, sobs spilled out, before she could stop them.

Brooke's arms came around her, and Beau hovered nearby. Lauren couldn't help it. The pain of loss held her in its grip.

―――――――

Jay leaned back in his office chair and stretched. He looked as tired as Grant felt. "I made some calls this morning. It isn't likely we'll get a summary judgment on your case."

"I didn't expect one."

"However, the deposition is being postponed until next Thursday, which will give us more preparation time. We'll need it. My secretary has rearranged some appointments the next couple of days, and I'll do more reading. Are you sure you don't want to delay this deposition further? You should have been told about it weeks ago."

"If we can prepare for it in time, I'd like to keep it as is. If the drug issue doesn't come up I don't see a problem. Even if it does, I never pressed the limit. I never overdosed."

Jay held up the stack of personal financial records Grant had produced for him. "Not a lot of assets for a doctor who's been in the business as long as you have."

"I spent most of our savings on cosmetic surgeries for Beau's face."

"I didn't realize the damage was that bad."

"The visible scars were minimal. The worst injuries were to the nerves on both sides. He doesn't have a normal smile, and until recently he didn't have a smile at all. Some of the nerves seem to have regenerated in the past few months, but now when he smiles it doesn't look friendly. It looks like a leer. I've taken him to the best surgeons in the state, three of them. They weren't covered by our HMO."

Jay closed his eyes and shook his head. "I don't know how I would have endured what you've been through, Grant." He shook himself and straightened in his chair. "Let's see, your house is paid for, and it has your sister's name as joint owner. Good move."

"Rita's name is also on my savings and retirement accounts. If something happens to me, she'll take care of Brooke and Beau." Probably. If things didn't change in the next few months. He thought of Lauren, a recently developed habit of his.

"I'll get to work on this stuff tonight." Jay pushed away from his desk. "Are you hungry? Want to grab dinner again?"

"I promised my mom I'd take her out to eat tonight." Grant noticed a slight stiffness in Jay's expression that hadn't been there before their initial meeting. It was barely detectable—maybe just his own paranoia. "Jay?"

"Mmm hmm?"

"Do you mind telling me how much a case like this would cost a paying client?"

Jay's mouth pursed, and he glanced at the wall behind Grant instead of looking at him. "Come on, Grant, you know the costs could vary wildly."

"I know it would be staggering," Grant said. "Up to fifty thousand for discovery. Up to a hundred thousand if a case goes to trial."

That earned a direct look from Jay. "I'm a man of my word. You know that. A case like this, for you, will cost nothing but time and painful memories . . . and maybe a tiny bit of public embarrassment if everything comes out. I just hope it doesn't come to that."

"I think I've surprised you. Maybe disappointed you, too." It bothered Grant more than he'd thought possible. He had always enjoyed the high regard in which Jay had held him for years.

Jay walked over to the hall tree, where he'd haphazardly flung his suit coat. "I think you're being too hard on yourself. You were taking legal medication for a good reason." He turned back to look at Grant. "You haven't disappointed me, my friend. I think maybe . . . I don't know . . . you've caused me to take a look at myself. You're taking this legal drug thing so much more seriously than I ever would have."

"The drugs may have been legal, but I'm not convinced that my use of them was ethical."

Jay shrugged on his coat and stepped over to face Grant again. "You haven't changed. You have the same moral integrity that I have always witnessed in your life. And if you were not guided by that strength of character, you could have chosen to lie about the drugs."

"Jay, aren't you listening to me? I manipulated the system. Never mind that I had myself convinced at the time that it was necessary. Never mind that it was legal. I told myself that the physician who had first given me the medication was being too tight with his prescriptions, and that as a physician myself, I had the ability to decide if I needed more, and so I made an appointment with another physician. He listened to my history, trusted me, and wrote the script I requested for chronic pain. I specifically chose this physician because I had noted, by treating some of his patients in the ER, that he was more liberal with his narcotic prescriptions."

Jay frowned at him for a moment, then shook his head. "You've already told me this, Grant. There's something I don't understand about you. You set higher ethical goals for yourself than anyone could humanly hope to achieve, and then you blame yourself when you can't reach them. If you do reach them, you give God the credit."

"That's because it truly is impossible to abide by God's standards of conduct on our own. When I tried and failed to do the right thing by my own strength, I had a crisis of faith. It lasted for two years. It wasn't until I realized I had been placing that faith on the wrong shoulders—mine, instead of Christ's—that I was able to accept that weakness in myself and lay the next crisis in His hands and not my own."

"Has it worked?"

"I haven't had the opportunity to test it."

Jay led the way out into the hallway and pressed the elevator button. "I hope you never do. Still, if the worst happens, this case could give you the opportunity."

"I'm sorry," Lauren said as she wiped the final tears from her face with the back of her hand.

Brooke dug into the pocket of her jeans and brought out a tissue of questionable cleanliness. Lauren took it gratefully. Why had she left her purse in the car? There was a whole packet of tissues in it.

Brooke and Beau remained silent as she struggled to compose herself.

"I'm sorry," she repeated.

"It's okay," Brooke said softly. "I know how it feels. We both do."

Lauren heard the thread of recognition in Brooke's voice. "Was your mother's funeral the last one you attended?"

Brooke and Beau looked at each other, then nodded.

"And you're willing to come here for me?"

Beau cleared his throat and winked at Lauren in a characteristic attempt to display humor. "You were willing to put up with Brooke while Dad's gone. It was the least we could do."

Brooke reached for his nose, but he blocked her grab, and the tension drained in a quick flight of teenaged play. For the moment, Lauren's tears were forgotten.

She stared into the evening sky. The stars were brighter out here in the country, where streetlights and neon signs and traffic didn't interfere. She turned to the twins. "Thanks again for bringing me."

Brooke fell into step beside her. "Dad would have done it if he'd been here. We couldn't let you come by yourself, especially knowing how close you and Hardy were."

Tears threatened to attack once again. Lauren swallowed them back. She couldn't allow herself to dump all her pain on these two. They'd been through enough. She needed to lighten the mood, change the subject, if only for a few moments. She had to get herself under control before she stepped into this house.

A denim-blue Camaro shone in the glow from one of the pole lights, and Lauren saw her cue. "Oh, Brooke," she teased. "Guess who's here."

"Who?"

"A certain cousin of mine. Remember Jason?"

"Jason! Aha! I knew it," Beau said. "That's why—"

"That is *not* why I came here, Beau Sheldon," Brooke snapped. "I can't believe you would even think I'd be so shallow. How was I supposed to know he'd be here?"

"How do you think Evan would feel if he knew you endured riding in the backseat of the Volvo for a whole hour just to see—"

"That's a lie, and you know it. I came for Lauren. You know that, don't you, Lauren?"

"Of course I—"

"And besides, Beau, what does Evan have to do with anything? You act like we're boyfriend and girlfriend or something."

Lauren led the way up the broad slope of the front lawn, stepping across patches of tree-shaped shadows. "Brooke, you've got to realize he's crazy about you. As much time as you spend with him, he obviously thinks you feel the same about him."

"Oh, hel-*lo!* He knows better."

"You stayed out with Evan until midnight last Saturday," Beau said. "You're trying to tell us you were working on a school project?"

Her sudden silence was interrupted by louder talk and laughter from inside the house.

Lauren felt another attack of grief.

"I can't believe all the people who are here," Brooke murmured. "Hardy was sure popular."

"Hardy was . . . Hardy." How could she describe a man who had been a star athlete in high school and who wrote poetry and love letters to his childhood sweetheart until she'd finally broken down and married him? And how did one explain the kind of person who was willing to risk his own life to rescue a co-worker?

"He was a hero, then," Brooke said. "You told us he and Archer were good friends. Is Archer coming tonight?"

"He told me he was planning to stop by this afternoon." Lauren reached for the door. "Time to enter the fray."

———

Grant heard a piercing shriek as soon as he stepped out of his car. It sounded like the obnoxious *wheeeee* of a two-hundred-pound mosquito. He frowned and looked around the neighborhood, at the older homes that needed painting, at the yards that had been neglected for too many years, at the busy intersection just three houses south of Mom's, and at the convenience store across the street. Someone's fan belt must be acting up.

He went up the concrete steps to the kitchen door and hesitated at the top. The sound grew louder, and an acrid smell caught his attention. He peered through the window in the door and saw a pot on the stove, belching black smoke.

"Mom!" He jerked open the unlocked door and plunged into the gloom. He reached the stove, turned off the burner, and pulled the pot from the heat. The fierce cry of the alarm jarred his nerves. "Mom!" He coughed and bent forward to search for better air. "Are you here? Mom?"

He rushed into an empty living room, raced down the short hallway toward the bedrooms, and nearly collided with a figure coming out of the gloom.

"What is it? Grant?" She reached toward him and touched his arm. "What's wrong? And all that racket . . . is that. . . ?"

He slumped against the wall. She was okay. His heart could slow its beating. The house wasn't on fire. "Mom, your smoke alarm went off because something was burning on the stove." He reached up and pulled the battery from the alarm over his head in the hallway. The relief was immediate. "Were you cooking something?"

She stared up at him in confusion for a moment, then her expression cleared and she nodded. "Pot roast. Oh, phooey, you mean it's burned? I thought we'd have a nice family dinner tonight." She waved at the smoke in her face and stepped past him toward the kitchen.

"No, Mom, don't go in there yet. Let's get some windows and doors open and turn on the exhaust fan. Family dinner? I thought we had decided I would take you out to dinner tonight."

The confusion returned. "We did? When was . . . oh, yes, that's right. . . ."

"It's okay. We'll get the house aired out, and then we'll go." *Lord, help me. What's wrong with my mother?*

CHAPTER 15

A s soon as Lauren stepped into the overheated, noisy atmosphere of home, the memories accosted her. Hardy's face smiled at her from framed school pictures on the built-in shelves next to the staircase of the big old farmhouse. She could almost hear his teasing, cracking voice the day he bragged to her that his notches had surpassed hers—when Daddy measured their height each year, he had carved those notches into the corners of the staircase threshold for each child to measure yearly growth. Hardy outgrew her at the age of fifteen.

She reached up and traced those indentations with her right forefinger. Simple pencil marks weren't enough for Herbert McCaffrey. They had to be carved into the wood deeply enough to withstand a coat of paint. Hardy had done the same with his little girls as soon as they were big enough to stand up straight beside the threshold. He was—had been—a proud daddy himself.

Brooke and Beau crowded through the door behind her, hovering, waiting patiently. But for a moment she didn't want to move past the entryway. Her friends and family filled the rest of the house with life, but they had left this vestibule private. She wanted a couple more minutes to delay looking into the grief in her parents' eyes. She needed to fortify herself to comfort Hardy's wife, Sandi, and their two children, but how could she possibly do that? She couldn't tell them everything would be okay.

She could tell them only the truth—that Jesus was near and he understood their pain. She knew those words would sound trite after being spoken so many times by family members, but they were true. In times past, when she'd suffered heartbreak, that was when she'd encountered God's loving presence most clearly. She needed His presence now. They needed it the most.

"Lord, protect them," she whispered. "Comfort them."

Brooke touched her on the arm. "Need to go for another walk?"

Lauren turned and patted her hand. "No, thanks, honey. It's too late. I need to get in there." She inhaled the scents that drifted from the kitchen. This big old house was constructed so that the rooms downstairs interconnected. The kitchen aromas accosted her from both sides.

Here in southern Missouri, a death in the family brought out friends and relatives from every pastoral acre, all with their best-cooked recipes of fried chicken, chicken and dumplings, chicken and dressing, chicken and nood—

A thump on the stairs behind her was quickly followed by two long, strong arms wrapping around her from behind. "What kept you?" growled a male voice in her left ear.

She smelled her brother Roger's citrus aftershave as he pulled her against his chest in a grip like a grizzly. Roger. Her youngest brother. Her only living brother now.

She felt the tears burn her eyes. "Sorry I'm late. They had trouble getting a replacement for me at work, and I had to hang around until we knew for sure the shift would be covered. We're having all kinds of nursing shortages at the hospital lately, and I've been picking up a few more shifts than I usually have." Chatter mode. Anything to keep the present circumstances from caving in on her.

His arms tightened, then he released her and let her turn around to give him a proper hug. "Let them hire a temporary nurse. We need you here right now. Sandi and the girls need you." His voice rumbled with the gruffness that he always used to cover his emotions.

"How are they doing?" She released him and stood back to look up at the dark circles beneath his tired green eyes. Those were the McCaffrey eyes. The rest of Roger's features—the long narrow face and dark hair—also resembled Daddy's side of the family, while Hardy and Lauren had taken after Mom's Nordic ancestors.

"Not too good." Roger hugged Brooke and Beau, then laid a hand on Lauren's shoulder and walked with her to the wide threshold that led into the huge, crowded living room. Heads came up from conversations, and greetings were called out.

Roger gestured toward the kitchen, which had a breakfast bar that served to divide the two areas. Past that divider Lauren saw their sister-in-law Sandi huddled beside the stove, as if she couldn't get warm. The girls, Faith and Sierra, sat at the kitchen counter with two of their cousins, Roger's boys, all intent on their coloring books. Mom worked at the table nearby, replenishing food and paper plates on the bar, which was already heaped with food. Aunt Geraldine, Mom's sister, and Roger's wife, Cindy, worked with her.

Typical for Mom—she always buried her grief or worry in work after she bathed it in prayer. There were telltale signs of fresh tears on her face, and a tightness around her mouth that wasn't ordinarily there, but there would be a quick smile and welcome for every person who walked into the house tonight.

Daddy would be outside with some of the men of the family, huddled under the hood of a cantankerous pickup truck or peering at the motor of one of the farm tractors. Every few minutes he would saunter off into the shadows alone, look up into the sky, blow his nose. Sitting in the living room with all that noise and commotion was too wearing on him, and he would grieve hard.

While Roger started to escort Brooke and Beau into the living room, Lauren took the long way to the kitchen, through the deserted back hall and basement landing. She heard the shrieks and pounding footsteps of children playing in the upstairs hallway. Ordinarily, Faith and Sierra would be up there, shrieking as loudly, playing with as much abandon as the others.

Lauren stepped through the back entrance of the overheated kitchen.

Eight-year-old Sierra looked up from the coloring book. "Aunt Lauren! Mama, she's here!" Scrambling from her stool, the child tossed her crayon to the counter.

Lauren met her halfway across the room with open arms and nearly stumbled backward at the impact as the blond-haired child hurled herself forward. Faith and their mother, Sandi, joined them, and the tears began once more.

Beau stood between Brooke and Roger just inside the expansive threshold that led from the entrance vestibule to the rest of the house. He stared at the thirty or so people crowded every which way in the long, broad living room. Some lounged in sofas, some in chairs, a few on the raised hearth of the fireplace, and some of Lauren's teenaged cousins huddled around a card table in the far corner of the room. He could tell that many of them had been here for quite some time, because the initial hush of shocked grief had abated and, typical of what he'd witnessed of the McCaffrey clan when they got together, things were getting lively.

Good-looking, blond-haired Jason McCaffrey caught sight of Beau and Brooke from that far corner and gestured for them to join the circle of others who hovered around a board game.

Brooke reached for Beau's arm to drag him with her, but he evaded her grasp and stepped backward. He had no intention of laughing and playing games while people were grieving. On top of that, shyness had attacked him with sudden abandon. He looked for an empty corner where he might be less visible.

In spite of what he considered slightly inappropriate behavior so soon after a man's death, he envied Brooke as she sauntered past groups of friendly faces—greeting those she knew and allowing herself to be introduced to others.

Thanks to Lauren, he and Brooke knew many of the people here. Lauren's family was very close-knit, and different ones had driven to Dogwood Springs to attend church with her, or have lunch with her, or even visit her at work. When she'd been hospitalized in the summer for mercury poisoning, the whole clan had turned up at the hospital and practically camped out in the waiting rooms until they could be assured she would be okay.

He shoved his hands into his pockets and ambled toward a bare space along the wall next to the fireplace to his left.

"Beau Sheldon, don't you disappear until I get my hug!" called a husky female voice from across the room.

He turned to see Lauren's oldest sister, Sarah, wave at him from the love seat beside the front window. She smiled as she stood to walk toward him.

Lauren's family was a kissy, huggy one. Lauren was a hugger, too, although she didn't force her hugs on someone she sensed didn't want them. Beau didn't mind at all.

"Aren't you getting more handsome all the time, just like your father." Sarah was five years older than Lauren, heavier, and she wore glasses. She also talked more. But she had Lauren's wide smile that seemed to warm the air around her.

She reached up and enveloped him with plump arms and a hint of sweet perfume. He loved those motherly McCaffrey hugs, and he returned the favor.

"My goodness, those shoulders just keep getting broader." She leaned back and beamed up at him. "Where are your father and sister?" She turned and looked around the room. One of the McCaffrey aunts and two cousins waved and called a belated greeting to Beau.

Suddenly he didn't feel quite so shy. He waved back as he answered Sarah, "Dad had to go to St. Louis, so Lauren's staying with us for a few days."

"Oh, she is, is she? Good for her. Where's that sister of yours?"

"Brooke's over there with Jason and the others." He pointed toward the far corner of the room. He liked Lauren's sisters. He liked all of Lauren's family. They were loud and friendly country folks, generous and outspoken. "Brooke and I didn't want Lauren to drive here alone."

"Thanks for taking care of her for us." Sarah leaned closer. "How's Lauren holding up?"

"Not great."

"Didn't think so. She and Hardy were just like *that*." She held her right hand up, with her first and second fingers crossed. "Always sticking up for each other. Hardy's the one who gave us all a good chewing out when Lauren moved from Knolls. He accused us of driving her away with our constant attempts at matchmaking. He was probably right."

Beau nodded. Of course. They still did it, most recently with Dad, and he caught gleams of speculation in the glances from several people in the room. He darted a look toward the kitchen. How would Lauren react to those speculations? In the past she had always changed the subject when anyone suggested there might be some kind of deeper relationship developing between her and Dad. Beau had never brought it up, but he wondered about it more and more lately. He knew his sister did, too.

"Hey there, Brooke Sheldon," Sarah called over the din of the room. "Why don't you come and give your auntie a hug?"

With a grin, Brooke stood and made her way back through the crowd.

Once again, Beau wondered how Lauren felt about all the talk and laughter. When Mom died, their church had provided food for the family, but Beau had been in the hospital until the day of the funeral. Granny and Grandad Case, Mom's parents, had flown in from Arizona and stayed for two weeks, helping take care of him and Dad. He didn't remember anyone laughing. He did remember Grandpa and Grandma Sheldon fighting when they both arrived at the same time in Beau's hospital room.

The McCaffreys liked to "discuss" differing opinions at the tops of their lungs, but he doubted they ever actually fought.

"Hi, Aunt Sarah." Brooke reached out for the expected hug as soon as she reached them.

Sarah didn't disappoint. "There's my beautiful girl. How're you, darlin'? I can't tell you how much I like the sound of that name coming from your lips. Too bad Lauren didn't hear it." Sarah released Brooke and craned her neck to glance into the kitchen, where Lauren continued to huddle beside Hardy's family. "This is going to be so hard for them, but you'd know all about that, wouldn't you? Bless your hearts."

She glanced from Brooke to Beau as if they would know all the answers for a grieving family, and suddenly a sheen of moisture filled her eyes. "I can't believe this is happening," she whispered. "It's a horrible shock. I want to take those little nieces of mine in my arms and love all that pain away, but I know that can't be done. Still, I hug on 'em whenever I get a chance." Her voice cracked and her chin dimpled.

Beau forgot about his attack of shyness completely and put an arm across her shoulders. "I'm sorry about Hardy. I think your family is going to be a lot of comfort to Sandi and the girls. I wish we'd had support like this when Mom died."

"Me too," Brooke said.

Sarah dabbed at her nose with a tissue from her shirt pocket. "You don't have a lot of family?"

"Not a big one like yours," Brooke said. "And Dad wasn't released from the hospital in time for Mom's funeral."

"Was he hurt that bad?"

"He had a pneumothorax with associated rib fractures . . . uh, a couple of broken ribs and a dropped lung, and some pulled muscles in his back," Beau explained. "They had to put a chest tube in him for the dropped lung. He didn't get out for over a week."

Sarah's softly lined face filled with sympathy. "So the two of you went alone?"

Brooke touched Beau's arm. "Dad missed the fireworks, didn't he?"

Beau nodded.

Brooke sighed. "I hope Dad's doing okay up in St. Louis. I think one reason he wanted to move out of the city was so we wouldn't get dragged into so many of the fights. You'd think after more than twenty years of divorce, Grandma and Grandpa would learn how to hate each other a little more quietly."

"One would think that, yes." Sarah sighed. "You two have been through so much. I hate to see it, but it'll help you to learn empathy for others who are going through similar things. Just remember—'. . . in all things God works for the good of those who love him. . . . ' I know it's hard to see what good can come of Hardy's dying, but we've got to trust."

"You know," someone said from behind Beau, "twins run in the McCaffrey family, too."

He turned to find Lauren's pretty, blond-haired mom bearing down on him with a tray of deli meats and crackers. Her eyes were haunted by shadows, the same way Lauren's were.

She held the tray out to them. "I bet you're hungry. Have some. My sister had twins, and my grandmother was a twin. Can't you imagine having another set of little Sheldons running around the house, what with you two in high school?"

Beau did a mental hustle to keep up with her abrupt change of subject, then nearly dropped a cracker on the floor when he realized what she meant.

Brooke giggled.

"Mama," Sarah chided.

"I wouldn't mind," Beau said. "I like kids."

"Me too," Brooke agreed.

Mother McCaffrey's eyebrows rose. "Well—"

"Brooke!" Jason called across the room. "It's your turn, and your team's losing!"

Brooke excused herself and battled the crowd again. After one more hug from Sarah, Beau let himself be drafted to help with the food.

"It's a homecoming for him, Lauren. You know that." Mom's round, pretty face was pale and pinched with grief, but the evidence of what she believed was in her eyes. "I'm just going to miss him so much."

Lauren took her in a hard embrace, gritting her teeth to keep from crying. She squeezed her eyes tightly shut and concentrated on breathing deeply.

"He admired you so much, Lauren."

Be strong. "I know. I loved him, too. I wish I'd told him that more often."

"He knew it, darlin'." Mom patted her shoulders briskly, then stepped back. "I just keep telling your daddy that we can feel sorry for ourselves, and we can grieve for Sandi and Faith and Sierra, but we can't feel bad that our boy has been promoted to glory. He's walking streets of gold and arguing with the apostle Paul about a woman's place in the church."

Lauren tried to laugh through the tightness of her throat. "Hardy loved to argue."

"It's a family trait." With a final brisk pat on Lauren's shoulder, Mom turned to greet a newcomer, and Lauren was engulfed in surreal images of memory once again.

She stood in uncharacteristic silence, looking into the beloved faces of family in the crowded living room. For the fifth time in her life, she realized why families banded together when they suffered a death. There was such a spiritual bond that held them, that healed them, that helped them grow—and they all needed that healing tonight. *She* needed it.

Strange that she never thought about it much at other times, but the connection felt so precious to her now, and she wondered at the wisdom of the distance she had put between herself and her family when she moved to Dogwood Springs.

Here in the Ozarks, funerals and visitations were still observed with town-wide focus. The dead were held in respect, the family was comforted by the turnout, and friends and family were given their final opportunity to reconnect with the deceased one last time. It was an act of respect and caring. It also was somewhat of an opportunity for family reunions.

Lauren knew that tomorrow night at the visitation the funeral home would be packed with a crowd of townsfolk showing their respect. If it was anything like the visitation they'd had for Dwayne Little last year, there would be a line of mourners all the way out to the street, and they would take an extra hour to file through to hug the weary family, cry and shake their heads at the casket, and exclaim over all the pretty flowers.

At some point during the evening the laughter would get too loud and people would stop and look at one another and duck their heads in shame. Quiet would descend for maybe three minutes, and it would start all over again. And the family wouldn't mind that much, because they would be engrossed in the process of bringing Hardy back to life in their hearts with the help of friends and relatives.

Lauren entered the fray of the living room at last and eavesdropped on nearby conversations.

"Remember when Hardy played the lead in the school play and ripped the heroine's wig from her head?"

"Remember when Hardy pitched an egg instead of a softball during the tournament three years ago?"

"That ornery Hardy and his practical jokes! Remember when Aunt Geneva burned the turkey for Thanksgiving, and he—"

"Lauren McCaffrey, they said you'd be here, but I didn't think you'd be able to get off work, what with the nursing shortage!" The booming voice reached Lauren seconds before a beefy arm fell across her shoulders and swung her around.

She looked up into the handsome features of a lovable giant, Clarence Knight. His dark hair was sprinkled with a lot of salt, and his dark brown eyes, the color of untouched coffee, held a little extra moisture tonight. A gentle, generous spirit shone from those eyes. But something was missing.

She gasped in awe when she reached up and gave his solid shoulders a tight hug—she was able to get her arms all the way around him. "Clarence, you've lost more weight!" At least a hundred pounds since she'd seen him last. Had it been that long?

His laughter rumbled. He picked her up and swung her around in a circle, obviously proud of this new ability. A year ago he could barely walk because of his overwhelming weight, which at one point had been over five hundred pounds.

"My friend, you look wonderful," Lauren said.

He patted his belly. "Slender and pretty as you are, you'd never be able to guess how good it feels to have all that lard off."

"How much do you weigh now?"

"He weighed two hundred and fifty-three and a half pounds when he stepped on the scales this morning," came a sweet voice from behind him.

A young lady of twelve poked him in the side with her elbow as she stepped around him. Her dark eyes were framed by the glasses she'd started wearing last winter, and she appeared to have grown at least four inches since then.

"Hi, Lauren."

"Tedi Zimmerman, I can't believe how grown-up you look!"

The young lady's face beamed. "It's Bower now." Tedi had dark hair just like her mother, and she was filling out in all the places that once held a tiny amount of baby fat. "Lukas legally adopted me three months ago. That's what Dad would have wanted." She gave Lauren a hug, the top of her head even with Lauren's eyebrows. She looked as if she might grow taller than her mother's five feet eight inches. "I'm sorry about Hardy. He was such a neat man."

"Thanks, sweetie. I know he was."

Tedi poked Clarence in the arm. "You'd better not be flirting with Lauren, or one of your girlfriends might catch you."

"Girl*friends?* " Lauren asked. "He has more than one?"

Tedi held up two fingers.

"Hey, I don't have any girlfriends," Clarence growled. "They're just friends. Buddies."

"Sure, Clarence, that's what they all say." Tedi rolled her eyes at Lauren. "Clarence is going to nursing school, did you know that? His girlfriends are nursing students, too."

"Ted!" Clarence glared down at her. "You weren't supposed to tell."

"Nursing school?" Lauren asked.

Clarence made his point with a final glare of amused outrage at Tedi, then leaned closer to Lauren and lowered his voice. "Seemed like I kind of had a knack for stuff like that when I started helping out Arthur and Alma Collins at the Crosslines clinic, so they went behind my back—mind you, I had nothing to do with it!—and told Ivy I should get some training in the medical field."

"Yeah," Tedi said eagerly, "and you know how bossy Grandma is—she talked to a bunch of her rich friends in Knolls, and they gave Clarence a scholarship to Burge in Springfield, and so now he's all buried in homework, and he stays in Springfield during the week, and he's trying to graduate early so he can come back home and get to work and pay back his debt to society and—"

"And Tedi talks too much," Clarence complained.

"But he's getting straight A's," Tedi said. "And did you know his sister, Darlene, got married last month to my old fifth-grade teacher, and Grandma Ivy may get married to Dr. Heagerty?"

"Doc Heagerty?" *And Mercy's mother?* Lauren didn't think Ivy Richmond would ever remarry, especially another physician. "I knew they were sweet on each other. Good for them."

"Yes, and Clarence is now one of the most eligible bachelors in—"

Clarence cleared his throat and shifted positions, managing to give Tedi a gentle nudge. "So, Lauren, when are you coming back home to stay?" His voice seemed to boom with a deep bass, and it carried well. A little too well.

The roar of conversation that, only seconds before, had seemed to fill every room in the house now dropped to a whisper. With peripheral vision, Lauren saw Brooke and Beau turn toward her.

She gave Clarence another hug. "What makes you think I'm coming back to Knolls?"

"That empty spot you left in this town when you moved. It's still here."

"And I miss you, too, my friend, but I've got a mortgage to pay and a job to do."

Still in the edge of her vision, Beau and Brooke returned their attention to Lauren's younger cousins.

"Lauren, do you have a boyfriend?" Tedi asked.

"Nope, not me."

"Oh, really?" Clarence asked. "Funny, I heard different."

"You know how rumors fly." Lauren would have to possess a stone heart and be deaf as a fishing pole not to have caught the drift of conversation tonight.

When she'd agreed to let Beau and Brooke come with her, she had considered the possibility that her family might use it for ammunition. Her instincts had been correct. She also realized that the twins retained an interest in her plans for the future. The thought stirred mingled emotions of tenderness and alarm. She had grown to care a great deal for Grant's children. A very great deal.

"Lauren?"

She looked up and saw the kind, bespectacled blue eyes of Dr. Lukas Bower. Beside him stood his wife, Dr. Mercy. Together they engulfed her in hugs, and for the first time, she didn't feel awkward about hugging Lukas in front of Mercy. There had been a time, before their marriage, when Lauren's crush on him had been obvious to everyone in Knolls, and humiliating to her.

"He didn't suffer, Lauren." Lukas gave her a gentle pat on the back. "They brought him to the ER as soon as the accident happened."

She felt the sting of moisture in her eyes. "Yes, Daddy told me. I'm so glad it was you."

"Hardy was gone before his body reached us. From all evidence, it was instantaneous."

"Thank you."

Mercy handed her a tissue, then engulfed her in another tight, consoling embrace. "Are you going to be okay? I know you two were close."

"I'll be fine. I can't help wondering if the rest of my family will suffer, though, because of my selfish decisions."

Mercy kept an arm around Lauren and gently guided her away from the crowded room, back into the vestibule where a younger Hardy smiled at them from the wall.

"Lauren, honey, what's going on here? Why the guilt?" Mercy kept her voice low.

"I can't help wondering if I've made a mistake," Lauren said. "Maybe I should never have moved away." Why was she telling Mercy this? But then, who else could she talk to about it? Mercy had the foundation of maturity and wisdom that came from suffering. Her empathy and compassion were well known, and her family practice clinic was booming because of it.

"What makes you say that?" Mercy asked. "You had a good reason to move, Lauren. You're a grown woman, and frankly, your dear mother tends to smother you."

"But this has been my home forever. It's still home. Why did I leave? Now it won't be so easy to check on Sandi and the girls. I've got friends and family here who need me."

"Are you sure?"

"What do you mean?"

Mercy raised an inquisitive brow. "Honey, Sandi and the girls have lots of friends, and they have their church, your parents, Sandi's parents and brothers and sisters. . . . Need I continue the list? Sandi won't lack for help in the community. What would bring your mother great joy— what would bring all of us joy—would be to see you happy and settled."

"If you mean I'm supposed to get married—"

"Did I mention marriage?" There was a hint of a smile in Mercy's eyes. "I believe if your parents knew for sure you were fulfilled in your life, they wouldn't be so anxious to see you married." She turned and gestured toward Lukas, who stood talking with Clarence and Tedi, and her gaze grew tender. "I never dreamed I would remarry, but when Lukas proposed, I knew it was right, in spite of the problems I expected to have with Tedi learning to accept a stepfather."

"But Lukas and Tedi have such a wonderful relationship."

Mercy turned back to her. "Exactly. And you seem to have a good relationship with Grant's children, or they wouldn't have been so eager to come here with you. So, Lauren, how do you feel about stepchildren?"

Lauren ignored the heavy hint. "I think Lukas is the most blessed man on earth to have Tedi as his stepdaughter. She looks more like you every day."

Mercy nudged her with an elbow. "That isn't what I meant, and you know it. Beau and Brooke are enchanting."

Lauren glanced toward the twins, who stood in the center of a group of cousins. They had, indeed, made themselves at home. Brooke flirted with Jason. Two other second cousins—female—hovered near Beau. Lauren had learned to see past the partially paralyzed features of his handsome face to the emotions that played behind those wire-framed glasses. He looked comfortable in spite of the gravity of the circumstances—possibly even *because* of the circumstances, since he, too, had such a compassionate heart.

"I'm happy single," Lauren said at last.

"I was, too, once upon a time," Mercy said. "Much happier single than with Theodore, believe me! And at that time in my life, I believe God wanted me to be single. But our lives change. What God calls us to be at one time in our life might change just as soon as we get good and comfortable."

Tedi strolled back to her mother's side and hugged her. Lauren couldn't miss the expression of contentment in Tedi's eyes now, compared to a year ago. The child obviously knew how cherished she was by her mother and stepfather. Her dark eyes no longer looked haunted by fear. She had once been terrified of her alcoholic father, who had retained custody of her until a few months before his death. But, in an ironic twist of fate, the man who had once nearly killed his daughter in an alcoholic rage had, in the end, sacrificed his own life to save her.

Mercy gave Lauren another hug. "I'm not trying to tell you what choices to make, and I'm glad you've learned to be content living alone.

But don't you think that could be only one of many goals God has for your life?"

"I'm sure it is, but that doesn't mean—"

"Don't become so content that you miss the next step God intends for you to take."

CHAPTER 16

B eau strolled through the darkness toward the car, taking point between Brooke and Lauren, since he had been given responsibility for Dad McCaffrey's big fluorescent flashlight. At this distance the front porch light didn't chase away enough of the shadows.

Lauren's father reminded Beau of Dad, and his voice still seemed to echo, saying, "You all be careful, now, and don't try to race home. You ride those brakes on the curves, you hear?"

Had Lauren heard the catch in her father's voice? The special reminder that he'd already lost one child this week, and that he couldn't bear to see anything happen to the others?

"Lauren, how far is the city of Columbia from here?" Brooke asked.

"I'd say it's about a four-hour drive."

The keys jangled in Beau's hand as they approached the car. "That means it would take about three hours for Brooke."

"Shut up, Beau."

He stopped and aimed the beam of the flashlight into the shadows, into other cars . . . nothing suspicious, but it didn't hurt to check.

"Why do you want to know about Columbia?" Lauren asked.

"It's where Jason's attending university next year," Beau answered for his sister. He'd overheard Jason talking about it to Brooke about an hour ago. "A month ago he wanted to major in agriculture. Now he wants to be a heart surgeon, so he's taking pre-med."

"So what's wrong with that?" Brooke demanded. "You want to be an ER doc. It wouldn't hurt you to check out Columbia yourself, especially since—"

Something skittered in the brush beside the car, and Beau jerked around, nearly dropping the light.

"Beau, would you relax?" Brooke said. "It's probably just a squirrel or a rabbit. Since when have you been scared of the dark?"

He looked across the roof of the car at her. Ever since the wreck last week he'd been jumpy, watchful. Afraid. He was so busy worrying he didn't even have opportunity to enjoy the fact that Brooke no longer complained about the girth of the Volvo. He couldn't help noticing, however, that almost every time her mouth had opened in the past ten minutes—which was several times—Jason's name had spilled out.

He ducked beneath the branches of sassafras and opened the passenger door for Lauren. She thanked him and gave him a smile that didn't spread past her lips.

She was grieving hard. Beau had been emotionally numb for weeks after the wreck that killed Mom, and he had continued to be so despondent that when the surgeries were scheduled to begin on his face, one surgeon had wanted to delay the procedure for fear that the depression would threaten the outcome. He could have been right. The outcome hadn't been so good.

On impulse, Beau took Lauren's elbow in a gesture of helpfulness as she slid into her seat. He knew she didn't need the help, but she needed to know she wasn't alone. He remembered needing the comfort of others, even though he'd hated seeing the initial shock in the eyes of visitors when they saw him swathed in bandages. He'd hated it even worse when he was left alone in his hospital room. His memories of the wreck still caused him more pain than the fact of Mom's death, and that reality was bad enough.

He circled the car and slid into the driver's seat. Brooke was still chattering from the backseat about Jason's school plans. She loved sitting where she could comfortably keep up a conversation with everyone in the car while watching the road and telling Beau how to drive.

When Brooke paused to take a breath, Lauren looked over at Beau. "Thank you for bringing me tonight."

"You're welcome." He checked his rearview mirror and studied the dirt road in both directions before pulling out of the drive. A guy would have to be pretty good at dodging bullets and bad guys on computer games to be able to miss all the potholes on this road.

Brooke was silent for a full two minutes before she spoke again. "Lauren?" Her voice was meek—even tentative. Uncharacteristic.

It caught Beau's attention. He looked at his sister's dark silhouette in the mirror, hit a rut, winced.

"Yes?"

"Did you mean that when you said you weren't moving back to Knolls?"

Silence loomed in the car when there should have been quick reassurances. Beau looked over at Lauren. Her face was mostly in shadow, except for a bright sheen in her eyes.

"I'm . . . not sure." There was a wobble in the softness of her voice. "Hardy's family might need some help for a while."

"But they already have help. They've got people all around them. Why should you quit your job and move all the way back from Dogwood Springs?"

"Because I'm single. It would be easier for me to find time—"

"But what about *us*?" The outburst was so sudden and so filled with disappointment that if Beau hadn't already known how his twin felt about Lauren, he would have no doubts now.

He pulled from the dirt road onto the paved county road and stole a look at Lauren. Her complexion was washed to white in the glow from the illuminated console.

"I haven't decided for sure, Brooke," she said.

After a moment of silence, Brooke's voice grew timid again. "I don't get it, Lauren. I thought you liked us."

"Oh, honey, you know I care a great deal about you."

"And I thought you liked Dad. You two could be more than just friends, you know."

"*More* than friendship?" Lauren asked. She turned within the confines of her seat belt to look over the seat at Brooke. "That's the most important thing in a relationship."

"Oh, come on, I know it takes more than that for marriage. Dad's a great-looking man—lots of people say so. Even Jade Myers has a thing for him."

"The mayor?"

Beau had caught the switch Brooke made from *friendship* and *relationship*, to *marriage*. He wondered if Lauren had caught it.

"She knows a good thing when she sees it," Brooke said. "She thinks he's hot."

"Brooke, I know I'm not exactly experienced when it comes to marriage, but I'm pretty sure it takes more than high temperature to make it work."

"Dad has what it takes," Beau said.

Lauren turned her attention to him. He continued to watch the road.

"Did you ever consider the possibility that your father might enjoy a dinner out with Jade?" she asked them.

Brooke gasped. "No, and please don't say anything to him about it."

Lauren chuckled. "Don't you like Jade?"

"I like her as mayor, but can you imagine what she'd be like to live with? Have you ever actually *met* her? She never stops talking!"

Beau snorted.

"Shut up, Beau. It's why she makes such a good mayor—she talks so much nobody else ever gets a chance to say anything. Norville Webster's been out to dinner with her a couple of times, and Evan says he thinks she not only orders her own meal, she orders Norville's, too."

"Tell Evan it isn't nice to make up stories about people," Lauren said. "Norville's been out with her?"

"That's what Evan told me. But really, can you imagine her and Dad getting together? Talk about your nightmare—"

A chuckle escaped Beau's throat before he could stop it.

Lauren's laughter echoed his own.

"What are you laughing about?" Brooke demanded.

"Jade sounds a lot like you," Beau said.

There was a sigh of impatience from the backseat, and finally a peaceful silence settled on the interior of the car. Beau had learned to enjoy the break while it lasted. Brooke seldom pouted for long.

Grant felt like a traitor.

But it had to be done. Rita was his sister—she had to know. He waited for the third ring, preparing to leave a message on a machine, when Rita answered.

He cleared his throat. "Hi, sis. It's me." After they got the preliminaries out of the way, he hesitated. "Have you spoken with Mom lately?"

"Not since Thanksgiving. Same old argument, though. You know how it is. She wants to know if I've seen Dad lately. If I tell her the truth, she's hurt because I'm paying more attention to him than I am to her. If I lie, I feel guilty for the next week." Rita sounded tired. Grant knew how she felt.

"Have you noticed anything different about her lately?" he asked.

"Different? Like what?"

"Does she seem forgetful?"

There was a short silence. "She repeats questions sometimes, but I don't think that means anything. I repeat questions, too. Life's just too hectic these days."

"You don't forget important facts about your own family."

"Sometimes I do. I called Patrick by the dog's name the other day."

"I'm serious."

There was a slow sigh. "Grant, what are you saying to me?"

For the next few moments he downloaded the details about Mom's problems with her memory. Rita was silent after he finished.

"I've made an appointment with a neurologist," he said. "I doubt she'll cooperate, but I hope to be able to convince her how important this is. We'll need to run some tests."

"What kinds of tests?"

He closed his eyes. "It could be Alzheimer's."

There was a quick intake of breath.

"I don't know yet," he rushed to assure her. "I'm an ER doc, remember, so I don't work with this kind of thing. I just wanted to prepare you for the worst."

"Oh, Grant, poor Mom. What if it is? She'll go nuts if she has to move into a home somewhere."

"Would you relax? She isn't that bad yet."

"But what can we do to help her, with both of us living so far away?"

"I'm not asking you to do anything at this point, but I thought you needed to know."

Rita had always been closer to Dad, which kept her in defense mode with Mom most of the time. Since Grant had always kept in closer contact with Mom, living in the same city until six months ago, it had made for some interesting—and painful—family dynamics over the years. Somehow, Grant and Rita remained close in spite of the geographical distance between them, and he understood why she and her family had chosen to live in Kansas City—a four-and-a-half-hour drive from Mom.

To Grant's regret, he and Rita had tried and failed several times to bring about even an illusion of peace between their parents for the sake of the grandchildren. Although there had been a break in tension from time to time when Dad was on one of his numerous extended vacations, everyone in the family despaired of ever seeing the two of them come to any kind of agreeable terms.

"Well, you know Mom wouldn't let me do anything for her," Rita said at last.

"May I make a suggestion? Try harder. If this is what I think, it's hitting her fast. I didn't notice a problem last time I was up here, and that was just three months ago. Maybe I've been living in my own busy world lately, but I would think I'd have noticed this kind of forgetfulness. She asked me the same question seven times last night."

"That's awful." Rita sighed. "I should probably try again to make peace with her while we still have time. But it won't be easy."

"I'll talk to Mom about it first, then maybe I can convince her to call you."

"Lots of luck."

It would take more than that. "Good night, Rita." He hung up.

A shadow moved in the hallway. Grant looked up to see Mom's familiar shape outlined by incoming neon. He felt a sudden shock, and a chill spread through his gut.

She stepped into the living room and switched on the lamp beside the sofa. "What are you supposed to talk to me about, Grant? What are you and Rita up to?"

"So, speaking of romance," Brooke said, breaking the silence after an amazing ten-minute reprieve, "I finally figured out who the Todd is that Levi and Cody were talking about the other day. What do you think of Gina's little fling with Todd Lennard?"

Awkward silence filled the car.

"Hasn't anybody warned her about the dangers of messing around with the wrong person?" Brooke continued.

Beau groaned aloud. "Brooke, can't you wait and talk about this kind of stuff when I'm not stuck in the car with you?"

She didn't listen. She never minded embarrassing him. "I'm always trying to talk my friends at school out of sex. I can tell they think I'm whacked out. They're nice about it, but they don't listen."

"Frustrating, isn't it?" Lauren said softly.

"Yeah. It's like"—Beau heard Brooke's characteristic slap of her forehead with the palm of her hand—"get some brains! And they always break up. I mean, it isn't like they're making any kind of commitment, even when they say they are. And when they get pregnant? They come crying to me. Right, like I had something to do with it? And I've learned I'm never supposed to call it a baby when they're talking about 'getting it taken care of.' "

Beau rolled his eyes. His sister was never afraid to speak her thoughts. He complained about it a lot—and had to brace himself, at times, for Brooke's next one-liner, knockdown punch—but her brazen honesty was one of Brooke's more dependable qualities, even though it wasn't always one of her most attractive features. At least he seldom had to guess what she was thinking—except for this project with Evan.

"Brooke, are you sure they don't listen?" Lauren asked. "Ever?"

"Afterward." Brooke snorted. "Like it's going to do them any good for me to say 'I told you so.' "

"You never tell them that, I hope."

"She tells me that all the time," Beau said. "When she thinks she's right."

"I just hold them when they come crying to me afterward."

"Then maybe they learn eventually," Lauren said. "Maybe your words touch them in the long run."

"If they have, nobody ever said anything to me about it," Brooke said. "So. Has Gina . . . you know . . . been stupid with that two-timing creep?"

Beau groaned. "Brooke—"

"Relax, I'm not talking to you. It's the latest hot topic for Fiona Perkins, and you know how she spreads it at the hospital."

"That's what they're saying?"

"Yes, but who's more likely to know the truth, Fiona Perkins or Lauren McCaffrey, Gina's best friend?"

Lauren slumped in her seat. "Some best friend I am."

"You'd better pray hard for Gina," Brooke said.

"Thank you, Pastor Sheldon," Beau said. "Do you mind if we change the subject now?"

Brooke gave a heavy sigh and sank back into her seat. Asking Brooke to shut up was cruel punishment, and he knew she felt strongly about what she said. She'd had a friend in their school in St. Louis whose father had an affair with a woman at work. It had destroyed something vital in that family, and they'd never been the same since.

Just like Grandma and Grandpa Sheldon.

———

Grant sat in the lamplit living room of Mom's house, staring at the constant reflection of the green-and-purple neon sign that flashed from the convenience store across the street through the filmy curtain of the bay window. He riffled through his mind for some believable explanation that wouldn't be hurtful but also wouldn't be a lie.

He couldn't think of anything.

And Mom sat in the rocking chair facing him, waiting for a reply. At this moment, of course, her mind seemed sharp and clear.

"Mom, what do you think about moving out of this house?"

She blinked at him, lips held in a firm, straight line. "Is that what you were talking to Rita about?"

"Not exactly, but it's something we will want to discuss before long."

"Why?" That same uncompromising line.

"Because things have changed since Rita and I grew up here. All the old neighbors have moved out. Your new ones aren't as friendly or as helpful."

"I have friends at the senior center, and I can still drive wherever I need to go. I can take care of myself. Just because you don't want to live here anymore doesn't mean I'm leaving." She crossed her arms over her chest. "Why are you all of a sudden so worried about my neighbors? And why are you gossiping about it to Rita?"

"I'm not gossiping, Mom. It's just that we're . . . we want you to be safe. This isn't a safe neighborhood anymore."

"And you think I'd be better off somewhere else?" Her gray eyes narrowed, and she leaned forward in her chair. "You're *not* talking about a retirement home!"

"What would be wrong with that?"

She gasped. "Grant Sheldon, how dare you! Shipping your mother off to live with a bunch of strangers just because you feel guilty that you and your kids don't want to be around me anymore?"

He winced. She could have kicked him in the stomach and it wouldn't have hurt as much. What made it so painful was that he could not avoid the fact that her trouble began after he and his kids moved away. "No, Mom, that isn't it. I called Rita because I'm . . . worried about your health. I'd like you to make a visit to a doctor I know about."

"What kind of a doctor is he?" She started rocking back and forth in her chair, short bursts of restless energy, almost as if she knew what was coming next.

"*She's* a neurologist."

"You think I've got a nerve problem?"

"No, I think you might be having trouble with short-term memory." He took a deep breath. This was harder than he'd ever dreamed it would be. "I'd like to make sure your health is okay, and then I think the doctor will want to run some tests."

"For what?" She rocked faster, no longer making eye contact, but staring blindly out the window.

"It could be any number of things, Mom. I'm just concerned because you seem to be forgetting so many things lately, and—"

"*What* specific test do you want to run on me?" she demanded. The rocking stopped, but she still didn't look at him.

"Among other things, I would want her to screen you for . . . Alzheimer's."

She deflated like a hot-air balloon that had been blasted out of the sky.

"That doesn't mean it's what you have," he said quickly. "There are many other possibilities, especially since the onset of Alzheimer's isn't usually this sudden."

She covered her face with her hands.

He knelt in front of her chair. "Mom, the smoke alarm scared me. And there've been times in the past couple of days when you didn't remember that Annette is . . . gone. Please, just help me find out what's wrong so we can take measures to fix it."

She uncovered her face and looked at him. Tears dripped down her cheeks. "I'm getting older, Grant, but I'm not useless yet. If you promise not to farm me out to some nursing home, I'll . . . I'll take those tests."

He hated the sound of fear in her voice. "I'm not farming you out anywhere. I've already spoken with this doctor. She's a friend of Jay's, and she promised to make some time in her schedule to fit you in while I'm here." He felt a great urge to get home, and yet Mom needed him. She wouldn't accept Rita's help, and in the past she had been reluctant to listen to anyone but her "doctor son."

Had he done the wrong thing by taking his children so far away from her? At the time, it had seemed so important to distance them from the conflict that had become the primary focus of her life years ago.

Whatever it was, she couldn't continue to live alone under these conditions, but before he made any further decisions he wanted to talk to his children. They had a right to know that their lives might once again be turning upside down.

Beau drove in comfortable silence past a tiny town with abundant Christmas lights around the welcome sign. There was a manger scene on the front yard of the courthouse. He wondered how long they would be allowed to do that. This year he'd barely noticed the passing of Halloween before Thanksgiving had arrived, and now they were racing toward Christmas.

Around Halloween time, too many other things had been going on—things more frightening than goblins and pointy-hatted witches. Real spooks crept the streets of their little town, meth manufacturers and drug dealers, people who carelessly tossed their noxious waste wherever they wanted.

As for the holiday season, with all the lights and music blaring at him every time he stepped into a store, he sometimes felt like a scrooge. It had been that way for the past two Christmases.

"Dad would never have had an affair on Mom," Brooke muttered, obviously unable to remain silent any longer. "They had a great marriage. Isn't that right, Beau?"

"Yes. He worked a lot, but when he wasn't at work he was home with us."

"I don't doubt that," Lauren said quietly.

"He was a good husband," Brooke added.

"Of course he was."

"And he's a good father," Brooke continued. "He isn't one of those strong, silent types who doesn't know how to express their love."

Lauren sighed. "I know that, Brooke. Remember? We're friends. I know your father. We're not talking about a stranger—"

"And he would be a good husband again."

Lauren glanced over her shoulder at Brooke, then sighed again. "Are you finished with the sales pitch?"

"I wasn't giving a—"

"You two need to understand that no one will ever fill your mother's place in his life, or in yours."

"No, but—"

"Anyone else would come with a different set of values, habits, likes, and dislikes. It would be awkward and uncomfortable, and it would never be the same as what you had before."

Beau waited for more argument from Brooke. None came. Lauren straightened in her seat and repeated the expressive sigh once more. The silence lingered as Beau turned onto the highway that would snake through the final stretch of Ozark hills and valleys that led home.

He glanced at one set of colored lights in the front yard of a farmhouse, and he blinked and looked at it again. Someone had parked a tractor there and had outlined it with Christmas lights. What would they think of—

"But you don't try to take Mom's place," Brooke said at last. "That's why we . . . that's why I thought we had something special with you. I used to be afraid that Dad might start dating someone who would be jealous of Mom's memory, or of us. I wouldn't worry about that, because I thought you cared about . . . us."

"Brooke, stop with the guilt trip," Lauren said.

"You and Dad are a perfect match, you know."

"Why do you say that?"

"Because you understand him so well. And you've been through some of the same things."

"I've never been married, Brooke."

"You've lost someone you loved."

"Most people my age have lost someone dear to them."

Brooke huffed. "You're not making this easy."

"I'm sorry, but I'm not letting you or anyone else talk me into doing something that could have a major impact on my life, your life, and other lives for the rest of our lives."

"But what if I'm right?"

"What if you're wrong?"

"Lauren, have some compassion," Beau interrupted. "How many women do you think Dad's going to meet who already understand the hazards of knowing Brooke? And your family actually likes her. I mean, how rare is that?"

Brooke smacked him on the shoulder. "Beau, I'm trying to be serious."

"I'm being serious."

"If you can't help me, keep your mouth shut."

They rode in brooding silence for several moments, and Beau was glad, because he wanted to concentrate on the road that twisted and curved between the flicker of forest shadow and the light of an almost-full moon that had finally made its way from behind the clouds. He saw the stop sign at Highway 65 south of Branson and eased on the brake, ever conscious of his passengers.

"Is there anything wrong with the friendship we already have?" Lauren asked.

"Nothing," Beau said. "It's great."

"Then maybe we shouldn't confuse the issue right now. And while we're talking about your father, I need to ask you a favor. Unless he specifically asks, would you please not tell him about Hardy's death just yet?"

"Why?" Beau asked.

"Because he has enough to worry about right now without dumping my problems on him. The news can wait until he comes home. He didn't know Hardy that well, and—"

"Don't you think that's kind of deceitful?" Brooke asked.

"I didn't tell you to lie—I asked you to keep the news to yourself."

"I think that's a little cold, Lauren," Brooke said. "My father can make his own decisions about how to handle the news."

Lauren sighed and sat back. "Okay. I guess you're right. Sorry."

"Actually, our family usually operates with a bit of secrecy," Beau said. "Mom and Dad started doing that years ago. Mom took care of everything at home because Dad was so busy at work, and so I guess he never realized just how busy she always was. Dad did it, too. He never told her about the bad stuff that happened to him at work."

Brooke leaned forward. "So, Lauren, I guess that means you'd be a perfect addition to our family."

CHAPTER 17

A t eleven-thirty Monday morning, Beau pulled a chair from beneath a table in the high school commons area, where the aromas of institutional cheese and frying beef floated through the air with cloying heaviness. He placed his own paper-wrapped lunch parcel on the table and breathed a particularly passionate prayer of thanks for a father who had taught him how to cook and who believed in organic, gourmet fare. Beau loved cheese, but the stuff the school used made him gag.

He unwrapped his sandwich and opened a bottle of apple juice. He'd packed Lauren's lunch for her today, too, and she had appreciated it. After their intense conversation about her and Dad on the drive back from the McCaffrey farmhouse, he and Brooke had done everything they could think of to express their sympathy about Hardy's death— and to prove to Lauren that living with them wouldn't be a hardship on her.

"Hamburgers again." Evan smacked his tray onto the table and jerked out the chair across from Beau, then leaned over and looked at Beau's food with a predatory gleam. "I want to move in with you. What kind of sandwich is that?"

Beau hovered over it protectively. "Free-range turkey with goat cheese on a multigrain roll with roasted garlic spread."

Evan edged his tray toward Beau. "Want my spinach? It's healthy."

"No."

"Are you sure you wouldn't like a nice greasy hamburger dipped in saturated fat? It won't make your breath smell like garlic all afternoon."

"I want to smell like garlic. It keeps the girls away."

Evan slumped into his chair. "Figures. You have to use garlic repellent to keep them away. I, on the other hand, have the talent to scare them off with just one glance from my beady eyes."

Beau bit into his sandwich, shaking his head at Evan's usual lunchtime banter. He had just completed his first taste when he caught the sound of someone shouting at the other end of the commons.

"Tell you what," Evan continued. "You pack a lunch for me every day, and I'll give you twice what I pay for my lunch—"

There was another shout, this time closer, and Beau raised his hand to silence Evan's offer. "What was that?"

Evan frowned and turned to look behind him. Several junior high kids came running into the commons area from the far hallway. Brooke was with them. Her face was pale, her eyes wide.

Beau stiffened. She looked horrified.

Evan shoved his chair back and jumped up. "Brooke, over here!"

She saw them and plunged through the mob, stumbling past tables and shoving aside chairs. Her cheeks were flushed. She paused to catch her breath when she reached Beau and Evan.

"The kids said Oakley Brisco just collapsed downstairs!"

"Oakley?" Evan squeaked.

"In the junior high rec room."

Beau dropped his sandwich. "Just now?"

"Yes!" She turned to Evan. "Did you hear me? It's Oak. They need to know. We've got to tell somebody what we—"

"Has an ambulance been called?" Beau demanded.

"Yes, and someone's doing CPR."

Beau jumped from his seat and ran, pushing his way through the crowded hallway where classmates huddled in groups, whispering shocked questions at one another. Oakley Brisco, a skinny eighth grader he'd seen in the principal's office a couple of times, was popular and excelled in sports, and Beau had heard he lived with his grandfather. So what had happened to him?

Beau reached the rec room and saw the crowd in the hallway,

peering through the open double doors. He pushed through and saw two of the junior high teachers bent over the body of the scrawny eighth grade boy, attempting resuscitation.

Before he could reach them and offer help, the ambulance attendants came charging through the crowd with their stretcher and portable monitor unit. He could do nothing but stand and watch helplessly as they ripped aside Oak's shirt and slapped monitor patches on his bony chest. Beau knew that they would first check to see if the patient's heart rhythm was in ventricular fibrillation—shockable.

It wasn't.

The EMT placed a bag-valve mask over the boy's nose and mouth and squeezed the bag to force breathing while the paramedic attempted a quick IV. The needle found a home, and the paramedic attached a line for drugs, then just as rapidly established an airway by the successful placement of a breathing tube through his mouth into his throat.

Beau was impressed. He was also frustrated that he could do nothing to help. The rhythm didn't change while the EMTs rushed their patient out the door toward the ambulance, following proper resuscitation protocol.

As far as Beau could tell, it did no good.

Gina Drake came running into the department and joined the code team. Her face was flushed, the bright strands of her short hair mussed in disarray. "Sorry I'm late," she muttered. "I was . . . taking an early break."

Lauren nodded. "It's okay, the ambulance is just now pulling in."

No one said a word when lanky Todd Lennard entered just a few seconds later. Gina's expressive face reflected more than a hint of embarrassment. There was no time for Lauren to consider those ramifications.

Gina looked up at her. "Lauren, you doing okay?"

"I'm fine. Thanks." They'd had little contact the past few days, and Lauren continued to battle hurt feelings. Not a word about Hardy's death. Not a card. Not a squeeze of the hand. But Gina was fighting battles of her own, and she didn't need a cold shoulder.

They huddled at the entrance doors as the attendants wheeled the stretcher into the department. The boy had the pale skin of a cadaver, and Lauren's heart squeezed as she sensed the aura of death that surrounded him. She raced alongside the EMTs, directing them to the room and preparing to reconnect the leads to the hospital monitor. She caught a brief glimpse of Dr. Caine's expression. His face was ashen and beads of sweat filmed his brow. The hum of the monitor and the shuffle of movements by the staff—hovering, awaiting the doctor's first order—filled the department.

He swallowed. "Epi, one milligram, now." He dabbed at his forehead with the back of his hand. "Get a . . . a blood gas." His voice trembled, and the tension mounted in the room. The staff was stretched to the limit, and the irritating buzz of the unanswered telephone seemed louder with each ring.

Vivian rushed into the room with a chart. "His parents don't live in town, Dr. Caine. His grandfather has temporary custody."

"Have you contacted him?" Caine snapped.

"Yes, he's on his way in." She leaned toward Lauren. "You know those feuding farmers who nearly came to blows last summer after their cars went over an embankment? Brisco and Scroggs? Poor old Brisco's this boy's grandfather."

"Atropine, one milligram," Caine snapped. "Any more information from the school about what happened?" he asked Vivian.

"Not yet," Vivian said.

"Intercept the grandfather when he arrives. We need medical information so we'll know what to treat as soon as we resuscitate him."

"I'm sorry, Dr. Caine," Vivian said. "Med Records didn't have anything."

"Find something!" His voice sounded on the verge of panic. He stared at the monitor. "Stop CPR. And get somebody to help answer the phones!"

"We don't have any extra—"

"Just do it!"

The school bell rang, but no one noticed. Beau eased his way past crying classmates and whispering teachers and found Brooke and Evan huddling beside Evan's open locker with their backs to the hallway.

Evan held his cell phone to his ear, then glared at it and pressed the Off button. "Still no answer."

"I can't believe this," Brooke said. "It's crazy! What if they have, like, an emergency? We can't have the wrong number, can we?"

"What wrong number?" Beau asked.

Brooke whirled around and grabbed him by the arm. "Where've you been? We're trying to contact the hospital and nobody's answering."

"Why?"

"We think Oak might have had an overdose of meth," she said.

"Why do you think that?"

"Does it matter? We've got to reach the hospital and let them know."

Beau took the cell phone and punched the number he used when he wanted to reach Lauren at work. "Now, tell me why you think Oakley is on meth."

"Because we saw him with Peregrine out on the street last night," Brooke said.

"Last night? I didn't know you went out last night." The telephone rang once . . . twice . . .

Evan closed his locker door. "Oak was the one we saw him with the other morning, too. You know, the morning we got that picture of Peregrine, when you told us to mind our own business."

"I didn't tell you to—"

"I think Peregrine was setting Oakley up as another contact at school," Brooke said.

"And you didn't tell me? Did you call Sergeant Dalton?" Nobody was answering. They would all be busy with the code. But they needed to know.

"We got him a few minutes ago," Evan said. "He's on his way here."

———

It was too late. Lauren knew that, even as Dr. Caine paced the crowded room like a caged panther, wringing his hands together in frustration and barking increasingly sharp orders to the code team. It had gone too long without results. The buzz of the monitor mocked them, and the tension stretched so tightly that Lauren felt as if it were a physical force bumping up against her.

The telephone at Lauren's station interrupted an order and added to the cacophony of the department.

Caine growled a curse at the offending sound and raised his voice to be heard over it.

The strident nag ended abruptly when Vivian snatched it up and snapped a warning that her nerves were frayed and this better be good. Her grumbling ceased almost immediately.

"What's that? Who is this? Beau?"

Lauren looked up from her position beside Oakley Brisco's left arm. She listened to Vivian's voice.

"What kind of drug? When? The kid took an illegal drug right there at school?" Vivian whirled an about-face and waved toward Dr. Caine to catch his attention. "Beau Sheldon says the patient might've taken a methamphetamine—"

"I heard." Caine muttered a soft curse. "What makes him think that information will do us any good at this point?"

Irritability lowered Vivian's graying brow. "I don't know, Dr. Caine. Maybe he's just crazy enough to think we could actually do a successful resuscitation here in the emergency depart—"

"Hey!" Someone shouted from the reception window, out of sight of the hallway. "Where is everybody? Where's Oak? Somebody lemme in there!"

Lauren recognized that voice. "Dr. Caine, that's our patient's grandfather." The irascible farmer had been a patient in the ER a couple of times in the past. He'd shouted then, too.

The doctor stood staring at the monitor.

"Dr. Caine, do you want me to go talk to Mr. Brisco?" Lauren asked.

Caine whispered something.

"I'm sorry, I didn't hear what you—"

"I asked," Caine growled, "what good it would do." He pointed to Vivian, who was keeping the records for the code. "Time—" he looked at his watch—"twelve-ten P.M." He snapped off his gloves and threw them in the trash. "This patient is dead."

Without another order he stalked out to the reception area. There were murmured words, a cry of mortal pain, and then the sound of Brisco's sobs. Seconds later, Caine swept back through the ER proper at a speed that discouraged questions. He plunged into the director's office and closed the door. The lock clicked, and there was a crash, like the sound of something being thrown against the wall.

For a few more shocked seconds, no one moved. Lauren touched Oakley's arm and could still feel the warmth of his body through the thin material of her gloves.

"That's it?" Gina said. "He's just letting it go?"

Todd started to pick up the mess on the floor. "He took it longer than I expected, hon."

The endearment became the sudden focus of the entire code team in order to block out the tragedy and loss that surrounded them.

"But he just left that poor old man out there in the waiting room, crying!"

"It's okay." Todd spoke softly and laid a hand on her arm. "I'll go talk to him."

"But the doctor—"

Todd placed a finger against her lips. "Shh. I'll take care of it."

He walked out of the room. Lauren watched him go, then looked back at Gina, who had pressed her fingers against Oak's gradually cooling shoulder.

"The world's gone crazy," Gina whispered. Tears filled her eyes. Gina Drake had never been good at handling bad outcomes in the ER, but lately she'd been even more tearful, more emotionally spent whenever she experienced a traumatic session.

Lauren, too, felt the sting especially hard so soon after Hardy's death. She wished she could shut her emotions down for a few days, but it was no use. The numbness that had given her occasional relief the past few days crumbled away and left her defenseless.

Someone touched her on the arm. She looked up into Gina's unique copper-colored eyes, still glazed with moisture. "Are you sure you're okay?"

Lauren nodded. "I've got work to do." She had to call the coroner. Though Dr. Caine hadn't instructed her to, she also needed to call the police, if they didn't call first. Since Beau was aware of the drug involvement, he would very likely call Tony Dalton himself. There would be an autopsy. Knowing Tony, there would be an immediate, complete investigation.

"Okay, guys, keep everything clear for the exam. I'll make the calls."

CHAPTER 18

Tuesday afternoon Archer Pierce leaned over the elderly lady in exam room four and said a silent, heartfelt prayer for her health. It was a selfish prayer, he knew. He didn't want to lose Mrs. Piedmont. She was one of the dearest people in the world, and after the shock of Hardy's death last week and young Oakley's tragic death yesterday, Archer didn't think he could face another loss.

In spite of the tension, he had to suppress a yawn. The past few days of grieving and comforting and intensive plans for his wedding this coming Saturday had robbed him of sleep. He didn't want to disturb this patient, but her eyes fluttered open, and she looked up at him.

"Pastor, when did you come in?"

He smiled down at the welcoming gleam in Mrs. Piedmont's eyes. "Sorry, Cecile, I didn't want to disturb you." He pressed his fingers on the thin, wrinkly flesh of her right forearm. "How are you feeling?"

She attempted a smile but couldn't quite dislodge the grimace of pain that had set into the line of her mouth. "I'll be fine." She looked past him toward the doorway, then gestured for him to lean closer. "I miss Dr. Sheldon."

"I know, so do I."

"How is Dr. Caine taking care of his own practice and working here, too?"

"Dr. Caine's here?"

"I saw him in the hallway."

"Has he been in to see you?"

She shook her head. "Dr. Jonas is on duty."

"How about a quick prayer before all your kids come barging in here to rescue you?"

"I'd like that. I'm sorry I didn't make it to church Sunday. I just didn't feel well at—"

There was a brusque knock at the open door, and the tall, white-coated form of Dr. Mitchell Caine materialized in the threshold. "Reverend Pierce, I need a word with you."

Archer didn't move his hand from Mrs. Piedmont's arm. "Of course, Dr. Caine."

"In my office."

"I won't leave my patient alone. As soon as someone else—"

"*Your* patient, Reverend?" Caine's focus narrowed to Archer's eyes. "I wasn't aware you had a license to treat patients in this facility."

Archer suppressed a sharp retort. He hadn't been aware that Mitchell suddenly had his own office in this department, either.

For a moment, he made no reply at all. It had been a difficult few days, and everyone was experiencing the stress. He'd heard from more than one source that Oakley's death had taken its toll on Mitchell.

Still, the man didn't have the right to make Cecile uncomfortable with his personal irritations.

"I'll stay with Mrs. Piedmont until someone else can come in and sit with her." Archer let his words fall with gentle authority. "My whole reason for being here is to provide comfort."

Mitchell pointedly checked his watch. "I'm here for a meeting with the department directors in thirty minutes. I want to see you before that." With that order he turned and stalked from the room.

Archer gave Cecile's arm a reassuring squeeze and felt some of his own tension drain away. "Feeling okay?"

"Better every minute." She laid a weathered hand over his. "I'll let you escape as soon as you say a prayer for me."

"You've got it all wrong, Cecile. You *are* my escape." Still, he said a quiet prayer for God's comfort and peace, not only for Cecile, but also for her grown children. They were grandparents themselves and still doted on their mother. She had developed heart problems in the spring.

For her to come into the ER on her own, without one of her children forcing her to do so, was an admission of illness indeed.

Archer finished the prayer and gave Cecile a peck on the cheek, then turned to find that Lauren had joined them. She, too, looked as if she were barely keeping pain at bay.

"Hey, pal, how're you holding up?" He reached a hand out to her and she took it. He drew her forward for a quick shoulder-hug, then released her.

"I'll be fine." Her focus centered on Mrs. Piedmont's kindly gaze.

He'd had little time to talk with her alone, and he knew she was struggling with yesterday's tragedy combined with her brother's death. She'd missed church Sunday, and the substitute teacher who had taken her Sunday school class had passed on the news that Lauren and the Sheldon twins were attending church with her family in Knolls.

She stepped to Mrs. Piedmont's bed, and her expression showed that she, too, found solace in the older woman's presence. "Calvin's on his way here, Cecile. He just called. Did you know he sent flowers for Hardy's funeral? Your kids are some of the nicest people . . ." Her voice wobbled. She swallowed. "They take after their mom."

Cecile reached her arms out, and Lauren leaned into the comfort of them, expertly avoiding the monitor leads and oxygen line.

Archer gave Lauren's shoulder a final pat, then stepped out into the hallway. He was in no hurry to face Mitchell, but he might as well get this over with. His own temper was his worst enemy at the moment in this sleep-deprived state. He had to remind himself that Dr. Mitchell Caine hadn't always been so hard.

When Archer entered junior high, Mitchell had been a senior, the darling of Dogwood Springs. Nowadays, the seventh and eighth grades held classes in the lower level of the new school building, while the upper grades used the rest of the campus. Twenty years ago, before the townsfolk deemed the older teenagers to be a dangerous influence on the younger students, their classes were all held in the same huge building, and Archer often passed Mitchell in the hallway.

Mitchell was his hero, a senior who acknowledged young underclassmen, and he did so with grace—or so Archer had felt at the time. He played basketball and football like the fearless athlete that he was, and yet he was never too busy for a friendly smile or a casual wave at the kids he passed in the hallway. It made a big impact on Archer. Mitchell's golden laughter had filled the corridors, and his sense of humor was legend.

After graduation, it wasn't until Mitchell was in the middle of his family practice residency that Archer saw him again, and the meeting was due to extreme tragedy. Mitchell's parents had been killed in a boating accident on Table Rock Lake. He came home long enough to bury them, then disappeared until after the completion of his residency.

When Mitchell returned to follow in his father's family practice footsteps a year later, Archer noticed a difference in him—a heaviness of spirit, as if life had suddenly become too serious for laughter, and smiles were a waste of his resources. Apparently, his loss combined with the stress of medical school and residency had stolen his youthful joy.

And years later another tragedy altered his personality for good.

Dr. Caine stood waiting for Archer in the doorway of Grant's office, arms crossed over his chest, without a hint in his expression that he had ever been acquainted with humor. His hovering presence made Archer feel he had reverted to immature childhood.

"Are you ready now?" The raw flick of undisguised irritation threaded the man's voice.

Archer inclined his head and stepped into the room. "So, Mitchell, what can I help you with?"

"Have a seat." Mitchell closed the door behind him.

In spite of a rebellious inclination to refuse, Archer did as he was told.

The doctor took a seat behind the desk—Grant's desk. He leaned back and studied Archer's face for a moment. "Dr. Sheldon hasn't seen fit to clue me in to his reasons for this little 'prayer program' you pastors seem to think is so important, but as the acting director, I take exception to your interference in this emergency room."

Acting director? Grant was only in St. Louis for a few days—he wasn't dead. "I'm sorry, Mitchell, I didn't realize I was getting in your way." Archer kept his voice calm and conciliatory, but he saw the doctor's frown at the familiar use of his first name. "Are you referring to my interference, in particular, or to the chaplain program as a whole?"

There was a measured silence while Caine seemed to be trying to decide if Archer was mocking him. "As a whole, the program disturbs me. I disagree with the ethics of non-medical laymen marching into this place like saviors on white horses, offering helpless patients false hope for—"

"Oh, but the hope we offer isn't—"

"Tell me something, how many patients have you prayed with since you came in this morning?"

Archer leaned back in his chair and stretched out his legs, crossing them at the ankles. He refused to allow this to become a game of intimidation. He was a grown man now. "Actually, I didn't come into this department until this evening to—"

"I saw you before lunch when I came to check on a patient of mine."

Lord, guide me here. Help me to see the young star he once was. Help me to understand the emotional pain that has changed him. "I was visiting a church member on the floor and stopped by for a moment to talk to Vivian about something." He would not apologize for his presence here.

"Tell me, how many members have you added to your church rolls since our new director started this program?"

Archer smiled at the implied criticism. "Are you asking how many people I've frightened into joining us for Sunday worship?"

The doctor raised his brows, as if to imply, "You said it, I didn't."

"One of our chaplain directives is to refrain from proselytizing. Ordinarily I don't even tell patients my denomination, because I'm not here to represent the Baptists, I'm here to represent Christ."

"Christ." Mitchell made it sound like a curse.

"I show them where they can find hope."

"False hope."

Archer's smile remained tender. A few months ago Jessica had told him that she sometimes felt as if she could look into someone's eyes and see a heart breaking. She said it didn't happen until her own heart was broken for the first time. Afterward, it was easier to recognize the symptoms. Archer had no children, of course, and so he couldn't identify with Mitchell as a father, but he could imagine how his own father would feel. And he could look at Mitchell with eyes of compassion for the suffering he had experienced in the past few years.

"I believe in the power of prayer, Mitchell." *Lord, speak through me. Break through his wall of anger. And control my reactions.*

Mitchell steepled his fingers together and rested his chin on them. He gave a subtle shake of his head. "I heard your father speak those same words from the pulpit a few years ago."

"The truth hasn't changed."

"Then God is still as absent as He has always been to me." He said it like a judge making a final decision on a case.

Archer continued to watch Mitchell with sorrow. The man's bitterness festered so deeply inside him that only the God he continued to deny would be able to heal him and his family.

Mitchell broke eye contact and stared at the floor. "How can an intelligent man continue to believe after so many unanswered prayers?"

"After all the prayers I've seen *answered*, there's no way I could refuse to believe."

"Oh, stop it, Archer! You haven't been on this earth long enough to discover a healing for pain. You've never suffered, you've never had a child choose a life of drug addiction, and you've never had a money-grubbing, manipulating wife who's so stupid she continues to pay for those drugs." Mitchell stood to his feet and stalked over to the window, as if Archer's presence suddenly offended him. "Obviously, *my* prayers never mattered to *anyone*."

"Prayer is a two-way conversation, Mitchell. Complete prayer cannot take place until we are as ready to listen to God as we are to tell Him what we need. He cannot converse with us until He has our attention so He can tell us His will—"

"His will! That's ridiculous!" Mitchell spat the words. "You people claim to know all the answers about life. Why do you make such fools of yourself when God—if there is such a being—does what He wants, no matter how it affects our puny human lives?"

"But, Mitchell, haven't you read the latest literature on the power of prayer? I don't know how you could have missed the articles that have peppered the medical journals in the past few years. I've read them myself, and I've been surprised by their honesty. The medical community can't help noticing the obvious results of so many separate studies."

Mitchell's eyes narrowed. "Do you know how many dangerous drugs have been favorably acclaimed in those same medical journals, following those same double-blind studies? If your God is real, he is a tyrant without a heart. He does what he wants, blesses whom he wants, and the devil take the rest of us."

"That's precisely what God does *not* want. He does answer prayers."

Mitchell paced around the desk and leaned over Archer with a glare. "Are you trying to tell me my daughter's drug addiction is part of his will? Are you trying to tell me that Oakley Brisco's death was God's will?"

"Those were results of free human choice, not God's will. But, Mitchell, I can tell you that what you are going through—no matter what it might be or how horrible it might seem to you—is something that can have a better ending if the right choices are made and if you ask Him for help."

For a moment the doctor's eyes glazed over as if in memory.

Archer placed a hand on Mitchell's arm and felt the resistance beneath the layers of lab coat and dress shirt. "He isn't some genie in a bottle, He's God of the universe, and we're living and acting in a world and a time of His creation. He isn't required to act in ours."

Mitchell held his breath. Archer could almost hear his thoughts, could almost feel the rhythm of his heartbeat. Then, with an oath of disgust, he jerked free of Archer's grasp and spun away. "Take some good advice and call off your wedding plans."

I'm failing him, Lord. He won't listen to me. Please touch his heart. "Mitchell, I know things have been difficult for you lately. I would be glad to pray with you if you'd like."

No reaction. No reply.

"I'll be praying for you anyway."

"No." Mitchell's voice filled with contempt. "Don't waste your breath."

Archer watched the man's stiff shoulders and wished he could break past that barrier of time and pain. "I'm sorry, Mitchell. I wish there was something I could do to help you."

"You have nothing with which you can help me." Mitchell turned back to him. "I don't care what Grant Sheldon does when he's here.

While I'm directing this emergency department, the clergy call program is suspended."

Archer froze for a moment, and then he replied quietly, "You don't have the authority to make that decision."

Mitchell's shoulders stiffened, then he smiled with slow deliberation. "Oh, but I do. With the hospital administrator out of office, I can implement changes as I see fit."

"The call program is volunteer only, Mitchell. If the patients need someone to pray with them while they're here, you can't deny them that, and Grant is still the director even when he isn't here."

"I'm chief of staff."

"And I respect that—"

"I don't think you understand that I have authority over the director of this department."

"Not when the director is acting administrator."

The steel gaze sharpened with anger.

The telephone buzzed from the desk, and the open speaker announced an urgent call for Archer.

"Go ahead and answer it," Mitchell snapped.

"Archer?" came a faltering female voice when he lifted the receiver. "Thank goodness I've found you!" It was Caryn, Sergeant Tony Dalton's wife. "Can you come to the house?"

"Sure, Caryn, what's going on? Is Tony okay?"

"No, I think he's lost his mind, and he's about to take mine, too." She paused and sniffed. "His ophthalmologist called today. Tony has a chance to take part in a clinical trial out in California. There may be a way to restore his sight—"

"What? Caryn, that's great! Hallelujah! When would—?"

"He's decided not to take the offer. Archer, please come and talk to him. He's acting crazy!"

"Give me fifteen minutes."

There was a sigh, and the line disconnected. Archer looked at Mitchell, whose grimace of disgust only deepened.

He turned away. "Go jump on your white steed and rescue more victims, Archer. Just don't try to make me one of them, and stay out of my way while I treat the *real* injuries."

Beau tried to ignore the voices that carried through the vent in the ER storage room, but the more he attempted to concentrate on his work, the louder the conversation became. Dr. Caine had a distinctive voice. So did Archer Pierce. Beau was not an eavesdropper by nature, but since the door to Dad's office had a large window, and that window overlooked the storage room entrance, it would be impossible for Beau to exit without observation by the scariest face in the ER—Dr. Caine's.

By the time the conversation between Archer and Caine ended and the office door opened and closed, Beau had given up hope of escape. Now there was no reason for it.

There was a muttered oath of frustration, and then silence fell in the office. Beau moved quietly as he stacked four-by-four-inch gauze pads onto the metal shelf in the supply room and checked them off the list.

Why in the world were they being supplied with this many gauze pads at one time? They wouldn't be able to use them up for weeks. Of course, if they ran out of blankets for the exam rooms, they could always break out enough gauze pads to keep the patients warm. Unfortunately, they might need to do that, since the requested blankets had not yet arrived from Housekeeping.

That wouldn't be a problem if the air conditioner hadn't suddenly decided to transform the department into a freezer compartment. But every time someone complained to Maintenance, the reply was that they were working shorthanded. Big surprise.

Why were all these departments working shorthanded? It was Beau's personal opinion that people were leaving because Dogwood Springs Hospital had lost its heart. Dad was fighting litigious people in St. Louis, Mr. Butler was still out on sick leave, and a dark mood had infiltrated the core of administration in the person of Dr. Mitchell Caine. That was the word in the halls. Beau was trying to be sympathetic because Dad had instructed him to do so. Right now, that was hard.

Something about Dr. Caine had always made Beau uncomfortable, and it wasn't just the man's antagonism toward Dad over reduced shifts in the past few months. There was an irritation that filled the man's eyes when he was dissatisfied about anything. Those eyes, which were the color of a stainless-steel knife blade, often relayed his dissatisfaction. So did his voice.

The calculator buttons tapped in Caine's temporary domain, and then there was a whispered oath, another series of tapping, a shuffle of pages. Caine snatched up the phone and punched some numbers.

Beau had almost half the cart empty by the time the waiting silence ended.

"We have a problem."

Beau froze in position and felt a surge of adrenaline at the icy charge of words. What problem? Did the doctor know he had an eavesdropper, perhaps? Maybe he was talking to security. Maybe Beau should have—

"I can't balance the checking account. Do you know why?"

Beau slumped against a shelf. *Stop being so jumpy, stupid.* As the doctor awaited some kind of reply from whomever he had called, Beau straightened and glanced at the open door of the supply room. He had to leave. Now. He did not want to be privy to—

"Don't give me more excuses, Darla. You've been using the debit card, withdrawing the cash limit every day for a week, sending it to Trisha, no doubt. . . . No, don't use that tone with me, you . . . Don't you think I have enough brains to figure that out for myself?"

Listening silence again, while Beau cringed at the intimacy of the moment. He glanced again toward the hallway. He could not leave now. The doctor could see the supply room door. Resigning himself to whatever fate awaited him, he continued unloading the supply cart.

"You're coddling her to death. Do you think she's buying groceries and paying the rent with that money? Of course not. It goes straight to Simon Royce's account. You're supporting Royce. Don't you know that?" His words clipped in short bursts, with rising anger.

"Oh, no? Then why does she live in that one-room apartment with a bathroom down the hall? Why do we receive her medical bills? Why won't she ever show her face in our home? You're helping her kill herself, and I will not be part of it. If you want to siphon cash into Royce's drug system, siphon it from your own account, and *you* can earn the money for it." His voice could have frozen a volcano. "I will not let you spend *my* income for our own daughter's slow suicide." The phone slammed down.

Beau continued to work. Quietly. He listened to the increased rhythm of his heartbeat in his ears and controlled the volume of his breathing while he tried not to dwell on what he'd just heard.

Caine sighed, then picked up the telephone receiver again, punched another number, waited. "Yes, this is Dr. Mitchell Caine. I need to speak to Betty Rivers, please."

Beau breathed a whisper of a prayer as he listened for the raw flick of Caine's voice again.

"Hello, Betty, I need to make three transfers of funds, and I need to do it today. Now." He gave the numbers of three separate accounts. "Yes, I realize that. No, I don't plan to close the accounts, and you will *not* contact Mrs. Caine about these transactions. I need someone to come to the hospital for my signature. I can't leave. . . . Fine. Thank you."

He punched more buttons and waited, then, "Ray?" There was a deep sigh. "I need an appointment. I need you to handle a divorce for me."

Beau became a concrete statue, barely daring to breathe, refusing to listen further. His last class of the day on Tuesdays and Thursdays was Health Occupations, and so on those days—which in the past he had always looked forward to with great anticipation—he rushed to the hospital to work extra hours, free of charge. This was the first time he regretted coming here early.

At last the chair—Dad's chair—squeaked. Footsteps echoed, and Beau tensed when he heard the office door open and close. He looked up in time to see Dr. Caine walk past the open entrance to the supply room.

The doctor's left hand was clenched so tightly his knuckles shone white. His face was a mask of tearless misery so profound he looked like a man sentenced to death, a man who had aged ten years in fifteen minutes. It was a look of utter despair.

He paused in the hallway and turned to gaze around at the activity taking place at the desk. He pivoted on his heel suddenly, as if sensing Beau's presence. Their gazes met and held.

Dr. Caine's expression altered. His gaze of steel hardened. He *knew*.

aryn Dalton's eyes were the color of an Ozark river on a cloudless day, and Archer knew her well enough to see the evidence of angry tears in them when she opened the door and nodded him through it. Since Tony's accident last summer, she had cut her beautiful hair short and had stopped wearing makeup because she didn't have time to spend in front of the mirror. Her uniform of choice was faded jeans and one of Tony's old T-shirts. A veil of sadness had become an aged mask. At thirty-four, she was too young to look so old.

"He's on the telephone right now, Archer. He heard me call you, so now he's all mad." She closed the door. "That's nothing new lately."

Archer could feel her frustration and could imagine Tony's. "I'll talk with him, Caryn, but you and I both know that once he's made up his mind about something it's a done deal."

"You're the one who kept him from giving up on himself when the accident happened."

"You know better than that," Archer said. "Tony isn't a quitter."

"That's right." The strong tone of Tony's voice came from farther back in the house. "So I hope you didn't come here to try to talk me into quitting now."

Archer walked down the hallway and entered the Tony Dalton branch of the Dogwood Springs police force, where Tony sat brooding behind a precisely ordered desktop. This was where he masterminded the drug task force for Dogwood Springs. There were at least eight separate stacks of files within his reach. Archer knew that Tony was well acquainted with each of those files, thanks to his wife and other assistants who came to the house to help.

Tony leaned back in his chair and looked at Archer—his sightless gaze beneath heavy, dark eyebrows found Archer with uncanny accuracy. "I told Caryn she wasn't going to win this argument, so she decided to find someone she thought could change my mind. Won't work, Archer."

"Not even to regain your sight?"

The brows lowered further. "It's a trial, Archer. An experiment. I don't have time for experiments."

Caryn brushed past Archer and leaned over her husband's desk. "Tell him the truth, Tony! It's already been done successfully in California and Thailand." She turned back to Archer. "The doctor explained it to me. He said they would take cells from Tony's own eyes and use them to regenerate his corneal tissue; that way there would be no rejection."

"Yes, there will be." Tony pointed a thumb at his own chest. "Me. I'm rejecting it. I don't have time for this."

Caryn swung away from the desk with her hands spread wide in an "I can't believe this man is so stupid" gesture.

Archer had grown accustomed to their arguments in the past few months as they both adjusted to their drastically altered lifestyle—Caryn had quit her job in the office at City Hall to become Tony's assistant here at home, to be his eyes. Still, it hurt to see these two people, who had always been so much in love, and who had endured so much with Tony's job, suffer this additional heartbreak.

Archer sat down at the chair next to Tony's desk—the spot usually reserved for Caryn. "I have to agree with your wife."

"Yeah, well, you always were a soft touch for a sad story. I think you sympathized with her for marrying me in the first place."

Archer relaxed. At least Tony's deadpan humor was still in working order. "If you can't do it for yourself, can't you do it for her? It couldn't possibly take that much time."

Tony leaned forward and grasped the desk with both hands. "Later, Arch."

"Later could be years!" Caryn cried. "If you don't do this now, you may not have another chance."

"She's right, Tony."

"You two aren't getting the message. I don't have *any* time to spare right now. None. Zilch. You've noticed, haven't you, that kids are dying?" He held up a copy of an autopsy report on Oakley Brisco. "Meth. There'll be more if we don't do something to stop it. We must continue the drug education program we've started in our schools, because the kids are the primary target."

"You have officers who can do that," Archer said. "Trust them. Trust me. I'm not exactly a slouch at relaying the specifics, and I'll take the classes you're scheduled to teach."

"You're getting married Saturday."

"How much time does it take to have a wedding?"

"I'm your best man. If I'm not there, you'll never convince me that Jessica was actually crazy enough to go through with it."

"Tony," Caryn pleaded. "Stop joking. This isn't funny."

"You could get your sight back," Archer reminded him. "How much better could you fight then?"

"By then it could be too late. Trust me, I know what I'm talking about."

"I don't," Caryn snapped. "Why don't you try again to explain it to me."

"Peregrine's failing," Tony said.

"How do you know?"

"I see the signs. He's been a high intensity abuser for too long. He's getting paranoid, and that makes him a threat to anyone around him, particularly those in authority. He's our key to this town. He's the one on the inside track."

Caryn gave an exasperated hiss and paced across the room. "You don't know that for sure! You're jumping to conclusions and risking your future—*our* future—on guesswork."

"I know what to look for." Tony held a hand out to Archer. "Would you just listen to me for a few minutes? Then tell me if you don't see a frightening pattern."

Caryn pulled a chair from the dining room table—the table that had been pushed against the far wall to accommodate the desk. She slumped into the chair with a sigh of defeat.

"First of all," Tony said, "we all realize that Simon Royce, aka Peregrine, is the kingpin for drug traffic in Dogwood Springs. That's an established fact based on information from several sources. He was the one who passed the meth on to the Brisco boy."

"But how do you know that?" Caryn demanded.

"Private sources that I can't reveal."

"Not even to me, Tony? I'm your wife, and you're saying you don't trust me enough to—"

"Trust has nothing to do with it, my love. I gave my word I would not breathe a word about my source to anyone, and if my word isn't—"

"But *why?* What's so special about this one—"

"May I continue? Just listen for a moment. Please?" He held up two fingers. "Second point, we know, also from those sources, that Royce has held an iron-fist control over several meth manufacturers because of his customer base, and his vicious temper, and his lack of conscience."

Archer knew what he meant by lack of conscience. There was a difference between a human being who was depraved enough to sell dangerous, illegal drugs—drugs that might very well kill the customer—and a human being whose mind was diminished in function to the point that he would not hesitate to kill any living being—even a child—with his own hands.

Tony pointed to his own eyes. "Case in point. The booby trap that caused this had his fingerprints all over it. And that, my friend, is my third point. Two years ago Simon Royce would have left no evidence. He's getting careless. This means we are closer to catching him than ever before. What frightens me is that we won't catch him before he strikes at our children again, and we have no idea where that will be."

"But that could happen with or without your presence in this town," Caryn said. "Why don't you give your men some credit? Why can't you trust them?"

The muscles of Tony's jaws worked silently. His right hand clenched. "I tried that. I trusted my partner not to move before I gave the signal, and look what it got me." A strain of bitterness seeped into his voice.

Archer had noticed the bitterness a few times in the past weeks, and it disturbed him. This was not the Tony that Archer knew, but Caryn had mentioned that her husband was struggling with bouts of depression. Archer knew how depression could affect a person's whole outlook. He also knew that Tony had a logical thought process, and in the end that was what would guide him. But when would that end come? And would it come in time?

"You're making this too personal," Caryn said.

"It *is* personal, don't you see?" Tony's voice rose steadily and cut more sharply with each word. "I *want* to feel the personal responsibility to stop this monster before he hurts or kills someone else, and now is the time to prepare for a strike, immediately after the shock of Oakley Brisco's death. I want the *pleasure* of catching this guy myself. I can't take the chance that I'll be tied up in some hospital with strangers trying to play God with my eyes. I can't take the chance that I'll come to depend on a source of vision that might or might not let me down at a crucial point." He turned his face toward Archer. "Can't you understand what I mean?"

"Yes," Archer said, "but are you allowing a need for personal revenge to cloud your judgment?"

"No!" Tony hit the desk with his fist, scattering a stack of papers. "*I'm* the one who gathered the facts and drew the conclusion that Peregrine's mind is failing. *I'm* the one who found the evidence that he's tweaking more and more often. What makes me sick is that one child has already died, and others are in extreme danger." Anger deepened in Tony's face. "Now is the time to strike, not next month."

"No one is disagreeing with you about the danger, Tony," Archer said. "But the danger I'm worried about is permanent loss of your sight. That's important. You have a whole future to do what you're doing now, and you'll be able to perform better when you can see how—"

"Arch, listen to me." Tony overpronounced his words, as if trying to explain to someone who was hard-of-hearing. "The drug has taken over Peregrine's life, and he's taking more chances out of desperation to find a high that is no longer there. His natural endorphins are shot because the drug has forced them into his system too many times."

"I know all this, Ton—"

"He's in a continually depressed state, and the inevitable spiral downward is going to kill him." Tony's voice deepened with offense. "No one had the foresight to report that to me. I expected that to be obvious to anyone with the same set of facts. I had to figure it out for myself. How can I trust anyone else to do my job? It's my calling. I have to do whatever is necessary to stop this animal."

Caryn stood up and paced the length of the room again, combing her fingers through the short strands of sparrow brown hair. "I'm sorry, Tony, but I can't take this any longer."

"But it isn't going to *be* that much longer, don't you understand that? We're in a crucial period that could affect the whole future of this town."

"No, stop it." Caryn held her hands up in front of her as if in an automatic gesture to protect herself. "You accuse the doctors of wanting to play God with your eyes, but you're doing the same thing with your job. You can't take the responsibility of the whole police force on your shoulders, because it's landing on my shoulders, too, and I can't keep carrying it."

"I never asked you to—"

"Yes! You did, Tony. You asked me to assist you. I work beside you every day. I've put everything else in my life on hold so I could be your guide while you preside over this task force, but I can't keep doing it!" She rubbed her hands across her face. "I can't take much more of this. It's all you ever talk about, all you ever think about. It consumes you, and it's consuming our marriage!" Her eyes filled with horror as she caught the echoing impact of her words.

Silence hit the room like an oppressive wall.

Tony closed his unseeing eyes, and pain etched itself across the lines of his handsome, worry-lined features. "You don't understand." His voice was a hoarse whisper. "I truly believe I'm doing what I've been called to do. I've never been more certain of anything in my life. I've seen how much worse things can get, and I can't let it happen. Not here. Not in our town."

Archer reached across the desk and laid a hand on Tony's thickly muscled arm. "At least pray with us about it." He held a hand out for Caryn to join them.

"I'll pray about it," Tony said. "I've been praying, and I will continue to pray. But unless God tells *me* to stop, I'm with this thing to the end."

———

Lauren was returning to the ER after a break late Tuesday afternoon when she rounded a corner in the hallway and nearly collided with a redheaded spitfire. Gina Drake's short hair was disheveled, her face blazing, fists bunched at her sides.

"The man has no brain," she muttered as she passed Lauren.

Lauren turned and followed her. "Gina? What's wrong?"

"I've never seen anyone treat staff with such callous indifference."

"What man are you—"

"If I could afford to move, I'd quit this job so fast—"

"Hold it. Gina, what's—"

"He doesn't have an ounce of intelligence." Gina stopped and turned so abruptly that Lauren had to scramble to keep from slamming into her from behind. Tears of temper filled her eyes. "I don't know if I can go back in there and face him without punching him in his stupid face."

"Whose face? Who are you going to punch? Did you and Todd have a—"

"No, not Todd!" Those copper eyes flashed. "Could you possibly, for once, leave Todd's name out of a conversation? My problem isn't Todd, it's that . . . that . . . Mitchell Caine. I refuse to call him Doctor when I don't have to."

"What did he do?" Obviously, Gina was in the middle of one of her mood swings, and the best thing to do was to get out of her way. It occasionally happened when her blood sugar dropped. "Have you eaten?"

Gina scowled at her.

"Sorry, Gina, but I have to ask."

"I'll eat in a minute—didn't get a chance earlier. Would you listen to me?"

"Of course. Go ahead."

"For some reason Caine's all bent out of shape about the way his clinic is receiving test results, and every chance he gets he comes barreling into the hospital to complain about whichever tech or therapist or director has offended him in the past hour."

"Has he said anything to you?"

"Not yet, but our director's about to quit over it, and if Sarah goes, the whole department will be a mess. Fiona told me one of the lab techs already walked off the job. Just walked off! It'll get worse if Mitchell Caine keeps throwing his weight around."

Lauren groaned. Even though Dr. Caine wasn't on duty today, she'd seen him in the department at least three times.

Gina took Lauren's arm and drew her to a small meeting room and closed the door. "I tell you, Lauren, that man's always been a jerk, but something happened to him yesterday. Oakley's death did something to him. I mean, didn't you see him? He was shaking during that code yesterday. Todd told me later that he overheard Caine shouting and cursing in the office after they took Oakley's body away."

"I heard." It had concerned Lauren, too.

"I think something snapped, I really do."

Lauren frowned. "There's something else going on with him, I think."

"Alcohol, maybe? Drugs? You know what time he does his hospital rounds? Todd's seen him coming in at eleven at night."

Lauren checked her watch. A few minutes left of her break, and she was still worried about Gina's blood sugar. "So, how about a snack before I go back to work?"

"No, that's okay." Gina dabbed at the moisture on her forehead. "I've got a late break coming up."

"Good, then I'll walk you there. You don't look that—"

"I'm meeting Todd, okay? We're going to eat together in a few minutes. He didn't get off for his lunch break at the usual time."

Lauren couldn't hide her disappointment, and she could tell from Gina's expression that it was obvious.

"Would you just give him a chance, Lauren? I know he's got some problems, but I think they're going to get worked out." Gina avoided looking Lauren in the eyes. "He's so thoughtful. He brought dinner for the kids and me last night, and he was careful to make sure we got enough to eat. Do you know how good it feels to have somebody watch out for you like that?"

"I know it feels good," Lauren said softly. "It might even feel *right,* but—"

"I don't want to hear your *buts* right now." Gina raised a hand to silence her. "If you're my friend, you'll be happy for me. I can't remember how many times Todd has told me that our friendship has had nothing to do with the breakup of his marriage. That would have happened anyway, because his wife has some habits he just can't stand to live with any longer."

"Everybody has habits."

"I don't think it would take too much for us to develop a . . . deeper relationship . . . if you know what I mean." Gina looked down at her hands as she folded them in her lap.

"Oh, Gina, no!" The cry of alarm sounded from Lauren's lips almost before she realized she was speaking her thoughts. "Honey, that isn't for you."

Gina looked up at her sharply.

Lauren lowered her voice. "I mean, I know it seems like it's none of my business, but—"

"You're right, it isn't," Gina snapped.

"Please, just listen for a moment." Lauren reached out, but Gina snatched her arm away. "Gina, you can't possibly realize what you're getting into." She knew she was pushing past the boundaries of their friendship, but she had to try.

"Don't you think you're being a little melodramatic?" Gina stood up and took a few steps away, with her back to Lauren. "I mean, it isn't as if we're virgins."

"You are to God."

Gina snorted.

"When you became a Christian, you were washed clean. You became a child of God. He wants his children to remain physically pure."

A shake of the head. "You mean we're supposed to be like nuns and priests and not have sex?"

"That kind of union is intended for marriage," Lauren said softly. "It's a physical covenant. I'll show you some Scriptures to explain what I—"

"I don't need any Scriptures to make me feel guilty, Lauren. I just think I'm different from you. It's, like, when you've had *that* kind of a relationship with a guy, you need to have it again."

"You don't—"

"How do you know? You've never—"

"I know what's right. Don't you think I've been tempted?"

Gina turned her head and glared over her shoulder at Lauren. "Okay, fine, you're stronger than me. Is that what you want to hear?"

"No. What I want to hear is that you can see through this guy and see the pain this relationship is causing other people. Children. Wife. Parents. Todd is a parent who is rejecting his own family so he can be with you, don't you see that? Gina, I don't care what Todd says, your friendship with him is impacting his marriage."

The glare deepened and hardened on Gina's face. "No. I've had it with this guilt stuff. Don't talk to me about it anymore. I don't need a friend who slaps me up the side of the head every time I do something she doesn't like. I'm tired of living under your shadow, under your rules."

"But they're not my rules. I would never dream of being so presumptuous. They're God's rules, and they exist for a reason, to keep from destroying—"

"I want to see Todd. He makes me feel better about myself than anyone else ever has. He wants *me,* not what I can do for him, or—"

"Don't you think he treated his wife the same way, once upon a time? If you can't think of her pain, think of your own kids. If you and Todd did get married, he's already proven he won't stick with it. How do you know he won't leave you and your kids just as he's leaving his own family right now, and Levi and Cody will suffer rejection all over again. Gina, I know you. That would break your heart."

Gina held her hands in front of her face. "Stop, Lauren. Just stop it. I'm not going there with you anymore. Leave me alone!" She swung away and stalked from the room.

Lauren sighed and looked at her watch. Time to get back to work.

She'd risked their friendship for honesty, and it looked as if she'd lost.

CHAPTER | **20**

Archer pulled into the church parking lot and saw Jessica's Outback, and for an instant he considered driving on by. After all, the florist's van was parked there, too, and he recognized the car that belonged to the church pianist, Melissa. They were making last-minute plans for the wedding, and he wasn't sure he wanted to face Jessica right now, not with the doubts that had ebbed and flowed in his mind since yesterday. If he drove on through the lot, no one would know he'd been here.

The temptation shocked him, and he parked immediately. He met the florist coming out of the building and saw Jessica pulling on her coat just inside the foyer.

Her beautiful face filled with joy when she saw him. "Sweetheart! I was just getting ready to go find you at the hospital." She rushed up to him and kissed him. She looked more closely at him. "I thought you'd . . . be . . . busy." Her joy was replaced by concern. "Archer, what's wrong?"

He suppressed a grimace. One reason he loved her so much was because she saw deep into his heart, and she accepted him as he was. That very same insight, however, was what had tempted him to avoid her.

She leaned close and put a hand on his arm. "Sweetheart? What is it?"

He shoved his fists into the pockets of his simulated-leather bomber jacket. "How about a walk around the neighborhood? I need to work off some excess energy."

She studied his eyes for another few seconds, then linked her arm through his. "Let's go."

They strolled along the tree-lined sidewalk for nearly a block without speaking. How could he even bring up the subject that disturbed him most without damaging months of progress? And how could he even think about—

"It must be bad," she said at last.

He shouldn't even—

"You might as well spill it, Pierce. We're in this together from here on out."

He swallowed and kept walking.

Her steps slowed. "Archer?" There was a thread of fear in her voice.

He pulled his hands from his pockets and turned to look at her. "I've been doing some intense Bible study since yesterday. And I've been praying. Suddenly it seems as if those prayers are bouncing back in my face."

She nodded. She didn't even ask what those prayers were about. "Me too."

He waited for her to continue, but she didn't. Finally he swallowed past the lump in his throat. "Oakley Brisco's funeral is Thursday. They're already finished with the autopsy, and the methamphetamine overdose was confirmed. My telephone hasn't been silent all day. Kids are hurting, parents are terrified. I have to be honest, Jessica, after losing Hardy last week I haven't been functioning at my best. After yesterday's tragedy I find myself wondering about some things."

She turned her frowning attention on him, then her eyes widened and she caught her breath. "You're wondering about the wedding."

He swallowed again.

"You're wondering how we can have a celebration when everyone else is suffering grief," she said.

He nodded. "And yet we can't call off the wedding. No way."

She tucked her hand inside the crook of his elbow and tugged him forward. "But you're feeling guilty?"

"I think it's only natural."

"Of course, but I don't think Hardy would want you to cancel our wedding because of his death. In fact, isn't his family attending?"

"Yes. All of them are."

They walked another moment in silence, then Jessica cleared her throat. "If you truly feel it's God's will for us to get married Saturday, why would you feel guilty? He knows we can both serve Him better together than separately."

It was exactly the thought that had come to him again and again these past twenty-four hours. He felt a stirring of warm comfort.

"And maybe we could add a song of memorial to the service, as close as you and Hardy were. I mean, he was going to be an usher. Heather has a beautiful one in her repertoire."

He bit his lip. The answer settled into place as if it had come straight from God. Archer had choked up more this past week than he had in the past year, and his vision blurred once more.

"Do you know how much I love you?" he whispered.

"Yes. So tell me what else is on your mind. There's something more bothering you."

And so he told her about Tony. And she listened, and their shoes scuffed the few remaining leaves on the sidewalk as they continued to walk.

"Tony has made his own decision," he said after a complete explanation. "And he won't listen to Caryn or me or anyone else."

"He obviously has good reasons."

"But we're talking about his eyesight, Jess. Think how much more he could do if he gets his eyesight back."

"But look at the good he's done since he *lost* that eyesight. Even though I don't agree with his decision and can identify with Caryn's frustration, I respect his decision, Archer."

A brief whisper of irritation streaked through Archer's mind, and he allowed silence to fall between them. *She* hadn't been friends with him since childhood. Of course, he hadn't exactly been best friends with Tony all that time, either.

Jessica strolled beside Archer in blissful ignorance of his chaotic thoughts, easily matching her stride with his. "I can't imagine how rough this must be on Caryn. I don't think it would be easy to be married to everyone's hero. Look at the price she's paying."

"I keep wondering about the price *he's* paying," Archer said. "And I've been asking myself if I would do the same thing."

"You already do, sweetheart." She hugged his arm. "You live your life for Dogwood Springs Baptist Church."

"Working overtime in an overheated church office isn't the same as being blasted by a booby trap set by a dangerous drug dealer, or rushing to the rescue of a fellow worker and getting caught in an explosion, the way Hardy did."

She slowed her steps and looked at him. "You fight in the trenches right along with them. You put your heart on the line, you—"

"No, I think I've always straggled along behind both of them. Hardy's always been a hero. Tony's the best at anything he does. Nothing's changed in twenty-five years. At nine, Tony had all his Scripture verses memorized before anyone else in Sunday school class. He was the valedictorian of our class. And now he's willing to sacrifice a very precious opportunity for renewed wholeness in order to catch the bad guy. I just feel helpless because I couldn't convince him otherwise."

"You sound irritated with him."

"Wouldn't you be irritated with a good friend who's throwing away his chance to regain his sight?" He cleared his throat. There was more, but he didn't want to discuss it right now. He changed the subject. "Is your dress finished?"

"I had my last fitting today. It looks great. And the rest of the tuxes are at the shop. They're the wrong color, but if they can't get the right color, we'll have to go with them."

"You're going to be the most beautiful bride who ever walked down an aisle." And every day he grew more eager for their wedding day, and every hour he had more trouble keeping her out of his thoughts.

"Thank you, Archer." She unlinked her arm from his and slowed her pace, then caught his hand with hers. "Okay, what else?"

He shortened his steps to match hers. "Hmm?"

Her hair glowed in the dappled sunlight. "The last time we spoke, you were planning to visit the hospital this afternoon. What else has upset you? There wasn't another death, was there?"

"No."

Jessica squeezed his hand. "Pastoral or patient confidentiality?"

He would never get accustomed to her on-target insight. "Neither." He strolled a few more seconds in silence. "Something happened at the hospital today that must have upset me more than I'd realized."

Jessica waited. She had always been comfortable with silence.

"I have been warned that if I continue to try to proselytize in the ER, I could be dropped from the call list."

"You're proselytizing?"

"I didn't think I was. I know I'm not supposed to tell people what denomination I pastor, but in a town this size it's kind of difficult to keep that a secret. Actually, the chaplain call program might be in danger if Grant doesn't come back soon."

Jessica released his hand and stopped mid-stride. "Who would tell you something like that? Grant wouldn't—"

"Not Grant. Dr. Mitchell Caine."

"Who's that?"

"He's a family practice doc who moonlights in the ER, and he's throwing his weight around. I've known him since I was a kid." Lately, it seemed to Archer as if he'd known everyone in the world since childhood—and the world was getting a little cramped. "He graduated a few years ahead of me in school."

"So he's a hometown boy. That doesn't give him the right to tell you what to do." She started walking again, and Archer followed.

"He's chief of staff this year."

"That still doesn't make him your supervisor."

"He's got a lot of patients, and he can influence those patients simply by his title. You know what bothers me the most? I'm more upset about the threat of being dropped from the call list than I am about Mitchell's own pain. I'm a pastor. I need to get my priorities straight. In fact, Dad was Mitchell's pastor about five years ago. That's where I should focus."

"You're saying this doctor was a member of Dogwood Springs Baptist?"

"Once upon a time, he and his wife and daughter attended. They never joined, but nearly every Sunday for about six months he dragged Darla and Trisha to morning worship."

Archer remembered that there had been an almost expectant quality in Mitchell's attendance, as if he were looking for the physical presence of God in that building. In contrast, his daughter never lost the bored expression from her face, and his wife always seemed irritated about something. It hurt Archer to realize that no one in the Caine family ever seemed to encounter God in the church.

"Dad always felt as if he had somehow let them down. And that meant he had let God down."

"Why?" Jessica asked.

"I guess because Mitchell decided he wasn't going to find what he was looking for in church."

"What *was* he looking for?"

Archer shook his head. "What do most people look for? Help with their problems. Soon after he and his family stopped attending, Trisha ran away from home, driving the car her parents had given her for her sixteenth birthday. His wife made their problems a matter of public record by writing a letter to the editor of *The Dogwood* with a plea to anyone who might have information about her."

Jessica groaned. "Oh, wow, talk about desperation. That must have been humiliating. Did it get the desired results?"

"The police found her in Springfield about a week later and arrested her and Simon Royce for grand theft auto."

"Simon Royce?"

"Aka Peregrine. He's our famous hometown drug pusher."

"Oh, Archer," Jessica breathed softly. "How that must hurt her parents."

"I can't help thinking Mitchell and Darla knew something was going on with Trisha long before she ran away, and that was why they tried church. Dad attempted to visit them several times, but they always had other plans. I know he and Mom prayed for them. There was never a connection, I guess. The fact that Mitchell Caine was even willing to try church shows he must have cared about his daughter."

"How could the police arrest Trisha for being in her own car?"

"Mitchell actually put it in his own name when he bought it for her so he wouldn't have such high insurance premiums. Since Peregrine had *not* taken Trisha across a state line, and they were in a car that was actually in her father's name, the police couldn't hold Simon without also holding Trisha."

"Ouch."

"I know. Mitchell and Darla endured a lot of pain. I'm afraid they blame God for everything."

"Which is why he's taking it out on you now?"

"It's a typical response. I just don't handle it well."

"What ever happened to Trisha?"

"A few months after they brought her home she left again, and she hasn't been back."

"Do you think she's doing drugs?"

"I don't know. Every so often word trickles down that she's somewhere in Springfield, living on an inheritance from her grandmother."

"That family needs our prayers, honey."

"Yes. They don't want them, but they're getting them anyway."

She took his hand with both of hers and held it against her cheek. "That's what I like about you, Pierce. You pray for your enemies, even if you have to force those prayers down their throats."

He smiled, but he felt a pang of guilt. The prayers didn't come without resentment, and though he knew from past experience that forgiveness and a more tender heart would come to him as he continued to pray, he hadn't yet achieved that goal this time. Mitchell Caine was a very real threat to the call program, and he was capable of revenge. From what Archer had heard from other members of the hospital staff, quite a few people were unhappy at work lately.

"Come on, keep walking." She tugged on his hand and drew him along the sidewalk.

This was an older section of town, where the residents were slower about clearing the streets of their aging autumn splendor. The rustle of the leaves, the peace of their surroundings, and the gentle flow of Jessica's voice soothed something inside him. Would married life offer more of this taste of heaven on earth?

"Remember Tito? My Chihuahua?" Jessica asked. She kicked a thin layer of leaves and watched them flutter down.

"Of course I remember him." It had ruined Archer's macho image in Branson when he fell in love with Jessica's feisty little dog. He'd been devastated when it was hit by a car and killed a year and a half ago.

She held her right hand up in front of him, displaying where three small scars marked the deepest of the wounds she had received the day Tito had been hit. "I only touched him. He was in so much pain he didn't realize what he was doing. He sank his teeth deep and held on with all his might, and I know he didn't intend to hurt me, Archer. That's just what animals do when they're in pain. They strike out blindly. I think a lot of people do that, too."

"People like Mitchell Caine."

"Yes."

"Thanks for the reminder." His hand tightened around hers and sighed. "Jessica Lane, will you marry me?"

"Let me think about it."

"I don't know how I was ever called as a pastor to this church without your steadying influence."

"Must I remind you that we were already engaged when they called you?"

"And will you promise to forgive me on those rare times when I get jealous because you're more popular than I am?"

"Aha! So you finally admit it! *That's* what's really bothering you." Her laughter filled the street. His joined with it. She knew how to make him feel better.

He was marrying the most wonderful woman in the world.

CHAPTER 21

Wednesday evening Beau sprayed disinfectant on the vinyl surface of the bed in exam room seven, wiped it dry, and spread a clean fitted sheet over it, all to the tune of "Silver Bells." He was getting tired of the canned, artificially cheery music and lights, which did nothing to cheer the patients. Most of them had been doing too much Christmas shopping with too little money and were no longer in the best of spirits. With over two and a half weeks to go before Christmas, how bad would it get?

Voices jumbled with the music from several different exam rooms. Two of the rooms had at least three children each, because the mothers decided that, since they were getting one child checked, the others might as well be seen, too.

Lauren and Muriel were on duty today, and they'd kept Beau busy ever since he'd come in two hours ago. He liked being busy. It kept him from thinking about the recent tragedies.

He was tossing the used sheets into the bin at the end of the counter when the distant trill of the triage bell outshouted the buzz of the telephone at the central station. A new patient needed to be seen. Lauren was assisting Dr. Caine with a suture repair two doors down, and Muriel was keeping a close eye on a man with chest pain in one. Lester, the other tech on duty, was taking a patient down the hall for x-rays. The float nurse, who would ordinarily come down from the floor, was swamped with three new admissions. Business was great at Dogwood Springs Hospital.

The bell rang again, twice, and Beau looked over his work to make sure he'd cleaned the room thoroughly.

Muriel poked her head out of the cardiac room and caught sight of him. "Oh, there you are. Doctor Beau, honey, would you check out that triage and do some vitals?"

"Sure." *All right, some hands-on!*

"Let me know if it's bad."

"I will. I'm on my way."

"Thanks, Doctor Beau." She grinned and winked at him.

"You're welcome." He rushed to the scrub sink and washed his hands.

Doctor Beau. Muriel knew he loved the sound of those words. He suspected, however, that wasn't the only reason she called him that— she enjoyed irritating Dr. Caine when she could get by with it. No one had missed the doctor's grimace when he heard the title she gave Beau the first time.

Besides Lauren, Muriel was Beau's favorite nurse in the department. She was all muscle and solid as a rock. Beau had seen her in action one day when an old man fell on the slick floor out in the waiting room. Before anyone else could reach him to help, she'd picked him up all by herself and eased him into a wheelchair. She had the underbite of a bulldog, but she had the gentle brown eyes of a newborn fawn. They were kind eyes that reflected a kind heart.

Beau took the stethoscope from around his neck on the way to the triage room. As a medical technician he couldn't fill out charts for the nurses, but he could take vitals and write down the results, and he could escort patients to the exam rooms. He loved the personal interaction with patients, and he looked forward to the day when he could do more than just tech.

He stopped just inside the door of the triage room. There sat Dru Stanton from school, the one with the shy smile, who worked in the office during her free hour. Her face was flushed to an unhealthy red, and her eyelids drooped. She looked miserable. An older woman—a little old to be her mother—sat in the chair to her left.

"Hi, Dru." He stepped over to the supply counter and reached for a thermometer. "Not feeling too well today?"

She shook her head. "I feel awful."

The woman beside her eyed his blue scrubs. "You know my grand-daughter?"

"Oh, sorry, I should have introduced myself. I'm Beau Sheldon. I have a couple of classes with Dru, and I'm an emergency technician here at the hospital."

She studied his face with close deliberation, and her mouth formed a bow with radiating frown lines. "You're in *high school*?"

"Yes, ma'am. I attend Dogwood Springs High."

"And you're allowed to work unsupervised with patients?" There was more than a shadow of doubt in her voice.

"When we're busy I get to do the basics, and I take every chance I can get. I'm sorry, but the nurses are all tied up with emergencies right now, and I've been asked to check Dru's vital signs so we can be a step ahead when a nurse gets free. If you would prefer to wait, I'll go—"

"Please." Dru's face grew brighter red, and she slumped farther down in her chair. "Grandmother, let him do his job."

The woman hesitated, then nodded. He could tell she wasn't convinced.

He jotted Dru's name on a blank notepad. "Dru, I'm going to check your temperature and heart rate and see what your blood pressure is." He took her temperature while counting her respirations.

He nodded and replaced the thermometer on the counter. "No wonder you feel bad."

"What do you mean?" her grandmother asked.

"She has a temperature of 102.6. I think anybody would feel sick with that, but you'll probably feel better as soon as we get it back down closer to normal." He placed the blood pressure cuff on Dru's arm and the pulse oximetry probe on her finger.

"So now you've proven she's sick, why don't you get a nurse?" the grandmother asked. "What do you think it could be?"

"I don't know. The doctor will look at the readings I've taken, and then—"

"When's that going to be? I don't want to wait around here all day."

Beau felt sorry for Dru. "I'll get this information to a nurse as soon as I can—"

"I still don't like this. What kind of a hospital hires teenagers to handle emergencies?"

The woman's voice carried a little too well, and Beau flinched. He was accustomed to working with grumpy people. The ER averaged probably one really irritable person every couple of shifts, and more during the holiday season. He had been instructed by the best—Dad— to allow the complaints to pass unchallenged, apologize when appropriate, and treat the patients with courtesy and respect at all times. Ordinarily he could handle that, but for some reason Dru always made him nervous—probably because Brooke kept telling him Dru had a crush on him.

He had a little bit of a crush on her, too. Crushes made him goofy.

He checked vitals on the machine and wrote them down. The heart rate was above a hundred. She was certainly sick, but part of that rate was most likely due to nervousness about her grandmother's complaints.

Beau removed the cuff and pulse oximetry probe. "It'll be okay, Dru. I'll get you into a bed as soon as possible." And then he forgot himself and did something he never did around strangers. He attempted to smile. It came automatically, the way it used to before the wreck. He did it just to reassure Dru, but weeks of practice in front of a mirror reminded him that other people didn't see a smile, they saw a twisted grimace. Almost like a leer.

Dru stared at him. Her grandmother gasped. And then he realized the import of his word choice. Oh, boy, he'd done it this time.

"*What* did you say?" The woman stood up, the pale wrinkles striating across her face.

"Sorry, I realize that didn't sound the best. I just meant I'd see her to an exam room as soon as one is avail—"

"No, you will not." She reached for the curtain. "I want you out of here. I don't know what the people in this hospital are think—"

"Grandmother, stop it," Dru begged.

Before the woman could reach the curtain it snapped open, and a tall, white-coated form loomed in the doorway. Dr. Caine. Lauren entered behind him.

Beau groaned inwardly. It was getting worse.

"What's going on in here?" Dr. Caine asked.

"This young . . . kid is trying to make a pass at my granddaughter," the older woman growled. "Right here in front of me!"

"No, please," Beau said. "That wasn't what—"

"I'm sorry," Dr. Caine said. "This tech was here without my permission."

Beau handed him the page of vitals. "Dr. Caine, the nurses were all busy, and so I came in to do a triage on this patient so we could get her into an exam room more quickly."

"That isn't what you said," the woman accused. "And you should have seen the look he gave her." To Beau's humiliation, the woman did a parody of his awkward attempt at a smile. It was hideous.

He didn't look that bad, did he? "I'm sorry, I've had some facial damage—"

"I don't want this masher near my granddaughter," the woman snapped.

"Of course, you don't have to worry about that," Dr. Caine assured her. "Beau, who requested you to do these vitals?"

"Well, Muriel asked—"

"Muriel doesn't have the right to authorize your services."

Beau felt his face begin to burn. "I've done them before when we were busy." Lots of times. Just not when this doctor was on duty. The other doctors trusted him. This one wouldn't even give him a chance to explain, even if he *was* a student in the Health Occupations class, a *nationally recognized* program.

Dr. Caine stepped aside and gestured for Lauren to approach the patient. "Nurse, I want you to take this patient's vital signs and ignore these numbers." He tossed the sheet with Dru's vitals into the trash bin. He looked at Beau. "Until you learn decent bedside manner, I will never let you near another patient on my shift. You are dismissed."

Lauren's eyes flashed green fire. "Dr. Caine, we need Beau. We're busy."

Beau caught her with his gaze and shook his head. No more. He just wanted to get out. He escaped the department as quickly as he could.

Lauren's hands shook so badly she had trouble forcing her fingers to punch the correct buttons on the computerized drug dispenser. She had to clear it and start over before she got it right.

If the ER weren't so busy, she would go looking for Beau. As it was—

A shadow fell across the counter, and she sensed someone close behind her. She pivoted almost directly into Dr. Caine's chest.

"I can see you are having some kind of problem tonight, Lauren." He paused until she looked up and made eye contact with him. "I'm sorry if you're upset about the unfortunate incident with Beau, but I need you to speed things up a little. Patients are waiting."

Anger shot through her like electricity. She reached down for the drugs from the dispenser. "You're right, I have a patient waiting for this. We're busy because our help was dismissed." She turned to leave, but he grasped her shoulder.

"When there's more time, we need to discuss the situation."

"Excuse me, but my immediate problem is this." She pushed against his arm, effectively breaking his grip on her shoulder and his attempt to intimidate her. "You're supposed to lay hands on the patients, not on the staff." She caught a curious look from Lester Burton, who wheeled an elderly man past them in the hallway at that moment, and saw the shocked surprise in Caine's face.

She was surprised herself. Seldom did she lose her temper, especially on the job. This was the second time in less than two weeks.

"I beg your pardon." Caine raised both hands out to his sides and took an exaggerated step away from her. "I didn't realize you had such an *extensive* personal—"

"And I do object to the way you treated Beau Sheldon tonight." She was on a roll. "He didn't deserve to be humiliated in front of an audience of patients and staff."

"It isn't your job to object to my treatment of a hospital staff member. It's your job to follow the orders of your superiors and be a patient advocate. When a patient complains about the care she receives, that reflects on all of us."

"That patient didn't complain, her grandmother did, and I got the impression she was just looking for an excuse. And when a doctor humiliates an earnest young tech just because of a misunderstanding due to a disability, *that* reflects on the very heart of human compass—"

"What?" Dr. Caine frowned in apparent confusion. "What are you talking about? What's this about a disability?"

Of course he wouldn't know. Beau didn't talk about it, and neither did Grant. "Beau was in an automobile accident two and a half years ago that not only killed his mother, it damaged his facial nerves." She felt as if she were betraying Beau in some way, but they hadn't attempted to keep the facts a secret; Beau just didn't like to talk about it to strangers.

The steel in Caine's eyes flickered with deepening confusion and something else—was that dismay? "How could I have known something like that? His father and I are not exactly bosom buddies."

Oh yeah? And whose fault is that? "Beau tried to explain about it tonight, but nobody was willing to listen. So now you know." She collected the medications from the dispenser and walked away. Maybe she could get her old job back in Knolls after all. If she continued to spout off at Dr. Caine, she probably wouldn't have this one much longer. And if she had to work with him many more shifts, she didn't want it.

Beau pushed through the unlocked door into the business office and heard the slow *click-clatter-click* of a computer keyboard from the far corner of the cavernous room. The door swung back into place with a *phlunk*. The clicking ceased.

"Who's there?" came a sharp demand filled with stress. It was Brooke.

"Just me."

"Beau! Thank goodness."

He strolled to the aisle on the eastern side of the room. "What's wrong?"

There was a soft squeak of a chair, and Brooke's silhouette popped up from behind a partition. Dark spikes of her hair stuck out in angles from her forehead, as if she'd combed her fingers through it several times. With glue. Mascara smudged her face.

She'd been crying?

"Beau, I can't do this job. I mean it. Why did I ever tell them I could type?"

He joined her at the desk where she was working. Manila file folders decorated the floor like confetti. "Because you can. Kind of."

"Not three thousand words a minute!" She gestured to the data stacked on the desk beside the keyboard. "I terminated the lives of three patients between four o'clock and quitting time. The supervisor had to enter them again from scratch to resurrect them. And then she was crazy enough to leave me here to finish up. I mean, is that stupid?"

"So don't do it. Wait until tomorrow."

"I need this job."

"Your supervisor probably needs her job, too. What's going to happen when *her* boss finds out she left a fumble-fingers alone to do the job she probably should have done herself?"

"Thanks," she snapped.

Beau picked up two of the folders. "I didn't mean it like that. It'll be okay. I can—"

"And I can't let word get out about this. It'll humiliate Dad, and—"

"I'll do—"

"How will we ever make our next car payment if—"

"I said I'll do it. Relax."

She stopped mid-complaint, and her smudgy eyes caught a gleam of hope. "You?"

"Well, I don't think you'll call your supervisor back in now."

"You can do this stuff?"

"Sure. I did some data entry this summer between my shifts in the cafeteria. Remember when half the staff was out because of the mercury poisoning? They were desperate. I learned how to do a lot of clerical work." In fact, it was probably his destiny in life to hide behind a computer monitor and enter data. He could do that well, and computer monitors didn't complain when he tried to smile. What had he been thinking when he tried that with Dru? He was truly losing his mind. What had made him think all of a sudden that he could be normal?

Brooke grabbed him in a sudden impulsive hug and gave him a loud smack on his unsmiling cheek. "Oh, Beau, I love you!"

He squirmed away from her, but the contact eased some of the sting of Dr. Caine's words.

She dabbed at the offended cheek to remove all traces of her lip gloss. "Won't they miss you in the emergency department?"

Hardly. "If they want me they can call." He knew they wouldn't.

Brooke watched him in silence for a few seconds. Her eyes darkened with a knowing frown. She'd always been able to pick up on his slightest mood change. "Are you okay?"

"I'm great."

"Dad call?"

"No."

"Did you kill a patient?"

"No!"

"Cut yourself?"

"No. Brooke, would you just—"

"Needle stick? Those are dangerous, you know. Lauren was telling me the other day about some geezer doc in Knolls who—"

"Brooke, I didn't get stuck by a needle, okay?" He took her gently by the shoulders and turned her toward the door. "If you don't leave me alone to enter this data, even I won't be able to finish it in time."

"Okay, I'll go. You'll get a ride with Lauren?"

"Sure. She's working overtime tonight." Especially with a tech missing from staff.

"Good, then I'll pick up Chinese takeout on the way home." She checked her watch. "And maybe I'll have time to drop by Evan's and check out the new article he's doing."

"Then you'd better go to the bathroom first."

"What?"

He bared his teeth at her in his ugly grimace-smile. It was okay. She saw it for what it really was. "You look like a raccoon," he said.

"Evan won't care. He won't even notice."

"The guys at the China Garden probably will."

"Oh. I'll wash my face on the way out." She winked at him and left.

He sighed and sat down at the keyboard. Brooke would find a way to repay him for this, and he really didn't mind it. Sure beat showing his deformed face to frightened patients in the ER.

"The man has the personality of a pit viper." Muriel scrubbed beside Lauren at the sink, her movements short and sharp, her chin jutting forward in anger. "No, strike that. He's not that friendly."

Lauren nodded in agreement. She had ached to follow Beau and reassure him, but there had been no time, and before she could break free, they'd received word that he was over in the business office, helping enter data. She'd talk to him later.

"I know what his problem is." Muriel jerked a paper towel from the dispenser and dried her hands. "He resents Dr. Sheldon, and he's getting back at him through Beau."

Lester stepped toward them. "Muriel, would you lower your voice? I heard you halfway down the hall. If Caine—"

"I hope he does hear me." Muriel stood with fists on hips. "Did you know he applied for the ER directorship last year and was turned down? Mr. Butler's too wise for that. So now comes the power play with that chief of staff title while the real administration is out."

"So, did you even hear me say shut up?" Lester hissed at her. "He isn't in the best of moods, and he has a reputation for firing nurses in his practice."

"Will Butler won't let him fire me."

"Butler isn't back yet, in case you haven't noticed," Lester reminded her.

"He will be soon. I saw him yesterday at the grocery store, and he's doing great. He's itching to get back to work, and when he does he'll put a stop to some of Caine's shenanigans."

A voice of hard-packed ice struck them from behind. "Define shenanigans."

All three of them turned to see Dr. Caine stepping around the corner, arms crossed over his chest, lips pressed together.

Muriel didn't falter. "Tricks. You know, as in humiliating people in front of an audience—like you did to Dr. Jonas when he came in late because of a delayed flight, and Beau, when you blasted him loudly enough for the whole department to overhear it."

"Then here's another trick for you." Caine leaned into his words, as if he were relishing them. "Find yourself another job, Muriel, because you're fired."

Her eyes flared with momentary shock. "On what grounds?"

"Insubordination."

"You can't fire me."

"Check my job description."

"Dr. Caine," Lauren said, "if you fire Muriel, half the nursing staff will walk out."

Caine turned his attention on Lauren. "And then they can be hauled into court for abandoning their patients. If you wish to try it, be my guest."

Beau stared out at the street, where a cold drizzle dampened the blacktop and reflected a muted image of the big red letters of *Emergency* from the sign above the ambulance bay. Weather reports assured every-one that the temperature would not drop to freezing tonight, but he still felt a chill all the way to his spine. He still stung with humiliation. How could he ever face Dru at school again? How could he face the others?

"Ready?" came a soft voice behind him.

He turned and looked at Lauren. It could just be the lighting, but she looked wiped out. "Sure."

"Let's get out of this place." She led the way through the waiting room door.

He had to rush to keep up with her as she made her way across the parking lot toward her pickup truck. Okay, she wasn't wiped out; she was upset. Mad, even.

She unlocked the door and climbed in, waiting until he was buckled up before she spoke. "He fired Muriel."

For a few seconds the words didn't register. Then he felt a sick anger in the pit of his stomach. "Why?"

"You don't want to hear my opinion right now."

"But can he just fire her for no reason?"

"He overheard her complaining about him." She looked at Beau through the darkness, then shook her head and remained silent as she backed out of the space, pulled from the employee parking lot onto the street, and negotiated the negligible traffic.

"She was defending me, wasn't she?" Beau asked.

"Of course she was defending you. She's as angry as everyone else about the way he treated you tonight."

Beau felt a stab of guilty pain, and he allowed it to attack him in silence for several moments as Lauren turned onto their street, slowed, pulled into the driveway.

"I wish your dad were here," she said.

"So do I."

"I may be looking for a new job, too."

He blinked at her. "Why? He didn't fire you, did he?"

She inhaled deeply, pressed the automatic garage door opener, and removed her foot from the brake. "I hate what he did to you. I let him know it. That probably wasn't a smart thing for me to do, but I don't care." She pulled into the empty garage. "Brooke isn't home yet? Did she say anything about—"

"She's probably at Evan's. I saw her just before she clocked out."

Lauren parked and looked at him in the dim glow of the overhead light. "Lester said you'd called, but we were so busy I didn't get a chance to talk to you. I can't believe Dr. Caine is being so—"

"Could we . . . not . . . talk about this for a little bit?" It was just making him more miserable. By the time he got to the hospital tomorrow, everyone would have heard about it. Ugly Beau Sheldon scared a patient. It hurt.

"Of course, Beau. I'm sorry."

They entered the house in the shelter of companionable silence.

Lauren raised her head and sniffed the air, then plopped her purse into a chair and headed to the kitchen. A few seconds later came an exclamation of joy.

"Chinese! All right! Are you hungry?"

He was.

They ate sweet and sour shrimp and rice noodles in front of the television. Beau thought he sensed Lauren's occasional attention focus on him, but he never caught her watching him.

Still, he could almost hear the questions she wanted to ask, and he felt bad for shutting her out. After all, she'd come to his defense. She'd risked her job, just as Muriel had, and in spite of the pain, the guilt, he felt a sense of warm strength lap over the recent wound.

He finished a final chunk of shrimp and pushed away the cardboard carton, and when he noticed Lauren wasn't watching the television, he turned it off. "Did you ever read the story about the tangerine bear?"

She dabbed at her mouth with her napkin. "I don't think so. Why?"

He couldn't help noticing how, as soon as he spoke, she focused her whole attention on him. It was the way she always listened. She didn't just do it with him, but also with Brooke, and with Dad, and with patients at work. She probably didn't even realize how it drew people, or how her natural kindness seemed to radiate from her eyes. Unlike Brooke, Lauren hardly ever wore makeup. Dad liked that about her. Mom hadn't worn makeup, either.

Mom would have liked Lauren a lot. They would have been good friends. In another life. If things were different.

"What's a tangerine bear?" Lauren prompted gently.

He released the memory of Mom. If she were here, he'd be talking to her about this, and she wouldn't want him to dam it up inside. Brooke wasn't here right now, and neither was Dad.

"I don't remember much about it, except it was a stuffed bear with his smile sewn on upside down," he said. "He was placed in a shop with other misfits, and no one wanted to buy him because he was a freak."

Lauren's face relaxed in lines of understanding.

He couldn't believe how stiff his throat suddenly felt. It was just a children's story, but he felt as if he were spilling deep secrets that he'd never shared with anyone except close family.

She leaned forward, elbows on knees. "Do you remember anything else about the story?"

"Not a whole lot. It's just that . . . I guess . . . when I was a kid I felt sorry for the bear, but now I can identify with him."

"Was there a happy ending?"

"Yes, but it wasn't the ending he had expected."

"Does that matter? The older I get, the more I learn that we can't predict what's going to happen in our lives. And you can't allow one little incident in the emergency room to color your world, or your future."

"You sound like a Sunday school teacher."

"And you sound like an intelligent young man who will be one of this world's best doctors someday. Stop listening to people like Dr.

Caine, and start listening to people like your father and Archer Pierce."

"And Lauren McCaffrey."

She grinned. "And me."

"Thanks. I think I will." He tossed their trash and leaned back. "Want to split Brooke's cashew chicken?"

"What, do you think I'm suicidal?"

He opened the lid of the untouched cardboard container and waved it in front of her. "There are extra cashews—that's her favorite part—and she can't scream at me, because she owes me a big favor. Come on, Lauren, you'll never get another chance like this. She always playing practical jokes on us."

"And I'd like to live through the next one, thank you very much."

Okay, so she wasn't perfect. But she was close enough.

CHAPTER 22

On Thursday before school, Beau sat in his father's home office reading the most recent literature on the treatment of headaches within the ER. The article was long and dry, filled with abbreviations he didn't recognize, and it didn't keep his attention. He was worried about Brooke.

She hadn't arrived home last night until after ten o'clock curfew, and all she'd told him and Lauren was that she and Evan had some last-minute research to complete. He'd taken that to mean pictures or snooping, but he'd given up trying to control his sister. Almost. She wouldn't listen, and who was going to back him up—Tony Dalton?

He was about to shove the periodical aside and start breakfast when the telephone rang beside his elbow and startled him. He glanced at the caller ID. It was Grandma Sheldon's number.

He snatched up the receiver. "Hi, Dad."

"Beau? It's good to hear your voice, son. How are things down there?"

"We're okay. A little busy at work."

"That's nothing new. I didn't wake you, did I?"

"Nope, I was just getting ready to do some cooking. Don't you have your deposition today?"

There was a tired sigh. "Postponed. I thought I might drive home last night, but . . . there's been a little problem here."

"What kind of problem?"

"It's your grandma. I don't feel comfortable leaving her here by herself right now."

Beau's grip tightened on the telephone receiver. "Why? Is she sick? Did something happen?"

"That's what I called to talk to you about. Is Brooke there? I need to discuss something with both of you before I make any decisions."

"What decisions?"

"Get your sister. Has Lauren already gone to work?"

"No, she's sleeping in today. Hold for a minute." Beau left the receiver on the desk and stole through the house, taking care to silence his footsteps as he passed the closed door of the guest room. Lauren had to work tonight.

He knocked on Brooke's door and waited. No answer. She probably had her head buried under her pillow.

He knocked again, then cracked the door open. "Brooke, Dad's on the phone. He wants to talk to both of us."

No answer.

He pushed the door wide and saw that her bed was empty. Unmade. She never made her bed. "Brooke, where are you?" He sniffed the air and caught the aromatic combination of soap, perfume, and deodorant that always wafted from her room after she got ready for school in the morning. But it was too early. He glanced toward the dresser, where she always plopped her ten-gallon purse. It was gone.

"Brooke!" Her bathroom door was open and the light was off. He went to the kitchen, thinking she might have slipped past him and could be sitting at the kitchen table, but all was quiet. He saw the bright square of a sticky note on the refrigerator and snatched it off.

She'd left for school early, caught a ride with Evan.

Beau went back to the telephone. "Sorry, Dad, Brooke's already gone to school."

There was silence. "You're kidding."

"Nope, I found her note just now."

"Okay, what's going on? Is she sick? She barely gets to school on *time*, much less early."

Beau sighed. "I don't know, Dad. She's been acting stranger than usual. She and Evan are working together a lot on some articles, and . . ." He would not tell Dad that they were ostracizing him from their special little project. He'd given up tattling when he was ten years old. "And we've had some major things happen."

"Like what?"

"An eighth grader died of an overdose of meth Monday. His name was Oakley Brisco."

"Brisco? I know that name." There was a deep groan from the receiver. "Oh, no. I treated his grandfather. He died at school?"

"Yes. They rushed him to the hospital, but they didn't get him resuscitated. It was horrible, Dad. When I heard about it I ran downstairs to try to help out, but the ambulance got there quickly and they didn't need me. They did everything right, they just couldn't get him back. A lot of people are upset, and I'm one of them. Evan's probably writing a piece about it."

"I'd better just talk to you," Dad said. "Beau, we need to do something about your grandma. She has Alzheimer's."

Beau sat down hard in the office chair. "When did you find this out?"

"I've suspected it since last week. It's just one of the reasons I didn't get home over the weekend. Jay pulled some special favors and we had an appointment with a neurologist Monday. We're trying some new medication with her, but we can't tell yet if it's going to work. Meanwhile, I may have found someone who will stay with her, but if this arrangement doesn't work out I need to know what you and Brooke think about asking your grandma to live with us."

Beau swallowed. "Of course."

"That's it? Just like that?"

"This is Grandma. We're her family."

"I don't know if she'll be willing to leave St. Louis. She's lived here all her life."

"Maybe you should talk to her about it when she's . . . you know . . . thinking straight."

There was a soft sigh. "I'm glad you feel that way. Thanks. I hope your sister—"

"She'll say the same thing." Eventually. Brooke could be opinionated, and she liked her own way, and living with Grandma would probably drive them all nuts, but they would drive her nuts, too. It was their family way. His sister had a deep sense of responsibility. She'd do the right thing.

"So how's it going down there today?" Dad asked. "You worked at the hospital last night, didn't you?"

"Yeah."

There was a waiting silence. Dad could read him almost as well as Brooke.

"Dr. Caine was on duty," Beau said at last. It would come out sooner or later anyway. He kept telling himself it wasn't a big deal. "He wasn't exactly friendly. I did something stupid, and a patient's grandmother took it the wrong way, and I was banished from taking vitals when Dr. Caine is there."

"What do you call stupid?"

Beau related his experience to the tune of Dad's sympathetic monosyllables.

"I know that must have been humiliating for you at the time," Dad said when Beau finished.

"It was. I didn't think I was going to live through it, but I did. Someday we might even laugh about it. I just can't believe I tried to smile like that."

"It's your natural compassion, Beau. It's the kind of person you are. How do you feel about another attempt at surgery?"

"No. Not yet. The others didn't work, and we got our hopes up for nothing."

"But I spoke with Dr. Taylor Monday, and he's had some success—"

"It's okay, Dad, really. Maybe later." Dad was already in debt because of the other surgeries. If the plaintiff won this malpractice suit, their bank account might not see daylight for years to come. And he didn't want to go through all that again.

"Beau, remember a few years ago when that kid was picking on you in sixth grade?"

"You mean the one Brooke beat up?"

"Oh, yes, thanks for reminding me," Dad said dryly. "When you came to your mother and me about it, your mother suggested that you pray for him. It helped, didn't it?"

Beau remembered that it had, unconventionally. "Sure, especially after Brooke heard me praying and decided to beat him—"

"Okay, yes, I know. Why don't we try to leave Brooke out of it this time? I don't—"

"You want me to pray for Dr. Caine."

"It's what we're supposed to do. Pray for our enemies."

"It won't be easy, Dad."

"Lots of things aren't easy, but they need doing. I'll see you soon. I love you, Beau. And keep an eye on your sister, will you? My father's intuition tells me she's up to something."

"Sure, Dad. Bye."

Grant hung up the phone with a bit too much force—just a little bit. It was a good thing he was in St. Louis right now instead of Dogwood Springs, or he might be tempted to pull a "Brooke move" and beat someone up.

How could Mitchell Caine be such a jerk? How could he treat Beau like that? After everything Beau had endured . . .

Grant took a deep breath and let it out and flexed his fists as he went to the kitchen to start breakfast before Mom could beat him to it. He took a little too much satisfaction breaking the eggs into the hot grease in the skillet. Mitchell Caine would have some questions to answer when this was all over. He had no right taking his frustrations out on Beau.

Breakfast was almost cooked by the time Grant calmed down enough to think about something else, and with the change of focus came the worry once again. He knew he was in partial denial. Mom's mental status seemed to have deteriorated since Monday, but her sleep patterns were a mess, so her daytime confusion could be from sleep deprivation.

She'd been up three times last night, wandering the house, checking the locks on the doors, staring out the leaded panes of the front door at the lights across the street. Still, in spite of her wanderings, she was usually up by seven-thirty, cooking breakfast for him. Twice she'd spilled eggs on the burner, and the smell lingered even after his attempts to air out the house.

He was pulling toast from the toaster when she came padding into the room in the house shoes that were a size too big for her.

"Grant? What are you doing up so early?"

He looked at the clock. "It's seven-thirty, Mom. It isn't that early. And I have some arrangements to make and another meeting with Jay before I go home, so I need to leave before eight."

"When are those snoops coming to inspect the house?"

This was going to be a kick-and-scream operation, he could tell. He took a breath to relax himself. "Comfortable Companions is supposed to send someone over to meet with us at three this afternoon. That's why I need to get everything else done before then." He poured her a cup of tea, pulled her chair out, and waited for her to sit.

"I don't want somebody else living here with me," she muttered.

"She won't be living here; she'll be staying here nights and then preparing your meals in the mornings for the day."

"I don't want anybody else in my kitchen."

Grant sighed. "Just meet her, okay? It won't hurt us to talk to her."

Mom eased herself down on the chair, leaning her elbows on the table, combing her fingers through her hair. "Why don't they call it what it is? A baby-sitting service."

"You're not a baby. If you don't like this companion we can look for someone else. The only other option I can think of is for you to come to Dogwood Springs and live with us."

She blinked up at him, and her gray eyes seemed to fill the circumference of her round, owlish glasses. "Live with you? I can't go traipsing off across the state to the middle of nowhere. And what would your father have to say about you taking the enemy to live under your roof?" Ancient bitterness hammered through her words.

Grant didn't want to think about that. Brooke and Beau had been dragged into their grandparents' fights all their lives—controversy over who would go where for holidays, who had spent more money on whom—until Annette put a stop to that by establishing holiday celebrations at home as a family, promising to visit the grandparents separately at other times.

She'd been firm about not dragging the kids into any conversations about the "other" grandparent. She had been unpopular for a while with both Mom and Dad, but Rita and her family supported Annette's stance and did the same thing. In the end it had made for smoother relations—until Annette was killed and the family was thrown into chaos.

It was a shame when children had to be sheltered from their grandparents.

Bringing Mom home with him would be bringing the battle into their home again if he didn't take and hold a firm position the same way Annette had done. "I can't leave you by yourself, Mom, not until you get better."

She spooned sugar into her tea. "Am I going to get better?"

"You could with the right treatment. We'll just wait and see."

"And what if I'm not? Are you going to stick me away in some nursing home?"

"Not as long as we can keep you home."

"This is home. Your place isn't."

"We'll do what we can, Mom. I'll take all measures necessary to take care of you. Please just trust me, okay?"

The darkness of hurt suspicion remained in her eyes, and it cut him deeply. He reached forward and laid a hand on hers. "Mom, I love you, and you know I'll take care of you."

"Even if your father kicks up a fuss because you're spending more time with me?"

"Even if he cuts all ties. I can't leave you stranded like this. I'll take care of you."

She sat back, and though the pain of loss continued to chisel her face with sorrow, the suspicion cleared. "I don't think you're going to give me a choice."

CHAPTER 23

B eau arrived at school twenty minutes early—giving himself time to look for Brooke and Evan to make sure they were actually on school property and not skulking around in the shadows spying on questionable characters. He found them in Publications, hovering over a table with a computer at the far end of the cavernous room—the same computer they used for all their skulking work and articles. They hadn't even turned on the lights.

He stepped in silently enough that they didn't notice his arrival.

"That's him, the one who was with Oak the other day." Brooke's voice was unnaturally soft. She picked up a small square of paper that looked like a photograph. "See? Here he is again, with Kent. I could pick him out of a lineup. Good work, Evan. You could set up your own photography business when you graduate."

Beau moved in closer, and the shadow of his movement must have alerted Brooke. She slid the photographs beneath a manila folder and turned to the computer where Evan hovered. They both kept their attention on the screen without looking up.

" 'Peer pressure can be a powerful incentive,' " Brooke read aloud. " 'It's hard to say no when everyone around you is saying yes.' So far it's good, Evan." Her voice was a little too loud and shrill.

"Okay, that works." Evan enunciated his words too clearly. "But we need to segue into the rest of the article. Listen to this. 'You may think you have—' " He looked up at that moment, as if he'd just noticed Beau had entered the room. "Oh. Hi, Beau. You're at school early."

Beau sighed and shook his head. "Don't let me stop your momentum," he said dryly. He took a few steps closer to the computer. "Why don't you read it to me?"

"We're polishing. It isn't done yet," Evan said. "And it's just a bunch of boring facts."

"Oh, come on, you two, how stupid do you think I am?" Beau pulled a chair from beneath the computer table and slumped into it. "You're still sneaking around, snooping where you shouldn't be, taking pictures, taking all kinds of chances. Brooke, Dad called this morning and he wanted to talk to you, but you'd already left for school—*early*. That's twice in a week and a half. How weird is that? When are you ever early for any—"

"Has it occurred to you or Dad that I might have finally found something that holds my interest?" Brooke snapped. "Give me a break, Beau."

"You two are doing surveillance for Tony Dalton again, aren't you?"

"We've talked with Sergeant Dalton, if that's what you mean," Brooke said.

Beau reached beneath the manila folder and slid the photos out before they could stop him. The shot on top was a side view of a scruffy-looking man with spiky blond hair, wearing a dirty sweater and jeans. He was holding his hand out to a kid Beau didn't recognize. The background was dark.

"What's this?" he asked.

"It's a picture we took last night, okay?" Evan snatched the pictures from Beau's hand. "Satisfied? It's a drug deal, and it's happening right out there on our streets when the kids go cruising during the—"

The overhead lights came on. "What's going on in here?"

Evan gasped and shoved the pictures beneath the manila folder again, and the three of them turned to see Miss Bolton walking to her desk carrying her purse and the large canvas bag she always used to cart work home with her.

"Webster and the Sheldons, I should have known. Are you finished with that article yet?" She set her things down. "We need to get it into tomorrow's edition if possible."

Evan swallowed. "Tomorrow's. . . ? But I thought—"

"All the kids I've talked to are staying after school for Oakley's funeral, and we're going to have a packed gymnasium." She shoved her hands into the pockets of her jacket and strolled back toward them. "It's no secret that Oak died of an overdose. You hit them with a good article tomorrow and public outrage about the drug problem will shoot sky-high." She leaned against a nearby desk. "So let's hear it. What've you got?"

Evan scooted closer to the monitor and cleared his throat. "Okay, I'll read you what I've got, but don't critique it yet. It's really rough."

"Let's hear it."

He cleared his throat again. " 'Let me tell you what peer pressure can do to you. It can ruin your love life, damage your relationship with your parents, and eventually it can kill you. It happened to me.' "

Beau straightened in his chair. "Peer pressure killed you?"

Evan peered up from his screen. "I said don't critique. You'll knock me off my stride."

"Sorry."

Evan scowled and punched a few keys. "Fine, then, how does this sound? 'I know, because it recently happened to one of our own, and it almost happened to me.' "

"That's better," Beau said.

"Good. That's all I'll need to say about Oakley. So listen to this, 'Don't get me wrong, sometimes peer pressure can be a good thing, especially when public opinion forces you to drive cautiously, study hard, and be kind to little old ladies. But there is a dark side.' " He looked up and gave Beau a warning glance.

"I didn't say anything."

Evan sighed and continued. " 'When a friend entices you to try a drug, that person is no longer your friend. Our fair community, deep in the heart of the Ozarks, with strong ethical standards, is a town on the edge of a dangerous precipice.' " He looked up at Beau again.

"I thought you didn't want my opinion," Beau said.

"I don't. I can read it in your expression. So far you're not gagging."

"No, I'm not, but are you ever going to get to the point?"

"Fine. Here goes. 'Our fair community is drowning in the drug scene, and our poison of choice is methamphetamine, which some of our own citizens are manufacturing.' "

"Cut the purple prose," Brooke said. "And don't say 'fair community.' It sounds like something in a political speech."

"Later, okay? I'm flowing with it. 'The pills are bad enough, dangerous enough to kill, but even if that first dose doesn't hurt you, the high gets old. At this point you are a low-intensity abuser. But it will draw you deeper. You discover, soon enough, that the real trip comes when you snort it up your nose or inject it with a needle. By then, you've already stepped into the zone of red alert, and there will be no warning.' " He looked at Miss Bolton. "Brooke's probably right. I think the rest has too much purple prose. Maybe we should wait—"

"No, I want to hear the rest," she said. "Just stop trying to bias the reader against the drug. If they're the least bit resistant, they'll rebel against everything else you have to say. Let the facts speak for themselves—that's all you'll need."

Evan nodded. " 'Do you see what I'm saying? You'll crash without a safety net, and when you hit, you'll hit hard. And remember this—if you never remember anything else—you'll never again feel the same ability to enjoy life without the drug. You will have become a high intensity abuser. The scientific explanation is that it depletes your body's natural endorphin supply. No matter how many times you shoot up or snort, you will never find the same high again—and yet you'll *have* to *have* it!' " He punched a few keys. "I see what you mean. I do sound a little prejudiced."

"At least you have some scientific stuff in there," Beau said. "Let's hear the rest."

"Let's see . . . okay, here we go. 'At this point you have traveled out of the reach of redemption, and even if you've never believed in a devil before, you will believe in him now, because he will snatch your soul.' "

He looked up at his listeners. "What do you think? Scary? Will it make the readers think?"

"They'll probably complain that you're forcing your personal convictions down their throats," Brooke said.

"I've done this kind of thing before, and nobody complained."

"So read us the rest," Miss Bolton said.

Evan beamed at her. "I got your attention, didn't I? You want more. I can read it in your—"

"Would you just read it from the screen," Brooke snapped.

Evan chuckled and returned to his work. " 'The final consequences are gruesome to behold.' "

"I still think you're using too much purple prose," Brooke said.

Evan shrugged. " 'The victim of the drug has now become the very evil that lurked in those shadows, the evil that is not afraid of killing. The drug abuser gets high and stays high for days, even weeks—without sleep. And then, after sleeping from one to three days straight, he becomes a 'tweaker' looking for his next high—and he'll do anything to get it.' "

"Objection," Brooke said. "You're using the masculine pronoun."

"I'll deal with it later, Brooke. 'Even if he—or she—is serious about trying to quit, about sixty to ninety days out he realizes that he has brought someone back with him from that dark world of illusion—the specter of depression, a permanent companion.

" 'And so our vicious victim turns to alcohol to blunt the sharp pain of depression, and another companion joins the first. Paranoia. If you see eyes that flick back and forth in a crowded room, you'd best keep your distance. The victim has become the aggressor. There is no going back.

" 'This could be you, my friend, if you listen to the voice of seduction.' " He sat back and sighed, then looked at Miss Bolton. "What do you think?"

"Too long," Brooke said.

"I don't know," Beau argued. "Even if it is a little too dramatic, I think it'll keep their attention."

"Keep the dramatic slant," Miss Bolton said. "Get that thing rewritten and ready to go. Beau and Brooke, help him edit, but don't hit him too hard. We can get away with more emotion right now."

The bell rang, and Miss Bolton shooed them out of the department.

At two-fifty on Thursday afternoon Grant entered his bedroom and closed the door while Mom got ready for company. As he had begun to do in this room twenty-four years ago—after becoming part of the body of Christ—he knelt beside the bed and buried his face in his hands.

"Lord, your compassion and blessings are overwhelming, and I know I can never repay you for them. I can only stare in awe at the wonder of belonging to you. I feel I have no right to ask for more blessings, more compassion, and more protection, but I'm asking anyway.

"Please, Lord, protect my mother, and guide us as we stumble through this confusion together. Show us your way, your will, and give my mother peace. Show her you, Lord. And guide me toward the right decisions—the necessary measures—to help her in the very best way."

Necessary measures. The term struck him. Many times the measures one had to take were not attractive. They were often painful and difficult.

"And please protect Brooke and Beau. If I seem to place their welfare above serving you, please forgive me and show me your most perfect way. I know you love and understand them better than I do, so please guide them. Give them wisdom, and please, please, Lord, protect them. They are so precious to me. I know they're precious to you. Help me to place my faith in that fact."

He heard the doorbell, heard Mom's voice calling out to him, and he started to get up. He couldn't. He wasn't finished. Reluctantly, he settled back onto his knees.

"Grant?" There was Mom's familiar click of fingernails on the door. She did that because it hurt her arthritis to knock with her knuckles.

"Let them in, Mom," he said. "I'll be out in a minute." She would have to get accustomed to company. He could hear her breathing as she stood another few seconds outside the door, then she shuffled on down the hallway.

He laid his forehead against the edge of the mattress again. *Just say the words. Ask God to bless Mitchell.* It didn't take overwhelming, heartfelt love for the man. It only took a whisper of compassion, and then God would do the rest. It was yet another necessary measure.

It would be easier if Mitchell hadn't attacked Beau. It was easier to pray for his own enemies than for his child's. Just last night Grant had prayed for the plaintiffs in his malpractice lawsuit. True, he'd prayed for them to come to their senses, but he'd also prayed for God to bless them.

He had also prayed for the other physicians named in this case, who were now willing to cast aspersions on him to protect themselves.

And yet his anger with Mitchell Caine was so harsh, his pain for his son so fresh, he could not say the words. In spite of the truth he knew, his own spiritual resistance held him silent, and there was no more time—

There was another click of fingernails on the door. "Grant! That woman's here! You need to get in here and tell her what you want, because I don't know."

"Coming."

Another rap of nails to let him know she meant it this time, then she moved away again.

"I'm sorry, Lord. I need help with this one. I know I'm overreacting to Mitchell's actions, but I can't . . . can't do it." He got up and opened the door, straightening the collar of his shirt, and he stepped out to meet the nice lady in her sixties who would be Mom's new companion . . . if this worked out.

───────

Lauren sat pressed between Brooke and Beau in the bleachers of the high school gymnasium. Taped organ music floated over them as Mr. Brisco—that feisty old farmer who had come to blows with his neighbor last summer—staggered toward the front of the auditorium between an obviously grief-stricken middle-aged couple.

Brooke leaned close to Lauren's ear. "That's Oakley's mom and dad with the old guy, I think," she whispered. "They live in Little Rock, Arkansas. Can you believe it? They sent Oak up to live with his grandpa because they couldn't control him."

Lauren shook her head. How did they handle their grief? She was having a hard enough time dealing with the loss of her brother, but to lose a fourteen-year-old son . . . "I can't imagine how they must feel."

Brooke reached over and took her arm and squeezed.

Lauren patted her hand and tried hard not to cry during the eulogy and prayer, but when the high school's mixed chorus sang "Amazing

Grace," the tears flowed. She heard Brooke sniffing beside her and handed her a tissue. She glanced at Beau. His face was red and the muscles at his jawline flexed. When the singing ended and the overhead speakers fell silent, Lauren heard sniffling all around her. Many in the crowd—adults and kids alike—were sobbing openly.

She saw Sergeant Tony Dalton and his wife, Caryn, down on the floor where chairs had been arranged between basketball court lines. Just down from them sat Archer Pierce. Several members of the Baptist congregation were peppered throughout the gymnasium.

Brooke blew her nose and sniffed one last time. "We're going to get this guy," she muttered.

Lauren leaned closer to her. "Who's that?"

"The guy who did all this." Brooke gestured around the room. "The guy who sold him the dope in the first place. I just wish I could get my hands on him."

Lauren patted her knee as one of the local ministers stepped up to the lectern to give the homily. "It looks to me as if there are a lot of people here today who feel the same way."

"Good," Brooke said. "Then maybe he won't keep getting away with it."

———

Beau was cleaning exam room four when he heard the voice of Dr. Caine behind him.

"I think we have something to discuss."

For a moment, Beau didn't realize that he was the object of the doctor's interest.

"Sheldon."

"Uh, yes?" He turned to find his doorway blocked by the man in the white coat.

"It seems I was not fully informed about a particular condition. Because of that misunderstanding, I may have been uncharacteristically outspoken yesterday."

Uncharacteristically? "Okay."

"I apologize for hurting your feelings."

"Thanks, Dr. Caine. It's okay. Everybody makes mistakes." He returned to his cart, but the uncomfortable sense of Caine's presence did not disappear.

"You understand, of course, that my first concern must always be for the patient."

Beau suppressed a sigh. With Dr. Caine, this couldn't be just a simple apology. "Sure, I understand."

"You know . . ." Dr. Caine said slowly.

Oh boy, here it comes.

"It wouldn't hurt you to develop a better bedside manner."

"Okay, Dr. Caine, I'll work on it." *And have you checked on yours lately?*

"Is there no chance for reconstructive surgery?"

Beau picked up a cellophane package of syringes. He didn't want to get into this discussion. He didn't even like to talk about this with friends, and Caine was no friend.

"Am I talking to an empty room?" the doctor complained after a moment of silence.

Beau sighed, making no attempt to suppress his own impatience. "My father took me to the best plastic surgeons he could find. There seems to be some nerve regeneration recently, but I've been told my face can*not* be repaired." He risked a quick glance up at the doctor and saw the typical focus of scientific interest that he had encountered several times in the medical community.

"That's a shame, Beau." A trace of pity threaded his voice and floated across the room like cold bacon grease, cracking at the edges. "A smile can be one of your best allies when you're treating a patient." He showed his own smile suddenly, a beautiful set of straight, white teeth. "I would say it's as vital as a stethoscope. In fact, it could be even more important. Some physicians don't even use stethoscopes anymore, and often it's just a prop, something for the patient to believe in. Medicine has changed, and we have to change with it."

"Yes, Dr. Caine." *Just stick this out a little longer.* The man didn't know how to apologize. He had no humility. Did he even know how to *use* a stethoscope? Beau had begun to listen to Dad's before he went to kindergarten. That connection to the heart of the patient was vital. Human connection was vital.

"You wouldn't dream of becoming an actor on stage without a full range of facial motion," Dr. Caine continued.

Beau could feel the flush across his neck. "I wouldn't dream of trying to be an actor. I don't want to be an actor, and I don't want to be on stage." What he wanted was to punch this man. "I'm going to medical school because I want to be a doctor who helps people."

Caine showed no offense, which probably meant the full meaning of Beau's statement had probably sailed right over his head. "I can't believe a good surgeon couldn't repair a few simple facial nerves. Smile for me."

"What?"

"I said smile. That accident didn't injure your ears, too, did it?"

"No."

Caine reached up and pressed the first two fingers of his right hand against Beau's left cheek and jawline. "Smile."

Beau obliged with the offending grimace, bracing himself for further scrutiny.

Dr. Caine palpated Beau's face and frowned. "Hmm. I would definitely advise you to refrain from that when you're with a patient. I see what the woman meant."

Beau pulled back and turned away. He didn't need to hear this. He already knew—

"You said you think there's some regeneration?" the doctor asked.

"I have more movement in my right cheek than I had last year at this time."

"Then how can any surgeon in his right mind tell you that your face cannot be repaired? I think you and your father need to seek another consultation."

"We've already been to the best."

Caine shrugged. "Suit yourself." He turned to leave, then hesitated and turned back. "One more thing." He took a step closer to Beau and lowered his voice. "I hope you don't make a habit of eavesdropping on private conversations."

"No, I don't."

"You spent quite some time in the supply room the other day. I suspect you were privy to some personal matters that I would prefer to keep to myself."

"I'm not a gossip, Dr. Caine."

Caine nodded. "Then you did overhear the fact that I am experiencing some . . . difficulties in my private life."

"I heard."

Another nod. "My personal problems are no one else's business."

"Neither are mine, but it doesn't keep people from talking about them."

There was a softening in Dr. Caine's expression. "Just so we understand one another." He glanced at his watch. "I have patients to treat, and you have bedpans to empty. We'd better get busy."

CHAPTER 24

I t was a groggy two o'clock on Friday morning when Grant walked into the emergency department. In spite of his weariness from the long drive and the lateness of the hour, he reveled in the familiarity of the surroundings and the friendly face of the secretary at the central workstation. All appeared calm. No crowds lined the hallway, no monitors beeped, no bad smells emanated from any exam rooms.

Becky looked up from the depths of a novel, and her lips parted with a pleased smile. "Dr. Sheldon, is that really you?" She took off her glasses. "It is!" She placed the novel facedown on the desk and got up to greet him with a typical Becky-beam. "You've been gone so long I was afraid you'd left us for good. Didn't I hear Beau say you'd be stuck up there a little longer?"

Yes, it felt good to be home. "I had a chance to get away and I couldn't resist the temptation. I miss my kids." He missed Lauren. "And I don't want to miss the wedding." He turned to scan the quiet department. "Where is everybody?"

Becky shrugged. "Lauren's taking a break, and I think Dr. Caine is asleep in the call room. Lester's down the hall visiting with his buddies in the—"

"*Lauren's* here? Is she covering for someone?"

"Oh, she didn't tell you?" Becky glanced toward the closed door of Grant's office. "Uh, maybe I shouldn't be the one to . . . Why don't you check out your desk, and maybe you should talk to Lauren while you're here."

"I think you're right. The last time I looked she wasn't scheduled to work tonight."

"A lot has changed, Dr. Sheldon. You'd better see for yourself."

"How much can change in eleven days?"

Becky shrugged and shook her head. "You'll see."

Lauren sat staring into the shimmering blackness of her third cup of coffee this shift and chewed endlessly on a sawdust-and-cheese sandwich from the vending machine. Why hadn't she allowed Beau to fix her that wonderful chicken sandwich he'd offered?

She had to stay awake. The doctors who worked nights were expected to sleep when they had a chance—and were provided nice call rooms in which they could have their privacy. Nurses, on the other hand, could be fired for dozing on the job.

Of course, the doctors often worked excessive hours, stretched between private practice, night and weekend call, and shifts in the emergency room two or three times a week. Grant was trying to get that changed here, but it was a tedious process. There weren't enough doctors to go around. Lately, there weren't many nurses, either, or staff in other departments. Because of the shortage, patient complaints were on the rise, and Mr. Butler wasn't on hand to reassure them.

Lauren let the sandwich plop down onto a napkin and braced her elbows against the table. Just a short break . . . if she could close her eyes for a few minutes . . .

She rested her forehead against the knuckles of her clasped hands. It was a trick she'd learned in school, though she'd seldom used it. Her roommate had taught it to her when they were studying for finals at the end of one particularly busy semester—just a short doze, until she lost her balance and caught herself—would help refresh her brain. If she had known then that she would be stuck working with cranky doctors on unpopular night shifts for the rest of her life . . .

"When did you become a night owl?" came a deep voice from the hallway.

Lauren jerked upright and blinked. She had not fallen asleep—she'd just been resting her eyes. That voice . . . She turned around and saw Grant standing there in black jeans and a sweater of soft blue, and a joy of unnamed proportions rushed through her, waking her like a splash of refreshing spring water.

"Grant! You're home!" She pushed away from the table and jumped from her chair, nearly tipping her coffee in the process. She wanted to hug him. She wanted to shout for joy. She did neither of those things, but simply walked toward him, grinning like an idiot.

"It's good to see you, too," he said softly.

"What are you doing here at this time of night?" she asked. "Have you been home yet?"

"No, I just thought I'd stop by here first. And I might ask you the same question. What are you doing here?"

She held her hands out from her sides and glanced down at her purple scrubs. "What does it look like I'm doing? Trying to stay awake and praying that I don't lose concentration. The kids are safe at home in bed. I just spoke with them a few hours ago. They've got Archer and me on speed dial in case anything goes wrong. I'm sorry, I didn't want to leave them alone overnight, but lately I haven't had much of a choice."

He sighed and leaned against the doorjamb. "Lauren, I'm not concerned about that at all. I just want to know what's going on here. Why the shift change? Dr. Caine wasn't scheduled to work tonight, either, but according to Becky he's in the call room."

Lauren leaned against the edge of the table and crossed her arms in front of her. "Are you sure you want to hear this? It's a long story, and it might be easier to handle after you've had some sleep."

"It can't be that long, I've only been gone since—"

"You've been gone over a week and a half. I've discovered a lot can happen in that amount of time," Lauren muttered.

"Why didn't I hear about any changes when I called home? It isn't as if I was in outer space."

"You're busy fighting a malpractice suit. Besides, what could you do up there in St. Louis? Want some coffee?"

"I think I'm going to need some."

Lauren kept her gaze averted as she poured a cup of freshly brewed coffee, set it on the table, and pulled out a chair. She sank down with a sigh. "I hope you realize you have been sorely missed."

"Thank you. I think." He sat down across from her and leaned forward, elbows on the table. "What's going on, Lauren? I'm surprised my kids haven't mentioned any problems."

"I . . . uh . . . I asked them not to."

His gray eyes, always so expressive, reflected his disappointment. He continued to watch her, obviously waiting for further explanation, while he sipped his coffee.

"Please don't blame Brooke and Beau."

"I'm not blaming anyone for anything. But are you going to tell me what's going on?" His firmly chiseled features were pale and drawn, outlined by a dark evening shadow.

"Yes, I'm just trying to decide where to start."

He groaned.

"Okay, here's the good news. You have raised your kids right. They have been compassionate and supportive of me through a very difficult time." To her embarrassment, she felt her throat swell with the threat of tears. This was not a good time. She was tired. Her defenses were down, and—

His attention focused on her more completely. "Lauren," he said quietly, "Beau told me about Oakley Brisco."

"His funeral was this afternoon at the school gymnasium. The gym was packed, and the tears could have filled Farmer Brisco's pond. Grant, he was only fourteen."

Grant studied her face carefully. "What else happened, Lauren?"

She swallowed. She would let Beau tell him about the Tuesday night debacle with Dr. Caine if he hadn't done so already.

He leaned forward, resting his chin on his fist. "Lauren, there's something else. You said the kids helped you through a difficult time. What happened?"

She hesitated. "Hardy . . . he was killed in an accident at work last week."

He gave a soft grunt, as if he'd been kicked. His fingers whitened around the coffee mug, and he sat back in his chair with a slow, deep breath. "Oh, Lauren, no," he whispered.

She felt the reproach, though she couldn't tell if it was some unspoken thought betrayed through Grant's body language or if it was her own personal remorse. "I'm sorry," she said. "I should never have kept it from you, I can see that now. At the time it had seemed like the right thing to do because of what you were going through. I didn't do it to hurt you, I just didn't want—"

He raised a hand, and his exhaustion was evident in the gesture. "I know you didn't." His voice was gentle but sad. "When did it happen?"

"Just before midnight last Tuesday. The funeral was Friday. If I'd known the deposition would be postponed—"

"That doesn't matter, Lauren. You obviously don't realize, yet, that I would have been here for you no matter what the circumstances in St. Louis. My attorney is a friend, and he would have helped me out. I wish I could have . . ." He sighed and held his hands out in frustrated helplessness. "How are Sandi and the girls taking it? How are *you* taking it?"

Lauren swallowed. Fresh grief welled to her eyes. "As I said, the kids have been great. They drove me to Knolls the night after he was killed, and they returned for the visitation and for the funeral."

"But my kids can't serve as a stand-in for something like this, Lauren." He rubbed his bloodshot eyes and leaned back in his chair. He watched her for an awkward moment of silence, then gave her a hesitant smile, as if making an effort to shrug off the issue. "Are we rubbing off on you?"

"What?"

"I'm sure you've noticed these past few months that my family has a tendency to try to 'protect' one another from bad news. I've done it with the kids in the past. I didn't notice that they'd been doing it much, lately, until the wreck, when Brooke and Beau both seemed to be trying to shield me from the impact and the injuries."

"Well, I should tell you, then, that Brooke was offended by my suggestion to . . . uh . . . 'protect' you from the truth."

"But she did so anyway. Lauren, you haven't told me how you're holding up."

She looked away. "Better, thanks. How's your mother?"

"Oh, no, you don't. You're not brushing this whole thing off that easily. I want to know how you're doing, how your family is doing. I want to know what caused the acci—"

"I will, Grant. I promise to talk about it later. It's just that . . . everything's still too fresh, and I'm tired, and I'm not handling my emotions that well right now anyway, so—"

"I'm sorry. You're right."

"So why don't you tell me how your mom's doing," she suggested.

He held his hand out and rocked it back and forth. "Iffy. I have someone staying nights with her, and two of her friends have promised to check on her at least once during the day. But she hates it, and I'm not sure it's going to work out. I already spoke with Beau about asking her to come and live with us."

"That may be the best thing for her."

Grant rubbed his forehead wearily. "I want to do what's best for everyone concerned." He studied her face carefully for a moment, then looked away. "I don't know if there is such a thing. I don't want to drag my children back through the old family feud."

"Then just don't let your parents feud in your home. If your dad doesn't like it because you're taking care of your mother—which would have been *his* responsibility if there hadn't been a divorce—then he doesn't have to come around. It would be a shame, but it would be his decision."

He thought about that for a few seconds, nodded, grinned at her. "You seem to have some strong feelings on the subject."

"I've seen it happen with some of my relatives. That's one good thing about being related to half of Knolls County, you get a great education on human dynamics." And here she was, spouting off again.

"You haven't told me why you're here tonight," he said. "Are you working to pay someone back for taking your place last week?"

"Not . . . exactly."

"Then what—"

There was a knock at the threshold, and Becky stepped through the open break room door. "I thought I'd find you here. Lauren, we have a patient waiting for triage. A woman with belly pains."

"Coming." Lauren pushed wearily from the table and put her mug into the sink at the far side of the room. "If you want to know what's been happening around here lately, Grant, check out your office. Dr. Jonas gave notice two days ago, and he was removed from the physician schedule completely."

"But why?"

She glanced over her shoulder and lowered her voice. "He's upset about a reprimand he received from Dr. Caine within the hearing of patients and staff. Muriel is no longer with us—Dr. Caine fired her." She wouldn't tell him, yet, that she herself had seriously considered submitting her own resignation and returning to Knolls. "We've lost some staff in other departments, as well."

"Let me guess. Dr. Caine?"

She nodded. "Primarily. Are you sure you don't want to go home and take a nap before you have to face this place?"

He looked more weary than when he had come in. "I don't think I can afford to let things go for eight more hours."

Lauren turned to walk from the room, then reconsidered and pivoted back. "I'm sorry, I didn't ask. How did your deposition go?"

"It was postponed again, rescheduled for next week if one can believe the schedule." He picked up his cup and stood from the table. "Apparently, I wasn't the only one caught off guard by the sudden announcement of the date. Now I think I'll check out my office and see if I can do some damage control."

"One more thing before you go. About Oakley Brisco's death—I think it hit Dr. Caine pretty hard. That could be one reason he's been so antagonistic this week."

"Sure, it might explain this week, but what about last week?" Grant's tone was uncharacteristically sharp. "And the week before that?"

Lauren shrugged. "I just thought you'd want to be warned."

Grant switched on the overhead light in his office and stood in the threshold for several seconds. Time to shake off the disappointment and get on with things. He didn't want to burden Lauren with guilt because she mistakenly thought he should be protected from the news about Hardy's death. And he didn't want to blame Brooke and Beau for doing the same. Hadn't he done that with them in the past? It was one of the millions of love languages of dysfunctional families.

He stepped into the office, bracing himself for whatever he might discover. He wouldn't be surprised to find that Mitchell Caine had arranged for the room to be redecorated while he was gone, but the curtains had not changed, the desk was still the same, the chairs familiar. He strolled to the bulletin board where he kept all the staff schedules.

The red marks gave him his initial clue to the extent of the changes Lauren had mentioned.

Each of the ER schedules, from nursing to secretaries to physicians to surgeons on call, contained changes. Lauren had been relegated almost exclusively to night shifts for the rest of the month. She had *not* mentioned that. How many other things had she neglected to mention?

Mitchell had crossed Dr. Jonas from the list and replaced it with his own name in neat, familiar script. Phil Jonas only worked a few shifts a month to supplement his family practice in Branson. He was part-time at this facility, which was the only way Mitchell Caine could legally remove him from the schedule so quickly after receiving notice.

After further checking, Grant discovered that two of the less experienced nurses had been placed together on weekends—an unwise move, since this emergency department saw about fifty percent more volume on weekends. Muriel was missing from the schedule altogether.

In a surge of anger Grant ripped all the schedules from the board and stacked them on his desk. He punched the number to the call room and drummed his fingers on the desktop while he waited for it to ring three . . . four . . . five times. *Stay calm. Caine is the chief of staff. He has authority over the ER director, and he's a confused, hurting man.*

There was a click, and then a grumpy voice echoed over the speaker-phone. "What is it?"

"Mitchell? This is Grant Sheldon."

There was a grunt of surprise and a muffled groan of bedsprings. "What time is it?"

"Two-thirty in the morning. I just received word that you have a patient waiting for you."

"Patient?"

"Lauren is with her now. If you don't mind, I need to discuss some concerns with you when you get a chance."

"Fine."

"I'll be waiting in my office." He punched the button to disconnect.

He would call Phil Jonas in the morning and make amends, praying the doctor would accept an apology, because he filled a vital role in this facility, particularly when two or more of the regular docs wanted off for vacation or continuing medical education at the same time.

Grant would also call Vonda Slinkard, the nurse director of the ER, and arrange to rescind Muriel's termination and restore the schedules as they had been before he left. He jotted instructions to himself and stuck them onto the respective calendars. There was a slight chance that he was risking his future here at Dogwood Springs by bucking the chief of staff, but it wasn't a serious risk. William Butler had final call on these matters. William would back him.

By the time Grant completed the delicate task of schedule changes, his anger had spent itself. Almost. *Just remember, most physicians aren't like Mitchell Caine.*

Long ago, Grant had discovered the special bond of brotherhood that existed between doctors when they didn't allow their egos to get in the way. It was probably the same for nurses or attorneys or teachers, or any other calling. The medical field was a tough profession.

If they stumbled along the way, Grant could hardly blame them. It didn't mean the calling wasn't there—it just meant they had lost sight of their first call. He, too, had stumbled. Now it was time to deal with a comrade who seemed to have stumbled hard along the way—and he needed to do it with compassion.

He was half-dozing at his desk when the knock came on his office door. He looked up to find Mitchell Caine hovering at the entrance. The doctor's stained lab coat hung in wrinkled folds, and fatigue lined his face.

"You wanted to see me?" The voice was not antagonistic, but it wasn't friendly, either. It was hesitant, cautious, like a truant schoolboy who thought he might have been caught skipping school but wasn't sure.

"Yes, Mitchell. Please come in and sit down."

Caine stepped inside, but he did not sit.

Grant gestured to the sheets of scheduling on his desk. "I notice you've been putting in a lot of hours here lately."

A muscle twitched in Mitchell's right jaw. "I don't see what choice I had. You were out of town, and Jonas chose this week to abandon ship."

Grant nearly choked on his tongue. "I understand the situation. I'll call Dr. Jonas in the morning and talk to him. Meanwhile, I hope to be here at least until next week, and probably longer. I'll be able to do the scheduling. I'm sure you'll be relieved to see that you will be working only the hours you were previously scheduled. That should give you a chance to catch up on some rest."

Mitchell's shoulders straightened and his winged eyebrows lowered. "I spent a great deal of time and effort rearranging those schedules."

"Thank you, Mitchell. I appreciate your efforts, and I'm sorry my absence has made things difficult for you." Grant picked up the sheets in question and kept his voice soft. "I can't use them as they are. The safety of our patients is my first concern, and we need more seasoned nurses on these weekend shifts." He just hoped they hadn't lost half their nursing staff over this outrage. "We also need our night nurse back. I'll call Muriel in the morning." Might as well spill it all out at the same time.

Caine's eyes flared. "You can't do that. I fired that nurse for insubordination. I refuse to work with a member of the staff who is blatantly disrespectful. A nurse *has* to be willing to take orders from the physician on duty and—"

"I'm aware of the situation," Grant said. He didn't mention the fact that he had found a copy in his mail of a grievance report Muriel had filled out. "I understand that it's difficult to maintain order in the ER when a staff member is insubordinate, but I feel this is a special case—we need this nurse, Mitchell. Our hospital is short-staffed as it is, and we can't afford to lose a competent, experienced nurse over one instance of insubordination."

"I can*not* work with her."

"I will review the paper work and speak with her, Mitchell. I'm sorry if she irritates you. We can arrange to have your shifts scheduled so that you can work with nurses with whom you feel most comfortable."

Grant tried to curb his own rising animosity, but he couldn't help thinking about the way this man had treated Beau.

"Will that be all?" Mitchell snapped.

"One more thing." Grant picked up a sheet of names and numbers that had been placed in the center of the desk. "This is the list of ministers in the area who take part in the chaplain call program. I'm curious to know why it's been taken from the bulletin board. Is there a problem with their scheduling?"

A sigh and a nod. "The good reverend called you, did he?"

"Reverend? Nobody called me."

A glimmer of surprise crossed Mitchell's expression, and he shook his head. "Okay. I'm . . . sorry. I . . . was wondering if your . . . if Beau told you about our misunderstanding."

Grant curbed a sharp retort. "Misunderstanding? I don't think those were the exact words Beau used, but yes, he told me what happened. He tends to blame himself more than he should when something bad happens."

Mitchell looked up, and for once there was no coldness in those steely eyes, only the barest glimpse of sorrow. He looked down quickly. "There was a considerable amount of misunderstanding, which began with the guardian of one of our patients and unfortunately escalated before I realized the facts about Beau's situation." His lips gave a sardonic twist. "Lauren was quick to point out my mistake, as was Muriel, and I came in early this evening to express my . . . misgivings to Beau about the unfortunate incident."

"I'm sure he appreciated that," Grant said. "And so do I. Thank you."

Mitchell nodded. He stared down at the floor for a moment, then said in a quiet voice, "He may have told you about the divorce, as well."

"Divorce?"

A long silence. Then another sigh that seemed to reach to the very edges of Mitchell's lung capacity. "Mine."

"No, Mitchell, Beau didn't say anything about that. I'm sorry to hear it." That tight band of anger loosened a little more from around Grant's heart. This was a very viable explanation for so much of Mitchell's poor behavior lately.

"Yes, well, I'm sure you didn't call me in here to listen to musings about my private life," Mitchell said, turning as if to leave.

"On the contrary, I'm here to listen to you any time, and if you prefer professional or spiritual counseling, I will help you contact—"

"No." The hard edge of steel rebounded in his voice. "I have no interest in baring my soul to a stranger, religious or otherwise. As for the chaplain call program, I want nothing to do with it. It's in your hands."

"Good. I believe it is one of the most helpful programs we have at this hospital. They offer a great deal of comfort for the patients and support for our staff. If you change your mind about—"

"I won't." A muscle worked at Mitchell's left jawline. "As long as those ministers refrain from stuffing their programs down the patients' throats—"

"I don't think that will happen. Most patients are closer to prayer in this facility than at any other time."

"That's my point." Mitchell's voice grew stronger. "The ministers take advantage of that."

Grant winced inwardly. He had known that Mitchell was not a believer, but he hadn't seen this depth of animosity before. "I know we're both tired," he said softly. "Neither of us is at his best. Perhaps we should continue this conversation after we've both had a good night's sleep."

"That would probably be best." Mitchell turned on his heel, like a soldier in stride, and left the office.

As Grant watched him go he felt an uncomfortable surge of empathy for the man. Mitchell was obviously in the first stages of grief over the loss of a marriage, and he showed many signs of serious depression. He must be overwhelmed by the pressure, particularly since he didn't seem able to bring himself to rely on anyone but himself. If the pressure continued, the cracks in his relationships with others would become more and more obvious, and his self-control would grow weaker.

What would happen when Mitchell Caine lost his ability to continue the facade? Just as important—how long would it take?

"Lord," Grant whispered at last, "please bless him. Touch Mitchell Caine's heart, and protect him. Heal his wounded spirit, and heal his family." As he prayed, he felt only a whisper of the pain Mitchell must be feeling, the overwhelming darkness. "Show yourself to him, Lord. You are, and always will be, his only hope."

He sat back and finally felt the relief of obedience. He felt the beginning of forgiveness.

CHAPTER 25

U ntil this past June, Tony Dalton had never really heard or felt the power of his own heartbeat. He'd never focused on the exquisite pain of an adrenaline rush through his system. He was never so cognizant of his remaining four senses until after the attack that had robbed him of his most cherished one.

This morning would be, he hoped, the culmination of years of learning, months of teaching, and weeks of strategic planning and detective work from some surprising sources. He'd scheduled everything with detailed precision and much help.

His natural high could end in frustration, however, if he focused on the things he could no longer do. He had to depend on others for the simple act of spying.

A tap of keys on a laptop echoed through the van like a muffled spray of ricocheting bullets.

"The last officers are in place," announced Officer Henry Fulton. "No sign of activity."

"How long until daylight?"

"I'd say ten minutes. Getting cold in here, want some heat?"

Tony reveled in the cold. "Nope, leave the engine off."

"Fingers are getting stiff."

"Sit on 'em for a little bit. That'll warm them up."

They had arrived under cover of darkness. They would wait until first light. Henry—who did his best work behind a keyboard—would be

Tony's eyes. Tony knew Henry couldn't forget the accident last summer. During a raid, Henry had been told not to enter a building until Tony gave the order. He hadn't waited. If Tony hadn't jumped forward when he did, Henry would have taken the full blast of ammonia in the face. Instead, that blast had caught—

"It'll go great, Tony. The guys know what they're doing."

"Anything could happen," Tony growled.

Tony knew Henry hadn't forgiven himself for the accident. This was his first raid in six months, and the tension was thick in his voice and permeated the van.

He was right about one thing, though. Tony's people knew the upcoming sequence in their sleep. The plan wouldn't work everywhere, for every drug raid. It had been custom designed for this setup, this town's drug boss, and these particular raiders. Tony had drilled them, encouraged them, admonished them, and often shouted at them when they didn't want to listen.

He'd told Archer, the other day, that Peregrine was failing. The smell of their production could alert a good agent, who could quickly get a search warrant. A good drug dog was a treasure. But the slippery, more experienced meth producers had made a habit of setting up shop, cooking a batch or two in a short period of time, then dismantling and moving on to escape authorities.

Peregrine was becoming more and more careless, however. Strict surveillance showed that for the past four months he had frequented five rental houses scattered throughout Dogwood Springs. According to sentries, all five houses had been occupied last night. Tony expected his people to find evidence of production in every single house, and they were prepared with protective gear, camouflage, and gas masks.

Today's raid was made possible by private citizens of this town. Since Thursday's funeral the telephone calls to the police department had quadrupled. Public outrage over Oakley Brisco's death was a powerful force. Evan Webster's article in the school paper yesterday had been a clincher. Students and their parents were moved to action, and Tony and his men had been able to work out last-minute details from information they had received from some of these brand-new sources. Tony could kiss Evan Webster.

A few minutes later, when Henry's teeth had begun to clatter almost as loudly as the keyboard, the key-clatter stalled out. "Getting light, Tony. Sun's halfway up, just like you wanted."

Tony spoke into his mouthpiece to the forty-five people who awaited his go-ahead. "Everyone get ready."

The tension mounted and he loved it. Officers had come from all over the county, many on their day off, to work this raid. Peregrine had last been seen entering the house a block down the street, and the sentry had not seen him leave. The stealth with which Tony's raiders moved in would aid them greatly in the surprise attack. Other raids had been successful on Saturday nights in the nearby countryside at rural rave parties, but a dawn surprise attack was perfect today.

Okay, we're ready. We can do this. He pressed the button, gave the word. "Now. Move. Go."

He sat back and listened to Henry's stressed-out breathing. Now was the time to pray. *Please, Lord, no leaks this time. Protect my people. Vengeance is yours, but I intend to revel in the afterglow.*

Henry cleared his throat. "They're going in, surrounding it just as you'd planned."

This was a pivotal point, vital that they stop any communication from the house—any warning to the other places. *Lord, bless our men and women, and when this is over, just let us match faces to photos.*

He heard the first gunshot echo only minutes after his order. He heard Henry's sharp gasp.

"What do you see, Henry?"

"Nothing." The word trembled from the man's throat. "I can't see anything! You want me to g-get out and—"

"Stay here. They know how to take care of themselves." What they wouldn't know how to handle was Henry when he tripped over his own feet.

Another shot, and Henry groaned. He held his breath for a long moment, then started to breathe again. "They're coming out. Look, that detective from Blue Eye's got one handcuffed."

"I can't look right now, Henry, if you know what I—"

Tony's cell phone rang and he pushed the talk button. "Dalton."

"Hi, Sergeant, are those extra ambulances still on standby?"

"Yes. Is the house secured?"

"Yes. Four people in this one, one gunshot wound, one inhalation distress."

"Who's hurt?" He braced himself. He couldn't bear to lose a raider.

"Two of the suspects."

"I'll call an ambulance." Other than that, he could only pray that they had prepared enough.

And pray, he did.

Beau stood in front of the bathroom mirror and practiced his grimace. No changes. It still looked like a lascivious leer. Today he would concentrate on not smiling. It would be hard.

He was a closet romantic. He loved weddings. He loved the tearful smiles, the pageantry, the candles, the music. Most of all he loved the joy of hope. Every time he attended a wedding he imagined how happy his parents must have been on their special day, how beautiful Mom must have been walking down the aisle in clouds of white, and how Dad must have gazed at her with utmost reverence and awe.

Tears came to Beau's eyes as he thought about it—though Mom was dead, he could still feel the power of the love his parents had shared. It was the power of their love that had given him his sense of connection in this family from his earliest memories—that and Brooke's voice, presently raised in complaint about the fit of Dad's tuxedo.

"Those are too tight! You can't wear them, Dad, I won't let you! You look like some . . . some gig—"

"Don't go there, Brooke. I don't see what I can do about it now."

"But why are they so tight? Did the shop get your order mixed up with Archer's? You know he has a flatter stomach than—"

"Watch it."

"I didn't mean you're fat, I just meant that Archer's so much younger than you, he still has—"

"Brooke!" Beau called through the open door of the bathroom. "Shut up, or Dad won't let you catch the bouquet."

"What would I do with a bouquet?"

"Never mind. Just leave Dad alone. He looks great."

"Thank you, Beau," Dad said from the other side of the wall.

"Oh yeah?" Brooke said. "You haven't seen him in the past ten minutes, have you? Come in here and take a look."

"I'm brushing my teeth."

"I hope you're not wearing your jacket. I stopped Dad just in time to keep him from wearing his good shirt to cook breakfast."

"*You* didn't try to cook it, did you?" Beau called to her in alarm.

The ensuing silence twanged with her irritation.

Dad's soothing bass voice came with gentle humor. "I cooked a good breakfast, and it's staying warm in the oven. Now, if Brooke will stop reminding me that my waistline has expanded along with my time-line—"

"That wasn't what I meant," Brooke protested. "I just think they ordered the wrong—"

"Maybe it was supposed to be Hardy's tux," Beau said. Lauren's brothers had both been ushers initially.

Beau crossed the hall and strolled into the master bedroom. "Or maybe they confused it with the one for Mr. Netz. Archer called him to take your place if you didn't get back from St. Louis." He studied the tux with feigned disinterest. He hated it when Brooke was right. It wasn't that Dad looked bad in the tux, but the color was wrong for him. Jessica normally had great taste, but she obviously had grown accustomed to working with flashy colors on stage. Dad looked like a pine tree in his Christmas green tux. It was supposed to be burgundy.

"I don't understand why those people didn't just do the deposition and get it over with," Brooke complained. She sat on the dressing chair beside the bureau, wearing blue jean cutoffs and a T-shirt, painting her toenails with clear polish. "Now you've got to go all the way back up there and fight it again. Who wants a malpractice suit hanging over his head? It's a frivolous suit—anyone with half a brain knows that."

Beau patted Brooke's arm, as if she were a small child. "Sis, we could be talking a jury trial. The plaintiff's attorney will try to keep anyone with more than half a brain out of the jury box."

"They can only do that so many times."

The muted buzz of the telephone, still set for night-ring, floated from Dad's bedside stand. Dad answered.

He listened for a moment, while Brooke continued to apply the polish and Beau sat waiting on the corner of the neatly made, king-sized bed that Mom and Dad had shared for years.

"How many did they get?" The sudden tautness of Dad's voice alerted Beau and Brooke in concerted attention. "Officers wounded?"

Brooke fumbled the open bottle of polish and it dropped to the floor. She stared at Dad, hand suspended in midair, her artificially darkened eyes opening wide in agitated excitement, ignoring the bottle. Beau leaned over and picked it up before it could spill its sticky contents on the carpet.

"The sergeant is there? You are aware he's the best man at a wedding today? Yes, of course I understand the gravity—" He sighed. "Yes." He checked his watch against the time on his bedside clock. "I'll be there." He replaced the receiver and gave a low groan.

"Dad?" Brooke said softly. "How many did they get?"

Dad frowned and turned slowly to look at his daughter. "How do you know what I was talking about?"

Beau caught the bare flicker in Brooke's eyes before she replied. "Simple. The only person I know who is a sergeant, and is also a best man today, is Tony Dalton. Officers wounded? What am I supposed to think?"

"Last time I checked, you weren't a member of any local police force, young lady, and the police should be the only ones with foreknowledge about a drug raid."

Brooke didn't reply.

Dad reached for the top button of a pair of slacks that were far too tight—just as Brooke had said. "I have to change, you two. Finish getting ready. Brooke, you and I will talk about this later. I have to make a detour by way of the hospital."

"But, Dad," Brooke complained, "if you go to the hospital you might not get out in time for the wedding."

"You're right. We'll need some help clearing out the patients. Beau, why don't you come with me?"

Yes! Beau tried not to gloat. "Sure, Dad."

"Me too," Brooke said. "I want to—"

"Brooke, you get ready and go on to the wedding," Dad said.

"What? No, Dad! That isn't fair!"

"Save a place for us."

"But why does Beau get to go with you—"

"Because," Beau said, "I don't scream, throw up, or faint at the sight of bleeding people."

"Neither do—"

"And I know how to stay out of the way and keep my mouth shut—most of the time—in the exam room. Save us a place, Brooke. I'll try to make sure Dad makes it on time."

"But—"

Dad put his hand on the edge of the door and pointed her out of the room. "Later. I'll give you all the gory details as soon as I get them. Just get to the wedding. Go early if you can."

"No way. Archer was crazy enough to ask Evan to take informal pictures before and after the wedding today. Do you know what kind of pest he is when he's trying to catch the perfect shot?"

Dad gave Brooke a kiss on the forehead and nudged her out the door. "Just get dressed and get to the church. We'll fill you in on the details later. And then *you* can tell *me* why you suddenly know so much about secret police business."

———

Even blind, Tony could feel the stares of officers and hospital staff alike as he sat in the center of the ER bustle in his wedding slacks and ruffled shirt, sans bow tie and coat. He didn't care. He was relishing this moment with supreme abandon.

Three of the detainees from two of the meth-lab houses had engaged the officers in gunfire, and two had been wounded in the process. Another had attempted escape after he was handcuffed. He'd fallen into a hole in the yard and had sprained or broken an ankle. Two had inhaled damaging amounts of fumes from their own production in their panic, and one had attempted to swallow the evidence and was now getting her stomach pumped. Did she appreciate the fact that the nurses were trying to save her life? Oh, no. She swore at them all the way through the process—only garbled a little once the tube was in place.

To Tony's joy, no officers were wounded, and in all they had made fourteen arrests. It was just possible that the major artery of drug flow in Dogwood Springs had finally been severed, thanks to the recent increase of cooperation from private citizens.

A familiar stink hovered in the department, of course, although Tony's decontamination people had done their job. Most people would not even recognize that particular smell for what it was, but he could have gagged at the odor.

He spoke softly into his voice-activated recorder as he downloaded orders to be carried out later. One reason Henry was his temporary right-hand man again was because of the wedding, and Caryn's insistence that she be allowed to attend without being called in to take notes.

Another loud complaint streaked through the central section of the ER. Tony suppressed a smile. He probably shouldn't be enjoying this so much, but the success was—

"Sergeant."

"Yes, Henry?"

"You'd better take this call." The man's voice sounded strained. He placed a cell phone into Tony's right hand.

"Okay, what is it?" Tony asked into the receiver.

"Sergeant, you're not going to like this."

"Wilson? Are the houses all secure?"

"Yes."

"Then what's wrong?"

"Our main target got away."

"Royce?"

"That's right."

"But he couldn't have escaped. I ordered four officers on that man. I received report that he had been subdued." Simon Royce could not have gotten away from—

"Prints didn't match the guy we brought in. It wasn't him."

Disappointment mingled with frustration mingled with rage. He could control himself. "The photos. We have the photos—

"Not the same guy."

"Okay, that means Royce is still out there somewhere." It did, didn't it? Tony couldn't bear the thought that he might have gone to all this trouble to catch a man who wasn't even in the area. Evan had said

Peregrine's physical appearance had changed drastically, but the kid had a good eye for detail, and he'd seen the pusher. Tony was going to stick with that hypothesis.

"The houses are secure?" Tony asked.

"All covered. We've got twelve guys booking, five teams securing evidence."

Tony slumped back in his chair. He couldn't believe this was happening.

Archer stood at the open window of his office at the church and listened to car doors slamming and voices of church members greeting one another as they made their way in their wedding-day best toward the entrance. As he had expected, people were arriving early to get a seat. Evan Webster was wandering around the parking lot with his trusty little camera, taking candid shots of the early arrivals. The guests took his antics with good grace.

Except for Evan's clownish attempts to get his subjects to smile, Archer and Jessica had managed to tone down the festivities in honor of the recently deceased. Heather, Jessica's sister, would be singing an extra song to commemorate Hardy's life and heroism. It would be hard on the family, who would be here today, but he also knew it would mean a lot.

He looked at his watch. It had moved forward two minutes from his last check. Heather wasn't here yet. Neither was Grant or Tony. Why not? It was nine-thirty, and the wedding was scheduled for ten.

Lord, please let this day go well. I know it's a selfish request, but—

There was a knock at the door.

"Yes?"

"Archer? It's Caryn. I need to tell you something."

No, Lord. Oh, please, no. He walked to the door and opened it. Caryn wore a dress of light blue silk, and she was wearing makeup. He concentrated on these things, because he didn't want to think about why she was here.

"Tony and his men made a big raid a few hours ago." There was an excitement in her voice and life in her eyes that he hadn't seen in quite some time. "Big raid. Archer, they called in units from all over the county, got all kinds of stuff. There was apparently some gunfire and a couple of accidents. At last report, none of the officers were injured, but Tony might be late. He's at the hospital."

"Is he okay?"

"Hyper as all get-out. He won't be okay for weeks, considering the paper work we'll have to complete. He doesn't need illegal drugs to get high. A raid like this will last him for months."

"Then maybe he'll agree to the clinical trial."

"Wouldn't it be great?" She sounded almost like the old Caryn.

"I'll see about delaying the wedding as long as possible." What else could he do? Tony would get here as soon as he could.

Tony clenched and unclenched his fists as he forced himself to remain seated in the staff break room. Peregrine had done it again. He had evaded capture. One of the suspects had admitted, just moments ago, that Simon Royce—aka Peregrine—had been with her last night, teaching her the latest meth recipe, and when the batch was completed he had slipped out into the darkness and walked away.

Had he taken any of the drug with him? No. He had given himself an injection just before leaving—but had not taken any drugs with him—and left with instructions to sell the rest and hold his share of the proceeds until he returned for them. The suspect had volunteered the information that she thought Peregrine was drinking, as well.

Tony felt comfort in the fact that their prime suspect was still in the vicinity.

A quick call got Wilson on the telephone again. "I want you and Brymer under cover," Tony said. "Find Peregrine. I want Johnson and Deleuth and Spaldron and Baler under cover, as well. Wear your bullet-proof gear."

Three two-man teams could cover the places Peregrine was known to frequent. Maybe he'd slipped up. Maybe he'd stopped somewhere before he got out of town. Sloppy as he'd grown lately, that was always a possibility.

"He has a couple of girlfriends he's been seen with in the past few months." He gave Wilson the names and addresses. "Check them out. Look up our informants." The thing was, most of the people who worked closely with Peregrine were now being booked. "Keep in close contact with the booking officers. They may get more information from our suspects."

"Sergeant, he's going to be dangerous."

"Don't I know it. That's why I want you to use extra caution. Put out an APB, notify all local agencies. Do you know if he had access to a car?"

"That hasn't been established."

"No reports of stolen vehicles?"

"No, but I'll check again."

"Be sure everyone has a copy of the most recent picture we have of him, and don't forget that description of the light-colored four-by-four Dodge truck he might be driving. I want this guy stopped before he kills somebody. Don't give him time to find a new hideout."

"Okay, Tony. We're on it."

Tony hung up and began praying in earnest. If Peregrine was tweaking, he would be as dangerous as a small troop of officers.

Were they missing something? Did he have contacts they didn't know about?

Pressing this guy into a corner could be dangerous, and Tony didn't want his people injured. But he didn't want any citizens injured, either.

He felt the face of his Braille watch. The wedding was almost ready to begin, and typically a best man should be somewhere in the vicinity of the altar when the ceremony took place. He knew Archer would appreciate it if he made an effort to attend church today.

Okay, this could still work. All was not lost. Even though Tony had apparently encountered a roadblock, Archer trusted him. Tony would be here. The wedding would take place, and this next week was going to be wonderful, with no interruptions. No trips to the hospital. He expected to suffer severe withdrawal pains from his cell phone—for perhaps five minutes. Dad was filling the pulpit for the next week, and Jessica didn't have a show for eight days.

Christmas madness was threatening to implode on them when they returned home, but for a week they would have peace.

The parking lot continued to fill, and Archer checked his watch again. Would the world end if Jessica walked down the aisle fifteen minutes later than planned?

Better check and see.

He strode through the fancy reception room—the decor of which the reception committee and the kitchen committee had battled over for the past two years—knocked on and opened the door to the bride's dressing room, and stepped into the hushed, carpeted haven of floral bouquets and ficus trees.

"Oh, no, you don't, Pastor!" Mrs. John Netz honed in on him the moment he stepped over the threshold. She charged toward him like a mama elephant protecting her calf. "You'll see her soon enough."

A bright flash alerted him, and he turned to see Evan grinning at him from the hallway, glasses reflecting the overhead light, making it impossible to see his eyes, just his white, slightly crooked teeth. He must have lost his contact lenses again. Of course he would be thrilled at catching a pose of his pastor being barred from the bride's dressing room.

Archer turned back to the self-appointed guard. "I understand how you feel, Mrs. Netz, but I've received word that there might be a delay."

"Nobody delays a wedding for more than five minutes without bringing bad luck on the bride and groom during the honeymoon." She gave him a look over the tops of her glasses. "You don't want that to happen, do you?"

He saw the twinkle in her eye just before opening his mouth to reprimand her for believing in luck instead of the blessing of the Lord. He grinned. "Would you please just tell Jessica that Tony's been delayed?"

"Archer, the photographer's on a tight schedule today. We might have to go on without him."

"I can do it, Archer!" Evan exclaimed, rushing forward eagerly. "I'd love to do it for you."

Archer held a hand up to control the young man's excitement. "Jessica's sister hasn't arrived either, and she's the maid of honor and the soloist. The photographer should have taken minor holdups into consideration."

Mrs. Netz pressed her lips together and nodded. "We'd better pray they get here."

Archer had already been doing that. He walked down to the church foyer, where family and friends in their finest clothes rushed over to greet him and compliment him on his tuxedo and the high polish on his shoes and the healthy flush of his face.

He smiled and thanked them and paced the full length of the vestibule before the door opened again. In walked Lauren and Brooke. Lauren wore a hunter green wool suit, and her hair fell over her shoulders in soft blond curls. Brooke wore a demure knit dress of soft blue green that brought out the blue tones of her pretty gray eyes.

"Smile!" *Flash*. Another chuckle from Evan.

"Evan Webster," Brooke said, "if you use that thing against me one more time I'll break one of your fingers."

"You look pretty, Brooke. Let me take one more picture. Please?"

"No. And remember, you're not supposed to disturb people. Stop using your flash." She turned her back on him just as he snapped another picture of her. She ignored him. "Archer, isn't it bad luck or something for the groom to be seen before the wedding?"

"No, and I don't believe in luck. Where are your father and brother?"

"Hospital."

He smiled and nodded, suppressing the urge to scream. *Hello? Lord, are you there? Would you please test my faith some other time?*

"They wouldn't even let me go with them," Brooke said.

"Two of the deacons have been pressed into service as ushers," Archer said.

"Sorry. It sounded urgent. Big bust or something."

"Bust!" Evan exclaimed a little too loudly. "Did you say bust? As in police?"

Brooke rolled her eyes. "Yes, Evan, that's what I said, but I didn't mean to announce it to the whole church." She eyed the camera. "Did you get those other negatives developed?"

"Not all of them." He pointed to his watch. "And not these. I haven't figured out how to download them yet."

The front door opened again, and a young woman in her early twenties breezed into the foyer, her long purple—*purple!*—hair shimmering across her nearly bare shoulders, black lipstick gouged in a straight line over her mouth. Someone gasped behind him. It sounded like Archer's secretary, Mrs. Boucher.

He studied the young woman more closely and felt a slow trickle of dread climb up his spine. It was Jessica's younger sister, Heather. He'd barely recognized her through the thick layer of pale makeup on her face and the heavy caking of black over her eyelashes. Worse, her dress—if it could be called that—was made of material disturbingly similar to the bridesmaid's dresses Jessica had chosen—but it wasn't the same style. It had spaghetti straps that appeared ready to snap, and the neckline plunged several inches lower than he ordinarily saw inside these church walls.

If he so chose, he could see her navel through the peek-a-boo lace cutout over her belly. He also saw pink fishnet stockings beneath a hem that ended several inches above her knees.

Flash! Chuckle. Heather's smile was broad and friendly and earned another flash.

Archer heard three more gasps and was afraid several ladies in his congregation would swoon if Heather walked down the aisle in that getup. Jessica had warned him. He should have been expecting something . . . but this?

Before he could recover, Lauren and Brooke had stepped over and introduced themselves to her. Brooke asked where she could find a pair of stockings like Heather's, and Lauren asked about the purple hair. He wished they wouldn't encourage her.

Sweat broke out on his forehead.

Flash! Chuckle.

Archer didn't want to have to injure Evan.

CHAPTER 26

I n the final moments of quiet organ music, while the bridesmaids congregated in the vestibule, Grant led the way toward the packed auditorium ahead of Beau, wondering whom the ushers had drafted to take his place to help seat this crowd. He wished he'd been here, but he'd had no choice. He and Beau hovered in the back, searching for the top of Brooke's dark head.

Someone nudged him from behind, and he turned to find Evan poised behind him, camera at eye level, grinning broadly.

"Smile!"

"Evan," Beau said, "shouldn't you be in your—"

Flash! "I'm helping with photography." Evan held the camera up as if it were proof.

"You're not supposed to disturb the guests," Beau said. "Turn off your flash, and don't be so conspicuous."

"Nobody'll pay any attention to me. Photographers tend to blend into the woodwork."

"This is a wedding, not a ball game."

"Beau, you're beginning to sound like Brooke," Evan complained.

"You'll thank me later for not letting you make a fool of yourself. Don't let all the hype about those articles go to your head."

"But Jessica said I could take pictures. She *asked* me to."

"She didn't ask you to make a mockery out of one of the most important days of her life."

"Fine, I'll turn off the flash. Will that make you happy?"

"And no jumping up to the platform. Stay in your seat and don't draw attention to yourself or Brooke will have to kill you later."

Evan scowled at him, then shrugged and preceded them into the auditorium.

"There's Lauren, sitting beside her family." Beau pointed toward the center section. "Brooke's beside her. Looks like they saved us a place."

Grant led the way down the aisle, where each pew was decorated with burgundy poinsettias tied with lace. The leaves matched the tux that lay across his bed at home.

He reached the pew where Lauren and Brooke sat, and he couldn't help admiring the way Lauren's hair tumbled over her shoulders, the way she sat with her shoulders straight, her head high. And she was wearing her best color.

He leaned down and whispered into her left ear. "May we sit here?"

She nodded and scooted while Brooke, seated to her right, glared at them and pointed at her watch. "You're way late, Dad," she mouthed soundlessly.

He nodded a greeting toward the occupants in the remainder of the row—Lauren's mother and Hardy's wife and daughters. Lauren's other brother, Roger, was ushering, but his family filled the pew behind them. The McCaffreys were out in full force.

Grant returned his attention to Lauren. "Thanks for saving a place for us."

She smiled, and he saw the quiver of her chin, the moisture in her eyes, and he knew she was struggling with this. Initially, both of her brothers had been chosen to serve as ushers. With Hardy's death, their father had stood in for him. Hardy should be here.

Grant took her hand and squeezed it. She squeezed back, hard. In his side vision he could see her mother nudge her sister. Grant found himself wishing Lauren's mother wasn't quite so obvious.

As enchanting classical piano music—with a stylistic country lilt—filled the auditorium, the seven-year-old flower girl, Archer's niece, Morgan, walked with slow, practiced confidence along the aisle. She carried a basket of long-stemmed dark red roses. After a few measured steps, a bridesmaid followed.

During the procession the three groomsmen paced themselves across the floor one at a time to meet the bridesmaids and escort them up the steps to the platform. Tony came in last, using the tip of his cane against the bottom step to guide him.

Grant relaxed. They had made it.

Archer had never cried at a wedding before, but he feared he might break with tradition at his own. He'd been uncomfortably emotional these past few days, and it didn't seem to be abating. Part of that emotion was grief over Hardy McCaffrey's death, especially linked with the tragedy of Oakley Brisco. He had to admit another part of it was from nerves. Heather and Evan headed his list of stressors, but Tony hadn't helped when he'd rushed into the pastor's office—which was doing double duty as a dressing room for the groom and his groomsmen—five minutes after the organ chimed its first lofty notes across the auditorium.

But most of the emotion that filled Archer was joy. How many times in the past year had he been convinced this day would never happen? Even this week he'd had his doubts.

Okay, just a twinge of that emotion was irritability. Evan Webster had taken Jessica's request for casual snapshots far too seriously. At least he was sitting down now, camera in lap, beside his father. The fact that his father, Norville Webster, was sitting beside Mayor Jade Myers had caused a great deal of commotion among the ranks of certified, self-appointed gossips.

Tony moved with grace and dignity along the front of the steps and stood waiting to escort Heather—

Heather!

Archer stopped breathing and gave his attention to the central aisle, where a beautiful young woman with golden blond hair and a demure dress in green silk—and a wicked grin—took her time coming down the aisle to meet Tony. No purple hair. No lace-covered navel or cleavage. No black lipstick.

Archer was able to breathe again, and he chuckled to himself, partly from relief, partly from amusement.

Tony escorted her up the steps with perfect grace, and she made her way across the stage toward the piano, where she was to sing. But first she paused in front of Archer and winked.

"Had you scared, didn't I," she whispered.

He returned her audacious smile. Someday she would get married—if she ever found a man with enough stamina to keep up with her singing schedule and her outrageous personality—and on that day Archer would enlist his wife's help to wreak vengeance on his sister-in-law.

Jessica had warned him that her family would require some adjustments, but he thought he'd done all that months ago.

The music changed as Heather took her place, and Archer looked toward the back of the auditorium. The congregation stood, and something expanded inside his heart—it was amazed joy.

Jessica's smile of adoration radiated toward him as she stepped down the aisle. She wore a simple gown of white silk and walked alone, holding a bouquet of poinsettias. She floated down the aisle as if escorted by angels.

Joy shone in her eyes as she looked up at him.

He stepped down to the bottom of the steps and took her arm to guide her up beside him. Together they turned and gazed out at the much beloved faces of family, friends, congregation. At this moment he knew he was the wealthiest man on earth.

He saw the glowing candles—which signified the eternal flame of their love as they remained connected to the source of true love. They had discussed who would do the honors of lighting the candles, since Jessica's mother had died years ago and her father, a near hermit, terrified of crowds, had barely been convinced to attend the wedding. Instead of using the traditional mother's candles, they had designated two of Archer's nephews to do all the candle lighting. Now the stage glowed with the gentle flames.

Heather's voice entranced the congregation with its purity during the love song "Perfect Moments," which Jessica had written. Archer and Jessica lit their unity candle and knelt together at the altar to pray while Heather sang "The Lord's Prayer."

They had written their own ring ceremony, and Jessica's voice quivered with emotion as she spoke the words that came from her heart.

Heather's song of memorial to Hardy drew Archer's tears at last, and Jessica reached out to take his hand, even though that wasn't in the script.

At the end of the ceremony, when the groom was finally instructed by the minister—Dad—to kiss the bride, Archer drew his wife into his arms with gentle tenderness. He gazed into her eyes and lowered his head to touch her lips with his own.

This moment belonged to him and Jessica alone. He forgot the congregation, forgot all the tension and stress. He held the love of his life in his arms, and nothing had ever felt more wonderful or more right.

Someone chuckled near the front row, and he released Jessica at last, holding that kiss in his heart as a promise of the joy that was to come, and they turned to face the auditorium as husband and wife. All their loved ones burst into spontaneous, energetic applause.

Life couldn't get any better. And no one could steal this joy.

At Archer's request, Grant checked out the decoy getaway vehicle, Archer's Kia, at the far end of the parking lot. It had been decorated with pink-and-blue ribbons and bows and was filled with tissue paper. The steering wheel had been chained, and a string of fifty or sixty keys—which Archer and Jessica would ostensibly be expected to try in the padlock until they found the right one—lay on the seat. Archer had "trusted" Roger McCaffrey with the care of the car. And Roger had fallen for his ruse. Grant hoped he wouldn't be disappointed when Archer and Jessica went driving off in Jessica's Subaru Outback, which was parked safely in Grant's garage.

He heard the sound of sneaking footsteps behind him, and he turned in time to catch Evan with the camera to his face.

Flash-snap-whine. The auto-advance was getting tired. The battery was running down.

"Evan, if you're not careful, that thing's going to grow into your eye. You'll be a cyborg, and you won't be able to run without batteries."

Evan closed the automatic lens cover and stuck the camera in his pocket. The broad grin, which had appeared to be a permanent fixture on his acne-marked face through most of the service, spread to an impossible width. "Three people have already asked me to be the photographer at their Christmas parties, Dr. Sheldon." He looked at the car, and his eyes widened. "Oh man, did you do that? Archer's going to kill you."

Grant smiled. He laid an arm across Evan's shoulders and walked with him back to the church dining room, where the reception was being held. "So, Evan, I hear you and Brooke have been lending your expertise to do a little undercover work for our local police department."

He felt Evan's shoulder tense. "Oh. Sergeant Dalton told you?"

"He told me." And that wasn't all they'd discussed. Grant couldn't help reacting like a father—horrified by the danger Evan and Brooke had placed themselves in, and proud of their courage.

He was also hurt by the fact that both of his kids had been keeping too many secrets from him lately. Time for a little talk.

Archer and Jessica took a break from greeting their guests, posed for their last picture, and tasted the cake and punch. Archer wolfed down a handful of mixed nuts and took another swallow of punch with two more forkfuls of cake. He and Jessica wouldn't have lunch until they reached Eureka Springs this afternoon. He'd made reservations. But he was starved right now.

Leaning close to Jessica's left ear, he whispered, "Roger fell for the decoy. He's decorated my car and locked the steering wheel. He did the same thing at Hardy's wedding, so I knew what to expect."

"My car's at Grant's, right?"

"Yes, but . . . I'd really like to play along if you don't mind the extra time."

She looked up at him, and her gaze grew tender. She cupped his chin with her hand and kissed him. "Of course I don't mind."

"The family'll get a big kick out of it."

"So will I."

He took her into his arms. "I love you."

"Grounded! What do you mean we're grounded?" Brooke's cry of personal offense echoed through the reception hall, attracting attention from several of the guests standing in line for cake and punch.

"And what do you mean we're *both* grounded?" Though Beau's

voice didn't carry as well as his sister's, his outrage matched hers in intensity. "I've been home taking care of things while Brooke's been driving all over the Ozarks with Evan—"

"Evan and I were being responsible citizens, making sure creeps like Peregrine didn't get away with—"

"You've *both* been keeping vital information from *me*." Grant leaned across the table, which he had chosen because it was in a far corner of the room that hadn't yet begun to fill with guests. "I'm well aware of our family's tendency to keep secrets from one another on the premise that we're protecting one another. I've got news for you—it doesn't work that way. I'm still your father, and no matter how grown up you two think you are, I'm *still* in charge." He saw Brooke's eyes widen as his own voice carried a little more clearly than he'd meant for it to.

"Sorry, Dad." There was still some discomfort in Beau's voice. "I know we should have told you about Hardy—"

"I'm not talking about Hardy—although I think I've made my feelings clear to Lauren about that incident. I'm talking about the stalker who rammed you."

Beau's lips parted in surprise. "Tony told you about *that*?"

"Tony assured me that he never promised to keep your secret, Beau. He's a policeman, and you're a minor. As your father, I have a right to know what's going on in your life so that I'll know how to protect you. I would never have left you two alone for a week and a half if I'd been informed about your activities."

"Lauren was with us," Brooke said.

"Lauren was working half of those nights, and she had a few nightmares of her own."

"But, Dad, if you hadn't gone to St. Louis you wouldn't have been able to defend yourself against that suit, and your whole professional reputation would have been ruined, and you wouldn't have found out about Grandma, and who knows what would have happened to her if—"

"Don't even try those excuses with me, Beau. You didn't know all those things were going to happen when you withheld that information—you were just trying to protect me. I don't need protection; I need

the whole story. I'm your father." He held his son's gaze until Beau nodded and looked away, then he looked at Brooke. "And *you*—"

"I know." She held her hands up in front of her face in a gesture of
self-preservation. "I'm a horrible daughter for making my father worry
about me and risking my life—"

"You're a wonderful daughter, and I'm proud of both of you. I still
haven't come to grips with it all, but I do know you're both still
grounded until further notice." He raised a hand when they both started
to protest. "It's for your physical protection. No cruising, no movies, no
'research' for one of Evan's articles unless you're with a crowd or with
me or another adult I trust."

Beau nodded first. "Okay, Dad. You're right."

Brooke gave Beau a glare that labeled him as a traitor, then she
slumped in her seat. "Fine."

Grant knew he would have to be satisfied with that for now. "I love
you both."

"Yeah, I know, we love you, too," Brooke said grudgingly. "Can we
get in line for some cake now? And you might check on Lauren and see
why she's sitting all by herself over there in the far corner of the room."

Grant followed the direction of her gaze. "I think I'll do that. Enjoy
the food, and don't forget you're on a short leash."

Lauren was still sitting by herself when Grant reached her. Mr. and
Mrs. McCaffrey were visiting with Archer's parents three tables away,
and the rest of the clan were still in line.

"Are these seats saved?" he asked.

Lauren pulled the chair out beside her at the round table, which
could easily seat six and would stretch to fit eight when needed. There
were seven chairs around it. "Just brace yourself for the family," she
warned.

"I like your family." He took the chair and gestured toward the bride
and groom, who stood greeting an endless line of guests. "I can't stop
watching Archer and Jessica." If he wasn't careful, he could step over
the line and commit the sin of envy.

"Archer's had that silly smile on his face ever since the kiss," Lauren
said.

Grant turned and watched Lauren in silence for a moment. "You've been quiet for the past hour. Are you doing okay?"

She nodded. If the joy was contagious, it hadn't reached her eyes yet.

"Want to go fishing?" he asked. If anything would perk her up, it would be a trip to her favorite fishing hole.

She looked at him. "It's cold outside. The thermometer read below freezing when I got up this morning."

Okay, so nothing would perk her up. He'd never seen her this quiet. It disturbed him. "Why don't you come over for a movie this afternoon. Brooke said she found a good comedy at Wal-Mart the other day, and the kids are grounded."

No reaction to that announcement. "Not today. I volunteered to stay and clean up after the reception."

"I'll stay too, then. We'll draft Brooke and Beau, and we'll ask Evan to take pictures of Brooke picking up trash."

That got a grudging grin out of her. "I can just hear what Brooke will have to say about that."

He'd grown very accustomed to that smile, and he missed it when he didn't see it. He liked to think that she seemed to smile more often when he was nearby.

"Lauren, I have a question for you."

She turned to him with polite interest. He did not feel encouraged. He did, however, intend to ask the question anyway, since it had been on his mind quite a bit this past week.

"Would you laugh at me if I asked you out on a real date?"

She raised a delicate blond eyebrow at him. "Has Brooke been nagging you again?"

"No more than usual. What do you think?"

"What do you call a real date?"

Well, she hadn't turned him down yet. And she wasn't laughing. "A real date is when I ask you to dinner at Lambert's and a show in Branson, just the two of us, and I pay for all of it, like the stick-in-the-mud male that I am, and I do the driving."

"So you're talking about one of those old-fashioned kinds of dates." A flicker of life had rekindled in those green eyes. It was a good sign.

"Yes, but I'm not finished. When I take you back to your house, I walk you to the door and give you a good-night ... uh, kiss ... and wait until you lock your door before I drive away."

"I haven't been out on a date like that—"

"Hold it, I'm still not finished. The next day I send you a bouquet of flowers—better yet, something that is green and hasn't been disconnected from its root system—that way it will match the living green of your eyes. And I would include a card to remind you about what a good time I—and hopefully you—had."

She sat watching him in silence for a few seconds. "Can I talk now?"

He nodded.

She gave him a real, Lauren-like smile this time. "It's no wonder Annette adored you. Do you know how many men would insist on seeing me safely inside and then resist leaving? Most men don't leave."

Grant suppressed a grin. "They *don't?*"

The resulting flush spread up from her neck. She was charming when she embarrassed herself like this. It was a habit of hers. "Uh, I'm not talking about myself. That isn't what I meant. I'll just say that it's been my experience that a large percentage of men who would go to all that trouble would definitely expect return favors, if you know what—"

"I know what you mean." He leaned forward. "You know me better than that. I have a great deal of respect for you, Lauren."

"Thank you." The flush receded, and she folded her hands carefully on the table in front of her. "It sounds like a dream date, Grant."

"Really?"

She stared down at her hands. "Yes. It does."

Her hesitation concerned him. "Of course, it would need to be with the right man."

That grin teased her lips once more. "Yes, I suppose it would."

"But it seems to me I heard you say, not long ago, that you didn't believe it was God's will for you to marry."

She nodded.

"Not that one date would constitute marriage," he said quickly.

"Of course not. Although my mother always told me never to date a man I wouldn't consider marrying someday." She paused, cleared her throat, and leaned closer. "You see, all my life I'd wanted to get married and have a family—so much so that I made a fool of myself a couple of times."

"So you say."

She grimaced. "So I *know*. Remember the rumors that spread through the hospital about Archer and me?"

"I seem to remember some silly—"

"—rampaging locomotive of gossip—"

"—which everyone knows wasn't true."

Lauren blushed again. "I suffered a lot for that one little slip of the tongue, and I wasn't the only one who paid for that rumor."

"I know."

"I mean, all I did was tell Gina, one time, that I thought Archer would be a great father and . . . and that I was—"

"Attracted to him. I know about all that, Lauren."

"But I'm not now."

Grant chuckled. "Would you stop trying to redeem yourself? You didn't do anything wrong, you know. It isn't a sin for a single woman to be attracted to a single man."

"Yeah? Well, for too long I went around developing crushes on the wrong men—oh, they were good, kind Christian men and all, but it always became apparent to me, a little too late, that they weren't interested."

He touched her hand. "Their loss."

"You know the night you found me at Honey Creek?"

"I'm not likely to forget that. For a while, there, I was afraid we'd lost you, Lauren." She'd been one of the hardest hit by the mercury poisoning because she regularly ate the fish and drank the water from the source of the creek.

"I had a kind of . . . oh, I don't know . . . a kind of epiphany that night," she said. "I was so hurt by the rumor Gina had told me about, and I felt so rejected. I asked God why He had never allowed me to have the husband and family I had always longed for."

"And He told you?"

"He showed me, step by step, that He wanted me to give my heart totally to Him, that I was to put no other gods before Him, and that included, especially for me, the god of husband and family. That was when I realized I hadn't given Him my whole heart because I had always been on the lookout for that special man. God wants our whole hearts, Grant."

"Yes, He does, but that doesn't mean you have to live the rest of your life without another human being for company."

"It isn't like that. He's put me in a family, in a way. I was here for Brooke and Beau when you needed me to be."

"And when will that need end? Did you ever consider the possibility that God might have intended to place you in a more permanent arrangement? Where you're very much needed?"

Lauren caught her breath. Grant knew he sometimes tended to be as bold and outspoken as his daughter. He wasn't sorry.

"You know I care a lot for Beau and Brooke. Friends can be family, but no one takes the place of God in my life."

"No one's asking that of you, but Lauren, godly, sincere people marry and make lives together and serve God *together*. Is that so unbelievable?"

"No, but there's nothing wrong with my state of singleness. And now I embrace it, and I shower God with all the love I would once have showered on a man."

"That's a good thing, but if you will remember a recent conversation we had, you reminded me that, even though I once thought my mission was to work in the ER in St. Louis, God might have had other ideas. He brought me down here for a reason. Couldn't He be doing the same for you? Now that you've reached that place in your life where you have embraced your singleness and have learned to be content where you are, maybe He's ready to move you on to another kind of contentment."

She paused, as if considering his suggestion for a moment.

"What I'm saying is that, with God, we need to be able to expect the unexpected. His mind doesn't work the way ours do."

She hesitated again.

"I always tell Brooke and Beau that, if they truly seek God's will in a matter, He will answer them in several ways over a period of time. They just have to be willing to *take* that time and be patient as they wait. I think—"

"I saw you two huddled over here together in the corner," came a cheerful greeting from behind them.

They turned to find Lauren's mother, Liz McCaffrey, pulling a chair from beneath the table. She sat down beside Lauren. She patted her daughter on the shoulder and gave Grant a conspiratorial wink. "Aren't weddings a wonderful way to bring out the romantic in us all?"

A gleam of stubborn rebellion suddenly shot through Lauren's eyes. Grant knew that look well, and he wanted to kindly nudge Liz away from the table. Didn't she realize that her loving manipulation drove her daughter crazy?

Sure enough, after a few moments of light conversation with her parents, Lauren pushed away from the table. "Looks like I need to get busy. People are leaving."

lmost home." Archer reached for Jessica's hand as he crossed the bridge over King's River late Friday afternoon. He felt the return pressure of her fingers and, for perhaps the millionth time in the past week, thanked God with great fervor for her presence in his life.

"So that's what honeymoons are all about," he murmured.

Her fingers tightened around his, then withdrew so he could replace his hand on the steering wheel. "I'm glad we didn't go to Hawaii," she whispered.

"We didn't need Hawaii." What they'd needed was that wonderful cabin in the woods—with no telephone, no cable television, and no visitors for a whole week. "We had each other."

"True."

He heard the hesitance in her voice. Their hearts had become so tuned to each other this past week that he felt as if he could actually hear her thoughts. "Jess, I truly don't think my macho pride is so muscle-bound that the difference in our incomes is going to cause me a lot of grief." Particularly since she had begun sending half her yearly income to support the Missouri Baptist Children's Homes all across the state. In spite of what she gave, however, they could have easily met the financial challenge of a trip to Hawaii. "Honest. I think I can learn to enjoy a working wife."

She didn't reply.

After the road widened once more, he again reached across the distance between them and touched her arm. "I mean that, sweetheart."

"I know you do. It isn't you I'm worried about, Archer—it's me. Helen said something a few minutes before the wedding, when we were waiting for Grant and Tony to arrive from the hospital."

"Helen *Netz?*"

"Now, don't get all excited. That's why I didn't say anything to you sooner. I knew you were already worried about the effect the stress of being a pastor's wife would have on me."

"You're right, I was." Was the church already causing trouble in their marriage? Their one-week anniversary wasn't until tomorrow.

Mrs. Netz should know better. That strong-willed lady's interfering husband had caused a well-intentioned mess last summer when he'd listened to an audacious rumor about Archer and Lauren McCaffrey. Thanks to him, Jessica still had her reservations about Lauren.

"Maybe I shouldn't have said anything," Jessica muttered.

"Too late. What did Helen tell you?"

"She said that she was sure I would receive my call from God sooner or later."

Archer bit his tongue until the irritated retort slid back down his throat. "And of course you were gentle when you set her straight."

"You don't think I'm going to receive a call from God?" Jessica's voice held that hushed quality that it always did when she was preparing to disagree with anything he said. It was a stubborn streak that had attracted him to her in the first place. Sometimes he was attracted by the most bizarre things.

"I have no doubt about your calling, and neither do you. People travel from all over the world to hear you sing."

"Maybe there's something I haven't—"

"And all that without showing a hint of cleavage."

"Archer, what I'm trying to say is—"

"That's pretty impressive, if you ask—"

"Archer!"

"Sorry. I'm just trying to say that you already have your hands full with that one very special calling, and we've already discussed this in detail. I never asked you to give up your gift in order to follow some silly church program. Church families are like natural families. They can, at times, be a little too possessive."

"But I'm your wife now—"

"Yes, that's become quite apparent to me these past few days. Yee-haww!"

"Archer Pierce, would you shut up and listen to me!" But even as she snapped the words, he could hear the humor in her voice. He wasn't in trouble.

"Yes, dear."

She giggled. Until this past week, he hadn't realized she was a giggler. She never giggled in front of anyone else, and never on stage. Only for him, in the privacy of their own home. Life didn't get any better.

"I can see I'm going to be forced to table this conversation until you can get serious," she said with mock sternness.

He felt guilty for about half a second. Then they crested the final hill into Dogwood Springs. Dusk had begun to slide across the sky, and now it hovered over the hillside city in a golden haze, enhanced by the iridescent Christmas decorations along the streets and quaint village shops.

"Welcome home, Jessica Pierce. Your presence here is going to show our citizens what true beauty, and true calling, are all about." In a few days they would celebrate their first Christmas together as husband and wife.

Could life get any better?

———

Darkness seeped over the sleepy town, and Simon Royce braved the blacktop road without turning on his headlights. His hands shook on the steering wheel, and he could hear the quiver in his breathing. He'd been hiding out like an animal for a week, only daring to sneak out at night for food. Every time he had gone near Dogwood Springs he'd seen a police cruiser. After nearly barging in on a raid last Saturday he'd headed for the densest part of the national forest and lain low.

If he hadn't recognized the outline of a police car in the darkness he would be in jail right now. So who had slipped up? Who had told the cops?

Every time he blinked he saw police! They were everywhere. He had hardly slept in two weeks and he needed to crash, but he didn't want to freeze to death, and he didn't want to get caught while he slept.

He hadn't eaten in three days. His familiar haunts in the forest seemed to mock him. Everyone he called on his cell phone refused to answer. *Backstabbers!*

He gripped the steering wheel in his hands, feeling he could almost bend it with the force of his anger. Someday he would break the thing.

He'd like to break some *heads*. After all he'd done for them, after all the money he'd brought in for them, they'd turned their backs on him. Gil Proctor, the moron, had probably let someone follow him home from the hospital the day he blew the new recipe and nearly killed himself.

The rumble of the truck echoed back from the buildings when he turned into an alley at the edge of town. A car was parked in the way. He slammed the brakes. The truck's motor died. He screamed a curse and kicked at the dash once, twice, three times until his anger receded.

He'd like to ram that car the way he'd rammed those teenagers in town that day—Webster and his stupid friends.

Webster. That little pimply-faced kid with the big mouth and the wimpy body and the big words. Those bleating articles about meth production had gotten everybody all stirred up.

Peregrine cranked the key, shoved the truck in reverse and backed out onto the street, stomped the brakes again, jerked the gear into drive. "I'd like to stomp Webster's face!"

Headlights flashed through the cab of the truck, and Peregrine froze. *Come on, maintain. Don't lose control. If you do, they'll catch you. Don't call attention to yourself. . . .*

Now, where could a weary man go to get warm and crash for a while? Who hadn't been arrested?

He drove a few blocks, studying the parked cars along the silent street until he saw a familiar house with a crumbling front porch and torn screens on the windows. That was where Jamey's mom lived.

Jamey . . . what was the last name? Younts. She didn't like his drugs, but she couldn't turn him in. She wouldn't. She thought he loved her, and she was going to have his baby.

He would check to see if she'd moved back in with her mother. If she was still at the motel, he could stay with her tonight. Meanwhile, he had to get off the street—had to hide the truck.

Lauren paused at the central ER desk at shift change and gave report to Muriel, who was back on the job. Dr. Jonas would be in soon to relieve Grant. Thanks to Grant's timely intervention when he returned home from St. Louis last week, hurt feelings had been soothed.

Meanwhile, there was a celebration of sorts taking place in Grant's office. William Butler, hospital administrator and veteran Lyme disease victim, had walked into the department fifteen minutes ago with Jade Myers. He looked well rested and happy. After appropriate treatment and a vacation to visit family in Ohio, he had returned to work this afternoon with renewed vigor.

Jade Myers looked good, too, with that short, midnight dark hair that set off her dark, deep-set eyes. And she'd appeared especially pleased to see Grant this evening—a little more pleased than a town mayor ordinarily was to see a doctor.

For some reason that bugged Lauren, and the fact that it bugged her *really* bugged her. Jade was dating Norville Webster now, so why couldn't she be satisfied with one man?

Unrestrained feminine laughter erupted from Grant's office once again, and Muriel paused in the middle of a question about a patient. She quirked her mouth at Lauren. "Honey? You okay?"

"Hmm?"

"Something bothering you?"

"No, why?"

"You look like you just sat on a tack."

"Nope. Here's the chart on Mrs. Reeves in five."

The celebration in Grant's office was especially notable because—typical of William Butler—he had been communicating with the insurance companies while he was "taking it easy" in Ohio. Today, when he walked into the ER with Jade, he had three impressive checks to show Grant from insurance companies that had been dragging their feet—and their funds—since the water poisoning.

"I guess you realize we'll all be able to breathe a little easier after the first of the year," Muriel said.

Lauren looked at her. "Why's that?"

"Dr. Caine will no longer be chief of staff. That was one of the reasons I decided to come back when Dr. Sheldon called me."

Lauren nodded. "I think Dr. Caine must have some problems with burnout." She recalled the way he had treated Jamey when she came in with strep throat. There had been a tenderness beneath that prickly exterior, and he had been deeply affected by Oakley's death.

Word had spread via the hospital grapevine that Darla Caine was no longer living with her husband. That might tend to make a guy behave like a jerk.

"Guess who I'm having over for company tomorrow night," Muriel said.

"Who?"

"William Butler."

Lauren allowed her delight to show on her face. "*Our* William Butler?"

When Muriel smiled, it always encompassed her whole face, and her eyes glowed with warm humor. "I checked, and there's no rule against it at this hospital. I think the man's a doll, I've thought so for years, and he's eligible now."

Laughter from Grant's office once more floated out to them.

"So why did you decide to do this all of a sudden?" Lauren asked.

"After Caine tried to fire me, I just got to thinking that my biggest regret wouldn't be speaking out when I shouldn't—although that's a bad habit of mine—but I would miss working where I could see a good, kind, strong man on the job every day." She shrugged. "I took the chance. Life isn't getting longer or easier, and I happen to know William is lonely."

"What about you?" Lauren asked.

"I'm lonely, too, but I can cope. I think women handle singleness a lot better than most men." She leaned closer. "They need us, sweetie. And if I don't make my move, someone smarter will."

"What did William say when you asked him?"

Muriel grinned, and those dark, doe-like eyes glowed with anticipation. "He's bringing dessert."

Lauren chuckled as she finished report, and she gave Muriel a quick hug—partly because it was good to be working with her again and partly because the older woman had answered a question that had nagged Lauren since last Saturday.

She'd prayed about it, she'd thought about it, she'd prayed some more, asking God to make the answer obvious enough even for her. She believed Muriel had just been used by God as an answer to prayer.

And so she waited until Jade and William left the ER. When Grant was alone in his office, she knocked on the threshold and waited for him to look up from his work.

It was impossible to miss the light that entered his eyes when he saw her.

"I've just drawn the amazing conclusion that a simple date doesn't *have* to lead to marriage," she announced.

His expression didn't change. "You're right, it doesn't have to. But what if it did?"

"What if it didn't?"

"We'd still have a good time. How about next Thursday? My deposition is that morning and should be completed by noon. I'll drive up to St. Louis Wednesday, check on Mom and spend the night there, endure the legal grilling, and be back here by five Thursday evening. We'll miss some of the weekend rush and get better seats at Lambert's Cafe."

"Are you sure you want to drive all the way back to Springfield after being on the road the whole afternoon?"

"I've heard some good things about Lambert's. Of course, if you wanted to stay closer to home there's this nice little Italian place down in the historical part of Branson by Lake Taneycomo."

"How about a picnic, like we did for Thanksgiving?" she said. "You pack some of your gourmet fare, and we can park your car down at the Table Rock Dam. Then after we eat we could hike around the lake with a fishing pole and get covered in mud—"

"Yuck."

She laughed at the look on his face. "So I'm weird. Sue me."

"You really *aren't* a romantic, are you?"

"You don't think fishing is romantic?"

"Lambert's Cafe is famous, with plenty of hillbilly cooking and entertainment. I think it'll be worth the drive."

"I love Lambert's."

"Pick you up at six Thursday?"

"The kids could come with us."

A smile spread across his face like warm honey. "Scared?"

These nice, warm, fuzzy feelings of friendship she shared with Grant Sheldon and his family could become something more than warm and fuzzy. They could become sharp and powerful. These past couple of weeks, Grant and his children had dominated a major portion of her thoughts. Not just the man, but his children, as well. A ready-made family took a much more challenging leap of faith than choosing to care for a man with no children.

His grin disappeared. "Lauren?"

"Okay. I'm in."

"Why, thank you, ma'am," he said dryly. "I'm charmed."

———

Archer and Jessica walked into their home to find that, while they were gone, some unnamed elves had found their way inside and left it looking and smelling like Christmas. A live tree stood in the corner, trimmed with crocheted hearts and nativity figures of lace and strings of berries and bell-shaped sugar cookies with green-and-red sprinkles. Archer remembered seeing nursing home patients crocheting those hearts earlier this month—those who still had fingers nimble enough to crochet.

On the mantel over the fireplace lay an evergreen spray with ribbons of brilliant blue, purple, and silver.

They entered the kitchen to find a plate of assorted homemade cookies covered in blue plastic wrap, and the refrigerator held a pot of beef stew.

Jessica stepped up behind Archer and put her arms around him. "And you thought being a pastor's wife would be a hardship on me. I think I'm going to love it."

"Lauren? You got a minute?"

The uncharacteristically timid voice came from behind Lauren as she stepped out into the hallway, purse slung over her shoulder, ready to head for home.

She turned to find her redheaded friend standing there, arms crossed in front of her.

"Gina? Is that really you? You're actually speaking to me?"

Gina's face darkened with color. "I'm sorry. I deserved that." She sighed and glanced along the hallway, then back again. "I was wrong, totally wrong about everything, okay? I feel really bad about yelling at you like that, and if you'll forgive me—"

"Hold it, wait a minute." Lauren put a hand on Gina's shoulder. "Don't just bare your soul out here in the hallway. You never know who'll be listening. Why don't we go to the cafeteria, then we can pick our eavesdroppers."

Gina gave her a hesitant smile. "How about we step outside for a few minutes? We've got our coats on, and it isn't that cold, and I've got a lot I need to—"

"Then let's get to it." Lauren led the way out.

"You were right about Todd and me," Gina blurted as they stepped out the door.

"I was?"

"I wish I'd listened to you sooner. The way I did things . . . just made it harder for everyone." Her voice cracked, and she stuffed her hands into her pockets and slumped to the edge of light from the glassed entryway. "That was really . . . difficult."

"I'm sorry. What happened?"

Gina shrugged, then sniffed. "I couldn't stop thinking about the things you said. It got to the point where I could no longer convince myself you were wrong, that you didn't understand what I was going through."

"You've changed your mind?"

Gina glanced over her shoulder at Lauren. "I still don't think you can understand how I felt when my husband left me. You've never been married. You haven't been rejected by the one person who is supposed to know you on a deeper level than anyone else in the world. You don't know how it feels to need the reassurance that you're an attractive woman—to need that kind of assurance from any man, just because you've been convinced of your worthlessness by one man."

"You're right," Lauren said. "I don't know how it feels, and what your husband did to you was wrong. Totally wrong." Lauren stepped to the edge of light and stood beside her. "You never talked much about it, but obviously it's something that still causes you a lot of pain."

"Of course it does! How's somebody supposed to get over being dumped like that? Not just me, but the kids . . ." She sniffed. "The kids, too." She dashed tears from her face and took a deep breath. "I thought he was going to work one morning, three days after Cody was born. I got a call from his supervisor an hour after he should have been there, asking where he was."

"You mean he just drove away?"

"They." Gina's chin wobbled, and she swallowed. "They drove away. They'd already made the plans." Her eyes filled with tears. "You knew he left me for another woman."

"Yes."

"And it finally began to soak in on me that Todd was doing the same thing. I don't know why it took me so long to realize that." Gina blinked and looked down at her folded hands. "I can't believe I was actually thinking of doing the same thing to someone else."

"But you didn't do it," Lauren soothed. "What did you tell Todd?"

"I told him about what happened to me. I told him to go back to his family."

"Is he going to?"

Gina shrugged. "He wasn't speaking much when I finished. I guess it made him mad, but I can't do anything about that."

"You did the right thing."

"The right thing would have been to avoid all this in the first place." Gina looked up at Lauren. "If you hadn't been so interested in my life—"

"Go ahead and call it what it really is," Lauren said. "I was nosy."

"You were my friend. After you said what you did I couldn't stop placing myself in her shoes, feeling her pain. Every time I looked at Todd, every minute we spent together talking and laughing and sharing, I felt like a thief. I was stealing minutes with him that she needed, that their children needed." Gina's shoulders slumped. "Lauren, I'm so ashamed."

"I'm sorry."

"Thanks for caring enough to talk to me about it."

"You're welcome. Why don't we start meeting for lunch again?"

"Okay. And walking sometimes in the evening?"

Lauren put her arms around Gina. "I'd love it. I'm proud of you, Gina. It's good to have you back."

Jamey's blue eyes widened with surprise—and a little fear—when she opened the door and saw Peregrine standing there. He had always enjoyed getting that reaction from people.

"Hello there, sweet thing." He gave her his most charming smile.

"Simon." She didn't seem happy to see him. "What're you doing here?"

"Coming to see my baby." He pressed his hand against her belly, then reached for the door and shoved it open. "Let me in, or our baby's going to have a jailbird for a dad."

She gasped and stepped backward. "But you can't stay here! I read the papers, Simon. They're looking for you, and some folks know about us. They'll find you here, honest!"

He kept going, shoving harder. "What're you saying, Jamey? Are you saying you don't want me here?"

"I don't want to do no drugs! I'm trying to straighten out! What're you doing?"

He slammed the door shut behind him and locked it. "Shut up. If you don't go telling anybody—"

"But I don't want to get in trouble with the police!"

"Then keep your mouth shut, okay?" He reached up and covered her mouth with his hand. "You know what quiet means? It means keep your stupid mouth shut!"

Tears filled her blue eyes. She gave a startled nod and stood motionless, as if afraid he might hit her. Yeah, he liked a woman who minded him. The younger ones were better at that. Jamey was . . . what . . . sixteen? Seventeen? Good age. By the time they hit twenty they didn't listen so well.

Trisha Caine had been like that, all nice and soft and sweet when he first met her. By the time he'd moved with her to Springfield he couldn't stand her mouth. He'd tried to slap it off a couple of times.

Jamey took a quivering breath and looked down at her hands, which were folded over her fat stomach.

"There now, that isn't so bad, is it?" He trailed his hand across her cheek and fingered the dull blond hair that fell around her face. "I'm not going to hurt you, okay?" He kept his voice gentle—couldn't have her screaming or carrying on loud enough to wake the neighbors. "I never hurt you, did I?" Without waiting for an answer he flipped off the light. The police might be watching her place, even now, in the middle of the night.

"Are you . . . you going to be here long?" she asked.

"I just got to sleep awhile, okay? Got to crash. Just leave me alone and let me use the bed, and keep watch out the window." He peered around the shabby room. There was only one window in the whole place.

He heard a soft sigh that sounded like relief. He didn't care. He just needed some sleep.

CHAPTER 28

A t nine o'clock Thursday morning Grant sat beside Jay at the large oval conference table of the plaintiff's attorney. It was an elegant room, comfortable enough to lean back in his chair and relax. He didn't feel like relaxing. At the moment he was thinking about the inconsequential fact that he had discussed the case with Lauren after having been told not to discuss it with anyone when he first received word of the suit. Silly worry, of course, but worry was an obsession of his.

Jay opened his briefcase and pulled out a folder. With a smile and a flourish, he slid it toward Grant. "Read it and celebrate."

"Celebrate?"

Jay glanced toward the entryway, then leaned closer to Grant and lowered his voice. "The short take is that your colleague, Teschlow, had to backpedal halfway through his deposition Monday. I think the hospital, and the plaintiff's attorney, realized we would only need one expert witness who could point out to a jury that his use of a depolarizing agent on a patient with myasthenia gravis—as Irlene Goodwin was—would definitely have killed her. Dr. Teschlow's decision to intubate her was a judgment call, and he can argue until the sun explodes that you did not give him a proper verbal report, but even the sparse documentation the hospital supplied on the case doesn't back him up."

"Meaning I came up here for nothing?"

"No, you still have to be present for the deposition and jump through their hoops, but once the other attorneys examine the facts and count the costs, I can't see them pursuing this. I expect the hospital to settle. Still, you'd better be on your toes for this."

There was a shuffle of feet on thick carpeting and a murmur of polite greetings. Grant leaned back in his chair as the other men in conservative three-piece suits filed through the doorway and endured introductions. Grant geared up for battle.

Jay had warned him to remain alert during the questioning, as the attorneys for the plaintiff might switch from the mundane, energy-sapping questions about times and dates and signatures to an indirectly worded question that could catch him off guard and confuse the heart of the issue. That confusion could immediately change the course of decisions made in the next few days.

Grant remained stoic during the process. He answered countless questions about his place of employment, his licensures, his associational memberships. He identified nine or ten exhibit documents relating to the treatment of Irlene Goodwin on the date in question. He answered multiple questions referring to the copies of medical records that had been so strangely absent from the hospital files. As coached by Jay, he gave only the information required by questioning, and volunteered no additional comments. He did not smile, he did not behave with antagonism.

This had to be the most boring, most wearying job imaginable.

Grant was stifling his first yawn and glancing at the clock on the wall when Mr. Duggins, the attorney for the plaintiff, paused and looked down at his notes. Jay cleared his throat and leaned forward. Grant stiffened. That was his cue to be alert. Okay, so maybe this wasn't the *most* boring job.

"Dr. Sheldon, on the night you treated Irlene Goodwin, on . . ." He frowned, looked down at his notes, and announced the date Grant treated Irlene for the last time. "When it became clear that your patient was having increased difficulty with her airway, why did you decide, against the guidelines for standard of care, to forego an intubation?"

Grant hesitated. Jay had warned him to tread lightly and not to answer any question without considering each word with suspicion. Duggins was attempting to confuse him with a leading, compound question that introduced damaging suppositions.

"What I think you're doing, here," Grant said pleasantly, "is attempting to get all the questions answered at once so we can have an early lunch."

Duggins did not smile. "I'm sorry, Doctor. If the question was confusing to you, perhaps I can word it more simply."

"No, thank you, but if you don't mind I'd like to give you a more detailed answer. In the first place, you're assuming that the longer Irlene was in the exam room, the more difficulty she had breathing. That was not the case. You're also assuming that it was standard of care to intubate under the circumstances of her illness. That, also, was not the case. It was a judgment call. She was doing well and her symptoms were improving when I gave report at the end of my shift. I was not—"

"Dr. Sheldon, I have here a plaintiff's exhibit of a document I would like for you to identify." Duggins held up a copy of a prescription, and Grant saw his own name as patient. It was a script for pain-killers.

Sudden change of direction. Another ploy to throw him off-balance. It was working, but he didn't let on.

Jay leaned forward to get a closer look at the exhibit, then frowned at Duggins. "Objection. Unless you're prepared to prove to the court why a prescription for medication about a totally unrelated case—"

"I fail to see how you can call it unrelated," Duggins replied calmly, "when the doctor could have been under the influence of this medication at the time of Irlene Goodwin's presentation to the ER the night before her death."

"*Could* have been?" Jay laughed. "Mr. Duggins, if you were to question the use of prescribed medication by every defendant you questioned in court, the judges would have you—"

"I merely wish to point out the fact that Dr. Sheldon's thought process might not have been the best," replied Duggins.

Jay gave a casual shrug. "We have three expert witnesses who were shown Irlene's medical records and agreed with treatment. Unless you intend to prove that their judgment was also hampered by some form of medication, may I suggest that this line of questioning only serves to prolong this deposition." He looked at his watch. "And I could use that early lunch."

There was a polite round of soft chuckles, and Duggins shoved the exhibit aside. Grant concealed his relief.

Duggins checked his notes again. "Dr. Sheldon, would you agree with the assumption that an emergency physician, upon the ending of his shift, is responsible to give a comprehensive report on all patients in his care to the relief physician for the next shift?"

"No."

Mr. Duggins paused and removed his glasses. "You disagree with my statement?" he asked, as if that were the most outrageous answer he'd ever received.

"A comprehensive report," Grant said, "listing every detail about each patient case, would be impossible to cover during a normal shift change. An adequate report would encompass the pertinent details of the case, which we call an abbreviated SOAP note format, which stands for subjective-objective-assessment-plan."

"And this is what you assert that you gave to your colleague on the date of these medical records?"

"That is correct."

"Did you, during that report, alert Dr. Teschlow to the fact that Irlene Goodwin suffered from myasthenia gravis?"

"Yes."

"You remember, specifically, that you gave him a verbal report?"

"Yes."

"And if you had forgotten to mention those particulars to Dr. Teschlow, or perhaps mentioned them to a nurse and mistakenly believed you had mentioned them to Dr. Teschlow because of a state of mental confusion due to the sedation of a pain-killer you had taken earlier, would you have recalled that oversight quite so easily?"

"I didn't forget."

"That was not my question."

Jay held his hand up. "Objection. This line of questioning is grossly misleading and argumentative."

Grant did not allow Mr. Duggins's comment to irritate him. Jay had warned him that the plaintiff's attorney would attempt provocation.

Duggins replaced his glasses and leaned forward. "Can you tell me how, two years later, you can remember the details of this case so precisely?"

"Because Irlene Goodwin had been my patient at least three times previously in that ER. The news of her death the morning after I treated her was a terrible shock, and at that time I reviewed the *comprehensive* facts on the case, including the personal notes I had taken the night before. It took me more than an hour. I made further notes, seeking ways I might avoid such an outcome in the future."

"So you concluded at that time that you could have been at fault?"

"No, I did not."

"What was your conclusion?"

"I found nothing I would have done differently."

Duggins leaned back in his chair. "I have no further questions of the witness at this time."

Grant watched him for a few seconds in surprise, feeling primed for a fight that hadn't taken place. He looked at Jay.

"None for me," Jay said. He gestured to Grant. "Do you want to read it or waive signature? You can read it for accuracy."

"Yes, I prefer to do that." The deposition was over. Grant could go home.

───────

Thursday evening, Beau sprawled across Dad's bed and watched him fumble with buttons. "So you're not getting sued now, huh?"

Dad dropped his comb, picked it up, leaned into the mirror and frowned at the forty-one-year-old lines around the gray, dark-lashed eyes. "That's what it looks like. I'm not sure yet."

"Dad, you're going to ruin a perfectly good silk shirt." It was a shirt Mom had bought him for his birthday not long before the wreck.

"I like this shirt. Brooke says it makes me look younger."

"It'll make you look like a clumsy fourteen-year-old on his first date if you don't fix your buttons. They don't line up. The collar's lopsided."

Dad checked the mirror, groaned, undid his button job.

"You said you're going to Lambert's, right?" Beau asked. "Lambert's servers go around the dining areas with extra helpings of fried potatoes and okra and beans and stuff. And they throw their dinner rolls and spoon out gooey molasses for the bread, even before you get your plate. Nobody wears a silk shirt."

Dad nodded at his reflection in the mirror and tucked the shirt into his slacks. He hesitated, and his gaze found Beau's reflection, his brow furrowing with concern. "You really think this shirt looks stupid?"

Beau felt a pang. "No, Dad, I didn't say that. It looks good on you. I just didn't want you to get it stained and then have to go to Jessica's Christmas show with a dirty shirt." He was beginning to sound like Brooke. What a horrible discovery. "Would you relax?"

"I'm relaxed."

Something stirred Beau's thoughts as Dad padded into the bathroom in his stockinged feet to brush his teeth. What would it be like to have someone else living here with them all the time? How would it feel to have another person—someone like Lauren—taking Mom's place with Dad?

But Lauren had already pointed out that no one would take Mom's place, and she hadn't been saying that just to be nice. She'd said it before she ever agreed to go out on this date with Dad. And they weren't even talking marriage. Still . . . it didn't hurt to think ahead.

Dad came back to the bedroom and sat down on his dressing chair to pull on his shoes. Beau noticed the sprinkles of water darkening the beautiful burgundy color of the shirt. He didn't remark on it. In just a few moments, his perspective had changed. Let Dad be happy on his date tonight. Don't make him worry about what might or might not happen to a stupid piece of cloth. The important thing was that he would be with someone who appreciated him for who he was—and whom his kids approved of with great enthusiasm. It didn't hurt that Lauren sometimes came back from the creek smelling like fish.

"Dad." He waited until his father finished tying a shoe and looked up. "You look great. Mom would be proud if she were here. Lauren won't be able to resist you."

Dad's smile came quickly. "Thanks, son. There's a lot of pressure here, you know. I haven't been out on a first date in"—he *tic-tic-tick*ed his tongue to mimic a calculator—"more than twenty years."

"Then this is a special occasion. You should dress up. Lauren deserves it."

The smile widened. "I think she does. Where's your sister? I thought she'd be in here all excited about this. She's been nagging me forever to take Lauren out."

"She called while you were in the shower. She's still at school."

Dad's smile froze on his face. "Why?"

"The school paper, remember? Christmas edition, final one of the year."

"So why aren't you there?"

"I wanted to come home and make sure you actually went on this date. Besides, you told us last week you didn't want the car parked in the school lot after hours."

Dad glanced at his watch. It was five-thirty.

"Dad, you're stressing. That's one reason Brooke and I never tell you anything anymore—"

"Okay, I'm sorry. How's she going to get home?"

"She'll call me and I'll go pick her up."

Dad hesitated. "Trade cars with me and take my cell phone."

Beau sighed. "You're overreacting again."

"No, I'm not."

"Nobody's seen any sign of Peregrine, and all his contacts are in jail."

"Don't argue with me on this, Beau, or I'll have to call Lauren and cancel our date. Brooke would never forgive you for that."

"Okay, where's your cell phone? And give me the keys to your car, quick!"

Dad caught him in a hug.

Beau would be relieved when this relationship with Lauren started taking a little more of Dad's attention.

———————

The sniveling coward, Kent Eckard, sat in the passenger seat of the truck, his hands clasped between his knees. "Look, I'm sorry. I didn't know anything about it, okay? How was I supposed to warn you when I didn't—"

"Shut up!" Simon wanted to rip the punk's face off, but he would bolt, and he would be no help then.

The fury blazed through Simon's body, and he gripped the steering wheel hard to control the shaking. Couldn't let on . . . it was getting worse. He was losing control. He needed more. He'd been seeing people standing in the trees out in the woods, staring down at him, eyes peering at him from the bushes.

"Just don't drive out on the street, okay?" Kent pleaded. "The cops are everywhere, man."

"Shut up! Don't talk about the cops! I gotta have another place to stay." The shaking got worse when Simon was mad, and it never went away completely anymore. "Jamey took off on me while I was sleeping last Saturday. I can't go back—she might have gone to the cops." His fingers clenched with fresh anger that shot through him even though he tried to fight it. He slanted a glance across the seat at the kid. "I can't sleep in the woods anymore, or I'll freeze to death. What about your place?"

Kent's eyes bulged. "You kidding? My pop would call the cops on both of us. He tried to kick me out when they suspended me from school. Why don't you just leave the state, man? Go to Arkansas. Nobody knows you—"

Simon grabbed Eckard by the collar of his scruffy T-shirt and yanked him halfway across the seat. The kid barked like a seal, mouth open, teeth bared in a grimace.

"That's right, nobody knows me. I got no contacts there. You tellin' me to get out of my own town?"

"N-no, man, no! I just—"

"Nobody strikes me down in Dogwood Springs!" He jerked the shirt tighter, loving the rush of power that pulsed through him as Kent gagged. Let him gag. This muscle boy thought he was so tough, let him see what a real man could do. "This is my town. The users know me here, and I can distribute my own stuff for a while, until I get some more staff. I try getting in on somebody else's territory and I could get dead real fast."

Kent choked, and Simon let up a little on the shirt, just enough to keep him breathing. "I've got to know who informed."

Kent nodded, his face bright red, eyes about to pop from their sockets.

Simon liked that. Just for fun he gave a final tug before he let the punk plop back into his seat. Push him any further and he'd probably have to change his jeans.

Kent fell against the door and stayed there, still breathing hard.

"Who informed? You?"

"No, not me! I never told nobody!"

"But you let that little fuzz-face Webster blast the school rag with all his propaganda."

"How was I gonna stop him? It was just a couple of stupid articles. I didn't know what they were printing, I didn't know anybody'd care about that—"

"Somebody cared, okay? Somebody's started singing to the cops. How'd Webster know about me unless somebody told him?"

"Look, it wasn't me! I'm the one that shut Webster up, remember? Got expelled from school for it." Kent rubbed at the red mark that lingered on his neck.

"But he didn't shut up, don't you get it? It's going to take more than a couple of bruises to convince him. Guess I'll have to do this myself, just like everything else."

"What're you gonna do?" Kent whined.

"First, I'm going to cook up some more stuff. I need a hit. And I can't let the customers down."

"Where're you getting the raw ingredients?"

"I've still got some things stashed out in the woods. We can buy or steal the rest."

Kent swallowed hard. "We?"

"Yeah. Hey, you still got the key you lifted from the chemistry teacher?"

The punk's eyes slanted away. He looked like he might puke.

"You've got it, I can tell." Simon couldn't believe his luck. "Then we're in business. They got beakers and everything. Let's go get that key." He switched on the clattering motor. "And as soon as we get our stuff cooked we're going to find Webster and shut his mouth for him. He's ruining everything."

Lauren's front porch light was on when Grant pulled into her driveway, and he took a moment to enjoy the little porch with the handmade wreath on the door and the drapes of lavender and dusky pink and sky blue. Gina had helped her select the fabric last weekend. The two women were obviously more comfortable together than they had been on Thanksgiving Day.

Grant loved the colors Lauren had picked out. He loved her style. He had been here often since he'd first met her—he and Brooke and Beau had even helped her paint the trim around the eaves and porch and shutters last summer.

He checked the time. She wouldn't mind if he was five minutes early, especially with his good news.

On impulse, he fastened the top button of his shirt. He pocketed his keys, got out of the car, then as he walked up the sidewalk to the house he unfastened that troublesome button again.

Why was he so nervous? This was Lauren, his co-worker, his fishing buddy, his sister in Christ. She'd seen him with the seat of his pants ripped out, with mud in his hair and a three-day growth of beard on his face after the mercury episode.

But this was special. *She* was special.

He rang the doorbell, then knocked, remembering that the doorbell hadn't worked in two weeks.

Lauren opened the door and stepped out. She wore a black, cowl-necked sweater dress, and her hair fell around her shoulders like molten gold—she'd dressed up for him.

"Wow," he whispered.

The smile she gave him was more brilliant than the glow of the porch light. "Thanks."

"Ready?" he asked.

"Ready. Nice shirt." She reached over and touched the sleeve. "Silk. Beautiful." Silently, her gaze seemed to measure the width of his shoulders. "You look great in silk."

"Thank you." The lady knew how to give a compliment as well as receive one.

She cleared her throat. "So how's your mother adjusting to the daily companion?"

"Much better than I expected. I haven't seen her so animated, or so happy, in years. I think it's going to work out, at least for a while." He opened the door for her and forced himself not to stare like a tongue-tied schoolboy as she slid into the passenger side of the Volvo. Lauren McCaffrey was beautiful. Her scent reminded him of lilacs. Was this the same woman who drove a pickup truck, fished in baggy overalls and her brother's old denim shirts, and could establish an IV in a patient's arm faster than any other nurse in the hospital?

"Beau called me and told me things went well in St. Louis," she said when Grant got into the car.

"He did? I had hoped to give you the good news myself."

"You can tell me all about the deposition on our drive to Springfield. I know you're relieved it's over."

He hesitated. "In a way."

As he backed out onto the street he felt her surprised attention. "Don't get me wrong," he said. "I was as outraged by the frivolous suit as any other doc would be, but as I drove home this afternoon I couldn't help feeling a sense of depression."

Lauren nodded. "I think I understand. No matter what happened in the lawyer's office today, a patient still died."

"Irlene Goodwin's memory should have been treated with more . . . I don't know . . . honor," Grant said. "As it is, the story of her struggle for life will be nothing more than a smudge on some legal documents. Her name will be tossed across a courtroom—"

"Grant, you really are getting gloomy."

"Sorry."

She put a hand on his arm. "It's okay. You want to spout, go ahead and spout. I've done it plenty of times."

He grinned. That was one of the things he loved about her. She knew how to say the right thing at the right time, and then she knew how to listen.

Beau paced across the kitchen for fifteen minutes, glanced at the clock, then strode to the front door and looked outside. Brooke wasn't there, of course. She'd said she would call him, but he hadn't expected it to take her this long.

He dialed Evan's cell phone number.

Evan answered before the first trill ended. "Yeah?"

"What's going on?" Beau asked. "I thought you would be done by now."

"I'm experiencing some . . . uh . . . complications."

"What kind of complications?"

"I'm trying to download some of these pictures from my watch camera."

"I thought you already gave those pictures to Tony."

"I gave him the ones from the other cameras, but I never could figure out the software for this one, and he wants these extra shots for positive ID on Peregrine so he can—"

"Why don't you bring your stuff here, and I can do it on ours?"

"Because I'm in the middle of this, and I've already downloaded the software . . . I think."

"I'll come and help you."

"Thanks. Meanwhile, we'll keep trying."

———

Peregrine pulled to the end of the alley in front of the school and stared with unholy anger at the glow of lights from the third story windows. Somebody was there!

He reached across and smacked Kent on the chest. Kent's grunt of surprise blended with the growling echo of the engine.

"That still the publications department?"

"Yeah."

"What're they doing in there this late?"

"I don't know," Kent whined. "I never took that class."

Peregrine switched off the motor. He needed his stuff. He had to have it. "Get the supplies. We're going in."

Kent caught his breath. "But somebody's in the building."

"Yeah. Somebody in Publications." Peregrine reached beneath the seat and pulled out a Sig Sauer, a beautiful weapon that gleamed in the pale glow from the school security lights. He heard Kent's gasp, and he smiled. "Maybe we'll make a social call."

CHAPTER 29

G rant had never been to Lambert's Cafe, but he had driven past it on Highway 65 en route from Springfield to Branson. Because of that he wasn't surprised by the number of cars in the brightly lit parking area or by the line of diners congregated out on the wooden front porch of the building. The "polished hillbilly" atmosphere and the noise and laughter—and particularly Lauren's friendly, "never met a stranger" attitude—lent a special warmth to the brisk night air.

In the surprisingly short time between their arrival and the moment they were seated, Grant and Lauren had become acquainted with the people in line around them, and Grant felt himself relaxing completely. As soon as they were seated at a booth in the raucous, laughter-filled dining room, the throwing of rolls commenced. The term "casual dining" was appropriate.

"Heads up!" Lauren was prepared and caught the first hot roll, then gave it to him and held her hands up for another one.

He turned in time to duck, and Lauren laughed. "There, now you know how it's done."

He unbuttoned the sleeves of his silk shirt. "Yes, and now I know why Beau didn't want me to wear this."

Lauren grinned at him, and he was captivated—this friendship had grown far past simple affection.

He rested his chin in his hands and allowed himself the pleasure of watching her as the party voices tumbled around them. A telltale blush across her cheeks told him she was affected by his scrutiny.

A server in denim overalls and a red-checked gingham blouse stopped and set plates and flatware on the table and asked for their order.

Lauren gave Grant a wicked grin. "Ever eaten hog jowls?"

"That isn't funny."

"*Have* you?"

"No, and I'm too old to be grilled by an attorney and eat a pig's jaw both in one day." Before she could argue he ordered chicken-fried steak and handed his menu to the server.

Lauren laughed and ordered the hog jowls. It was impossible not to be affected by her laughter.

"Did I ever tell you about the time I had a heart-to-heart with Brooke about my dating again?" Grant asked as soon as the server walked away.

Lauren tore a paper towel from the dispenser on their table and wiped her hands. "When was that?"

"When we first came here."

"Judging by her reaction to me the first time we met, I can imagine what she had to say."

He chuckled. "We were at City Hall when I casually mentioned that I was considering the possibility of dating again. In retrospect, I realize it was bad timing. It was a busy day there, and I wasn't familiar with small-town curiosity. Within twenty-four hours of the time she gave me her opinion, everyone in town knew about it."

"Of course," Lauren said. "I never have to wonder where I stand with her."

"Then you must realize that she's done a hundred-and-eighty-degree turn in her attitude since then, at least about you," Grant said.

"That much I've gathered recently. I do know that she doesn't think of me as a female John Boy anymore."

He laughed. "She told you about that?"

"She tells me everything. Sometimes I even appreciate it."

"Has she been nagging you as often as she has me about . . . us?"

"Probably."

He looked around the dining hall, gestured to the young man with the basket of rolls, and held his hands up for the pitch. He caught it and gave it to Lauren. "May I ask a personal question?"

"Depends. How personal?"

"What changed your mind about going out on this-here bona fide date?" He failed horribly at affecting the down-home Branson twang the server had used, but Lauren didn't seem to notice. "Did you just finally give in to Brooke's pressure?"

"No." She frowned, then shrugged. "Well, that could be part of it."

"Oh, really?" He was learning to appreciate his daughter's big mouth.

"Could be, but Brooke isn't the only one nagging me. Several friends have hinted that I may not have had a complete handle on God's perfect will for my life when I decided to remain single."

"They sound like good friends." *Thank you, Lord!*

"Something else that affected my decision," she continued, "was the discovery that my priorities have changed since last summer. Now having a relationship with God has become the most important thing to me. A few months ago I was more interested in getting married and starting a family before it was too late."

"And *that's* what convinced you it was okay to go out with me tonight? Because dating and marriage were no longer a priority?" *Oh well, whatever worked.*

Lauren nodded thoughtfully. "You know, it's like Paul says in the Bible, 'I have learned to be content whatever the circumstances.' I needed to become content as a single person in order to move forward with my life. And I have." Her smile returned. "But as you say, another reason was probably Brooke."

"My own outspoken, mischievous daughter, Brooke," he said lovingly.

"And Beau."

"My twins ganged up on you, then?"

"All the way back from Knolls the night they drove me to my parents' house after Hardy died, they gave me reasons why you and I should be more than friends."

"I'm sorry. They had no right to do that." He was going to give them both a hug as soon as he got home tonight.

"They're no worse than my family. Actually, they aren't as bad. Mom's worse than Brooke. She has no finesse. She can be a little wacky when it comes to her only single daughter finally getting married."

Grant had seen that for himself, but he knew better than to comment on it. He shoved his plate aside and leaned forward, allowing the din of voices around them to provide some privacy. "Lauren, I've been doing a lot of dreaming lately."

She dipped another piece of roll into the molasses on her plate. "What's your dream?"

"Someday I would like someone to share my life with again." He watched the flutter of her eyelashes and pressed on. "I've even found the courage to pray about it."

She put the bread down, and all evidence of humor left her face. "That's risky."

He nodded.

"I prayed very hard last summer for God to place someone . . . in particular . . . into my life," she said. "I received an answer I didn't want."

"That's always a risk, but you lived through it. If that's God's answer for me, I'll live through that, too."

A roving server stepped to their table with a large bowl of macaroni and stewed tomatoes. "Heads up!"

Grant leaned back, but before he was out of range of the plate, a diner passed by and accidentally nudged the server's arm. A few dribbles of stewed tomato juice spattered over Grant's upper sleeve.

He breathed a sigh of relief. "There. Now I don't have to worry about staining my shirt."

Lauren laughed.

Was it too soon to tell her he was falling in love with her?

———

Peregrine led the way to a stand of cedars beside the huge three-story school building. He needed his stuff. The whiskey he'd found with his stash of supplies had taken the edge off, but it wasn't enough. He felt as if he could wrap his fingers around somebody's neck and squeeze—

"You're not gonna cook the stuff right here at the school, are you?" Kent whined.

Peregrine ignored the question. "Give me the keys." He held out his hand and waited while Kent dug into his pocket and drew them out. "Follow me. Stay behind the bushes. And don't rustle the leaves!" He plunged into the shadows beneath the glow of light from the windows on the third floor.

He'd gone about thirty paces when he heard voices and froze. "Shhh! Listen." He grabbed Kent by the sleeve of his jacket.

All they heard for the next few seconds was the crackle of leaves beneath Kent's feet as he shuffled back and forth. Peregrine stomped down on the punk's toe.

There was a quiet grunt, then silence.

Three breaths later a young male voice floated down from above. "I got him!"

A surge of terror rocked Peregrine backward. He shoved Kent deeper into the shadows and ducked against the rough bricks of the building. Kent's breathing came in panicked gasps of air. Peregrine would have choked him right then if he weren't afraid they'd be heard.

They waited.

Nothing else happened. Nobody grabbed them—nobody aimed a light in their faces. Kent's breathing slowed.

Peregrine had almost decided the danger was past when they heard another voice, a girl, almost directly above them.

"Evan, why did you open this window? I'm freezing!" There was a noisy squeak of wood against wood, and the voice was cut off as the window latch snapped into place.

Peregrine listened to Kent's breathing a few more seconds, and then the rage hit him again with a force that made him tremble. "She said Evan!"

Kent didn't reply. The coward.

"We're going to Publications."

"Wait," Kent whispered. "I thought you wanted to cook a batch of—"

"Shut up and get in the building. We'll do it as soon as we settle a score with our biggest troublemaker."

"All right! It worked." Evan tapped his fingers on the computer screen and smiled proudly at Brooke over his shoulder. "Looks like this one was a perfect shot. What do you think?"

Brooke leaned forward and studied the picture that Evan had downloaded from his watch camera. "Perfect."

He basked in her rare praise. "Thanks. Not bad, if I say so my—"

"Now can you send it to Tony, so we can get home? Beau's going to come walking in here any second, and then he'll give us this long sermon about taking too many chances, and—"

"I think I'll e-mail a copy of these pictures to Beau. This downloads fast now that I've figured out how to do it. Let me do a few more, it won't take much longer." He pressed the Send key and waited. It didn't respond. "Where'd Miss Bolton go?"

"Library. She said for us to turn out the lights and lock the door when we're fin—"

"Rats!" He pressed the key again. No response. Nothing.

"What?"

"It froze up on me."

"Well, unfreeze it."

"I'm trying." *Rats!* He didn't want to have to start all over again. "I thought Beau would be here by now."

"Trust me. He'll come walking in the door any minute."

Evan leaned back in his chair and stared with disgust at the screen, which glared back at him with three enlarged pictures of Simon Royce— aka Peregrine. "I wish he'd hurry."

Lauren had never realized how much Brooke and Beau imitated their father. She'd never realized how much he used facial expressions and hands when he talked, particularly on the subject of his kids. She sat watching him in silent admiration as he described the harrowing experience he'd had teaching Brooke how to drive a car with manual transmission.

His deep voice imitated the grinding of gears as he mimicked the hand movements one would use with a four-on-the-floor, and Lauren's laughter rang out across the dining area. No one noticed. All the other diners were just as noisy.

"I'd never heard Beau laugh so hard." He lowered his hands to the table. " Of course, he was buckled up in the backseat. For three days I thought she'd given me whiplash. It's a good thing I have a low-stress job. I couldn't handle that much pressure."

"An ER medical director has low stress?"

"It beats being a driving instructor. Think of the terror those poor people endure every day. Beau was laughing so hard I thought Brooke was going to make him walk back to town."

Lauren laughed again as she imagined the scene. "I love those kids. One minute I think they're never going to speak to each other again, and the next minute Beau's helping her with something on the computer, or she's telling him what a good doctor he'll make someday." As she spoke she noticed that Grant's laughter dwindled and his expression grew serious.

"You mean that, Lauren?" he asked quietly.

"Mean what? That they have a special relationship? I had a good relationship with my—"

"That you love them," he said.

The question startled her. His seriousness alarmed her. "Yes, I do." And it was true. She had always wanted children. Before she met the Sheldons, she had never considered the possibility of falling in love with someone else's children—children raised and loved and taught by another woman. Those children would never be her own, and they would always have the memory of their "real" mother against which to judge all others. In the same way, their father would always have the beloved memory of that dead wife, and it seemed that the fact of her death would polish those memories to such a beautiful glow that no one else could ever measure up.

"I love them, too," he said softly. "I guess that just gives us one more thing in common."

Beau saw the lights glowing from the third floor of the old school building when he turned onto Hickory Street in front of the campus.

Obviously, Brooke and Evan were still up there, and they might be there for a while. No telling how Evan might have mangled the instructions for the software. Evan was a seat-of-the-pants kind of guy, and he seldom took the time to follow directions when he got excited.

Instead of driving into the student parking lot, Beau pulled along the curb in front of the building. Nobody was around to complain . . . well, hardly anybody. Miss Bolton's car was at the end of the teacher's parking lot about fifty feet farther down. And there was a vehicle parked awkwardly in the shadows at the end of the alley just across the street from Miss Bolton's car. Still, he wouldn't be here long enough to get in anyone's way. Dad wouldn't like this. There were supposed to be several other people here.

Beau got out of the car, locked it, pocketed his keys as he stepped onto the sidewalk, then frowned and peered through the darkness toward the alley again. Something about that vehicle in the shadows bothered him. As he stepped closer he recognized the shape of a truck. It was a light color, and it looked uncomfortably familiar. . . .

Fear tumbled over him like a landslide. It was the *stalker* truck! The one that had rammed them. From the glow of a school security light he could see the dent in its right front fender.

He pivoted and raced back to the car, unlocked and jerked open the door, and fell into the driver's seat. He pressed the automatic lock, pulse pounding in an adrenaline charge, and grabbed the phone. The guy was here. He was here! Watching the school building? Stalking Brooke and Evan? Or maybe he was just waiting to follow them when they drove home.

He punched Evan's cell phone number. *Don't panic. I could be wrong. Yeah, I'm probably wrong.*

The phone rang once, twice, then Evan answered in the middle of the third ring. "Let me guess, this is Beau? Brooke thought you'd be here by—"

"Evan, listen to me! I think our stalker is back. You guys need to lay low while I call the police."

"Very funny, Beau, but if you want us to do this at your house—"

"No, I'm serious. It's the truck that rammed us." As he watched, headlights flickered along the street, and a car came over the hill, casting the truck and the interior of the cab into momentary definition. It was, indeed, that same truck.

There was no one sitting inside . . . which meant . . .

"Get out of that room!" Beau screamed. "Get out of there now! Hurry, Evan, they—"

A muffled explosion and shattering of glass rocked through the phone line, immediately followed by an eerie *buzz-pop, buzz-pop,* and a feminine scream. Brooke!

There was another clatter of sound as Evan dropped his cell phone.

"No!" came Evan's voice over the receiver. "Brooke!"

There was a guttural sound of laughter.

Beau punched the End button with fingers that shook so hard they barely functioned. He keyed in 9-1-1 and prayed hard for God's protection for Brooke and Evan.

When the line connected he didn't wait for anyone to speak. "This is Beau Sheldon. We need help at the high school, old building, publications department on the third floor. Please come quickly—I heard a gunshot. There are people in there!"

He waited only for an acknowledgment that they'd heard him and the command to stay on the line before he disconnected. He jumped from the car and raced across the lawn. There was no way he could stay hidden in the car and wait for the police to get here.

He'd just reached the door when there was another muffled pop and the shattering of more glass.

"God, please!" he groaned as he yanked open the door. "Protect them, please!"

"Don't shoot her! Oh, Lord, please don't let him shoot her!" Evan stumbled over the wreckage of the other computers and stared into the face of hatred—the man held the barrel of a gun with a long silencer shoved just below Brooke's left ear. He held her throat with his other hand.

"Then tell me what I need to know!" The man tightened his arm around Brooke's neck.

She gagged, but to Evan's relief she didn't struggle. Her panicky glance traveled from Evan to the computer screen, and he knew what she was thinking. If Peregrine saw his own picture on the monitor—

"Who turned me in?"

"How should I know? Who are you?"

"You know who I am! You're the guy with all the answers. You're the guy with all the words. Who called the police on me? How do you know so much about me?" The rumble of his voice spiraled out of control, and his teeth glared yellow in the fluorescent light while he stared, unblinking, into Evan's eyes.

"The police? What are you talking about?" Evan forced the tremor from his voice with difficulty. He had to bluff through this one. The man was obviously paranoid.

Sure enough, Peregrine faltered. Evan saw Brooke signal again with her eyes toward the computer screen.

"Mister, I think you've made a mistake." Evan stepped around the side of the computer table, hoping to distract Peregrine from his forward progress toward it. "All I do is write about stuff I read on the Internet, and everybody's interested in—"

"Shut up! You think I don't know how to read?"

The man was crazy. Psychotic. And his buddy, Kent Eckard, just stood in the open doorway like an ice sculpture. He looked too scared to move.

Peregrine jerked Brooke along the inner wall of the cavernous room.

"You turned the whole town against me—people started staring at me everywhere I went. The police followed me all the time, wouldn't leave me alone!" His shouts grew in volume with each accusation, and still he dragged Brooke closer to the monitor. He was close enough now that Evan could smell the alcohol on his breath and the ripe odor of his body. If the man saw his own face staring back at him—

"We never followed you." Evan kept his voice soft and nonthreatening. It was true, they'd never followed him. They just took his picture when they *did* see him. *Why did I ever allow Brooke to get involved in this with me?*

"You told everyone!" Peregrine was within sight of the screen now. All he had to do was look down. He hadn't yet.

Paranoia. Bad paranoia. The guy was tweaking, big time, and that made him deadly. He looked around the room and, to Evan's horror, focused on the monitor screen.

"Somebody's coming!" The ice sculpture that was Eckard suddenly came to life, but not before Peregrine recognized himself.

His bloodshot eyes stared, then blinked. He frowned and shook his head, as if he didn't understand what he was seeing.

"Did you hear that?" Evan asked. "Kent said someone's—"

"You!" Peregrine's arm straightened, and he pointed the gun into Evan's face as Brooke stumbled away from him. "You're still doing it!"

Evan sucked in his breath. He was going to die.

"No!" Brooke grabbed for the man's arm and drew her knee up to stomp his instep, but before she could kick down he shoved her forward into a desk, took aim at her head with his pistol, and—

"No!" Evan hurled himself forward, but their attacker smacked him in the right temple. The room dimmed. Brooke's shout echoed in his ears as he fell.

Beau raced down the third floor corridor, listening to his sister's cry and Kent's pleading voice.

"Don't do it, Simon!" Kent cried. "Man, are you crazy? Don't do it! You'll go to jail. *We'll* go to jail! They might even give us the death—"

"Evan!" Brooke shouted.

Beau plunged through the open doorway and stopped in horror.

Peregrine straddled Evan's still, prone body, holding a pistol with both hands. He put his finger to the trigger and started to squeeze. Beau rushed forward. Peregrine switched targets and blew the computer monitor away.

Brooke lunged toward the man's right side and drove her heel down the side of his right leg with the full force of her body.

He roared with rage and stumbled forward. Before he could recover, Beau tackled him and knocked him to his stomach.

"Brooke, knock the gun away! Get the gun!"

Brooke scrambled over Evan's back and kicked the gun from Peregrine's hand. The Sig Sauer spun across the wooden floor and clattered to a stop against the far wall.

"Police! Stay down, don't move!" came a voice from the door.

Peregrine rose from beneath Beau, shoved him aside, and lunged away. He scrambled over broken glass and dived for the window, hitting it shoulder first. The pane cracked, and he stumbled backward.

"Stop! Police!"

Again Peregrine plunged toward the window. It shattered on impact. Shards of glass flew out into the night air. He jumped again, tripped, and screamed as he fell. His cry ended suddenly.

Evan moaned and stirred. "B-Brooke? Where's Brooke?"

"I'm here, Evan. It's okay. It's going to be okay."

CHAPTER 30

t's okay. It'll be okay." Lauren held Grant's hand, repeating the words to reassure herself as they rushed through the sliding glass doors into the ER waiting room. The two police cars outside could be there for anything.

"Hi, Dr. Sheldon. Hi, Lauren," Becky greeted as she hit the door-lock release for them to pass into the ER proper. "Dr. Sheldon, your kids are fine, but if they keep hitching rides on the ambulance you'd better upgrade your health insurance policy."

"I might do that. Which room?" He didn't slow his stride, and Lauren kept pace with him.

"We've got 'em corralled in nine," Becky said as they passed. "Dr. Caine wanted to keep an eye on them until you got here."

In the room they found Brooke, with a blackening left eye, perched on the edge of the bed. Beau sat slumped in the chair. He stood up when they entered.

Brooke slid down from the bed. "Dad, don't freak, it's not as bad as it looks. Dr. Caine says we'll be fine, and he already sent Evan home with more staples in his head and some superglue over a cut on his left eyebrow, but he wanted us to hang here till you guys arrived." She hugged her father with barely a break in her word flow. "I'm sorry Beau's such a crybaby and just had to call the restaurant and interrupt your first-ever date with Lauren—"

"Shut up, Brooke." Beau got up and hugged his dad. "How would he have felt if he'd heard about this over the radio or something?"

"They wouldn't have broadcast our names, dummy. How was the half-date?" She reached for Lauren.

Lauren pulled her into a tight embrace and held on, blinking at sudden tears. Welcome to the joys of loving a teenager with a death wish. "Lambert's was fun. The drive back here was horrible. We were so scared."

"Well, as you can see, we're fine," Brooke said. "So we ended your date for nothing."

"This date isn't over yet," Grant said. "You say Evan's already been sent home?"

"Yeah." Brooke made a face. "He's composing his next exciting article for the paper, telling them all about how he saw his lifeblood draining out on the floor. What a crock."

"Brooke," Beau said, "you need to take a course in compassion before you sign up for the police academy. Evan probably saved your life."

"Yeah, but I saved his first. Dad, they nabbed Peregrine a few minutes ago. We heard over the radio thingy they've got out at the desk."

"It's called an ambulance radio," Beau said.

"Anyway, the creep jumped out of a window in Publications. Third floor. It's obvious he fried his brains long ago."

"He must have fallen onto the glass from the window he broke out." Beau nudged Brooke aside and hugged Lauren. His arms were strong, and he was nearly as tall as Grant. "He got away, but he left some blood behind. Oh, and there's some good news. Norville Webster actually called Evan's mom to tell her about this, and she and Stan are meeting them at Norville's house."

"Is that a miracle or what?" Brooke exclaimed. "Evan says his mom and dad actually try to play nice sometimes, and he says it's because Jessica has been telling Lucy how important it is to try to get along. Too bad Jessica didn't interfere in that family years ago."

"Heads up in the ER!" Becky shouted from the central desk. "The perp is being brought here by ambulance."

"Dad, can we get out of here?" Brooke asked. "I don't want to see him again. I'm going to have nightmares forever after—"

There was a knock at the threshold of the room, and they turned to see Dr. Caine in the doorway. Lauren caught her breath. The man's face was nearly as pale as his lab coat. He looked ill.

"Dr. Sheldon, Brooke and Beau are doing well," he announced with a ragged voice. "I checked them thoroughly, but you may wish to make sure." He hesitated and glanced down the hallway toward the central desk, then looked at Grant again. "The police are waiting in your office to question them."

"Thank you, Dr. Caine," Grant said. "Are you feeling okay?"

"I'm fine," Caine snapped. He turned away as the familiar squall of a siren echoed through the ER. Lauren thought she saw a strange combination of contempt and determination cross his face. He straightened his shoulders and marched away from them, calling orders as he went.

"Well, gang," Grant said, "the police are waiting. Brooke and Beau, I want you to go with Lauren to Conference Room A down the hall from Mr. Butler's office. Use the employee entrance, and I'll meet you there with the police in a moment. I don't want you anywhere near this place when the EMTs bring their patient in, and it sounds as if he's almost here." He kissed each of his kids on the forehead and herded them out the door with Lauren in the lead.

Grant was on his way to his office to intercept the police when the rough growl of Mitchell Caine's voice caught his attention. Mitchell had donned a plastic apron, gloves, mask, and face shield. He stepped to the trauma room, where other staff members assembled to await the ambulance. "Okay, listen to me, boys and girls." He raised a hand to get their attention. "Nobody gets near this patient without protective gear. Keep in mind this is a hazardous situation, with multiple lacerations. I don't want to hear later that someone on my team let themselves be contaminated by this . . . patient. He could have any number of communicable diseases."

The ambulance and three police cruisers arrived with a blast of light and sound. The staff barely looked up from their preparations. They'd seen it all too many times before.

The attendants stepped from the cab of the van. With a sense of unreality, Grant watched as they joined the police officers at the back of the ambulance. They pulled the swearing, sweating patient out and wheeled him through the automatic doors.

Grant experienced a wash of ugly déjà vu when he recognized the grizzled face of the man he had treated during the mercury scare last summer. This man had been so freaked out on drugs he had broken one of the straps that secured him to the board and escaped the hospital before the police could arrive.

Tonight, four officers surrounded the cot with their hands on the butts of their pistols. Somehow, Grant believed they would keep their man.

"Police brutality!" the patient shouted.

"You're not being brutalized," one of the officers grumbled.

"I'm in pain, and these quacks won't give me anything for it!"

"You'll get your pain meds when we've found the source of your pain," an attendant snapped. "First we have to determine the extent of the damage."

"Damage! I'm in agony here, you stupid—"

Mitchell Caine reached forward and grabbed the man by the jaw.

"Ow! What're you doing?" Peregrine cried. "You're hurt—"

"When you do receive medication," Caine growled, "it will be directly by my order, not the attendant's, and certainly not yours. If you continue to cause trouble for this staff, that will delay treatment even longer." He glanced quickly at Grant, then turned his attention to the LPN, Todd Lennard, who waited beside him. "Strip him. I don't want him pulling a gun or a knife. Get the undershorts and socks off, too, if he's wearing any."

"You're crazy!" the patient shrieked.

Mitchell ignored him. The staff rushed to do as they were ordered.

"The police shoved me out a window!" he called out to anyone who would listen. "I'm dying here, and these people want a peep show! I need some pain-killers! My gut is killing me! My back hurts! Wait till I talk to my lawyer!"

"He's clear, Dr. Caine," one of the officers said.

"Strip him anyway," Mitchell ordered. "I won't risk the danger to hospital staff."

"My lawyer will tear you people to pieces!" Peregrine hissed. "You can't keep me in jail! You've got nothing on me!"

"Let's get him into the trauma room." Mitchell stepped over to Grant. "I told you I could handle this. Do you have a problem with my bedside manner?" There was a challenge in his voice.

"None." Grant lowered his voice. "Are you going to be okay? If you need backup—"

"I need space to treat this patient as I see fit, Doctor," Caine snapped. "I don't need a baby-sitter."

Grant nodded, excused himself, and went to his office to speak with the police.

Archer Pierce strode down the hallway of the brilliantly lit ER. Rancid body odors and a whiff of stale alcohol stung his nose, and the sound of angry swearing blasted his ears. He needed to be somewhere else—anywhere but here—and he would have been if he hadn't felt such a strong spiritual tug to come to the hospital after hearing about the kids. Two uniformed officers stood in the hallway outside the trauma room, and two more stood beside the bed where a naked man lay condemning the world—especially everyone in the ER—to hell.

Mitchell Caine stood beside the bed. "Emma, give Mr. Royce twenty-five milligrams of Demerol IV and twenty-five of Phenergan. That'll relax him until his flight arrives. Meanwhile, ladies and gentlemen, this isn't the only patient in need of our care. Tina, would you see about our lady in exam room five? Emma, six and seven need to be discharged as soon as Mr. Royce gets his medication. Officers, I'll be checking him for a few more minutes. If you don't mind, stay nearby, but stay out of my way."

Dr. Caine had everything under control. Still, Archer felt a powerful need to be here. Was it for Mitchell's sake? Mitchell Caine would not thank him for interfering, but he couldn't eavesdrop on silent prayers.

Archer paced along the hallway while Peregrine received his pain medicine. How would it feel to be treating the man who had seduced your own daughter? How difficult would it be to concentrate on saving the life of someone who held life in contempt? Archer didn't know if he could do it.

The pusher's voice grew less strident and demanding, and the relief in the department was palpable.

Emma stepped out of the room. She rolled her eyes at Archer. "That'll shut him up for a while."

Archer had turned to pace the hallway again when Mitchell came out of the room and called for Todd Lennard to take the patient to X-ray. He ripped his mask off a face glistening with moisture, nodded at Archer, and walked unsteadily toward the doctor's call room at the rear of the department. He snapped off his gloves and tossed them in a biohazard container as he passed it. He didn't close the door behind him when he reached the call room, just jerked his on-call bag from the closet and pulled an amber prescription bottle from an outside pocket.

As Archer approached, Mitchell shook two small white tablets into his hand and tossed them into his mouth.

Archer braced himself and knocked on the open door. "Need some water with that, Mitchell?"

The doctor jerked up straight and swung around with a look of startled offense. "No, I don't want water. What are you doing here?"

"I don't know." Archer couldn't miss the way Mitchell's hands shook. "For some crazy reason I keep finding myself where you are, and believe me, I haven't planned it that way." He winced at the bluntness of his own words, but he had to be honest. It wasn't his choice to spend so much time in the antagonistic presence of this man.

Mitchell gave an uncivilized snort and turned his back on Archer. "Don't tell me Jesus Christ made you do it."

Archer let that pass. "You're obviously not feeling well, and it can't be easy for you treating Simon Royce after everything he's . . . done." *Lord, am I way off base on this one? Shouldn't I be leaving now?*

For several seconds Mitchell didn't move. Archer braced himself for a backlash, but it didn't come. Mitchell took a shuddering breath, rubbed his face, turned around. "You don't have a clue about my feelings, *Reverend*. You don't know anything about me, and I believe you'd be shocked out of your shirt if you did."

"Try me." *Oh, Lord, what am I saying? Take control of my mouth!*

"You want a 'for instance'?" He leaned closer, until Archer could almost see his own reflection in the silver-stiletto blue of the man's eyes.

"The patient has multiple-system trauma. Probably internal bleeding. He could die, and I hope he does."

"I doubt anyone in this hospital would be surprised by your opinion."

"No? There's a crash cart down the hallway from the trauma room. We used it earlier today, but no one's had time to restock it. There are drugs in that cart that I could easily get to. I could fill a syringe and inject them into that sick monster's IV site, and no one would be the wiser when Royce died a few moments later. In fact, I think they would celebrate. So would I."

"You think *that's* going to shock me?" Archer said. "Try again."

Mitchell waved the remark away. "Brooke and Beau Sheldon are safe. I treated them and their friend with the utmost care. Those kids nearly lost their lives tonight, but they're safe now." He raised a trembling hand to his face. "On the other hand, my own daughter is still being held by that man's poison." His voice cut with a bitter edge.

"Yes, Mitchell, I know."

Mitchell stalked to the end of the room and back. "My wife is so insecure she insists on sending money to Trisha, even though I've warned her that she's supporting a drug habit."

"Mitchell, I'm sorry. I can't imagine the pain you must—"

"You're right, you can't imagine! But forget my pain," Mitchell snapped. He shoved his hands into the pockets of his lab coat and strode once more to the window that overlooked a central court where employees and patients went to smoke. "You Christians are always harping on the effects of sin, but isn't this hospital perpetrating the worst imaginable sin when we treat these depraved monsters who are killing our children? There's something outrageous about that kind of so-called service."

"I know it seems that way, but, Mitchell, you're doing the job you swore an oath to do to the best of your ability. You swore to uphold life. You're a doctor, not an executioner or judge or lawmaker. You can't take all those responsibilities on your shoulders."

For several seconds, Mitchell continued to stare out into the courtyard. "She didn't even think to tell her own father about . . . the baby." His voice broke.

Archer winced. *Baby?* Now he was shocked, but he tried not to show it.

"My granddaughter." Mitchell turned from the window, and Archer caught a brief glimpse of mortal pain before a mask of control replaced it. "It still amazes me that Darla didn't manage to broadcast that all over town, as well."

"Mitchell, I'm sorry. What hap—"

"It's strange, don't you think? It's as if everyone in town has a right to know all about my personal life, but when that baby was born . . ." The mask slid away again, just for a brief revelation of grief. "When that beautiful, innocent . . . flawed little life entered this world for such a short span of time, nobody knew."

"Your granddaughter." *Oh, Lord, what more can this man take?*

"I wouldn't have even seen her if a colleague of mine at the hospital where she was born hadn't called me. I drove to see her in Springfield—where she lay in the incubator, premature and fighting for her life because of the methamphetamine that was destroying her . . . my precious granddaughter." Mitchell was lost in bitter memories. "Even after that, Trisha never came home. She had her inheritance from her grandmother, and she lived off that until the money ran out.

"Do you know my daughter, my own flesh and blood, won't even speak to me? And do you know why?" Mitchell turned to look at Archer, and something threatened to rage out of control behind the steel blue of his eyes.

"No, Mitchell," Archer said softly. "Tell me why."

"Because I won't feed her addiction." The blood ebbed and flowed across his face, indicating strong, conflicting emotions. "Her mother says I'm—" As if he suddenly realized where he was and to whom he spoke, he caught his words as they formed, pressing his lips together. He took a long breath and squared his shoulders. "What are you doing here, anyway?" he demanded.

"I'm sorry, I thought—"

"If you have church members here, then visit them, pray for them, give them their last rites, whatever, just don't bother us in here. Can't you see we're busy?"

"Of course. I'm sorry." Archer backed into the hallway, and Mitchell came out and closed the door behind him.

"Dr. Caine, his BP is dropping dangerously low," Emma called to him. "The airlift will be here in approximately eight minutes."

Mitchell turned to Archer. "I may not have to do a thing."

Archer sat alone in Grant's office, attempting to rally his stray thoughts and concentrate on prayer, but the activity taking place in the next room made it difficult.

"Dr. Caine, his pressure's dropping again."

"And it will continue to drop until he gets blood." Mitchell's voice grew irritable. "Where is it? Do we have his blood type?"

"Yes, but no subtypes."

"No time. Go ahead and transfuse what you have."

Archer heard the familiar echo of rotary blades. The helicopter was getting ready to land, and then the patient would be out of this hospital. Mitchell Caine could finally relax.

"Doctor," the nurse said a moment later, "he's unresponsive."

"Get that blood going—"

A sudden shriek raced through the department, and Archer stiffened, shocked by the sound.

"What was that?" someone cried from the central desk.

"It was the patient," the nurse said. "Dr. Caine, there's no pulse."

"Start CPR."

There was a shuffle of activity, and the code team assembled as the helicopter drew closer. Archer knew they wouldn't be able to fly him out like this. Unless Mitchell and the rest of the team could resuscitate Simon Royce, he would die right here in this hospital.

Archer prayed as he listened to the code routine that had become familiar to him in the past few months.

Twenty-five minutes later, the helicopter flew away without a passenger.

"Well, that was a rough one." Becky stepped inside. "The patient didn't make it; I guess you heard."

Archer nodded. "Yes, I heard."

"I know exactly when it happened, too."

Archer watched her.

"Didn't you hear the death scream?" she asked.

"Is that what it was?"

"That's what Emma told me. It was sure eerie. I guess he won't be killing any more eighth graders."

Archer shook his head over a soul that had been lost long ago.

"Dr. Caine said it must've been internal injuries," Becky continued. "That wasn't a surprise to anybody."

An icy breeze skittered across Archer's shoulders. He suppressed a shiver. The sense of tragedy struck him with the usual sorrow over a soul lost for eternity, but added to that was the knowledge that countless other souls would follow in the wake of Simon Royce's influence. Even though the pusher's death had removed a small part of evil from this town, he'd already planted a foundation for growth.

———

Lauren strolled with Grant to the front door of her house. She was tired, and she had to work tomorrow, but she didn't want to say goodnight yet. She'd spent the past hour listening to the twins download to the police and hiding her shock at the ordeal Brooke and Beau had endured. She knew Grant was still recovering from a similar—but probably more intense—horror.

He stepped up to the porch and stood beside her. "You're sure you don't want to come to our house and watch a movie? We're all too stressed to sleep."

"How about a rain check?"

"Soon? Tomorrow night?"

"Thanks, I'd love to."

He gave her a surprised smile. "Really?"

"Yes, I would."

He gazed down at her for a few seconds, and then he took her hand in both of his. "Lauren, thank you. It meant so much to have you with me tonight."

"You like the way I catch rolls?"

"Among other things. I also like the way you keep the conversation flowing at a lively pace."

"That's a polite way of saying I talk too much."

"No." He reached for her house key and opened the screen door. "It's an honest way of saying I enjoy spending time with you. I enjoy sharing my thoughts with you, and I never have to be afraid that you'll judge me." He unlocked the door and handed the key back to her.

"Thanks for including me tonight," she said softly, "for understanding how important it was for me to see Brooke and Beau and realize for myself that they were safe."

He nodded. "I intend to make a habit of that kind of inclusion, as long as you think you can handle the stress." He reached up and brushed a strand of hair from her cheek, and his hand hovered there.

"I'd like to try," she whispered.

He lowered his head and pressed his lips gently, briefly, against her forehead, then lowered them to her mouth.

The kiss lasted only a few seconds. Lauren caught her breath and looked up at him.

"Good night, Lauren."

She nodded, smiled, stepped inside, and watched him walk to his car, knowing as she watched him that nothing would ever be the same between them again.

ACKNOWLEDGMENTS

A s always, we are deeply indebted to the Bethany House team: our editors, Dave Horton, Karen Schurrer, and Cheri Hanson. You not only help shape our words, but you help shape our lives. Thanks to Teresa Fogarty, Alison Curtis, Brett Benson, Alex Fane, and Jill Parker, who are all part of the team.

Thanks to Cheryl's mom, Lorene Cook, whose constant giving, loving support, and generous spirit have carried us through many hills and valleys. You are a treasure to us.

Thanks to Mel's mom and dad, Ray and Vera Overall, for always being there, for always encouraging, always loving.

We appreciate cousin Larry Baugher, P.I., whose experience fighting on the front lines in the drug wars has given us a wealth of help and information.

We owe a debt of gratitude to James Scott Bell for legal direction.

Thanks to Dr. James Brillhart for keeping us informed about Missouri state law.

Thanks to the huge Baugher clan (Cheryl's aunts, uncles, and multitude of cousins) for proving, once again, the healing power of extended family during the loss of loved ones.

We thank Jackie Bolton, once again, for insight into the working of the adolescent psyche and for editing with that in mind.

We appreciate Barbara Warren of the Blue Mountain Editing Service, who knows how to make the right call at the right time.

We also appreciate Brenda Minton, whose gentle suggestions and wise insight have served many times as inspiration.

I thank my God upon every remembrance of you.
(Philippians 1:3 KJV)

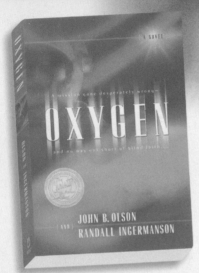